AMERICA'S PRISONER

The Memoirs of
Manuel Noriega

AMERICA'S
PRISONER

Manuel Noriega
and Peter Eisner

RANDOM HOUSE
NEW YORK

Grateful acknowledgment is made to Editorial Juventud, Barcelona,
for permission to reprint eight lines from "Los Caballos de los
Conquistadores" by José Santos Chocano from *El Libro de Oro de la
Poesia en Lengua Castellana*. Copyright © Ra Luz Morales.
Reprinted by permission of Editorial Juventud, Barcelona.

Library of Congress Cataloging-in-Publication Data

Noriega, Manuel Antonio
America's prisoner: the memoirs of Manuel Noriega /
Manuel Noriega and Peter Eisner.
p.   cm.
Includes index.
ISBN 0-679-43227-2 (alk. paper)
1. Noriega, Manuel Antonio.   2. Panama—History—
American Invasion, 1989—Causes.   3. United States—Relations—
Panama.   4. Panama—Relations—United States.   I. Eisner, Peter.
II. Title.
F1567.N67N67   1997   972.8705'3'092—dc20   96-27788
[B]

Random House website address: http://www.randomhouse.com/

Printed in the United States of America on acid-free paper

24689753

FIRST EDITION

Book design by Carole Lowenstein

To all who died in the U.S. invasion of Panama, December 20, 1989,
and to the American people, unaware of the dirty tricks played
by the establishment and its leaders.

Those who know do not tell.
Those who tell do not know.
—LAU TZU

All great events have been distorted, most of the important causes concealed, some of the principal characters never appear, and all who figure are so misunderstood and misrepresented that the result is a complete mystification. If the history of England be ever written by one who has the knowledge and the courage, the world would be astonished.
—BENJAMIN DISRAELI

ACKNOWLEDGMENTS

For administrative help in the office of Frank Rubino, Jon May and Jack Fernandez and their secretaries, Cristina Machin and Rita; Lena Montgomery; for their time, patience, equanimity in the review of the book's technical material, Lorena and Sandra Noriega; for spiritual support, Rev. Dr. Clift Brannon, Dr. Rudy Hernández, Tony Poncetti, Henry Black Aby, Franklin Dean, David Wideman, Jonathan Scott, Avery Willis, Hermana Doña María Flores and the Reverend Bill White of University Baptist Church.

Peter Eisner wishes to thank Les Payne, Knut Royce, Michael O'Kane, William Dorman and Richard Cole, among many colleagues and friends who provided encouragement. Musha Salinas Eisner, who transcribed and edited taped sessions, provided boundless love and support. This work is in memory of Bernard Eisner.

CONTENTS

INTRODUCTION

Rarely has a figure in this century been so universally vilified as Manuel Antonio Noriega. By 1993, when I was asked by Random House to interview Noriega—the deposed general and former leader of Panama, who sits in a federal prison in Miami—his infamy had become a matter of history. It had been four years since the United States invaded his country, killed untold hundreds of Panamanians and brought him back to the United States in chains to face drug charges. The name "Noriega" was employed to invoke images of vice, depravity and murder.

The resident wisdom told us that Noriega was the epitome of rank corruption and that while there might be lingering suspicions that something was wrong with the way the United States dealt with him, this foul man got what he deserved—a forty-year sentence for drug dealing and racketeering.

In post–Cold War America, Noriega was perhaps the first figure to be thus endowed with the inhuman qualities he is remembered for— pure "evil," in the judgment of retired General Colin Powell; a "crazed dictator," in the words of Washington policy makers; "just another crooked cop," in the words of the U.S. prosecutors, who later were found to have negotiated a deal with the Cali cocaine cartel to obtain witnesses to testify against him.

The U.S. government, Noriega's erstwhile benefactors, redefined him as a murderous drug lord and he joined the American government's panoply of villains of the decade—along with Moammar Gahdafi, Saddam Hussein and Fidel Castro.

The ignominy with which Noriega became known was accompanied by an almost religious fervor in the American republic—an uncritical and angry view that rejected any attempt to deconstruct or reconsider the image of this singular personality. Americans seemed to need a devil in the person of Noriega as a repository of that which was vile, base and degenerate, almost to the point of parody.

I was fascinated by the vilification. I had written about Latin America since 1979 and had seen the poverty and suffering caused by corruption and authoritarianism. I witnessed death and violence propelled by superpower politics in Central America. By comparison, Panama was benign. Why was so much hatred directed toward a man who, stripped of the media hype, was hardly a Latin American enforcer in the mold of General Augusto Pinochet of Chile, who crushed dissent and murdered his opposition; Anastasio Somoza of Nicaragua, who stole millions of dollars in U.S. earthquake relief money in 1973 while his people lived in squalor; Roberto D'Aubuisson in El Salvador, whom a UN commission determined was responsible for the Salvadoran death squads, which killed thousands while the United States stood by;[1] collectively, the nameless generals and colonels of Guatemala in the 1980s, responsible for tens of thousands of political murders? All of those men were supported to one extent or another by a succession of American presidents who turned a blind eye to their murderous abuses of power.

There is no way to defend the excesses of any military regime, including Panama's. I made numerous reporting trips to Panama in the 1980s; there were press restrictions, legal and political controls and

---

[1] Documents released by the CIA, State Department and Defense Department at the start of the Clinton administration revealed that Ronald Reagan and George Bush had reliable information that D'Aubuisson, who died of cancer in 1992, was a founder of the Salvadoran death squads, responsible for tens of thousands of political murders in El Salvador. Specifically, the CIA provided information to then–Vice President George Bush that D'Aubuisson, later the speaker of El Salvador's National Assembly, masterminded the 1979 assassination of Salvadoran Archbishop Oscar Romero. Bush and the Reagan administration contended they had no such information.

strong-arm tactics in Panama over the years, but it was obviously a safe haven from the war and destruction in most of Central America. Neither international human rights organizations nor the U.S. State Department could identify more than a scattered handful of politically related deaths in Panama in twenty years of military rule, nor did they cite huge numbers of political prisoners, massive exiles avoiding persecution or any of the other conditions of an extreme police state.

The reason for Noriega's demonization was clear: the Bush administration wanted to invade Panama. First, Panama's upper-class civilian elites—whose hatred for Noriega and the military ripened and increased during twenty years of military rule—had convinced the State Department, which in turn convinced Bush, that it was necessary to eliminate Noriega; second, Noriega's ability to survive the U.S. propaganda machine, his rejection of U.S. attempts to buy him off and his ability to survive an October 1989 coup attempt in which Bush came off as weak and indecisive made it seem as though the Panamanian general could successfully thumb his nose at the eagle. The effect on Bush's approval rating could be disastrous. And third, but not least, establishment of a government more responsive to U.S. desires could swing effective control of the Panama Canal back to the United States. As Noriega points out in his narrative, Panama was to assume superintendency of the canal for the first time on January 1, 1990—only twelve days after the U.S. invasion of Panama—and Noriega had designated the person to serve in that position.

Any government prepared to intervene and wage war must convince its countrymen of the necessity of such action; it must use its propaganda machine to bring the debate down to the personal level—there must be a particular target of hatred to counteract and divert potential opposition. Nicaragua's Sandinista government, by this view, was partly spared from direct U.S. intervention because the State Department ideological teams were unable sufficiently to imbue President Daniel Ortega, who avoided the center stage and who ruled with others, with the demonic qualities necessary for the job. Noriega was different; not telegenic, with poor public relations and more directly in control of his country, he could be objectified into the devil incarnate. Once done, the image passed into the realm of hardened resident wisdom.

President Bush said Noriega had to be ousted to restore democracy, echoing the rationale for U.S. intervention in the Dominican Republic, Grenada and Haiti. Less than a year after the Panama invasion, Bush nearly tripped into using the same justification for the Gulf War, except the idea of ascribing democracy to the emirate of Kuwait was so ludicrous that he had to divert attention toward nonexistent gas-laden missiles and work on demonizing Saddam Hussein, who was still receiving U.S. aid when the first U.S. missle attacks on Baghdad began. The cry for democracy rang hollow in the desert, much as it did in Panama, where the United States connived to create the country in the first instance[2] and then meddled in its affairs, with no interest whatsoever in popular suffrage, throughout this century. As late as 1984, the Reagan administration winked and nodded at the disputed election result that saw Nicolas Ardito Barletta take the presidency over perennial caudillo Arnulfo Arias. It served U.S. interests to see Barletta victorious. In that election, Noriega followed the script and kept quiet. As Noriega fell from grace, the theatrical tears of George Bush and Oliver North could not hide the central reality: in Panama the name of the game was power and control. Noriega was a useful tool, but when he dared defy American authority, he had to be crushed.

When I was told that Noriega wanted to tell all about his relationship with the United States and about the events leading up to his political and military demise, my reaction was a combination of fascination and great misgivings.

On the one hand, it was a fine opportunity to examine the man close-up and fill in the missing documentary evidence on Panama—no one had heard Noriega's version of events leading up to and during the 1989 U.S. invasion. To be sure, there was a historical value to that task. But how forthright would Noriega be? It was evident that with all the political subterfuge, vested interests and classified information, truth was very much a mutable commodity. Would the facts as I gathered them jibe with Noriega's story or with the popular assumption of Noriega's essential evil?

I remained fixed on one motivation for interviewing Noriega, rooted in memories of the smell of death after the U.S. invasion of

[2] Panama had been a territory of Colombia until 1903; when the Colombian Senate refused to approve a treaty with the United States for building the Panama Canal, Washington engineered Panamanian independence and concluded a treaty with the new state. In 1936, the United States paid Colombia $25 million (about $1 billion in 1995 dollars) as an apology for this act.

Panama, which I had covered as a reporter: I had the certain queasiness that journalism once again had not properly set the scene or described the consequences of a remote political war.

Beyond the damnation of Noriega and the pitfalls awaiting me should I undertake the project, I was driven by wanting to know the story behind the story. I shared in the rising skepticism about U.S. actions before, during and after the December 20, 1989, invasion of Panama.

I covered the Panama invasion for *Newsday*. I wrote about Noriega's capture on Christmas Eve 1989, his transport to the United States and processing in a Miami federal court and subsequent trial that led to his conviction in 1992 on charges of conspiring to deal drugs to the United States. He was sentenced to forty years in prison. I saw the madness of the post-invasion, slept with a cardboard sheet as my mattress at a U.S. naval base with other foreign correspondents, heard the gunfire, saw the human remains, smelled the smoke and the death and saw the fear and anger in the eyes of so many poor Panamanians. The invasion of Panama was the horrible and disgraceful result of American political folly.

Within the U.S. military, no one less than a retired general and former head of the U.S. Southern Command—based in Panama until he was fired six months before the invasion—told me that there was no justification for invading Panama and seizing Noriega. And he was not alone in his contention. Something was awry.

The U.S. invasion was a grotesque, shocking experience for Panamanians; theirs was a peaceful country, there were no wars, little violence. What could justify so much suffering at the hands of some distant, ignorant force? Panamanians experienced death, fear, wanton destruction, deceit and lies—the hidden truth about the invasion of Panama. Even newspaper publisher and banker Roberto Eisenmann,[3] one of Noriega's most ardent opponents, said that the invasion had created a "national psychosis" of unforeseen consequences for the future. Few Americans, least of all soldiers, who lived through the invasion of Panama thought it was their country's finest hour. The Pana-

---

[3] Eisenmann's newspaper, *La Prensa*, was closed by Noriega's predecessor, General Ruben Darío Paredes, for a time and then was closed again, subject to harassment, including the destruction of its presses by pro-Noriega thugs.

manian government, far from considering the U.S. invasion worthy of celebration, declared that December 20 would be commemorated as a national day of mourning.

Apart from limited appearances in the courtroom, Noriega's voice had not been heard since the invasion. But illusion needed to be sorted from reality.

So we set up some ground rules. Nothing was off-limits; I would ask Noriega questions, challenge and record his responses. Noriega was allowed to review the transcript of his words in both Spanish and English, and to make any corrections or revisions so that his version of events was exactly what he wanted to say.

Next, I would produce introductory and evaluation material, based on the interviews with him and with other sources. Noriega was not allowed to review or contribute to the introduction and analysis of this book, for which I take sole responsibility. Footnotes accompanying the text were also prepared by me.

The final product would be divided into three main sections: this introduction; the Panamanian general's first-person account of his rise and fall; and my afterword, which provides a ground view of the invasion of Panama and draws on interviews for an assessment of Noriega and the charges against him.

This book is the result of a three-year interview process, drawing also on my years of travels to Panama during crucial periods, including the immediate period before and after the U.S. invasion. The heart of this book is Noriega's account of his years in power, culminating in that invasion and the subsequent drug trial against him. The Noriega narrative is the result of dozens of hours of taped interviews, held mostly in the office of the deputy administrator of the prison.

I told Noriega that he would get a fair hearing, but my role in interviewing him would not constitute a defense of his actions; I had no reason to see him exonerated or to embellish his career. I would report his words and I would use them to analyze the record.

While Noriega said he would deal openly with all issues, he would not discuss the seamier charges against him. For example, he did not provide detailed information about his finances other than to say he had his own sources of wealth, that the CIA paid him more than the U.S. government admitted in public and that much of his money came through his job as commander of the Panamanian military. Stripped of the power, he said, he was stripped of most of his wealth. In any case, he said, accumulating wealth in Panama is not a crime in the United States.

Noriega also was not interested in discussing his own sexual mores or those of anyone else, other than to say that sex and charges of infidelity are irrelevant to his case and are part of the "demonization" process he was subjected to by U.S. propaganda, leading to the U.S. invasion. It was also apparent that he was protecting once-and-future friends, both American and Panamanian—not wanting to tell tales out of school in what he saw as an ongoing process. Clearly, Noriega had not given up hope of being exonerated. Noriega did not see this book as a confession in the twilight of his career. His decision to speak was tactical.

Like any politician or interviewee, Noriega certainly wanted to put the best possible spin on events. At times, his remarks were obviously self-serving, but often he admitted to mistakes and miscalculations.

Noriega surely will face peremptory criticism that his words cannot be believed. However, a dispassionate assessment of his claims and those of his accusers evens the playing field. His accusers all spoke in their own self-interest; all had a keen stake in providing their slant on history. Twenty-six of those who testified against him at the drug trial were fallen and convicted drug dealers or political and military rivals. A deeper investigation of those accusers shows that most had their own agendas.

Some of his accusers were U.S. officials, all with reputations to protect. Some participated in hiding a full inquiry into the truth surrounding Noriega's case, invoking secrecy provisions in the law. There is no inherent reason why Noriega should be believed any more or less than any of these sources; they were all participating in a soiled system of vested interests, which redefined what was true to mean what could not be hidden, and what was a lie to be anything the "bad guys" had to say.

Noriega's commentary is not a comprehensive memoir of his life and times: for the sake of brevity and interest, the arcane details of Panamanian politics and military relationships are not included here. Noriega said he hoped that his words will begin to revise the record about his life and times. He said he would continue to comment about Panama and the history of its relations with the United States.

Instead, these Noriega interviews focused on key elements of his career and then vaulted to the major events involving U.S. policy during his tenure as commander of the Panamanian Defense Forces, from August 1983 through the invasion of Panama and Noriega's transfer to U.S. custody.

My contribution is not meant to be an exhaustive biography or investigation. There are a number of sources, some cited in footnotes, that describe Panama, Noriega and his mentor, Omar Torrijos, at great length. Nor is the book intended to rehash the drug case against the deposed general. At least five major books have examined the drug charges, from various perspectives and with varying degrees of success. These books are also referred to both in the text and in the notes. Rather, my goal was to use the occasion of the Noriega interviews as an attempt to reassess the U.S. invasion of Panama and provide my analysis of the subsequent drug trial.

My questions were:

• What new information was there about Noriega's relations with the United States, particularly with George Bush, William Casey and Oliver North, and what was his role in U.S. affairs during the Central American wars of the 1980s?
• What were the untold stories about the U.S. invasion from Noriega's perspective?
• Was Noriega guilty of the drug conspiracy charges for which he was sentenced to forty years in prison?

Noriega dealt with these matters, but my analysis of the drug trial has nothing to do with his protests of innocence. I drew independent conclusions from the Noriega case:

• After sitting through the Noriega trial, reviewing trial testimony, interviewing lawyers, witnesses and investigators, intelligence sources and Noriega opponents, I found the drug case against Noriega to be deeply flawed and wholly circumstantial. Not only did the accounts by several scores of convicted drug dealers often not match on basic facts, but also, three years after the trial, at least half a dozen of those drug dealers were recanting or threatening to recant their testimony.
• I agree with an array of military, intelligence and political officers who said the U.S. invasion was unjustified on legal,[4] political and moral

[4] The charter of the Organization of American States, for example, Article 20, states, "The territory of a state is inviolable. It may not be the object, even temporarily, of military occupation or other measures of force taken by another state directly or indirectly on any grounds whatsoever."

grounds; it was wholly a result of hypocrisy and deceit in U.S. domestic politics. My analysis of the political situation and my reporting in Panama before, during and after the invasion brought me to the conclusion that the U.S. invasion of Panama was an abominable abuse of power. The invasion principally served the goals of arrogant American politicians and their Panamanian allies, at the expense of unconscionable bloodshed.

The Metropolitan Correctional Center, the setting for our conversations, is a mostly medium-security prison, located about twelve miles south of downtown Miami. Except for the razor wire and guard posts, the prison grounds are almost reminiscent of the well-sculpted campus of a state university, devoid of character and antiseptically neat and modern. One signs in at the visitor desk, then passes through a magnetometer, which is so sensitive that most people have to take off their shoes, because items as small as metal eyelets set off the alarm. Guards stamp an ultraviolet ink spot on the visitor's hand to mark outsiders should there be some question later as to the identity of people leaving the grounds.

Next, an escort leads the visitor through a waiting area, past photographs of the president and attorney general, portraits that changed from George Bush and Richard Thornburgh to Bill Clinton and Janet Reno in the course of the Noriega interviews. Two heavy electronic sliding doors are then activated, one at a time, creating a sealed guard space between the visitor's entrance and the prison yard. From behind smoked, bulletproof glass, another guard asks to hold the visitor's driver's license for the duration of the visit. The second steel-and-glass door trundles open and the visitor enters the prison yard, a series of low block buildings connected by cement pathways. Prisoners wearing neat khakis walk along, chatting quietly, or work in the yard, maintaining the smartly manicured lawns, swabbing the hallways or visiting the cafeteria.

For my first meeting with Noriega, in June 1993, I was led to a small holding cell at the institution, which was still being rebuilt following extensive damage from Hurricane Andrew ten months earlier. At that first meeting, Noriega, wearing an orange prison jumpsuit, and I were locked inside this solitary holding tank, a barren cement and cinderblock room containing nothing more than a stainless-steel table and toilet. Our conversation included an overview of events leading up to his imprisonment; Noriega repeated his pledge to discuss all aspects of his relationship with the Americans and his political history in Panama.

Noriega was at first reserved, evidently sizing up the reporter who had come to see him. While listening intently to what I had to say, he seemed almost to be cloaking his comments behind a dull mask. I could perceive an absence or withdrawal behind his eyes, as if he wanted to peer at me from a place in which his own personality was concealed. I talked to Noriega frankly about all I had seen in his country—both during the sometimes brutal 1989 election campaign, in which paramilitary thugs patrolled the streets, ready to bash heads, but also during the U.S. invasion, in which I told him about the piles of Panamanian bodies I encountered at the city morgue. My intention, I said, was to research events leading up to the U.S. invasion and the reasons behind it.

The actual interviews began on September 11, 1993. Noriega was isolated from the rest of the prison population. Depending on the officer of the day, other prisoners were locked down in their buildings when two guards escorted Noriega from his quarters to the administration building for our interviews. Occasionally a fellow prisoner would shout a word of encouragement to him from the distance. He smiled and chatted amiably with the guards, most of whom—like the majority of the prison population—were Spanish speaking. "He's very popular here among the prisoners," one of the guards told me. "Sometimes they cheer or applaud when they see him."

The only prisoner of war in the United States, Noriega has certain privileges under the Geneva Conventions, including the right to maintain contact with a U.S. military liaison officer, the right to his rank and uniform and the right to random meetings with representatives of the International Committees of the Red Cross. Noriega dresses for visitors in a pressed Panamanian Defense Forces general's uniform and sparkling patent-leather shoes. At our meetings he usually wore a green Eisenhower jacket to ward off the cold air-conditioning of the jail buildings.

At first I would meet him in the administration building; later, I was allowed to see him in his spartan quarters. The compound consisted of three small rooms, near clerical and medical offices in a small building separated from the main prison population by the winding cement paths. Noriega's living space added up to about 250 square feet. There was a small entrance anteroom, where a guard sat reading a newspaper by a collect-call-only telephone that Noriega assumed was monitored constantly by the government.[5] To the left of the entrance there was a small kitchen area, with a small table and microwave oven, where food trays were brought in to be reheated since, unlike other prisoners, Noriega ate alone. Beyond the tiny kitchen was a door leading to a small enclosed exercise area, where shafts of sunlight baked down through heavy wire grating onto a broken-down exercise bike. In one corner Noriega had small pots, where he was growing tomatoes and oranges culled from seeds from the produce served at his meals.

Noriega said he used the exercise bike frequently, his only source of recreation. Unlike the other fifteen hundred prisoners at the Miami Metropolitan Correctional Center, he did not have the freedom of going out in the prison yard.

In a separate small room to the other side of the entrance, there was a metal cot that served as his bed, a tall filing cabinet with a small color TV on top and a plain, lidless toilet and shower stall. Noriega's movements were monitored twenty-four hours a day via a video surveillance system overhead.

Noriega spent hours on the telephone talking to family and friends. His biggest complaint with his quarters was the air-conditioning, which produced a strong chill even at midday in Miami's subtropical summer. He laughed when, even with the door to his exercise area open to bring in blasts of hot air, visitors began shivering. "You should have brought a sweater, you can catch a cold," Noriega said. "I never get over the chill." Prison administrators said they could not control the climate in the room since it was attached to the medical compound, whose equipment had to be kept cool.

Because of the proximity to the medical compound, other prisoners were often hanging about outside Noriega's cell, sometimes calling words of encouragement. "Tony," they shouted, "hang in there."

"Manny," others called, adopting a nickname he has never used, "keep the faith."

"Always, they say friendly things," Noriega said. "No one is ever hostile."

[5] Tapes of Noriega's telephone conversations with his attorneys were the subject of a request for dismissal of charges against him, rejected by federal court judge William M. Hoeveler.

Lina Montgomery, the affable deputy administrator of the prison during most of the period of the interviews, said that Noriega had been easy to deal with and that his demands were few.

"One thing I have to say about Mr. Noriega is that he has never been the slightest trouble to anyone," she told me. "He is always polite and cooperative and never for an instant loses his dignity, despite all he has been forced to go through. Everyone respects him for that."

I observed closeness and affection for his wife, Felicidad, and his three grown daughters, Sandra, Thaís and Lorena, who all dutifully contacted his friends, handled correspondence and visited him when they could, according to the prison schedule. There were no conjugal visits allowed at the prison, however. Montgomery said that a guard was always posted in Noriega's compound when family, friends and lawyers came to visit.

Noriega was trim in appearance. He had no ailments of consequence, only occasional medical complaints—sporadic gastric distress or bouts with insomnia. He said he was well treated by the prison staff. He was disciplined and upbeat in the way he conducted a conversation, smiling easily, laughing, at times pointing to documentation he brought along with him to emphasize a point. The interviews were entirely in Spanish. His English appeared forced, although it improved in prison. He struggled when an English-speaking administrator spoke to him. The Metropolitan Correctional Center has a majority of Spanish-speaking inmates, mostly imprisoned on drug charges, but not all of its staff is bilingual.

In the course of dozens of hours of interviews, I saw Noriega lift the veil. He was personable and witty in his conversation and showed surprising ability to make literary and stylistic references in his descriptions. Yet despite glimpses of openness, Noriega made every effort to mask inferences of his own personal weakness. When Noriega spoke about his years as a young man, working as a government surveyor, he brightened at the memory of being the only person—by virtue of his small size—who could jump along the muddy ocean floor and place measuring devices without sinking. There was pride and an extra resonance in his voice when he spoke warmly about his brother Luis Carlos, his mother, who died when he was a child, and Mama Luisa, his foster mother.

Noriega was keenly aware of his image in the mass media; he tried to avoid self-pity and he showed an ability to sympathize with others. He was capable of friendship and empathy and generated loyalty from those around him. Yet experience taught him that friends were capable of betrayal.

At one point, I described my personal interactions and perceptions of Noriega with a friend who is a psychoanalyst. "You are not describing a psychopathic personality, you are rather describing a generally balanced individual, someone who has many elements of a healthy internal life," my friend said.

Often lost in the inflation of Noriega's image was his inability to navigate successfully in foreign political waters. Astute as he may have been in dealing with Panamanian politics, he was inept at handling or even understanding the U.S. system. His legal representation, for example, was chosen at random and with little regard to political and legal realities. Frank Rubino, who became his principal defense attorney, was a streetwise, charming man who learned about the political questions surrounding Noriega as he went along. Rubino, a former Secret Service agent, was joined by Jon May, a former federal prosecutor with appeals skills but no trial experience. These men inherited the case from Raymond Takiff, a Miami attorney, who became a paid government informant for the U.S. attorney's office in a local judicial corruption case even as he served as Noriega's lawyer. Takiff, in turn, had come to the case on a lark—a friend in the Canal Zone provided the entrée to Noriega, who accepted Takiff's offer of representation without paying much attention to the U.S. indictment against him. One highly regarded member of the defense team was Neal Sonnett, a nationally acclaimed criminal lawyer. "Had Sonnett remained on the case," Judge William M. Hoeveler told me in an interview, "I think the outcome could have been different—Sonnett could have won the case." But Sonnett, forced into the role of playing second fiddle to Takiff, dropped out of the Noriega defense at the imprisoned general's first appearance in Hoeveler's court. "He said he was resigning and gave me his card," Noriega told me. "I really didn't know what was happening and I never called him."

All of Noriega's lawyers signed U.S. government documents that forced them to accept the secrecy determinations of the Bush administration as to what they could reveal about political aspects of the case.[6]

---

[6] The acceptance of the security restrictions prevented the trial from becoming a political event and was not surprising, considering the lawyers' lack of understanding of the political realities that surrounded their client.

Lost in all of this was an attempt by famed political lawyer William Kunstler to contact Noriega with an offer to represent him for free. Kunstler, who died in 1995, represented Noriega's secretary, Marcela Tasón, on unrelated legal matters in New York. "But when I tried to offer to work with Noriega pro bono, I never got a response. I was quite surprised by this," Kunstler said in a 1993 interview. "I certainly would have highlighted the political aspects of the case. This was not really a drug case at all."

As a sign of his lack of knowledge and naivete about the U.S. system, Noriega said he had never heard of Kunstler and did not receive any such offer of representation, indicating Kunstler's offer was somehow intercepted. "I wish I had known that such a man existed and that he could have helped me," Noriega said. "But I was so isolated when the Americans arrested me. I had no idea about who Kunstler was or that he had offered to be my lawyer." Rubino, May and Judge William M. Hoeveler said they were also unaware of Kunstler's overtures to represent Noriega.

Noriega's comments were sometimes topical, other times ironic. He mentioned current events several times in the course of the interviews. Once, he was genuinely irritated when he read a news story that Colin Powell had been paid a $6 million advance to write his memoirs. "How can he be paid so much?" Noriega asked. "Who is he really but a yes-man for Bush? What did he really ever do?" My explanation that the market forces driving the publishing industry, along with Powell's potential presidential candidacy, had established the price did little to mollify his distress. "I am sure that in the course of history, my name will be remembered far longer than his," Noriega said.

Noriega's reaction to Powell was filled with irony. He was feeling the competition of the literary marketplace with the general who launched the invasion that led to his capture. "Powell is a traitor to his own people," Noriega said, having masterminded the invasion "which bombed so many black Panamanians in the barrio of El Chorrillo. He will have to live with his conscience."

Powell seemed from his autobiography to know little, and care less, about Panama. He paid lip service to the selective old Bush administration catch phrase of "restoring democracy" as justification for circumventing international law. Panama was Powell's trial by fire. After just twenty-four hours on the job as chairman of the joint chiefs of staff, he participated in the botched support and amateurish analysis of an October 3, 1989, coup attempt against Noriega.

The "plotters had to express a clear intention to restore democracy or we don't commit," George Bush told Powell. After the coup, Powell agreed with Maxwell Thurman, the general in charge of the U.S. Southern Command based in Panama, "that if we were ever forced to act in Panama, we would recommend getting rid of the [Panamanian military]. Max began to develop a plan to do just that."[7]

On another occasion, Noriega called me from prison shortly after the not-guilty verdict in the 1995 O. J. Simpson murder trial. I asked Noriega his opinion of the verdict. "Well, that's the American system and it doesn't surprise me," he said. "But really, let's talk about reasonable doubt. If there was reasonable doubt in the Simpson trial, what about my case?"

Another time, he used Britain's Princess Diana as an example of why it was sometimes best to allow rumors to lie fallow rather than dignify them with a response. Diana had just given an interview to the BBC in which she acknowledged having an affair with a British army captain after the collapse of her marriage to Prince Charles. "She didn't need to admit that. It didn't strengthen the rest of her case," Noriega said. "Once you raise the subject yourself, there's no end to it. People start examining the details and you're drawn further and further into the subject, which may not have been worth all the attention in the first place. Better to maintain silence and focus on the subjects that you find more crucial to your defense."

In the interviews, Noriega's shrewd defenses and analysis were always at work. He viewed his prison stay as an opportunity to patiently pick away at the U.S. government actions against him. With time and patience, he said, he believed he would win.

"It is important not only to get out of jail," he said, "but also to get out on my own terms—that is, with the American acknowledgment that they had committed the crime, not me."

While he was surprisingly upbeat, I saw some reflective moments. One day, seated together in the deputy warden's office, I saw him gazing out the window toward the parking lot, where visitors came and

---

[7] Colin Powell, *My American Journey* (New York: Random House, 1995; pp. 419–20).

went. "I've never seen the front entrance of the prison," he said. "Tell me what it looks like. I want to project in my mind to what it will look like on the day that I walk out of here for the last time, through the front door."

All the while, Noriega reminded me, he was prepared for letdowns, for some erstwhile friend to cross him as had happened in so many cases—his closest friends and aides had ended up being traitors. As he often said, in almost a lament, "He is a friend . . . if one can say that there are any friends in this business."

I reminded Noriega early on that we had met once before. The brief meeting came four years prior to our encounter in the Miami jail, on October 11, 1989, one week after a coup attempt that almost took his life.

At the time, the Soviet Union had not yet been dismantled. The Berlin Wall was still intact. Wars were still being waged in El Salvador and Nicaragua, although Central American presidents were negotiating around the United States toward a settlement that would end a conflict in which tens of thousands of people had been killed, and billions of U.S. dollars expended, in a supposed war to contain communism.

The United States was active in fighting a drug war in Colombia, and was controlling anti-narcotics forces in the South American countries of Peru and Bolivia, with the aim of destroying coca-leaf production, although endemic poverty was also at the root of cocaine production.

And in tiny Panama, a war was brewing. The United States had imposed economic sanctions on Panama after a federal indictment in Miami had charged Noriega, the U.S.'s longtime confidant on sensitive matters of international security, with drug trafficking and drug conspiracy.[8]

The United States financed and supported the Panamanian opposition's attempt to defeat Noriega's Democratic Revolutionary Party in May 1989 balloting. Noriega's government canceled the election count. The United States had invested money and prestige in the opposition candidates. By midyear 1989, the Bush administration had set

---

[8] The indictment charged Noriega with drug trafficking and conspiracy to import drugs into the United States.

up an invasion plan. Admiral William Crowe, chairman of the Joint Chiefs of Staff, and General Fred Woerner, the Panama-based head of the U.S. Southern Command, went to the State Department in early summer and voiced opposition to the invasion plan. They were both dismissed. Crowe, who was born in the Panama Canal Zone, was replaced by Colin Powell, catapulted in short order from staff aide to the highest rank in the military.[9] Woerner, criticized by conservatives and Panamanian opposition leaders for being too soft on the Panamanian military, was replaced by Thurman, who was given the task of setting up the invasion.

Noriega and his forces were tense. There were occasional and escalating provocations with U.S. forces, who not only lived in absurdly close proximity to but also worked alongside their supposed enemies. The Panamanian Defense Forces, formerly the National Guard, and before that the National Police, were created and fostered by the United States. Noriega was a graduate of U.S. military training courses and the liaison between General Omar Torrijos and the Americans. Torrijos died in a plane crash in 1981, amid charges and counter-charges, never proved, that the death was other than accidental. He was buried at Fort Amador, at a site that symbolized the absurdity of the situation. It was a small neck of land extending out into the Panama Canal, an enclave of ivy-covered administration buildings and tended greenery that evoked all the quaintness of the colonial protectorate that Panama had been since 1903. Amador and the Canal Zone at large had been returned mostly to Panamanian control in stages after the 1977 Panama Canal treaties, shepherded into existence by Torrijos and President Jimmy Carter. So now, next to Noriega's command office at Fort Amador, framed by the mausoleum where Torrijos was buried, were buildings still occupied by the Americans; the fort was guarded by a joint Panama-U.S. military checkpoint. It was a co-existence borne of the colonial relations between a superpower and its surrogate army. But the surrogate army was in open defiance.

Noriega saw a widespread conspiracy against him and against Panama. He saw journalists, especially American journalists, as tools of

[9] Powell says he first met Noriega in Panama in September 1983 on a trip with Defense Secretary Caspar Weinberger. Powell, in his autobiography (pp. 412–13), describes Noriega as "an unappealing man, with his pockmarked face, beady, darting eyes, and arrogant swagger. I immediately had the crawling sense that I was in the presence of evil."

that conspiracy, if not conspirators in their own right. And so, in the days after the October 3 coup, which found him huddled on the floor and praying for a swift and painless death, he banned the entry of American journalists into Panama.

I had gotten around that ban and was reporting on the growing war atmosphere. I had been seeking an interview with Noriega through his aides in Panama City, to obtain his version of the coup attempt. I was told that Noriega would be attending a diplomatic event at the Río Hato air base—a onetime U.S. Army air base, about an hour's drive up the Pacific coast from Panama City—and that this might be a good opportunity to approach the general. It was, indeed. Despite all the rumors about Noriega, about CIA plots and military plots to kill him, I was surprised to find that I could enter the Río Hato base easily and was waved through a guard booth without so much as having to stop or show an ID card. I drove until I came to a party facility, a long slab of cement with a thatched roof but no walls, which had a bar at one end. Traveling with some friends, I parked my car across the street and walked to the party area. A number of men were gathered in small groups all around, drinking beers and chatting, among them some foreign military advisors. I remember a Canadian and a French military attaché. I spoke for a while to the Panamanian ambassador to Haiti, and to several other Panamanians, all the time wondering when Noriega would make his appearance. "When does he show up?" I asked one Panamanian standing nearby, who looked bewildered.

"Oh, he's here," the man said, and nodded toward a figure standing to one side of the building, in the shadows of the thatched roof, very close to where we stood. It was Manuel Antonio Noriega, holding a long-neck bottle of beer, dressed in field fatigues and a baseball cap, looking perhaps a bit out of place. I was surprised again that there was no security entourage at the base, or anywhere in evidence.

"General," I said, approaching him and offering my hand. "I'm a reporter from the United States. I'd like to ask a few questions."

Noriega appeared startled by the approach. "But don't you know that I'm afraid of reporters?" he said. "I don't like talking to reporters."

"Well, no reason to be afraid of me," I said. "At least I speak Spanish. I don't see myself as being a bad guy."

Only the very start of a smile reached his upper lip. "Well, talk to my aide, López, and let's see if we can work something out," he said, and then walked off. Nothing was ever worked out.

Noriega told me he remembered the event that day, but did not re-member my being there. It was the anniversary celebration of the Rio Hato air base's relegation from U.S. to Panamanian control. Try as he could, he had no memory of an American reporter approaching him and asking for an interview. But it's true, he said, "I was always afraid of reporters, the way they were going to twist my words and what I was trying to say. I still am."

In the end, Noriega sought to avoid a tell-all tabloid account of sex and scandal; he wanted, rather, to correct the history of his life and times. During the 1992 presidential election, many people assumed that the imprisoned general would reveal some last-minute detail about George Bush or some other U.S. politician, perhaps a personal intrigue, perhaps information on a secret intelligence operation that would turn the tide of the elections. But Noriega said he had no such information—that the behavior of Bush and the hypocrisy and moral compromise of American policy were scandal enough. In part, Noriega clearly decided to take the high road. There were stories to be told in Panama about the drug use of one U.S. senator or the skirt-chasing ac-tivities of another, but Noriega chose not to tell them. If he had hap-pened to have a juicy story about Bush, however, he might not have been so restrained.

Noriega as a man was rather reserved, not effusive, not charismatic. This is the story of the conversion of Noriega from man to image: an image that the United States needed to be built up so that it could be destroyed. Such a story is important in its own right for those who seek to understand U.S. foreign policy.

For those prone to dismiss Noriega's words, they could do well to consider something that every lawyer knows: an honest man will get the facts wrong some of the time, and a liar must tell a measure of the truth. I take the odds, along with the measure of the man, in re-visiting the historical environment and the train of events that led to the December 20, 1989, invasion of Panama. One should not dismiss out of hand what Noriega has to say. It's certain that his percentages couldn't be much worse than those of the convicted drug dealers and the scheming U.S. officials who participated in his demise.

AMERICA'S PRISONER

CHAPTER 1

The Gringos
Spoil the Party

LOOKING BACK, I remember the sight of the bright faces, the cheers, the dark-skinned girls laughing in the sun, the babies held aloft by their mothers, a spontaneous street party as I marched along the main avenue from the Abel Bravo school to military headquarters in Colón that afternoon, December 19, 1989, the eve of the U.S. invasion of Panama.

There was a student celebration at the school: speeches, applause, inaugurations, ribbon cutting. I usually thrived on such events, enjoying the cheers, buoyed by the crowds. But this day I went through it mechanically, distant.

When the time came for me to go to the military barracks, I was uncomfortable; I felt distracted. Something was telling me, Get out of here, get out of here, get out! I tried to push things along, but protocol takes time. After the students had their ceremonies—I can't even remember exactly what the event was—the major in charge of the military zone insisted that we visit the Colón military headquarters.

Colón is a small, cheerful city; people of all ages gathered as they saw us coming. They were hanging over balconies, lining the street; there was music and there were kids running alongside us. *Panamá es una fiesta*—"Panama is a party"—and this day was no exception. We are never so intense and serious, never so engaged in business, never so committed that we cannot stage a spontaneous celebration—no matter what the occasion. It's something North Americans will never understand. Panama is always ready for a party, but never more than during holiday time. And yet for me, this day, it was muted, distant. I was somewhere else, seeing it from a dream.

When I arrived for the ceremony on the street in front of the military barracks, everything was in slow motion. How can this be taking so long? I asked myself. I felt feverish, sweaty, my clothes weighed down on me in the late afternoon heat. It got worse and worse. After the street scene, the officers and others insisted that the entourage move inside. I think the military wives were inaugurating a new cultural salon or something. And then, since no one had eaten, there was a late lunch.

I had gone to Colón, up the far end of the Panama Canal, the day before, on December 18, to try to mediate a dockworkers' dispute. They wanted more money and were ready to strike. It was a tough session, but we pacified them and reached an agreement.

I always enjoyed going up to Colón. I had spent my young days as a junior officer there under my patron, the late General Omar Torrijos. Returning always lifted my spirits, but this time I had a dull sixth sense that something was wrong.

At about 5 P.M. my aides began receiving reports about unusual activity by the Americans in the skies around the Panama Canal. For a while, nothing was said directly to me; eventually they told me that planes were landing, that the Americans were bringing in troops. But what did it amount to, really? For more than twenty years, this kind of thing happened periodically—maneuvers, troop movements, bombers arriving at Howard air base—it never followed a pattern. It was normal operating procedure. Nor did the Americans advise us, as they were supposed to do under the Panama Canal treaties, signed by Jimmy Carter and Torrijos in 1977.

During dinner, I was itchy to leave, but more obstacles appeared. A group of businessmen from the Colón Free Zone approached me with some projects they wanted to propose. I thought I would jump out of my skin, but I put up with it.

Finally, one of my officers brought information about the American troop movements. "Maneuvers, apparently," he said. We have reports that transport planes with soldiers leaving Fort Bragg are on their way." But no one made anything of it, particularly, and we let protocol take its course. The only concession I made to the maneuvers was in deciding how to return to Panama City. Normally, I might have taken a helicopter back to the capital. With the reports about all the air traffic, I told my bodyguards and the rest of our entourage of military and government officials to prepare for us to drive back to Panama City instead, about an hour's ride. I traveled with my usual convoy of three or four vehicles. I saw nothing unusual as we skirted the highway that courses along the canal the fifty miles to Panama City. We got home sometime between 6 and 7 P.M. There was still no tangible news about trouble. The atmosphere in Panama City was filled with Christmas cheer. We had no idea of what was to come.

As the United States prepared to invade my country, Panama was bathed in the normal excitement that precedes Christmas and the New Year. If the insanity of George Herbert Walker Bush's invasion of Panama had not been so cruel and deadly, the situation would have been laughable. Because while Panama prepared for Christmas that evening of December 19, his frogmen were landing near Río Hato beach, looking for where to station themselves to blow up highways and people; his soldiers were practicing land assaults; his communications specialists were preparing to control all the airwaves and radar channels. In one of the greatest examples of overkill in military history, specially trained U.S. pilots were practicing with their supersecret, billion-dollar Stealth bombers for a brave attack on a tiny air base named Río Hato that housed junior high school students and had few defenders, no planes or radar of its own. While his paratroopers were practicing combat jumps at seven hundred feet that would break the legs of scores of them and leave them maimed for a lifetime and his generals were tensely preparing for a massive invasion—the fourteenth U.S. military intervention in Panama since it was declared independent by the United States[1]—while all this was going on, Panama was getting ready to celebrate. The Christmas spirit was in the air—people were smiling, gathering in bars for a special drink with friends, running

---

[1] The invasion was the first intervention since the 1977 Carter-Torrijos treaties, in which the United States pledged it would never again intervene. For a history of Panama and the Panama Canal, see *The Path Between the Seas* by David McCullough (New York: Touchstone, 1977).

around buying presents. The wives of officers were gathering up gifts and toys for the needy and trees were being decorated.

True, I was feeling the tension. There had been a shooting involving American military personnel who had run a roadblock outside our headquarters in Chorrillo. And the Americans also said that a husband and wife had been accosted the previous Saturday night, December 16—sexual assault, they said. Bush, that noble defender of humankind, had gone on television, almost teary-eyed, saying that no American president would permit his country's women to be jostled by a bunch of thugs. It was as if I personally had gone down to headquarters and grabbed this woman. Actually, we couldn't find the woman, and the whole idea that American military personnel—who were restricted to base and were not allowed out to go to a movie or a restaurant—could have gotten so lost as to drive right up to the Panamanian military command headquarters raised more questions than it answered.

This was Christmastime and we went about our normal business. My troops had been reduced for the holidays; our bases had skeleton staffs, officers were at home with their families. This was not an army manning barricades; we were a professional force with thousands of troops, but we could scarcely even conceive of defending ourselves against an overwhelming blitzkrieg. We had never bothered preparing for an American invasion. The idea, then and now, would be idiotic. First of all, invasion of Panama would be a violation of international laws that protected our sovereignty. How does one plan for an invasion from the United States? After all, they were already there, a permanent invasion force. The Americans surrounded us all the time. Until 1999, they were to be permanently ensconced on our territory in fourteen bases that were home to more than twenty thousand soldiers from all branches of the U.S. military. We had no combat planes, and they controlled our air space whenever they wanted to. They probably would have had little trouble in killing me or capturing me whenever they felt like it. I knew all this. But I thought, naively, that the United States ultimately would honor its neutrality treaty with us and the principles of international law and adhere to the concept of nonaggression against any country. It is an umbrella under which civilized countries operate, so that this right is foremost, founded upon the 1945 UN charter of the great nations of the world.

We did in fact have contingency plans for dealing with emergencies, though not invasions. In a real sense, an invasion of Panama by the United States was a redundancy, so we couldn't exactly react in classic military terms. Instead, our strategy was to oppose any extension of the present American occupation. First, troops were to establish a safe perimeter around the Panamanian military command headquarters; my command would be at the rear guard in my home territory of Chiriquí province, from where our units could mount a military reaction force, a control center for the military command structure from which to base fighting and resistance.

Next, Panama Defense Forces troops were to be deployed with roadblocks all around the capital. We would then start organizing a civilian protest march into the city. We were ready for hand-to-hand local combat in such a situation. If the United States had tried that, it would have been bloody for them and they wouldn't have won. We had superiority because the civilian population had been organized into civil defense units, called the Dignity Battalions. These neighborhood forces were prepared to fight with the fervor of those who battle for the survival of their nation, their homes and their lives. Not all of them were under arms, but we had thousands of rifles, machine guns and rocket launchers at various secret munitions stockpiles. Upon the decision to launch our plan, our G-3 forces were to start distributing the weaponry so our civil defense could defend against any invaders on the ground.

The goal of our planning was to be prepared with measured responses toward establishing control and confrontation, but not to go beyond confronting whatever provocation developed. We never had any plan to take hostages or to launch a treacherous attack against any American target. We did have staging areas for troop deployment in high points overlooking Fort Clayton, where the U.S. Army was based. The U.S. ambassador's residence was a target for a retaliatory attack, if it became necessary. So were fuel storage dumps held by the Americans. These were key elements in establishing a defensive perimeter if the Americans left their bases and tried to take over.

But what we could not plan for was an aerial bombardment, which is exactly what happened. The bombing amounted to destruction of the armed forces, an attack on the civilian population and the rupture of our principal lines of communication. We were not prepared for such an assault, nor were we prepared when that aggression hit innocent people. By severing our communications, I could not issue orders via the chain of command. By cutting our air corridors, our ability to shuttle men and equipment was destroyed. So was my plan for retreat. When it became clear that we needed to put our plans in action, it was already too late. Air routes were blocked. I couldn't get through.

In retrospect, I should have realized what was happening. There were several reasons why I didn't. First, American maneuvers were no surprise; whenever they staged an operation, the Americans exaggerated—too many men, too many aircraft, too much ammunition.

Second, I was getting skewed information from a member of my own staff, whose name I will not identify. As I tell the story of the invasion and my imprisonment, I at times realize that I must shield the identities of some people who served with me in the National Guard and later in the Panamanian Defense Forces. Many of my colleagues still fear reprisals against themselves and their families for the simple act of defending their country against the United States. Others, who may have made mistakes and behaved dishonorably at the time, feel remorse for their wartime actions, but still fear reprisals. I reject acts of revenge against any Panamanian for his or her part in events leading up to and surrounding the U.S. invasion of Panama. Nor will I engage in a war of words with my Panamanian opponents over the years. Whether they realized it or not, our common enemies were the Reagan and Bush administrations, whose policies duped and overpowered us. My attention is directed toward highlighting those infamous acts.

After returning from Colón, I went to one of the alternate offices I had around the city—a PDF (Panamanian Defense Forces) facility in the Torrijos Memorial House on Calle 50, in downtown Panama City, one of the places dedicated to the memory of Torrijos, who died in a plane crash in 1981. A group of friends and military people joined me there, but the focus of attention was not on an invasion. Occasionally, more information on troop movements came in as we monitored American radio and television. There were several possibilities: that they were moving against Cuba; that these were maneuvers and a show of force against us, with a little harassment thrown in; that perhaps the movements had nothing to do with Panama. The previous weekend, I recalled, the United States had mobilized an attack on Colombia; at least one injured man had been airlifted back to Gorgas Hospital, a

U.S. military facility in the former Canal Zone. It was possible that the Americans were preparing for further action against narcotics-trafficking targets in Colombia or Cuba.[2]

All the while, there was the possibility of a commando attack by the Americans or another Panamanian coup attempt against me. So as a precaution against someone staging a raid, I decided to be a moving target; I ordered up a small convoy, composed of my bodyguard escort and the special forces team. There were fourteen brave men with me: Andrés Rodríguez, Iván Castillo, Omar Pinto, Simón Bolívar Herrera, Biviano Arboleda, Carlos Corcho, Nicolás Palacios, Santiago Padilla, Alcibiades Melgar, Marcelo Troechman, Antonio Sing, Marcos Saldaña and Jorge Juan Rodríguez. In addition, one man, identified only as J.F. for his own protection in Panama, was assigned as chief bodyguard for my family. He entered the Cuban embassy with the family and served as a contact for messages.

We used three vehicles: a four-door Hyundai, a Toyota Land Cruiser and a Mercedes sedan (I often brought along the Mercedes as a decoy vehicle). I rode in the Hyundai. Heading out toward the international airport, outside town, I planned to stop for a while at the Hotel Ceremi, located close to the entrance to the airport terminal. The hotel had become a military facility in recent years. From there, I had a special hidden telephone line from which I would contact our man inside the U.S. embassy to find out what was going on. By the time we were under way, it was approaching midnight. As we left the environs of the city along the highway that leads out of town, we saw the city streets almost empty; few civilians were out and there was little traffic, other than some Panamanian military vehicles speeding about. What we could not see yet was more significant than anything else: the skies above us were controlled by the Americans, who were poised to strike on many fronts—by land, sea and air.

Even if I had heeded the warnings and managed to get on an airplane earlier in the day, I still would have been a sitting duck, because the U.S. military started to take over our air space at perhaps four or five in the afternoon. So, if I had tried to get out toward the Atlantic, I would have

[2] On December 15, 1989, Medellín drug cartel boss Jose Gonzalo Rodríguez Gacha was killed by a Colombian strike force led by an American special forces operative. "U.S. Got Gacha" by Peter Eisner and Knut Royce, *Newsday*, May 4, 1990, p. 1.

been a fixed target; once in the air, trying to fly toward the Pacific to Chiriquí would have been just as bad, since either way they could monitor the sky from the same stretch of territory with their string of radar installations. The noose had already been set.

We made it to the Ceremi without problems. We hadn't been there long when I made contact with our U.S. embassy plant. His message was concise and to the point: "Evasion and escape: authorized to kill M.A.N." We began hearing bombs reverberating closer and closer to us. In similar circumstances, Charles de Gaulle had been forced to flee the invading Nazi army a half-century earlier. De Gaulle and his men made a battlefield decision to look for an innocent-looking civilian plane, managing to flee across the English Channel from Bordeaux to Heston, south of London. I did not have de Gaulle's good fortune; I had thought that a plane without air force markings might leave the international airport unnoticed and get to Chiriquí. I knew the odds made it almost impossible, but there were few other options.

I put on civilian clothes and jumped into the Hyundai with two bodyguards. The rest of the escort followed behind in the Land Cruiser. All of them showed great determination and poise, all prepared to fight for their lives and to protect their commander in chief and comrades in arms. As we pulled away from the Ceremi, we had our first clear view of what was happening. There, lit against tracers and the dim light, I could see hundreds of parachutes, an insane image of a Hollywood movie come to life. American paratroopers landing in Panama, ready to kill the enemy: largely defenseless Panamanians.

My mind raced as I took it all in. I had the clear sense that this was a personal battle, that all these machinations were directed by one man against another: George Bush had unleashed the power of the world's greatest military force, with one overriding target—me.

It was like a nightmare—like falling into a swimming pool and when you try to reach for the safety of a wall or touch bottom, you suddenly realize that the walls and bottom have fallen away. I couldn't grasp anything or stop my free fall. All I could see was an endless, limitless ocean and thousands of weapons and men hoping to find me in their sights. I thought of a conversation I had had some years earlier with Libyan leader Moammar Gahdafi, describing for me the U.S. bombing attack against his country. I was remembering his face and his eyes as he said this to me: "They attacked my family in the tent where they slept. They killed my little baby boy; they wanted to kill me."

I was jogged from these thoughts by an explosion to one side of our little convoy of private cars. What was an abstraction in the distance was now on top of us: war with the Americans.

"The paratroopers are still landing," shouted one of the men. We backtracked along the old Tocumen highway. On the radio, I heard a voice that sounded like Captain Heraclides Sucre. His voice was firm, speaking quickly, full of the adrenaline of desperation. "We are on the apron near the start of the runway, position Nilo Tango," he said. "Heavy fire—get the commander out of there!" The airport was plainly overrun with paratroopers, some of whom must have noticed us meandering down the road. We started taking fire, which kicked up dirt in the brush along the side of the road, as we advanced. The driver reacted well, swerving and then dodging in an irregular pattern to avoid the barrage. But in so doing, he caught a ditch on the side of the road and almost flipped us over. I remember getting my bearings as the men and I scrambled out. I could see helicopters all around and tracers lighting up the sky behind the Ceremi, parallel to the end of the runway, along with explosions and parachutes in the distance against the black night.

Everyone grabbed the weapon closest to him, looking for attackers, dodging incoming fire and taking shots in the direction of the attackers. The men fought bravely in a pitched battle against the American paratroopers. We were in an advantageous position, lower than the road surface; close by we could hear men barking and responding to orders—none of them were Panamanians.

I picked up an AK-47 and started fighting. Perhaps my American captors, who have no depths to their cynicism, will try to charge me, seated and railroaded in jail, with a war crime for having the gall to defend my own country. But that's what I did. I fired at anything that moved. We were firing into tall grass that separated the road from the runway—aiming machine gun bursts there, where the incoming fire was originating. And it is even possible that, firing back at the ambushers, I could have killed or wounded one of the brave young men sent by President Bush to capture me that day.

More than two years later, I found out about the American sergeant, Carlos Morleda, who led those men. I happened to be watching television in jail when I saw a story about him on a Spanish-language station. He was left paralyzed in the fighting. He and his platoon just happened to be jumping where we were driving. He described a group of cars coming up the road, an ambush and a fierce firefight. I don't believe he knows to this day that I was in the group he fought with. What a prize I would have been! He remembers it as a bloody skirmish and a turning point in his life. But he didn't see the far greater opportunity—the prize that eluded him in the distance, a Panamanian soldier taken from his command, with only his hands and his head and his heart, fighting against him.

I think the Americans and the Panamanians both were surprised by the intensity of the battle. Both sides lost men in that brief encounter. The American sergeant said they started out with eleven men and lost seven. We had about the same number.

I have no idea how long we were pinned down there—it seemed like an eternity, but in the rush of time and space, it could have been only minutes. Finally men from the Pumas de Tocumen, commanded by Captain Sucre, came to our aid. The Tocumen barracks were located not far from the airport, and by now they had been called to battle. We could hear the rising cadence of their gunfire as they moved toward us laterally. "Escort C-1, advance!" someone transmitted over the radio. "Pull out, situation under control. Over and out." Sucre's men provided cover while Castillo, I and several others piled into the Hyundai and drove away. It was pure luck and the bravery of those around us that kept us from being killed.

The whole time, the chief of my personal staff, Captain Eliecer Gaitán, was close by, trying to join up with us, listening to the radio traffic. He knew that the idea was for me to try to escape to Chiriquí or, failing that, to get to an underground bunker at El Chepo, on the road to Darien.

"It was close to the airport that my detail of six men and I had our first encounter with the American paratroopers," Gaitán was quoted in a newspaper interview about the invasion. "There in the main hangar, many Americans died; we shut down radio communications because they had a 100 percent chance of using that to pinpoint us. For the Americans, it was a technological war. We fought, but their attack was brutal. It was an unequal war in which we paid a high price in human lives."

We drove to a group of houses not far from the airport, but we couldn't get too far—our own Dignity Battalions had blocked the streets with cinder blocks and building material and cars and logs, just as they were supposed to do. It took us more than an hour trying to pick our way to safety; the quiet, deserted city of an hour or so earlier had become a battle zone of debris and staccato explosions and little fires all around. Our radios no longer answered; we had no telephones. The Americans had cut the lines. Headquarters was several miles away, and by now, perhaps 1 or 2 A.M., it had already come under bomb attack. This residential area, not far from the airport, was home to many PDF enlisted men and officers, including our driver. We used the telephone at his house to make some phone calls. We called my office at Fort Amador and a nervous enlisted man said that nothing had happened yet. No one answered the phones at command headquarters.

The crack Machos del Monte battalion, a highly trained special operations group, had moved from Rio Hato down to headquarters after October 3, when Major Moisés Giroldi, spurred on with help from the Americans, mounted a coup attempt against me. They remained on special duty in Panama City during the invasion and ended up defending the command headquarters against the invasion. They fought fiercely and valiantly, managing to shoot down two helicopters, although the Americans never admitted as much.[3] One of the helicopters crashed into a building and started a fire. The Americans then blamed the Dignity Battalions for burning down Chorrillo. That was a lie. They knew what had really happened: they launched a bloody invasion in close proximity to civilians and when they killed people, they hurled the blame, as they always did, at Panama and, specifically, at me.

We went back to the car, drove and drove through the chaos trying to get to the San Miguelito military barracks, which was close to the airport highway—it was there that I was to try to meet up with the general staff. We moved through well-to-do sections of the city, deeming it unlikely that they would be subject to attack. We zigzagged around the outskirts of Panama City, passing the statue of Teddy Roosevelt. There, we cut off the main highway once again and sought

[3] In a 1992 after-action report, the House of Representatives Armed Services Committee reported that "erratic rocket fire from a U.S. Army Apache helicopter probably started one or more fires in the Chorrillo slum area of Panama City that burned to the ground."

refuge in San Miguelito at the house of Balbina Periñan, the member of the legislative assembly representing the working-class neighborhood. It was a rough trip. On the way, we saw Colonel Moisés Correa and several other men standing near a yellow van not far away. I told one of my men to go talk to him; he returned soon after, saying Correa had taken off his gun and ammo clip when he saw his colleague approaching, in an apparent sign that he did not want to be a combatant.

What we saw when we got to San Miguelito was a full-blown invasion, tracers lighting the predawn sky, the sound of light weapons fire, aircraft, helicopters and explosions. My view of events was limited to what I could see from the windows of the Periñan home.

Since the invasion, I have had to rely on others: onetime friends bought off by the Americans and lawyers, judges and jurors who didn't speak my language or understand the political context of what was happening to me. My life under American imprisonment has been filled with treachery and a series of events that make a mockery of what Americans call their "system of fair play." I have been denied the privilege of telling my own story, blocked from providing my version of events; reviled by people who have bought the American establishment's story; ridiculed, slandered and maligned by the potency of that establishment's ability to propagandize. I now speak out, not in defense, because it is not my intention to take the weak position and acknowledge my attackers' victory. I expect to win, in the sense that I expect the vindication of history, not because I am belligerent, not because I am what I am expected to be—that ridiculous image of a man waving a machete, as if I would declare war on the United States. These are all images used by George Bush to soften the public for the carnage that took place on December 20, 1989, to create the image of an insane fighter, just another mad dictator who dared to challenge the supremacy of the United States.

I have not yet experienced the fabled American fair play that these people are raised on, that many of us Panamanians heard about while we were growing up—a fair trial, a fair hearing, human rights. I heard about fair play and the American way of life all the time in the jail where I am imprisoned, a prisoner of war—not a self-declared prisoner of war, but a prisoner of war under the independent determination of the International Red Cross, which is the sole arbiter of the Geneva convention.

The fact is that the United States waged war on an innocent country and killed thousands of Panamanians for no good reason at all. And I sit here proudly in my uniform, the last survivor of the Panamanian Defense Forces, a captive of that war, waiting to tell my story.

The crimes of the United States were well described by Mexican Catholic Bishop Mendez Arce, quoted by the Prensa Latina news agency on Dec. 22, 1989.

> The United States approved the unjust invasion and the consequent destruction, mistreatment and massacre of the Panamanian people. For us, it seems to be serious proof that systematic lies are capable of corrupting the American public. What a detestable and shameful panorama it is to see that a government that considers itself to be the champion of democracy and justice can ignore international order and assume the roles of police, judge, jury and executioner for everyone else.

I'm still waiting for that fair hearing and fair trial—I haven't seen it yet. Perhaps my words, telling my story, will give you the ability to judge me fairly, without any filter from politicians or judges. I'll let you be the judge, because I don't need to sell my position. These are facts that are easy to see.

It's important to say that I don't consider my words to be a defense. My ability to defend myself ended when the last gun was taken from my hands at the Vatican embassy in Panama City and I was imprisoned and taken to the United States.

Instead, this is a recitation of the wrongs committed in the name of the United States. I will tell you my view of what happened and how it happened. I will tell you about myself; and after it is all done, you can call me names, you can agree with me or not, or you can judge me by the size and treachery of my enemies. Perhaps you will be persuaded that the United States has no innocence in this story, that the enemy of the story is George Bush himself, who, reasserting American colonialism in Panama and all around the world before him, invaded a country to satisfy his political agenda, killed its people and seized its leader, who dared to defy his will.

Why me? Why, after being the man the United States could count on, did I become the enemy? Because I said no. No to allowing the United States to run a school for dictators any longer in Panamanian territory. No to the request that Panama be used as a staging base for the Salvadoran death squads and the Nicaraguan Contras. Lots of no's.

Combined with my defiance was lingering colonialism in the United States from conservatives like Reagan and Bush, who could not bear giving away the Panama Canal, especially to a leader who spurned their authority. So they conspired against the man they couldn't control; they made him into a "madman" and, what's more, a man who dared to consort with communists! Then, when they found something even worse to call him, they used that too. They called him a drug dealer, selling drugs in North America to destroy the United States.

Three times, however, they tried to force me into an agreement in which I would get every possible personal assurance, money, protection and safe passage, as long as I would agree to exile—and to leave the road clear for their control. I refused.

How do you deal with such a man who dares defy you? You destroy him.

Finally, factor in that you are a gutless man of weak character, a hypocrite, a liar—George Bush. You not only attack the "fiend" himself and his country, but also pretend that Panama is the enemy—and you kill anybody you want. No problem with the news media: you tell them that everybody you killed was the enemy, not unarmed, defenseless men, women and children. And you pretend that the Panamanians who did fight had no right to defend their country. You control the rules of the game. You are the establishment.

CHAPTER 2

In the Shadow
of the Conquerors

I WAS BORN IN Panama City, but I spent my early years in my mother's village in the Darien region, on the border with Colombia. My mother was a single woman. She became sick when I was a baby, took me back to her family home and placed me in the care of my godmother, Mama Luisa. My father, Ricaurte Noriega, was a public accountant in Panama City. He cared for me religiously, sending food and money periodically with my brother Tomás, who worked for a shipping company as a purser on one of the ships. Our family lived humbly, but there was food and I remember being a happy boy.

My little village was called Yaviza, in Darien Province, where Christopher Columbus landed on his fourth voyage to America. It was near there that Balboa crossed on his way to the Atlantic Coast. Balboa crossed the mountains, and it was nearby that he first saw the Pacific Ocean. When the Spanish conquistadors arrived in this part of the New World, they established a colony near Yaviza and built a mighty fortress to repel their enemies. The ramparts are still there. I remember climbing the parapets and the ruins of the fort, a collection of old stone steps and mazes, sixteenth-century ruins perfect for a little boy. My friends and I would scale the crumbling walls and balance on the towers and then, when we got hot as the sun baked down, jump into the Río Tuira, Panama's largest river, for a swim.

It is a jungle area and the river is much like you would imagine the Amazon jungle to look. As in the Amazon, rubber tappers had come to the Darien to earn money by bleeding the sap of the rubber trees, then transporting raw rubber to the markets of the city. There was a mixture of cultures in the Darien: some were descendants of African slaves; others were of indigenous stock; many, like me, were offspring of Indians, blacks and the original European conquerors.

In Yaviza, I began to get my earliest historic notion of Panama—who I was, how Panama was formed, the Spanish conquest, colonialism. We had a little school in Yaviza, where my cousins, friends and I received an elementary school education. My favorite teacher by far was my great-uncle, the brother of my grandfather. I am proud to say that the little schoolhouse in Yaviza still bears his name—José del Carmen Mejía. He was already an old man and had studied in Colombia, when Panama was a northern province of Colombia, before the United States conspired with the French and declared Panama an independent state. Seated on the banks of the river, atop the ruins of that historic Spanish fort, Uncle José del Carmen taught me and dozens of other kids over the years the story of the Spanish explorer Balboa and his drive toward the Pacific.

He told me how the Spanish conquered and killed any Indian tribe that dared resist them. There were barbarians among the conquistadors who thought nothing of humanity, only of gold. When Balboa came to the isthmus, crossing from the Atlantic, he came upon the mighty chief Caretas and greedily looked upon his village, all adorned with gold. The Spaniards were driven to distraction by the gold; so much gold, the tradition says, the chief even served water to Balboa in a golden goblet. Balboa and his men, of course, wanted to know where this wealth came from. "Go down into yon valley," the chief's son told them. "You will find much more gold than you have seen here or anywhere, all the gold that you need."

Balboa never found El Dorado, but this was how he became the first European to gaze upon the Pacific Ocean. In his greed, Balboa kept marching onward into Darien. Finally, he was killed by a rival Spanish conqueror, Pedro Arias de Ávila, who was angered by Balboa's having fallen in love with the Indian girl Anayansi. Ávila ordered his capture by soldiers. Balboa was seized and his captors chopped off his head.

The story José del Carmen told us was a tale of conquerors and the vanquished, the Spaniards and their massive force against the Indians;

subjugated Indian chiefs, indigenous people imprisoned, roped up and carried back to Europe as trophies of their conquest. It is the history of Latin America, relived and repeated by the conquerors, who are ever ready to impose their goals and their values on everyone else. Whenever I think about what has happened to Panama at the hands of the Americans, I can reduce it on some level to my uncle's story of Balboa and the search for gold.

Mama Luisa and I moved to Panama City. One of my earliest memories of those years was tagging along with the older boys as they organized protests against the Americans and the Filós-Hines military treaty they managed to renegotiate with Panama. The treaty would extend U.S. control of military bases, including Río Hato, in Panamanian territory.

Nobody liked the Americans and it was easy to organize protests. The Americans showed no respect for Panamanians. There were problems whenever an American warship docked in Panama City. Sailors caroused at the local night spots and bars, got drunk and started abusing Panamanian women. Fights broke out constantly.

Usually, when the student union organized a protest, little kids like me were expected to hand out fliers and carry around tin cans for contributions. Earnestly committed to what our elders had taught us, we then marched right back to deposit every cent we were given at the student offices at the National Institute, the college where all the anti-government activities were centralized.

One demonstration stands out from all the others. This was the big strike day organized just prior to December 12, 1947, the day of the planned ratification of the new Filós-Hines treaty at the National Assembly.

I was out on Avenida Central, in the middle of downtown Panama City, standing by a clothing store with the English name "Best Fit." The leaders of the protest that day were two students named Arístides Ureña and Moisés Pianeta; they marched at the head of the procession carrying the Panamanian flag. There were other student leaders there whom I can remember, people who later played prominent roles in the country, including Manuel Solís Palma, who later would become president of Panama. Solís Palma, one of the main organizers, was arrested that day, as were many other student leaders.

The student organizers knew they were lined up against powerful forces as they protested the signing of the Filós-Hines treaties. They were combating not just the Panamanian government; their targets were also the United States and the strong economic forces that controlled Panama behind the scenes. The term "banana republic" was coined in Panama and Central America—and a banana republic is exactly what we were. The United Fruit Company had massive holdings in Panama and throughout the region. It was in the company's interest to see the military ties between Panama and the United States strengthened and extended forever. When United Fruit wanted something done, it could wield its power. The company had huge plantations on both coasts of Panama. When a member of the National Assembly won election, it was usually with the backing and money from United Fruit. The same was true with presidents and, for that matter, with the National Police, the predecessor of the Panamanian Defense Forces. United Fruit became an extension of the will of the United States, especially in cases like the Filós-Hines treaty, which it very much supported.

The National Police at the time were under the command of Colonel José Antonio Remón Cantera, later to become a general and eventually president of Panama. He was under orders to repress the protests any way he had to—with gunfire, bullets, sabers and men on horseback trampling demonstrators, if necessary.

I was standing with my cousin, Yolanda Sanchez, a student at the Lyceum for Girls, when the cavalry, sabers drawn, started moving steadily toward the crowd. There were people as far as the eye could see. They were jammed in everywhere along Avenida Central, where it narrows down in front of Santa Ana Park, right up the street from the General Assembly. High school students, teachers, elementary school kids, students from the university, their professors, were all out on the street in support of the general strike.

As the cavalry drew near, people started to fall off and run to the side. Yolanda and I scrunched into a doorway as the cavalry moved into the crowd. But the protest leaders, Ureña and Pianeta, kept walking proudly in the lead, the Panamanian flag held high. The horses were breathing right on top of the crowd when one soldier sliced at Ureña's arm and cut the Panamanian flag right out of his hands. Pianeta, also covered in blood, fell to the ground.

I was deeply impressed by what I saw. I always thought about Arístides Ureña, and could see the image of him marching in front of me, just as he did that day. When I became commander of the Panamanian Defense

Forces more than thirty years later, I went to Santiago de Veraguas, where Mr. Ureña still lives, to tell him about my vivid memory. He wept when I told him how I saw the soldier cut the flag out of his hands.

After the attack, we all started running; the police were hurling tear-gas canisters. Yolanda and I choked and cried as we ran along Avenue B, stopping in the doorway of a little restaurant called the Café Duran. From there, we ran into the old market down near where I lived and went around the back way up to Avenida Central and into the park by the cathedral.

The demonstrators managed to regroup and were marching toward the Plaza de Francia, now renamed Las Bóvedas, right in front of the National Assembly; the debate on the U.S. bases was under way inside. The organizers needed to devise a way to keep the cavalry at bay, so the student leaders gathered all the little kids together and handed out little bags of corn kernels. They told us to throw as much as we could onto the cobblestones in advance of the horses. It was easy for us to do; we squeezed in among the crowd unnoticed and threw the corn onto the pavement.

It worked. The horses started slipping and falling to their knees on the cobblestones all along the route. This slowed the police down, giving the marchers time to escape along side streets once again and get back to the cathedral. The idea was to group right in front of the National Assembly and make enough noise to influence the deputies meeting inside.

But the police soon regrouped and this time they moved in on foot, rifles drawn. They opened fire. One student, Sebastián Tapia, fell to the ground. He was left paralyzed that day and became a hero to all.

As we ran, Yolanda was also hit; fortunately, she was only grazed, but some people picked her up and we went to the hospital. It wasn't serious. After that, we went back to my house, across the street from the market, a tiny flat at 27 North Avenue (Avenida Norte), on top of a store called Compañía Ávila. It was right up the street from the presidential palace.

The popular reaction to the protests and the subsequent embarrassment were too much for the National Assembly to bear. Despite the pressure from the United States and United Fruit Company, they rejected the treaties. It was a great day for the students, a great victory.

I was, of course, too young to appreciate much of this. But as I entered my teenage years, I shared the dominant attitude of my fellow students toward the Americans. Whenever there was any kind of a demonstration in town, there would also be problems in the Canal Zone. Students would taunt the Americans and throw rocks. As they always did on such occasions, the U.S. soldiers set up barricades on what was then known as Fourth of July Avenue; it is now known as Avenue of the Martyrs. That avenue separated Panama down below from the Canal Zone military administration area, situated on a hill overlooking the Panama Canal to one side and Chorrillo on the other. There were barricades with concertina on top that made it something like the Berlin Wall, dividing the city right down the center. The area was filled with U.S. soldiers and Panamanian police. The soldiers were stationed along every inch of the barricade, more than a mile long.

Anti-U.S. sentiment ran very strong, especially after the incident with the treaties. The disdain shown by the United States was a constant provocation for Panamanian young people, who were developing a sense of patriotism and were already antipathetic toward the Americans. And it was all centered right down there on Fourth of July Avenue. On one side of the street you had American soldiers, American policemen operating as if they were in their own country, speaking a different language, flying the American flag—the only flag you could see in the Canal Zone, even though it was Panamanian territory. A student walking to my school, the National Institute, had to pass by the Americans on the way from Chorrillo and other neighborhoods to get there. If you dared to walk on the wrong side of the street, the soldiers would push you and force you onto the other side. So it was pretty easy to see how the seeds of nationalism and pride for Panama could grow in such an environment. And if you take a look at the students of that period, you see some of the same people who helped negotiate the Torrijos-Carter treaties—people like Jorge Illueca, Rómulo Escobar Bethancourt, Materno Vásquez—all the people present thirty years later for the negotiations that led to the signing of the Panama Canal treaties.

I graduated from high school with general knowledge of many subjects. I had wanted very much to study medicine. Something had happened, however, that would change my life.

Of all my brothers, Luis Carlos was always my favorite. When he graduated from high school, he went on to obtain a law degree from the University of San Marcos in Peru. He then entered the Panamanian diplomatic corps and was posted to Lima, Peru. Although I was not at all interested in a military career, an opportunity opened for me to attend the Chorrillos Military School in Lima, and I seized the moment, realizing that this would also help me spend more time with my brother.

Chorrillos had a great military tradition, something that we in Panama did not have. I studied military engineering under a strict regimen. But the best and most memorable part of the week was Saturday afternoon, when we had weekend leave. I raced out of school to spend time with Luis Carlos, who became my tutor and mentor.

Luis Carlos was a great conversationalist; he was highly cultured and had a precise sense of history. He demanded nothing less of me. He would take me to museums, to readings on politics, to lunches among the Lima literati, where I developed a sense of culture beyond anything I had imagined. These were wonderful years for me—Luis Carlos could turn the most mundane subject into something memorable through his ability to recall anecdotes and events that brought history and literature alive. Our literary outings included intellectuals, writers, historians—he was great at making friends, especially among politicians, the wealthier people in Lima and the elder statesmen of the Lima cultural world. It was a rich, interesting time for me.

He demanded that I absorb the lessons of history. Luis Carlos was Bolivarian in outlook; that is, there was no greater source of political import than Simón Bolívar's march for Latin American independence in the 1800s. Bolívar's goal was to unite Spanish-speaking America. The followers of Bolívar are a breed apart—they study the minutiae of the great general's life; they place him as a model upon which to contemplate current events and political developments. And so it was with Luis Carlos; everything was a function of the Bolivarian ideal, Latin America's cultural independence, its unification and its freedom from colonial domination.

Yet there was nothing militaristic in this approach; strange as it may seem, militarism and armies were no more than an abstraction for me during my years in Peru, even though I was immersed most of the week in military studies. The reason was clear enough: as a Panamanian, I could not relate to a military future. Ours was a civilian police force, for most purposes in the employ of Panama's elite economic power brokers. The Panamanian National Police was not something that a young idealist or a student struggling to find his way could focus upon as a goal for the future.

Neither did my brother see his Bolivarian analysis in military terms. He was a civilian, a humanist, an intellectual to the core; he believed in diplomacy. While the military man sees the ultimate solution to conflict in weaponry and superiority of arms, the diplomat sees a solution in negotiations, meetings, in codicils to treaties. He believed that Panama's entire history could be understood by attention to the detail of history, hidden details that explained men's actions; that the only way for future Panamanian generations to overcome domination and humiliation was to understand and analyze the errors of the past.

Thanks to Luis Carlos, I developed an intellectual life. But another mentor would soon come along who would also be a profound influence, a man who would lead me into a new career in a new world—a new, professional Panamanian military force. His name was Omar Torrijos.

During Torrijos's term as leader of Panama, from 1968 until his death in 1981, and right up until the 1989 U.S. invasion, Panama was a changed country. For the first time, people from the country's poor neighborhoods—the son of the cook, the children of the women who sold lottery tickets on the street, housewives and peasants—rose up from poverty into the middle class with newfound social status, no longer pariahs in their own country. Suddenly, universities were open to them; there were scholarships to become lawyers, doctors and teachers. For the first time people from the lower classes could even think of rising up to be ministers, members of the supreme court.

Ask the powerful people of Panama and they will say that Torrijos was corrupt, that the system had to be replaced—that, thanks to the United States invasion, everything returned to the way it should be. The reality is different.

Since the founding of the republic, the predominant characteristic of the governing class has been that it is populated by rich white people. Everyone else was left to grovel in the dirt. They called them the *criollos*—or people of mixed racial background. They were slum dwellers, people of color, and they never had positions of importance; the very thought of finding a black person in government from 1903 to 1968

was virtually inconceivable. On the other hand, when Torrijos consol-
idated his power, after 1969, after the attempt to oust him, suddenly
we saw members of the middle class and descendants of the poor in his
cabinet, in high positions. And this is mirrored by the opportunities
given to the lower middle class, mostly people of color, who came to
have civil service jobs and other positions that before were a privilege
reserved for the Panamanian oligarchy and their closed society.

I came to know Torrijos better than almost anyone, intimately, as
the visionary dreamer that he was. Yet even though I believe now that
everything has a purpose, my chance meeting with Torrijos seemed an
incredible stroke of good luck for a lowly cadet just graduating from
military school.

CHAPTER 3

A Soldier
by Destiny

AFTER ALMOST FIVE YEARS in Peru, I came back to Panama as an adult, having matured greatly, thanks to the military academy and the tutelage of my brother. But the military still meant nothing to me—my plan was to settle in and find a job. I landed one in the International Geodesic Service. First I received additional technical training in cartography, and then was assigned to the field as an engineer.

I was well suited to the job. Our mission was to set up delicate cartographic equipment, an oceanographic monitor. We were operating at the time on the Pacific side in Azuero province at Punta Guanico. The equipment had to be placed along the rocks at low tide, but the rocks were slippery and the soft, sandy shore was loose. What was needed was a person light enough to walk on the rocks without sinking into the soft ocean floor. Most of my colleagues were older, fat and tall, but I was perfect for the job—at about one hundred pounds, I was the smallest man there. So they tied a life belt around my waist and out I went, onto the rocks, hoping they would support my weight. I was successful.

I was enjoying this work, had pretty much forgotten about taking the military seriously and was dragging my feet in signing up with the

National Guard, as the National Police had become known. I was earning enough money for a few luxuries, like a car and some decent clothes. I also had a girlfriend; life was treating me well.

I had settled into a routine and was looking forward to a solid, quiet life. I had no idea how dramatically things would change.

It all began during Lenten carnival celebrations in 1962, shortly after I returned from Peru. I drove into Colón with my girlfriend and a few other people for some party-hopping around town. We were on our way to the first stop when all of a sudden we got a flat tire. Everything was closed for the holiday and I didn't have a spare. So I started walking. We happened to be close to the local military barracks and I headed in that direction. I had friends there and knew they'd be able to lend a hand.

I walked into headquarters, looking for my friends. At first, I was disappointed that only a few people were around. But then there was some scrambling and orders being barked in the distance, followed by the sound of people approaching.

"Attention!" I heard someone say.

Instinctively, new cadet graduate that I was, even though I wasn't in uniform and hadn't reported for duty, I snapped to, clicking my heels as I did so. In strode the battalion commander, already a famous man within the military. He was tall, with a prominent brow and flashing eyes. He seemed to energize the room. His name was Omar Torrijos.

Torrijos had already garnered a reputation for being one of the new leaders within the National Guard, which was a far different institution back then. Largely subservient to business interests, it was still the repressive organization it had been during my student days, capable of putting down protest movements on behalf of the United States and the wealthy classes. Torrijos, however, had a reputation of being an independent thinker and was well respected among young recruits like me.

Panama is a small country, and at the time there were no more than several thousand people in the National Guard; very few were academy officers and fewer still had gone to the Peruvian Military Academy. Most men knew one another. I certainly knew who Torrijos was and Torrijos had heard of me from various sources. First, I was one of a handful of cadets who had trained in Peru. Second, I was the brother of a diplomat who was fairly well known. Perhaps, also, I had gained a reputation for having a mind of my own. Torrijos seemed to recognize me, although I didn't think we had ever met.

"You're Noriega, aren't you?"

"Yes, sir."

"Come upstairs with me."

I followed Torrijos to his office, forgetting all about my car, my girlfriend and the party. There I was, fresh out of school, a miserable second lieutenant who hadn't even started his formal service, and suddenly the local commander is taking me along with him. There is a big difference between a major and a second lieutenant, and I was in a state of shock.

We walked up to the second floor of the barracks, where Torrijos had his office, which is, by the way, still preserved as it was then. He addressed me informally.

"Let's have a drink," Torrijos said.

"Very well, sir, at your orders," I replied, as we were taught in cadet school. "I'll have a drink."

But Torrijos swept past the formalities, and the atmosphere became more casual. He said he had heard about my stint in Peru and asked me about my career and my future. I was honest with him.

"Well, sir, I've been involved in an engineering project with the International Geodesic Service and I'm enjoying it," I said. "I haven't really been focusing on the National Guard."

"That's happening to everybody these days, but it won't always be the same," Torrijos said, without making himself clear. "There are some of us who are looking for a new era ahead in the National Guard."

He left it at that conspiratorial tone and changed the subject.

"Listen," he said, "I'm the guest of honor at the *toldo*—the base carnival ball. Why don't you come along?"

"Well, I have some friends with me," I answered.

"That's okay, bring them along."

I gathered up my friends and we went off to the party. During the holiday period, we hold parties and dances and masquerades of all kinds, starting the weekend before and leading up to the big celebration on the Tuesday before Lent. He had invited me to the big carnival party in Colón. It was a great thrill to be swept along with him.

At a certain point in the evening, he brought up business once more.

"You see," he said, "there are those of us who believe that the National Guard could be more than it has been—that it could be restructured," he told me, still being vague.

Well, even to say this much was getting close to trouble. What he was saying, in so many words, was that there was talk of rebellion. The leader of the guard at the time, Bolívar Vallarino, was holding a conservative line and would not have tolerated a movement for change within the corps.

I was vague and theoretical in what I said as well. "I think that my military training has nothing to do with what I see of the National Guard as a police force," I said. "They run in opposite directions. Being a policeman has nothing to do with being a professional soldier."

The conversation went on like this for a while, until Torrijos said, "So now that you've graduated, what will you be doing? Would you like to work for me?" he asked.

This was a difficult question. My thoughts had been far from the military. My job was very satisfying. On the other hand, this encounter had taken me entirely by surprise. I found the conversation about the military very much in line with my feelings of nationalism, with my analysis of what the National Guard could be. I was unconsciously captured by Torrijos's style, so much so that I heard myself reply to him enthusiastically, "Yes, sir, very much. But I'm supposed to be starting a geography course with the International Geodesic Service. And I do have my job there."

"No problem" was all he said.

That was it. The offer of working for him seemed to get lost in the partying. Carnival came and went; I returned to the coast, back to my mapping work, slipping and sliding along the rocks on the coast, happy to follow my career working for the geodesic service. It was considered a plum job. I was paid well, I was getting praise for my work and I was getting to know the heart of the country.

About four months later, I got an urgent telegram from Luis Carlos, who had by this time returned to Panama as well. "The National Guard is commissioning four officers and your name is among them," the telegram said. "Get home as soon as you can."

Torrijos had not forgotten his offer. He had gotten in touch with my family, told them about the opening for officers and summoned me back to headquarters.

"What will it take to get you to start working for me?" he asked.

"Well, sir," I told him, "they're paying me five hundred dollars a month."

That was a great deal of money for a young bachelor like me. I was living with relatives and didn't need much to live on.

"Well, fine, come work for me and we'll find a job and some money for you," Torrijos said, adding that he would discuss the matter with General Vallarino.

And that's how I started working for Torrijos. Intuitively, he saw in me someone he could trust. His trust paid off for both of us. I was devoted to him; he knew that I was committed to doing anything he asked or ordered me to do.

But I was by no means his servant; or, sitting at his knee, I got no special treatment. In fact, whenever I did something wrong, he spared no punishment.

There was the time, for instance, when I was still a rookie that a couple of friends and I decided to jump the wall of the barracks in Colón and go out partying. It was December 31, 1962, the same year that Torrijos called me in to work for him. The others were Pedro Ayala, a full lieutenant, and Augustín Barrios and Luis Turber, both second lieutenants like me.

Colón was filled with clubs and bars; it was the perfect environment for a bunch of young soldiers out for a good time. But we were confined to base for some disciplinary reason. However, it was New Year's Eve and we couldn't stand being away from the action.

So we made a run for it. "Let's go dancing," Ayala said. We called some girls we knew and went out partying. There are plenty of night spots in Colón, but we picked the wrong one. After a short time, an old girlfriend spotted me with these friends and started making a scene. I'd been avoiding her recently and she was angry and ready to fight. "I thought you told me you were confined to base," she said. "Looks like you snuck out."

I told her to mind her own business. We started arguing.

"Okay, fine," she said, looking at the other girls, "go ahead and cheat on me." She walked away in a huff.

I didn't think any more about it. We stayed out all night; the boys and I slipped back onto base at dawn.

Everything would have been fine except my old girlfriend was out for revenge. She made up some story and told it to her father, who unfortunately was a member of the National Assembly.

With hardly any sleep, we were hauled into the office, charged with having been AWOL. Torrijos already had gotten a call from Commander Vallarino, saying that the assemblyman in question had called to protest my treatment of his daughter.

The girl complained that I had insulted her and had been disrespectful to her in public. Vallarino's message to Torrijos was a simple one: "Find Noriega and throw him out of the National Guard." My career didn't matter to this politician, who was abusing his power as a member of the ruling class by mixing personal business with someone's career. "Get rid of him" was all he said to Vallarino. And Vallarino passed the message on to Torrijos.

"What's this all about?" Torrijos asked.

"I'm not going to defend myself," I answered. "I accept whatever punishment you want to impose."

Torrijos was very angry. I had messed up his New Year's and he had to deal with Vallarino instead of getting the day off.

"You're right, sir," he told Vallarino. "He should be thrown out— he went AWOL and instead of defending himself, he stood in front of me and said he had nothing to say, that he agreed with whatever our punishment might be."

Torrijos told me what Vallarino said and I always remembered it. "I like this officer because he upholds his honor and his military demeanor. Punish him within the corps."

So Torrijos came back to me, shaking his head, his anger diffused. "Will you take a look at this?" he said. "I'm ready to let him get rid of you and he saves your hide."

From 1962 to 1969, I rose in the ranks; from lieutenant, I became a captain, then a major. They were important years, during which time I became very close to Torrijos; I learned about his dreams and his goals. He was on the road to becoming the leader of the National Guard.

What struck me most were his humanity and his ability to thrive in adversity. Torrijos was transferred from Colón to Chiriquí in February 1963, about ten months after our Lenten meeting. It was in Chiriquí that he gathered around him the young officers he would employ for change within the military and the country. I was one of the chosen.

Torrijos had seen the extreme poverty and social injustice in Colón, where a majority of people were left in the shadow of the giant U.S. fruit and shipping exporters, like the United Fruit Company, which controlled the Panamanian economy, along with its political leaders.

In Chiriquí, he was determined to promote improvements in the lot of Panamanian workers. He became an activist military leader like the country had never seen. He was interested in everything from highway improvements to rural development. The Chiriquí National Guard command became a social development center. Torrijos believed that the key was public participation in government. He organized local councils to discuss how to raise money for public works projects. He met with banana workers to discuss their problems, and he recommended that they form committees to strengthen their unions and demand better conditions. Soon, Torrijos was receiving a torrent of requests from the common folk, asking for help in setting up sewage treatment, clean water supplies and other projects. He reached out to the local city councilmen to incorporate this action within the local political structure.

Perhaps the most dramatic example of his innovation was in our dealings with the guerrilla insurgents who plagued both the interior of the country and the cities periodically in the late 1960s. The guerrillas were sometimes leftists with a cause, sometimes Guaymi Indians fighting for autonomy, sometimes mercenaries supported by the Arnulfistas—supporters of our perennial populist civilian leader, Arnulfo Arias.[1]

It was an emotional time for Torrijos, and I lived through it by his side. I played an important role in putting down the guerrilla insurgencies. I was sent to Chiriquí as zone commander with the mission of combating the Arias-backed rebellion there. It wasn't easy; we lost men and it was a tough, emotionally draining fight.

These were hit-and-run skirmishes, often cross-border raids from Costa Rica. I remember one in particular. In late 1968, a team of Ar-

---

[1] Arias won presidential elections in 1940, 1948 and 1968. He claimed that election fraud blocked him from the presidency in 1964 and 1984. He died in 1988 at age eighty-seven.

nulfista insurgents[2] launched an attack on the house of Eduardo
González in Boquete. González was the wealthiest, most prominent
politician in Chiriquí. I saved the lives of Eduardo González, his
wife, Marta, and his daughter that day. We had obtained information
that an attack would be taking place on a prominent target. Apparently, these men decided they would serve notice on the populace
that they would be challenging wealthy persons in Panama who supported Torrijos. A fifty-man commando team led by a Costa Rican
named Antonio Aguilar, "El Macho," launched an assault on González's ranch. My men and I repulsed the attack and saved González
and his family. Following that first attack, there was a series of border
skirmishes, many of them led by a Uruguayan mercenary named Walter Sandinas, who went marauding throughout the zone, attacking
and hanging opponents of Arnulfo Arias. Our men fought bravely,
and I was an active squad leader in the field with my men. When
it was over, Torrijos turned around and sent me to reach out to
the guerrilla fighters, who fled in defeat to exile in Honduras and
Costa Rica.

"You must extend a hand to them, personally. You must tell them
that you personally guarantee their return to Panama."

I went along with it. But there were perhaps four hundred fighters
and their families living outside the country, fleeing reprisals, in exile.

What a reaction when these people actually saw me, in Torrijos's
name, welcome them back to Panama and offer them the hand of
friendship. To have a high-ranking officer reach out to them was a seal
of approval, a guarantee that they could come home. And they did
come home, under the patronage of Torrijos, who had this remarkable
quality of forgiving his enemies.

The guerrilla threat eliminated, Torrijos launched into a rehabilita-
tion plan: restoration of guerrilla ranches destroyed in the violence,
grants and loans for rebuilding, grants for their children, indemnifica-
tion to the families of those who had been killed. Again, this is the
enemy we are talking about. There was an Indian rebel commander in
particular who struck me as a natural leader, Ariosto González. He was
an older man, but he fought in the mountains with mythic energy.

---

[2] Supporters of Arias, these fighters staged hit-and-run attacks around the country following charges of fraud in the 1968 elections.

When he engaged with National Guard troops it was as if he staged the entire attack by himself. His strategies were so intricate that nobody knew how he managed to get from one mountain to the next; he seemed to be a magician. González became legendary among the National Guard troops, who regarded him with a mixture of mystery and fear.

González was eventually killed in a National Guard ambush; after his movement was halted, Torrijos set out to find who this man was and whether he had a family. Gonzalez's widow and two children were living in San José, Costa Rica. Torrijos ordered that they receive a government pension on behalf of their fallen loved one. This was highly unusual in guerrilla warfare; I doubt that you'll hear much about that type of humanitarianism in many other countries as they dealt with the decline of their guerrilla insurgencies. But that was Torrijos; his humanism was broad and he broke the mold.

There was a military coup in 1968, and a year later, Torrijos was in sole command of the government. By that time it had been shown unequivocally that my loyalty was unswerving. "I can send Noriega out on any mission, from buying a present for a woman to marching into battle," Torrijos would tell people. "Noriega will always be there."

The 1968 Coup

Dr. Arnulfo Arias went to the movies with several members of his family in downtown Panama City on the evening of October 11, 1968. Arias, the perennial caudillo of the Panameñista party, had won sweet revenge for his loss amid charges of fraud in the 1964 presidential elections, won by Marco Robles. This time, Arias had won the election easily. Despite the angry, violent election campaign, he was now a happy man, enjoying the aftermath of the elections. In another part of the city, Colonel Omar Torrijos was packing his bags for a flight to San Salvador, where he was being sent into virtual exile as military attaché because of Arias's victory. The day would end quite differently for these men.

Despite the decisive outcome of the elections, it had been a contentious, angry election campaign, very bloody, very dirty, in which values seemed twisted. The election season had begun with intensified guerrilla actions by supporters of Arias in the mountains, who had taken their complaint of political corruption to the hills. Torrijos was responsible for defending against the guerrilla attacks, which were centered in my home province of Chiriquí, on the border with Costa Rica. The Arnulfista clashes with the military grew in intensity. At the start of the campaign for president, Arias formed a coalition with José Bazán and Arturo Delvalle.[3] The coalition was united in opposition to the civilian government of President Robles, whom the National Guard— along with its leader, General Vallarino—supported. The coalition organized demonstrations and protests and pushed for Robles's impeachment on corruption charges. In one notable protest, Torrijos was assigned the job of crowd control. When the demonstration got out of hand, Torrijos ordered troops to fire tear gas at the crowd. A number of prominent members of the Arias coalition were overcome by the fumes. That put an end to the civil disobedience, but it solidified the animosity between Torrijos, still a lieutenant colonel in the National Guard, and Arnulfo Arias. When Arias won the presidency, he showed his disdain by announcing that he would make his barber the head of the Secret Police; among the existing officers, Torrijos was one of the first to be blacklisted. At the time, I was still in Chiriquí, far from the leadership struggle in the capital.

Torrijos was only one of many in trouble with the new government. The Panameñistas came to power, bent on revenge. Arias's cabinet proceeded to dismantle the National Guard structure and banish National Guard officers they didn't like. Essentially, the new regime split the military between friends and enemies of the Arnulfistas.

Torrijos had been effectively removed from the center of activity. He was on the sidelines and knew nothing about the ongoing conspiracy about to unfold. As he prepared to leave the country, a group of conspiring officers—Boris Martínez, Federico Boyd, Ramiro Silvera, Amado Sanjur, and Humberto Jiménez among them—plotted against Arias. They knew that it was just a matter of time before they, too, would be blacklisted, banned or sent into exile.

Finally, on October 11, 1968, while Torrijos packed his bags and Arias enjoyed a night on the town, the men held a decisive meeting in

---

[3] Delvalle was the father of Eric Delvalle, who served as president from 1985 to 1988, during Noriega's term as chief of the Panamanian Defense Forces.

Panama City. After the meeting broke up, Martínez flew to Chiriquí and the coup sprang into motion. He seized control of key government outposts and radio stations in the province, detaining several prominent Arias party leaders. He and his friends then turned to extending their control to Panama City.

But when they went in search of the president, they couldn't find him. Only his closest aides knew where he was, and word came to Arias of the troop movements while he was still at the theater. Arias never returned home. He went directly to the Panama Canal Zone, seeking refuge with the Americans. Many other Arnulfistas followed him into exile, first to the Canal Zone, then on to Miami. Torrijos never left for El Salvador. He unpacked his bags and prepared for big changes.

Boris Martínez, as the key proponent of the coup, was the de facto head of the new military government, but Torrijos came into increasing prominence, along with Silvera, Luís Nentzen Franco and Sanjur. There was a swift reorganization of the guard, including formation of a staff structure. Torrijos was named commander of the armed forces, but Boris Martínez was a member of the high command and a man to be reckoned with.

The two men never got along well, and the dual leadership role strained their relationship much more. Martínez was more hard-line than Torrijos was, and quicker and more forceful in making decisions. He was opposed to the civilian power structure, and so was more radical in that sense, and very much anti-communist. All of this clashed with Torrijos, who was even-tempered most of the time and cultivated the art of diplomacy on all levels.

Each protagonist had his supporters. In the period between October 11, 1968, and February 3, 1969, there was constant squabbling. Whether in working meetings, the dining room or the barracks, the two leaders were always disagreeing. Torrijos was troubled by the weight of decisions upon him during this period. He confided his concern and anguish about Martínez to several members of his family. Torrijos started getting wind of a plan by Martínez and Boyd to oust him; he decided to react first. On February 3, Torrijos arrested Martínez and sent him on a military plane to exile in Miami, along with Boyd and other conspirators.

Thus Torrijos seized the reins and obtained full control of the military government. The problems abated, but the conflict was far from over. Lieutenant Colonels Amado Sanjur, Ramiro Silvera and Luís Nentzen Franco, some of the same men who had supported Torrijos against Boris Martínez, now were preparing another coup attempt. This operation was advanced, supported, aided and abetted by the CIA and U.S. military intelligence. The United States supported these men in trying to oust Torrijos, on grounds he was a communist sympathizer or at least a leftist. The coup plotters bided their time.

The strategy was to isolate Torrijos while he was traveling outside Panama. Finally, on December 15, 1969, Torrijos went on a trip to Mexico. He was troubled by events in Panama, but was not aware of the plot against him. The conspirators marched into headquarters and declared that the deed had been done: they were deposing Torrijos because he was a communist.

The coup was not successful. Lower-ranking officers, me among them, continued to back Torrijos. I helped Torrijos sneak back into the country on a private plane through Chiriquí. I rallied support for Torrijos from our base in Chiriquí and helped arrange for a secret night-time landing on a flight from San Salvador, the capital of El Salvador.

The plane flew out over the Pacific Ocean undetected. I had ordered jeeps and trucks to be brought down to the landing strip after dark, awaiting the arrival. When we made radio contact, I ordered the vehicles to turn on their lights. The plane landed and I saluted Torrijos as he alighted. There was a cheer from our men: *"Viva Torrijos!"*

We rallied our loyal units from there; by morning, the coup dissolved. Not a shot was fired. The coup plotters were jailed for two months, until the U.S. Central Intelligence Agency launched a clandestine operation that set them free. Torrijos assumed direct individual control of the National Guard for the first time.

Omar Torrijos's ascension to supreme command of the Panamanian armed forces was for me the fulfillment of the conversation I had had with him that carnival night seven years earlier: new thinking, a new concept of what it meant to be a Panamanian. Many people vastly underestimate or choose to ignore the revolution that came with Omar's ascension to power.

It was a social revolution that improved the lot of the lower classes for the first time. The wealthy classes had never paid much attention to the majority of poor people in the country. But under Torrijos, there was investment in public health care and education, roads were built, public sector jobs were created. In focusing on popular empowerment, in bringing about a significant change in the social conditions and mobility of a generation of Panamanians, Torrijos won the lasting enmity of the powers that cared little for the majority of impoverished, dark-skinned Panamanians, the class from which I came.

Because of this social agenda, the United States, which was naturally aligned with the tall, white-skinned oligarchy, came to regard Torrijos as a communist. Torrijos ridiculed the label. We were not tied to the Cubans, nor to the Soviet Union, although we sometimes had contacts with them—often at the behest of the United States. What is true about Torrijos is that he had a social conscience, a sense of concern for the peasant class, for the workers; and for that reason, some called him a socialist, and others called him a communist.

The American analysts would be referring to Torrijos all the time as a Marxist; this, in the thick of the Cold War, was the same thing as calling someone the devil himself. I remember once telling Torrijos about what the Americans were saying, and he began to laugh. "The only possible way you could call me a communist would be in matters of love," he said.

Torrijos's rise was also a political revolution that gave power to the new face of Panamanian nationalism; this too challenged the role of the United States and earned its suspicion. Omar and the military had already garnered the hatred of the traditional political classes, and that would not change. The American government recognized that it would be very important to keep tabs on Torrijos as he developed his social agenda and his plan to revise the canal treaties.

We had an interesting situation when Torrijos came back to Panama in triumph. Some people had jumped the gun on congratulating Omar's opponents. For a day or so, there was a flood of telegrams congratulating Nentzen, Silvera, Sanjur and the others for their great victory. The messages were published on entire pages of newspapers. I remember one in particular from a Panamanian consul somewhere in the Far East named Juan Gómez, who sent a telegram congratulating the new military leaders. Forty-eight hours later, of course, Torrijos was already back in Panama City, and we got another telegram from Gómez. This one read: CANCEL PREVIOUS TELEGRAM.

As we laid out the plot against him, it became clear that Torrijos had enemies all over. He was shocked. "But it's like everyone was against me!" he said in disbelief. "It seems as if I never had any real friends at all, that I was fooling myself."

We summed it up with the example of a supposed "dear friend," Enrique "Chino" Jaramillo, who owed his job as manager of the Banco Nacional to Torrijos. Jaramillo was a drinking buddy; he played piano at Torrijos's parties. When we had to sneak Torrijos back into the country, the first person we thought of was Jaramillo, asking him for money to pay for the plane to get the general back to Panama. Not only did Jaramillo refuse, but he also spoke out against Torrijos and in favor of the conspirators.

It came to the point where Torrijos would walk around headquarters, saying only half-jokingly, as if he were talking to himself: "Damn, Torrijos, whatever you do, don't let yourself get thrown out again. Because the next time, you won't have anybody left on your side."

I've often thought of this episode in later years. It's the nature of Panama, maybe the nature of mankind. Morality has the capacity to bend when power is concerned. It's axiomatic: there are no friends, only friends of the throne. The poor, humble man has a tighter group of real friends than the elevated, landed power broker. In the business of government and politics, you can trust no one.

As Torrijos analyzed the forces and circumstances that led to the December 15 uprising against him, his natural tendency to seek revenge softened with the overwhelming feeling that it was he and Panama that had to change. He reacted with a sense of forgiveness that was fascinating for me to observe. At the pinnacle of his career, here was a man who had the capacity to pardon his enemies. Perhaps he was even more disposed to pardon his enemies than he was to forgive those closest to him. He was very demanding of us.

This was the source of what is still known as Torrijismo. What grew from the consolidation of Torrijos's power was a popular movement founded upon the idea that Panama had to change its ways. Torrijismo became a national social program, a prescription for greater dignity and greater allegiance to labor, to the poor, to students, to people of color, all of whom never before had been a focus of concern from the wealthy power brokers. Hand in hand with this social revolution came the idea that Panama needed to express its own independence. And there was one focal point for our independence, a monument to Panama's existence and reason for being, there for all the world to see: it was the narrow seaward passage that cuts two continents from Atlantic to Pacific—the passage that has been the focus of American greed over our territory and our politics and our lives.

CHAPTER 4

Torrijos—the Man, the Secret Plan and the Canal

I F THERE WAS ONE THING that was self-evident to Panama under Omar Torrijos, it was that we could not be free while the Panama Canal was owned and occupied by the United States government. We could no longer tolerate the conflicts caused by U.S. control of the canal. It led to espionage, assassination threats, intrigue, political pressure and the threat of an invasion.

Understanding the relevance of the canal both to Panama and to the United States is important for anyone analyzing U.S. policy and the developments that provoked the 1989 invasion and my capture. The canal cannot be separated from any political or economic contact between Panama and the United States; we cannot forget that there were those in the United States who wanted to block the canal treaties at any cost; there were those who believed passionately that American interests would be damaged by Panamanian sovereignty over the canal. And even after the ratification of the canal treaties, American conservatives believed that the canal had been sold out and that it was their right to get it back.

With all the pressure against us, successful completion of the Panama Canal treaties was certainly Torrijos's greatest achievement. The treaties involved a combination of skillful negotiations, various pressure tactics and help from unexpected quarters.

First there was help from Japan, which took on almost mystical significance after the visit of Dr. Daisaku Ikeda, leader of a religious-philosophical movement known in Japan as Soka Gakai International—the "true Buddhism." The movement has branches around the world, including adherents in the United States and in Europe. He was a brilliant man, and he came to us via contact with my judo and martial arts instructor, Professor Chu Yi, the Soka Gakai representative in Panama. I was so impressed with Dr. Daisaku that I took him to meet General Torrijos.

Dr. Daisaku described his spiritual vision of the world in the year 2000; and in that context he thought that the peaceful transition of the Panama Canal to Panamanian control was vital to world peace. He predicted that the Pacific Rim would be very important in the next millennium and that Panama could be a centerpiece in a new world order, both commercial and cultural. He saw Panama's role as a bridge crucial in the development of these links.

He recommended that Torrijos seek alliances beyond the traditional sphere of American influence, that we turn our attention toward Asia. It was a long, long discourse, four hours or more, culminating in a prayer led by Dr. Daisaku. "Do not waste time fighting for what you already have," he said. "Expand your horizons. The world of the future is in the Pacific and you have made no contact with the people of the Pacific."

This was definitely the starting point for changing the orientation of what Panama was about and thinking about involvement with Japan. At the time, of course, the treaty negotiations had hardly begun and had borne few concrete results. We needed to consider other options.

By turning our attention to Japan, we were being practical. We were also pressuring the United States. Japan was keenly interested in the expansion of markets to Europe and the Americas. Entry into Panama and the possible participation in a new canal could have profound impact on their global economic growth.

The idea of Japan participating in or financing an alternative to the Panama Canal drove the Americans wild. But our conversations were logical. Japanese businessmen, led by a man named Shigeo Nagano, formed a chamber of commerce called the Japan-Panama Friendship Association to promote relations with Panama. They discussed with us the possibility of creating either a land-based alternative or an entirely new passage, a sea-level canal that would supplement the existing canal, to conform to the needs of growing maritime trade and Pacific trade in general, with larger and larger vessels in the twenty-first century. Mention of this possibility was included in Article 12 of the Panama Canal Treaty, in which it was specified that Panama could join with other partner countries in such an enterprise. The fact was that Panama had already chosen its additional partner, and that partner was to be Japan. The United States accepted this in the form of a treaty but never liked the idea.

We entered serious negotiations with the United States on the canal during the Ford administration, but there was little progress. By 1976, we were growing frustrated. The Republican administration was maintaining a hard line in the talks and there was no certainty that the talks would be successful.

Torrijos, committed to winning the earliest possible treaty for eventual surrender of the canal to Panamanian control, saw that both sides were just spinning their wheels. He had a plan to open things up. He trusted neither American politicians nor the U.S. military, blaming both for the 1969 coup that almost ousted him from power. But he saw the CIA in a different light, as perhaps being more pragmatic, even while supporting and being part-and-parcel of the American government.

He knew that the U.S. view on the canal treaties was divided: while on the one hand there was strong conservative, colonialist sentiment in the United States that the Panama Canal was a strategic necessity, there was, on the other hand, a recognition that it was untenable to maintain the Canal Zone as a U.S. outpost forever. Many politicians in the United States, living through Vietnam protests and watching the development of liberation movements in Latin America, were rightly frightened that student protest movements in Panama would turn increasingly violent and produce a guerrilla problem they could not afford.

As luck would have it, Omar found a sympathetic ear at the Central Intelligence Agency. We had close relations with the CIA for years, and both Torrijos and I felt comfortable with the succession of CIA station chiefs posted in Panama City. It should be noted that it was not at all unusual for world leaders to talk directly with the CIA—it was the natural order of things in dealing with the United States.

So Torrijos went to the CIA station chief, Joe Kiyonaga, seeking a back channel for advice concerning the canal question. He asked for total secrecy and isolation from the U.S. embassy and from Panamanian and U.S. negotiators. This was a request that, he reminded the CIA operatives, had its precedents. The agency had in the past been able to set up off-the-record operations with Panamanian help, especially when it came to diplomatic dealings with Cuba. The CIA man took detailed notes and said he would get in touch with Washington. Within a week, Kiyonaga was back, accompanied by an envoy from CIA headquarters and ready to meet with General Torrijos. A secret meeting was set up at the Hotel Panama in downtown Panama City. The envoy, a Spanish speaker, needed no translator for the top-secret, personal message he said he was delivering from George Bush, the director of the Central Intelligence Agency. Kiyonaga and I were there to hear the message.[1]

The envoy said Bush agreed with the need to push the talks along to a successful conclusion; the future president had not yet undergone his conservative metamorphosis. He agreed with those who said it was best to reach an agreement and turn the canal over to Panamanian control.

The CIA envoy's suggestion was to raise the political stakes and, recognizing that it was election time in the U.S., create the impression that it was too dangerous for the U.S. to protect the Canal Zone. The problem was that the American residents of the Canal Zone, called Zonians, were successfully lobbying in Congress for their rights. Many Americans saw the Canal Zone as God-given U.S. territory, and even raised the possibility of admitting it as the fifty-first state.

These expatriate Americans were claiming sovereignty over foreign soil; it was a story of colonialism gone awry. The Zonians, led by an activist named William Drummond, were mobilizing an advertising campaign in the United States that stirred up anti-treaty fervor on patriotic grounds among key senators and congressmen in Washington.

---

[1] Noriega says that he doesn't know the name of the envoy. Three CIA sources, including a subsequent station chief in Panama and a regional supervisor in Panama, said that Noriega's description here of a Bush role in the Canal Zone bombing plan is unfounded. In response to written questions, Bush denied Noriega's account. (See page 212.)

The possibility that the Canal Zone might remain a permanent U.S. enclave had always been opposed by Panamanian nationalists. And the problems in promulgating a canal treaty had spawned a new generation of anti-U.S. activists, young nationalistic protesters who rejected the U.S. presence in Panama. The students had begun staging small-scale demonstrations and militant acts around the Canal Zone PX and post office. What if, the Bush emissary suggested, the protests were suddenly to become violent and the Zonians' pleas for statehood were to be overwhelmed by the worst fears of the Americans, that a guerrilla and terrorist war was brewing in Panama?

The CIA proposal was to bring a group of Panamanian military men to the United States, train them in explosives and demolition tactics and then send them back to the Canal Zone for a high-profile but harmless bit of sabotage in the Canal Zone, which would add urgency to the canal negotiation by questioning the security of American residents in the area.

Torrijos liked the plan. He selected a group of ten or eleven men for the top-secret mission. Their prime directive was to be inconspicuous, to be good soldiers and to keep their mouths shut. They were sent to Washington, all expenses paid by the CIA. In Washington, they were fingerprinted and photographed, blindfolded for a trip to an airport, then sent off on a night flight in a plane with its windows darkened to undergo three weeks of training. Participants in the training session said they were never told where they were and could only surmise that it was within an hour or so from Washington, perhaps an island or a cove close to the Atlantic Coast.

The training camp was well equipped, with classrooms for theoretical training along with all sorts of equipment and field instruction. There was a small club and snack bar for after-hours recreation.

At the end of the three-week course, the men were given a final exam, which was a mock exercise on a training course to show they were ready for what lay ahead.

The newly trained commandos arrived in Panama under the leadership of a Spanish-speaking American army sergeant. The sergeant had received explosives training in Vietnam and was a member of the Green Berets, stationed in Panama at Fort Sherman. The sergeant's job was to target some locations for bombings and to assure that the mission did not cause any injuries. The first step for the commando unit was a week of review and mission training. They were kept isolated in an area of abandoned buildings on the Atlantic Coast, where they could conduct their dry runs in secret.

Ironically, the sergeant had to revise his mission when members of the Panama Student Federation started conducting small-scale operations on their own, including a firebomb attack on a car in the Canal Zone. The revised mission now included operations outside the main zone area. The American sergeant and our men placed small explosive charges at fourteen locations on the Atlantic and Pacific sides. The number 14 was chosen by Torrijos to represent a protest to the presence of all fourteen American installations in Panama. They left political leaflets at each site. As planned, no one was injured and material damage was slight.

The U.S. ambassador, William Jorden, who had been kept out of the loop on the CIA operation, reacted quickly to the bombings, contacting Aquilino Boyd, the Panamanian foreign minister, lodging his note of concern and warning that he had information that the National Guard was behind the bomb attacks. The head of the Southern Command, Lieutenant General Dennis "Phil" McAuliffe, was circumspect and reacted mildly, making no public remarks about the bombings.

Boyd delivered the ambassador's protest to Torrijos, who immediately asked for a meeting with Bush. He sent me to Washington as his envoy to meet with the CIA director. My first face-to-face contact with Bush ended up being a subtle charade, in which we both knew that the other was not supposed to reveal the substance of the little intelligence operation we had set up. At the same time, Torrijos wanted me to send a tacit message to the Americans that we would not tolerate being the fall guy for their political agenda—we would respect operational security on the bombings if they would keep the heat off us.

George Herbert Walker Bush

The CIA director came jauntily into the Panamanian embassy in Washington just before noon. It was December 8, 1976, about a month after the Republicans lost the presidential election. Torrijos knew that things would change with the arrival of President Jimmy Carter. He wanted our intelligence contacts with the new administration to be strong—he hoped my meeting with Bush, besides putting to rest the nonsensical charges about the bombings, would serve as a bridge to Carter that would lend further progress to the Panama Canal negotiations.

"Good to see you," I told Bush, shaking his hand. "General Torrijos sends his regards."

I was struck immediately by the fact that Bush came alone to the embassy; his driver, if he had one, aides and interpreter were not there. He carried no papers, not so much as a pen and pad of paper. *Aha,* I thought. No witnesses.

Bush was already well acquainted with Aquilino Boyd, whom he knew would do the translating for us. The three of us sat down in an anteroom of the embassy and engaged in a little chat before lunch.[2]

Substance was humorously lacking. Bush needed to be assured that I was not going to spill the real story of the U.S. involvement in the bombings. Yet he needed to do so gently.

"So," he said, "have you done a report on the bombings?" What he meant, I am sure, was *I hope you haven't written a real report about what we did.*

"Yes, I wrote a report and sent it to General McAuliffe," I told him. I understood this to mean *Don't worry, we're not talking.* It indicated that I had kept the information limited to what was already known, and directed the facts to the diplomatically proper channel—the corresponding U.S. military authorities.

"And he received the report?" Bush asked.

"Yes, I made sure of that," I said.

Boyd never knew what to make of this conversation. After his contacts with the U.S. embassy, he had expected some fireworks. Instead, he heard neither recriminations from Bush nor complaints and denials from me about our role in the bombing. In addition, he knew that my mentioning of McAuliffe was strange. The head of the Southern Command had nothing to say about the National Guard's role in the bombing. Yet Boyd would be the sole witness and would be able to tell other diplomats that there had been a meeting on the bombing, although, he might add, nothing important had taken place.

---

[2] Noriega is aware that his version of the December 8 meeting differs from other published versions, particularly an account of the meeting in *Our Man in Panama* by John Dinges (New York: Random House, 1990; pp. 84–90).

After this cryptic conversation, we were called to lunch and joined by our ambassador to Washington, Nicolás González.

Bush was relaxed, happy and friendly during lunch. The only substance to our chat was when he asked solemnly, one soldier to another, if what he had heard was true: "Is Torrijos a communist?"

"I assure you he is not," I answered. "It doesn't mean anything; he's no communist, he's a Panamanian, and that's as far as it goes."

This was all light conversation in the course of lunch, and despite the nature of the question, Bush was at ease and relaxed, changing the subject frequently.

"This embassy is one of the great old buildings of Washington," he said. "I really wish I knew more about Panama and its history."

"You're always welcome to visit," I said. "General Torrijos and I would be pleased to welcome you."

"You know, I'm particularly interested in the Panama Canal," the CIA director said. "How does it work?"

After Bush left, Boyd was clearly befuddled. There was no mention of the U.S. criticism of Panama for allegedly planting the bombs in the Canal Zone, he said. What, then, was the purpose of the lunch? He had expected an angry meeting with charges and threats, not the diplomatic display he had witnessed.

I told him not to worry, that everything was just fine: Bush had gotten the message. Sometimes, among intelligence operatives, no more than a word or a glance is needed to have a full understanding.

All of my subsequent contacts with Bush were cordial, as was evident in a photograph that has been mightily suppressed by the U.S. government. The occasion was a courtesy call Bush was making as vice president in December 1983 at Omar Torrijos International Airport. I had been armed forces commander for only several months. The meeting was ostensibly intended to brief President Ricardo de la Espriella on U.S. plans in Central America. In fact, I was attending to other duties and had not expected to see Bush. But on his arrival, I got a special request that Bush himself was asking to see me to pay his respects.

"General, it's good to see you again," Bush said when I arrived late at the VIP meeting room in the airport. Bush was ebullient and warm in his greeting, since I was the only person among the Panamanians he had met before.

We were paired up, the future president and future pariah, side by side. The visit lasted less than half an hour; then Vice President Bush pulled me aside. He congratulated me for having been named commander in chief and made a subtle reference to his request that the United States be allowed to use the Panama Canal Zone as a base for its counterinsurgency operations in El Salvador.

"I hope you'll be supporting my old friends," Bush said. "Our pilots are already chosen and ready to start flying." Neither one of us realized it, but the pilots included such men as Jorge Canalias, Floyd Carlton Caceres, César Rodríguez and Teófilo Watson, future cocaine traffickers transporting contra weapons in exchange for cocaine. They would later accuse me of dealing drugs.

I was noncommittal. Bush and company left Panama and my memory of him is vague and distant. As they say about George Bush the man, the meeting was so unmemorable that it did not even cast a shadow. At the time, however, the Iran-Contra operation was already in full swing. Later, El Salvadoran right-wing zealot and death-squad organizer Roberto D'Aubuisson—who was far too right-wing for me but with whom I maintained an ongoing debate about Central America—told me that Bush had flown to El Salvador to meet with him in San Salvador right after our Panama encounter. "He gave his blessing and a pledge of financial support to our operations," D'Aubuisson told me, using the word "operation" as a substitute for what he was thinking about—his plan to murder thousands of political opponents and leftists in an anti-communist frenzy. Bush and the Americans knew very well that D'Aubuisson was the real power. They didn't care, until successful protests in the late 1980s made it expedient for them to keep D'Aubuisson at a distance.

What we all know about George Bush is diabolical even without his dealings in Iran-Contra. Here is a man who, as a pilot in World War II, committed a war crime by shooting at lifeboats containing the survivors of two Japanese fishing boats he sank in the Pacific Ocean. The material is all on the record[3] and, if the U.S. media weren't so predis-

[3] See "The Question Bush Never Got Asked" by Mark Hertsgaard, *Harpers Magazine*, September 1993.

posed to worshiping their cold warriors, this truth, not my testimony, would have sunk Bush a long time ago.

I am fascinated by the way history repeats itself. Bush, proving his cowardice by attacking helpless lifeboat survivors in World War II, took just as cowardly a move in the invasion of Panama. I can see the young face of George Bush, dive-bombing a Japanese fishing boat, frightened, but hoping that others will see it as proof of his manhood. And then I can see the older, mature George Bush, on national television, speaking of the evil of Panama, ordering Stealth bombers to destroy a nonexistent enemy in Panama and manufacturing a mass version of his insecure vision of an evil empire challenging his manhood again. In English, they call it "the wimp factor." I am sure that this man's "wimp factor" will never allow him rest: once a wimp, always a wimp.

That is little solace to me, of course. But I can compare my emotional balance with his. I have a quality of measuring my emotional and mental reflexes in times of stress—during the invasion, under fire by guerrillas in the mountains, during a coup attempt, when I should have been killed. And I recognize stability within myself through times of trial, sensing only some natural rage at the grotesque figure of George Bush, sending brave, innocent American boys to kill so that he can defeat his cowardice. Yes, I resent the actions of a man within a system that can do what has been done to me. But I am also interested by the psychological profile it reveals. And I am committed to fight for historical truth, which still can rally me to victory.

With Ford, Bush and the Republicans temporarily retired from the scene, we started making quick progress toward a Panama Canal treaty with the new Carter administration. By the end of 1977, we were close to ratification of what was to become known as the Torrijos-Carter treaties. These treaties would guarantee full Panamanian sovereignty over the Panama Canal and U.S. abandonment of all its military bases, along with the U.S. Southern Command in Panama, by the year 2000. It was a monumental victory for Torrijos, for Panama and for the forces of anticolonialism.

But ratification involved approval by the U.S. Senate and we had our doubts about the resolution—it was difficult for us to believe that we had succeeded so quickly in rewriting the seventy-five-year-old treaty.

Considering all the anti-Panama, anti-treaty sentiment, we were not at all sure we would win and we were prepared for the worst. Torrijos had come up with a secret contingency plan, nothing less than a fully developed scheme to set off explosive charges to temporarily block traffic in the Panama Canal. I know of only a few people who were aware of this alternative at the time—on the general staff Torrijos, Colonel Armando Abel Contreras and me.

The contingency operation, code-named *"Huele a Quemado"*—"something's burning"—was neither conceived as a guerrilla operation nor a prolonged battle plan. It was a single event to demonstrate the consequences of a negative vote by the United States. For logistical reasons, the operation had several branches with independent teams. "High Road" was the group that would operate on the Atlantic, "Low Road" the group that would operate on the Pacific. In between them, at Gatun Lake and Pedro Miguel, and from Pedro Miguel to Miraflores locks, we set up another team, the "Mamati," disguised as innocent fishermen whose boats carried French rocket launchers. There was also a demolition team that would take out the transoceanic Panama-Colón railway. Each was operating separately; no operation team was in touch with the other and the discovery or failure of any one team would not affect the other.

The leaders of the operation were key members of the military, men who later became high-ranking government officials, diplomats and businessmen, still prominent and active into the 1990s. The leader of the High Road team, for example, was a specialist in nighttime military insurgency and had studied how to neutralize U.S. aircraft on the ground at Albrook airfield if that became necessary.

The Low Road included a contingent from the Pumas de Tocumen company; I won't mention the name of the commander, because its revelation could hurt him in his present assignment. The men on the Low Road slipped right past U.S. roadblocks—two hundred men who lived for two months right under the noses of the Americans on land owned by a Panamanian engineer named Julio Alcedo, who agreed to their presence, although he knew nothing of their plans. The American forces never knew that the innocent-looking Panamanian peasants behind their security cordon were really explosives operatives and frogmen ready to assault the canal. These were specialists in all sorts of commando activities, men trained in Israel for just such operations, forming an elite corps.

I was impressed and proud as I observed several dawn-to-dusk training sessions conducted in absolute silence and security in the field. It was like a movie, but there we were, watching the special operatives reach their objective and then head off, dripping wet, into the night. These men brought honor to Panama and to the oath and allegiance they swore before Torrijos: Lucinio Miranda, Nivaldo Madriñan and Luis Quiel, with units from the Department of National Investigations; Daniel Delgado and Felipe Camargo with troops from the Pumas Battalion; Porfirio Caballero with his technology squad; the renowned Edilberto "Macho" del Cid, leader of the Machos of Monte special forces; Fernando Quesada of La Chorrera barracks and Virgilio Mirones with his diving specialists and all the soldiers under his command.

As the U.S. Senate prepared to vote, all was ready. A signal was to be broadcast throughout Panama on Radio Liberty during the program of the popular radio personality Danilo Caballero. He was to announce a show segment, *"Boleros de Ayer"* as the signal to proceed, or *"Boleros de Ayer* has been canceled" to suspend the operation.

It was a historic moment for Panama, but nothing was so tense as the moment facing these men, who had trained and infiltrated U.S. occupied territory, thoroughly prepared to sabotage the canal if ordered to do so. Hearts were pounding as they waited. And, then, the news came: the U.S. Senate ratified the Panama Canal treaties by a two-thirds vote. The signal to suspend our operation was given.

The tension, the adrenaline levels needed physically and psychologically to carry out this huge act of destruction had been so high that the men, feeling the release of tension, were disappointed and some even wept as they prepared to withdraw.

One sidelight to the announcement was that Torrijos waited for the results in his office at headquarters, accompanied by President Aristides Royo and TV personality Barbara Walters. Torrijos was ebullient after the Senate confirmation; I remember looking up from the patio to the stairs above as the threesome made their way toward me.

"Noriega, *saque la gente*—get the men out of there!" he shouted, wanting to make sure that our sabotage contingency would not take place. "Make sure of it."

"Yes, *comandante*," I said, but I was shocked that he would mention such a sensitive matter in front of a journalist. Apparently, Walters didn't realize what he was referring to and didn't follow up.

Within moments, Torrijos was announcing the approval of the treaties in a nationwide television and radio broadcast. Spontaneous celebrations broke out all over Panama. And in the middle of his remarks, there was a special, elliptical mention of those unsung Panamanian patriots. "To those men who know what I'm talking about, I direct a special word of recognition for the great deed they performed by doing nothing at all."

As celebrations broke out throughout Panama, the United States never knew what we had planned—or that, one way or another, they would have lost the canal. We had been in control all along.

After that, despite periodic reports in the U.S. news media pumped up by American officials, there was never any plan ever again to threaten the canal. The canal was now ours, and come what may, it makes no sense to destroy your own house. Someone might have suggested it at one point, but I can honestly say that such a proposal was always immediately shot down. This canal was now a national asset. The only attack there ever could have been on it would have been some kamikaze operation by terrorists; we did everything we could to prepare for such a contingency. Any attack on the canal would have been opposed by all the means available to the Panamanian Defense Forces.

On the one-year anniversary of the canal treaties, there was an official celebration in Panama City. Torrijos did not attend. He felt something was missing, that the true demand for Panamanian independence had not been answered—our future was still under a security umbrella put up by the Pentagon.

Following the treaties, Panama kept up conversations with the Japanese. Shigeo Nagano, the Tokyo businessman who had led the earlier Japanese commercial mission to Panama, came for another visit and I took him to the western part of the country. We were still examining the possibilities of a sea-level canal. This had become more and more pressing as we saw reports about larger and larger ships being built, so large that they had to travel around the tip of South America through the Strait of Magellan. We became more interested in alternatives. We began evaluating specific sites. We took a helicopter to look at the hills toward Chorrera, and Torrijos named the spot where we stopped Nagano Heights.

The Americans sought to diminish and limit the Japanese presence in this enterprise. Japanese interest did not diminish. Our site studies included ecological evaluation and geological surveys, while the Japanese studied market conditions—the current size of shipments in both the Atlantic and the Pacific, future projections, existing fleets and capacities and the development of container shipping and how it was likely to change, along with technical development that would have an impact on shipping in the twenty-first century.

By 1985, Panama, Japan and the United States had created a formal commission, the Tripartite Study Commission on Alternatives to the Panama Canal. It was an international agency whose responsibility was to find means of improving the existing canal, faced with concern that it would otherwise be rendered obsolete.

The commission was envisioned under the canal treaties, which gave Panama the right to choose the third member of the commission, be it Japan, Germany or some other partner. But the Americans always came along as part of the bargain. They were not at all interested in making anything of this commission, preferring to impose their own decisions on us.

But once Japan entered the picture, they had to consider the situation seriously. I was invited to Japan in December 1986 to discuss the process of developing alternatives. In a speech before the Japan-Panama Friendship Association, I took the opportunity to criticize the United States for delays in making improvements to the canal.

In particular, I noted, the United States was delaying plans to widen the so-called Culebra Cut, a narrow portion of the canal, a project that would allow broader-berth ships to transit safely.

"This situation is regrettable, above all when we see that several sectors in Japan have made known their interest in contributing to the financing and execution of this work."

It was evident that our concern was well founded—either there would have to be a new canal or improvements on the one we already had. There was much sentiment that the idea of a sea-level canal was too complicated and much too expensive.

Nevertheless, engineering analysis took into consideration complicated factors—for example, the minimum acceptable level of water in Gatun Lake, the source of water that controls the canal locks. There were various analyses of different routes according to physical characteristics and other factors. Each plan had to be considered in the context of the technical requirements of the shipping industry. In that field Japan had practically all the information; they were the leaders in tankers and tanker technology, and they were making considerable advances in containerized freight. Meanwhile, the Japanese were forceful in calling for constant evaluation of ecological factors—preserving the ecological and biological species of whatever route might be considered.

The question was: could we push the Americans to allow us to increase maximum capacity in the canal, so that when we took control of the waterway, we would be able to handle the largest ships possible? Our efforts toward cooperation with Japan might pressure the United States into action.

There was a game being played here. As soon as the treaties were signed, the Americans backed off on work to improve the locks and entryways to the canal. They kept up their routine dredging and maintenance work, but they no longer dedicated themselves to the canal's improvement as they once did. The attitude seemed to be "We'll turn over the canal, but we'll turn it over the way it was when we signed the treaty—without anything extra."

All the while, from the formation of the commission throughout the final years before the 1989 invasion, the Americans sought every opportunity to pressure Japan to back off and not support Panama. We were stuck in a sphere of influence inherited from the first year of our creation as a country, in 1903; we realized that we had to extend our alliances beyond the Americans. This ran counter to American interests, which sought to turn over the canal but continue controlling Panama. They didn't want to see an independent Panama making deals with Asia.

Throughout the entire period from the earliest talks to the formation of the commission, I focused on the canal studies. My brother Julio, an engineer, was a member of the study commission; he was closely involved in the technical reporting on the system. We saw that the Japanese worked enthusiastically on the project.

The Americans knew that Japan saw Panama as a key link in its global development plan—the Panama Canal was a launching pad for exports to Latin America and Europe. The Japanese always maintained a basic level of support for Panama, but in the final years they sometimes did so at a very discreet level. They backed off in their economic support because the pressure from the United States was great, but they continued to extend loans, maintain exports and keep up strong diplomatic contacts.

For public consumption, the United States saw nothing wrong with Japanese industry and commerce providing technical know-how for canal studies. But under Reagan and Bush, there was something else at work—these men saw me as an obstacle because I was working on something that could unite Panama and free it from American economic dependence. Secretary of State George Shultz was a former executive of the multinational construction company Bechtel; Defense Secretary Caspar Weinberger had been a Bechtel vice president. Bechtel would have liked nothing better than to earn the billions of dollars in revenue that canal construction would generate. They were naturally interested in serving as a counterpoint to any Japanese initiatives to build a new canal.

I wonder if Americans think it's extraneous to analyze the economic precedents of the Panama invasion and the fact that two American cabinet members—not to mention many lower-ranking officials—had economic interests that conflicted with Panama's attempt to broaden its commercial relationship with Japan. I wonder if they think it's all a big coincidence, that I was a bad guy and the "well-intentioned" Reagan and Bush administrations had a good reason for attacking me and destroying Panamanian sovereignty. The Reagan and Bush administrations feared the possibility that Japan might dominate an eventual canal construction project; not only was there a misplaced concern about security, there was also the question of commercial rivalry. U.S. construction firms stood to lose billions of dollars; the government camouflaged that concern by saying that vital national security interests were involved in the Panama Canal.

I want to make it very clear: the destabilization campaign launched by the United States in 1986, ending with the 1989 Panama invasion, was a result of the U.S. rejection of any scenario in which future control of the Panama Canal might be in the hands of an independent, sovereign Panama—supported by Japan.

The Americans, of course, would say that I only do things for personal profit. But here we have a case in which I was working for nationalistic reasons with the Japanese—there was no financial gain involved. Americans like Shultz and Weinberger, meanwhile, masquerading as officials operating in the public interest and basking in popular ignorance about the powerful economic interests they represented, were building a propaganda campaign to shoot me down.

Under the Panama Canal treaties, U.S. superintendency of the canal was to expire on December 31, 1989; Dennis McAuliffe, the Southern Command general turned canal administrator, would leave his post. From January 1, 1990, and forever after, the entire canal operation would be led by a Panamanian.

But because of uncanny timing, the December 20, 1989, U.S. invasion blocked the designee for administrator, who had been approved by me as the Panamanian head of state in consultation with the Panamanian National Assembly. Instead, the choice was made eleven days later by a man who had been sworn in as president on a U.S. military base at the start of the U.S. invasion, a choice made in happy consultation with his American masters and benefactors.

And, in 1995, as I wrote about this episode, it was apparent that even the invasion and control of the canal was not enough for some. Jesse Helms, the North Carolina archconservative senator who used his position on the Foreign Relations Committee to influence my overthrow, introduced a resolution in the U.S. Congress calling for continued U.S. military presence in Panama beyond the year 2000. Negotiations began right away.

CHAPTER 5

Casey—the Master of Spies

ON A BEAUTIFUL SPRING DAY in April or May of 1981, a car pulled up in front of my hotel in Washington, DC. The scene was right out of a spy novel; a man designated as my liaison came to my room and announced we were ready to drive out to Langley, Virginia, in suburban Washington. I gave my military attaché and other aides the day off because no one was authorized to come along; this was to be a solitary affair, for me alone. It was also to be my first meeting with William Casey, the old OSS warrior who now had been appointed by President Ronald Reagan as the director of Central Intelligence.

The route was familiar; I had been to CIA headquarters a number of times in the past, including for several meetings with Vernon Walters, a former deputy CIA director and diplomat. But now, in the Reagan administration, I was once again to be the point man between Torrijos and the U.S. government. Both sides wanted the intelligence relationship between the countries to change.

Panama had always been a meeting place for espionage, a free port of call for East and West, North and South. But our government and our military never had much interest in spying. Two things changed that. First, the 1969 coup, which Torrijos blamed on the CIA, sensitized him to the necessity of intelligence operations; when he saw that his forces had been infiltrated by the CIA and others to organize the coup against him, he reacted by dismissing all those officials who had collaborated with the U.S. Army's 470th Intelligence Brigade, head-quartered at Fort Clayton, near Miraflores locks on the Pacific side of the Panama Canal. He did the same thing with the people accused previously of working with the CIA.

But at the same time he saw that the military forces could not isolate themselves, because that would provoke even more interest among the Americans to seek out intelligence by any means possible. He decided, therefore, that there must be a channel of communication. That is where I entered the picture. Fresh from having organized Torrijos's rescue in Chiriquí, I was brought in for the assignment: I was to be the sole person responsible for communications between Torrijos and the U.S. intelligence services, be it the CIA, military intelligence or the FBI. As the head of G-2, the military intelligence service within the National Guard, I was authorized to maintain contact at any level with the Americans. Torrijos even restricted his own contact with the Americans. During his entire time in power, he never met with any chief of the Southern Command. That was the measure of his resentment toward the U.S. military and the United States for its role in the 1969 coup.

The second reason for moving into intelligence and counterintelligence was the advent during the Nixon administration of serious preparations toward the Panama Canal treaties. That was when the United States began to tap telephones, especially Torrijos's lines, to keep a close watch on him. The United States was interested in anything that had to do with Torrijos—where he ate, where he slept.

We knew this and we reacted with countermeasures; we changed telephone numbers, planted false information and, significantly, we set up spy operations of our own. By the mid-1970s, we had successfully infiltrated U.S. forces in the Canal Zone. We reached out to civilian workers, office people and soldiers, the basic idea being to cultivate informants who had access to documents and data we needed. This was the same thing that the Americans were doing to us. We gathered intelligence by capitalizing on human weaknesses: women, alcohol—all of the vulnerabilities that made it possible to get people to give us information. We had Anglos, Puerto Ricans, quite a number of people.

Look at this picture. An American rotates into Panama every two years. He wants company, and all of a sudden, he is showered with it, being invited to Panamanian houses, going to parties, developing a warm relationship with a Panamanian family. Whatever it is, you win the true friendship of this person, so that you gain absolutely his or her sympathy.

Panamanian intelligence services came of age in the 1970s because we were able to establish significant access to information, right under the nose of the Americans. The most important group of U.S. informants came to be known as "the Singing Sergeants."[1] They were eventually discovered and caused great embarrassment to the U.S. Southern Command, who couldn't believe that any American would spy for Panama. The sergeants were very helpful in obtaining the material important to us: security information relating to Torrijos and the other commanders, as well as operational information. When they came up with other strategic information about the United States and its relations with other countries, it was of no interest to us and we simply destroyed it.

My philosophy in dealing with the Americans was to keep most intelligence contacts aboveboard, to establish an easy, frank conduit for providing information. It is said in intelligence circles that curiosity is the source of many mistakes; my job was to make sure the Americans would not miscalculate because of too little or wrongly developed information. I wanted to keep the Americans abreast of what Panama was doing; it was an effort to combat the rumors and misinformation spread about the country and about the canal. The source of these was an anti-military, anti-Torrijos, anti-nationalist lobby that included the wealthy classes of Panama, who opposed Torrijos, the military and me, and would do anything—invoke the Red menace, for example—to derail the treaties.

My assignment from Torrijos was to downplay spying, nurturing in-

---

[1] The U.S. military investigated at least three men as having been the "Singing Sergeants," including Army Sergeant Hor Brustmayer-Rodríguez who was honorably discharged and never charged with a crime. The case was the target of short-lived Senate judiciary subcommittee hearings, chaired by Senator James Allen of Alabama, one of the staunchest opponents to the canal treaties.

stead a relationship of respect and friendship and speaking openly with the U.S. intelligence services. We talked about our political goals; they could see that we were not communists. And as we explained ourselves to the Americans, a professional understanding developed, contacts that would avoid any confusion about purpose and motives. I started traveling to Washington several times a year, along with other Panamanian officials.

As a result of these efforts, the Americans began requesting that we carry out missions for them, pinch-hitting when the United States needed an intermediary. This was seen in our handling of Cuban contacts and in our help to the United States during the Iran crisis, when we gave asylum to the shah of Iran.

As a result of these dealings, it is always inferred that I was some sort of U.S. agent, which was never the case. I was a Panamanian official and I openly conducted myself as such in all my relations with the United States, for the good of my country, my army and with the full knowledge of my commander, General Torrijos.

My visit to CIA headquarters that spring day was with a full understanding on both sides of what the relationship had been. I was still a colonel and head of G-2, invited by Casey and on a courtesy visit at the behest of Torrijos.

There was, of course, always an air of intrigue on visits to CIA headquarters. The car pulled off the parkway after less than an hour's drive. Security arrangements were made at the front gate, and then I was driven into the CIA grounds, directly to the imposing administration building. I recall crossing the threshold, looking in passing at the globe of the world inlaid in the floor of the venerable old headquarters and at the stars on the wall, representing the CIA agents killed in duty around the world. There was a lone receptionist seated in the large foyer; the cavernous dimensions of this empty space gave no outward projection of the espionage and intrigue one could imagine going on throughout the premises.

I was ushered into a morning of meetings with staff aides; Casey, I was told, would meet us just before lunch. We spent the morning in a series of chats that set the stage for what they were thinking about: inevitably, the talks revolved around the strategic importance of Panama and the Panama Canal and their plan for the United States to remain in Panama after the year 2000. I can remember only faces, not names, in these talks; at the CIA, I don't think the use of names is a high priority. It may be Mr. Clark and Mr. Smith and Mr. Jones, but I had little thought that these were the real names of the people I was talking to; the only surnames mentioned with any certainty during the morning were those of Colonel Noriega and Mr. Casey.

There was an informal air to these conversations, but certain themes were repeated for emphasis. "Colonel, the United States is concerned about the security of the region; with the Sandinistas, we are worried about Cuban and Soviet influence all around your government," one of the anonymous men said.

"Colonel," said another, "Panama and the Panama Canal are a choke point for transport and communications throughout the hemisphere. We know how important you are to us."

As I reflected on these themes, it was clear that the United States was not talking about a little canal built three-quarters of a century earlier that was becoming obsolete and too small for the world's greatest commercial fleets. What value, I thought, did a tiny canal built in 1904 have?

No, the Americans were talking about their dominion over a geographical area that they saw as strategically vital, just as much now in the Cold War as it always had been. They were looking at a chess board. They controlled the pieces at an important stalemate: Panama was still the crossroads of the hemisphere. At the close of the century, the Americans saw Panama just as Teddy Roosevelt had seen it in 1904: this land was theirs and they wanted it all for their own.

In the late morning, I was ushered into the office of William Casey. He was not exactly an imposing man, standing there, hunched over and handling himself like any other American businessman, but with the appearance of a kindly old grandfather. Still, I was impressed with him. He seemed to be a classic, old-style intelligence officer and I found a great kinship in that; here was a man who had been consumed by the process and the art of intelligence gathering.

While many of the morning meetings were with Spanish-speaking intelligence officers, a translator was always present. This was especially necessary with Casey—my knowledge of English did little good. He cocked his head as he spoke from a turned lip with words that tripped out in ways I couldn't understand at all. And yet, with the help of translation, our chat, extending two hours or so over a luncheon in an adjoining dining room, was animated.

"Colonel Noriega," he said, "we want to do everything we can to maintain the cooperation we have established with you and your country."

"As do we," I told Casey. "General Torrijos has asked me to tell you that he looks forward to a friendly, open relationship." In addition, I told him, Torrijos asked me to describe our philosophy of openness— that we should talk frequently and openly to avoid misunderstanding. "The CIA ends up being blamed for every little thing because of the aura of mystery that surrounds it," I said. "We need to keep the lines open so we can change that."

Casey was interested in hearing about the CIA role in the 1969 coup against Torrijos. I told him what I knew. He smiled when I talked about the mystery we ascribed to the spy agency. "I'd like to come to Panama soon and visit with the general," he said. He wanted "a channel of communication with Cuba without any obligation."

The chats were in part protocol, in part an early attempt to raise the key issues that Casey and the Reagan administration wanted to promote. Central America, he said, was on the verge of being overrun by Communism. Panama was uniquely situated to observe events in Central America because our doors were open to all sides. The United States knew this and welcomed our openness and our help, he said.

I said little during this first briefing by Casey on the Central America plan. I never harbored any illusion that Washington really cared what I thought. It was a situation in which special foreign visitors, allies and potential allies are brought to the CIA for a briefing. The CIA representatives present their view of the world, ask polite questions of their guests and sit calmly and courteously when it's the visitor's turn to talk. This is what they call their foreign policy: supporting democracy worldwide. It is really a recipe for making sure that their own form of repression is being disseminated.

Casey gave no operations details of what was planned by the Reagan administration; instead, I got the party line, a general perspective of the struggle they had before them. Casey made it clear what he and Reagan and Bush thought the stakes were.

"The United States is concerned about the Cuba-Granada-Nicaragua triangle," he said. "We need to contain the communist threat because

Cuba and Russia will take any opportunity to subvert democracy. We plan to meet the challenge."

He said that the United States would take all possible steps, including covert action and mounting guerrilla insurgencies, to block Cuban- and Soviet-inspired designs. They were ready to do whatever they could to eliminate Marxist-Leninist insurgencies wherever they found them, and especially to repel and terminate any involvement, communication or dependence on Fidel Castro anywhere in Latin America. "Of course, we can't let the Central Intelligence Agency get involved directly," Casey told me. "We can't let it appear as though we are taking direct action here. We need help."

Over lunch, the chat was more anecdotal. As we reviewed the world scene, Casey was especially interested in my contacts with Israeli officials. I told him, for example, about having met Moshe Dayan and Yitzhak Rabin shortly after the 1967 Six-Day War.

Dayan, the triumphant general, took me on a tour of the war zone and described strategic planning that went into fighting the Syrians. We discussed Israeli theories of intelligence gathering. I recalled having met Dayan another time during a later trip at the Tel Aviv Hilton, riding down the elevator with him and a woman who was thrilled to have the opportunity to stand so close to the war hero.

"I met him; I shook his hand," the woman shrieked as she ran off into the lobby. Dayan smiled mildly. At the time, he was a civilian and was not in the government.

Rabin, I told Casey, by comparison was aloof and formal. My chat with him was about peace between the Arabs and the Israelis. Dayan was effusive and personal, making more of a lasting impression.

Casey listened intently as I shared my impressions of these men. I find this to be an important quality—he was a person who had the culture, social grace and intelligence to listen when others spoke.

This meeting was the start of a closer relationship with the CIA, which, for my part, was always characterized by equanimity. Over the years, my CIA contacts knew full well that I was a reliable conduit of messages from the United States to the Cubans; that communications link was defended by Casey and he could count on me to keep it open. He visited me several times in Panama at my home. When Casey and the CIA asked for passports and visas so that their operatives could carry out specific intelligence missions, for example, Panama, under my command, gave them that help and more. If, as was the case, the United States sought a channel of communication with the Russians, they knew that they could rely on me for clean and reliable transmission of information. We did not request or ever receive information on what any of these operations might have been. U.S. intelligence was highly compartmentalized; we never got an inkling of the targets or results in any such requests. Never did any double-dealing or bad information come out of Panama as a result of this relationship, which was handled always with a high level of respect. The Americans knew that they would get nothing more and nothing less from me than that.

Even in the depths of our bad relations with the Americans, certain intelligence information was protected. There was, for example, a National Security Agency center at the Southern Command known as "the Tunnel." Built into the side of a hill in Quarry Heights, the facility looked unassuming from the outside. Inside was the most complete, top-secret defense and spying center imaginable. It was used for tracking Cuba, for monitoring drug trafficking and spy planes. During our period of cooperation on hemisphere drug interdiction in the early 1980s, drug surveillance was handled from the Tunnel. We never told anyone of its existence.

I had been the U.S. contact person throughout the 1970s, and I was well known to everyone in the CIA; now, with Casey, the relations would become tighter. In 1983, when I assumed command, the CIA was pleased to have a direct connection with the leader of the Panamanian military. Even though I appointed my own G-2 intelligence chief, Casey came down soon after I assumed command to make it clear that his organization was happy to deal with me directly.

But I was under no illusions: neither Panama nor I was ever central to the game being played by the Americans; we, in turn, never allowed Panama to become a pawn in that game. Their Central American plans started to go too far. We viewed their support for the Salvadoran military and the crazed war they organized against the Sandinistas as irresponsible and unbalanced; this was not our battle and we thought it was wrongheaded.

Moreover, we supported the Sandinista revolution and understood the nationalist aspirations of the FMLN guerrillas in El Salvador. With the advent of their war, the United States began to make demands that we could not meet and applied more pressure than we could tolerate. Up until then, I had been Mr. Yes—the man on whom the Americans could always depend; now I had started to become known as Mr. No. And Mr. No, the Reagan administration decided, had to be destroyed.

Yet I am convinced that history would have been altered and the December 20, 1989, invasion of Panama never would have taken place if Casey had lived. Casey had the power and the inclination to defend me against the conspiracy that was developing against me, spurred on by Panamanian opponents and their friends in Washington.

Casey knew what was going on in Panama. The drug trial would not have worked if he were alive, because I would have had him as a living testament and defender; he knew the truth about all the charges against me. He knew the truth about the Spadafora killing and the drug pilots flying for Bush's contras.

Neither the Americans nor their allies ever understood why we would not help them: it was not in our strategic national interest to do so, it was not our belief that communism was about to overrun Latin America; it was not our intention to oppose liberation movements.

We weren't interested in helping the Americans in that way. Strategically, it made no sense. We didn't want to be the handmaidens of the Americans, and everybody in the region knew, whether they understood it or not, that this was our position. Because of this, our relations at times were strained with the closest U.S. allies—the Salvadorans and Hondurans and the Contras—because they knew that we had a different way of looking at the United States.

I had this argument many times with many different people. Three are worth mentioning: General Gustavo Alvarez Martinez[2] of Honduras, Captain Roberto D'Aubuisson of El Salvador and a lieutenant colonel from the United States named Oliver North. I was fascinated by all three—Alvarez because of how naive he was and because of what happened to him; D'Aubuisson because of his one-track mind on annihilating communism as if it were a disease; and North because of all the power he professed to have.

---

[2] Alvarez was Honduran military commander from January 1982 until March 1984; he presided over dramatic growth in the U.S. military presence in Honduras. He was assassinated in Honduras in January 1989.

Analyzing Three Zealots

The case of Alvarez was perhaps the most instructive example to me of how the United States dealt with its fallen friends. Alvarez, his army and the Honduran leadership were different from us. They had a strong ideology applauded by the United States: dedicated anti-Marxists, anti-communists, "anti" anything that was socially meaningful or beneficial to the people. Anything that had the word "social" in it for Alvarez meant "communism." He had a true fixation about Nicaragua.

"Manuel Antonio," Alvarez said to me one day, "I have a dream: I can see myself riding into Nicaragua on a white horse, freeing the country from the Sandinista communists and taking control."

Alvarez tried by all possible means to make his dream come true. Waving an anti-communist and anti-Cuban flag, he wanted to help the United States wage war against Nicaragua; all the time he was designing his war strategy.

It was this ardor in the struggle that convinced the United States to support Alvarez, helping him leapfrog over other officers and take control of the Honduran military. By way of giving thanks to his patrons in Washington, Alvarez opened Honduras up to virtual U.S. control. He and his military in the 1980s took over Panama's role as obedient servant to its North American masters. Alvarez said that it was all necessary to fight the Cold War. Yet where did his anti-communist zeal come from and what did it have to do with Honduras? There were virtually no guerrillas in Honduras, although a small group called the Chinchoneros did eventually emerge, seizing some hostages in Tegucigalpa, then negotiating their way out of the country with the help of mediation by foreign diplomats. Panama had a role in the negotiations, offering to send a plane to fly the guerrillas out of Honduras, guaranteeing their safety until they could leave the area. The Chinchoneros kept their part of the bargain, releasing the hostages, and we sent an air force plane to pick them up and take them to Panama City. Alvarez called me, asking me to renege on the bargain and send them back to Honduras. I refused, first of all because we had mediated in good faith, and second, because I knew this would be tantamount to a death sentence for the rebels.

Alvarez and I quarreled, but Panama was steadfast. "On diplomatic grounds alone, it can't be done," I told him. "These men were entrusted to our protection." We let the Chinchoneros go, some traveling to Mexico, others to Cuba. We found out later that Honduran intelligence got pictures of all of them, probably, we believed, from someone operating through the Red Cross. And when some of the rebels snuck back into Honduras, Alvarez was able to identify them and had them killed one by one.

Alvarez and I often argued, but we treated each other with respect. He knew that I was neither a Marxist nor a communist, but a supporter of these groups that he hated so much. The problem that ideologues had with Panama was that they couldn't figure us out. We made friends based on our own value system. Chile was a good example. The Panamanian military had respectful relations with its Chilean military counterparts, but when General Augusto Pinochet seized power from Salvador Allende on September 11, 1973, we set out to provide asylum to as many people as we could.

There was much concern in Panama upon hearing the news of the Chilean coup, since hundreds of our countrymen—students, leftists, even some opponents of the Panamanian military—were living there.

I called my counterpart as that country's intelligence chief, General Augusto Lutz, knowing he had become a member of the new military junta, and used that contact to help rescue many Panamanians, Chileans and others. My friend briefed me on events, then put Pinochet on the line. I recognized the general's distinctive voice; he told me he had a daughter living in Panama and feared reprisals against her by leftist opponents. Without his asking I told him I would guarantee her security, which I did, although there were never any incidents.

In the days that followed, Pinochet's military rounded up thousands of Allende supporters. Panama became a lifeline for people detained by Pinochet or threatened with arrest.

I asked our very able ambassador, Joaquín Meza, to go to the now infamous Santiago soccer stadium, where suspected leftists and opponents were later reported as having been tortured and killed. Panama managed to liberate at least 1,200 people—doctors, intellectuals, students—men, women and children. In particular I remember the case of a three-year-old girl named Macarena Franqui Marsh, whose father was a leftist activist. It was known that the father was in the hands of

Chilean Military Police, the DINA, but the little girl was missing and believed held captive, it was said, perhaps to apply pressure on her father. Meza heard the story and used his diplomatic prowess, along with the goodwill I had with Pinochet, to rescue the little girl. I was also able to help a United Nations official and members of the musical group Canta America, among others detained by the military regime.

Meza filled the Panamanian embassy in Santiago with refugees and when the building could hold not a soul more, Torrijos let us buy two additional buildings to hold more refugees under our diplomatic umbrella.

Years later, when I became commander of the Panamanian military, I went to Santiago for a hemispheric meeting of military chiefs. Pinochet invited me for a private dinner at his home with his wife and daughter. Ambassador Meza was also there.

Pinochet was in an ebullient mood. "Well, you Panamanians sure did save a lot of those Marxists—I'll bet it was something like two thousand of them," he said. "Tell me one thing, General Noriega. Have they ever thanked you?"

Alvarez's attempts to provoke a war proved his undoing. The United States wanted the Contras to overthrow Nicaragua and they wanted to act as an unseen player in that game. They did not seek a highly visible, overt approach, and that was what Alvarez was leading them toward. Eventually this meant that Alvarez, for reasons very different from the U.S. interest in getting rid of me, became a problem. I refused to help them in Nicaragua—Alvarez wanted to do too much.

So suddenly, one fine day, there was a coup in Tegucigalpa, coming from the quarter where one would least expect it: Alvarez's closest friends, fellow officers in the Honduran air force. The United States helped plan and instigate the coup. The armed forces seized their commander, tied him up and sent him packing out of the country, to Costa Rica.

The moment chosen for the uprising against Alvarez was important. The United States had been hosting a minicourse on military intelligence and operations at Fort Gulick, one of its military bases in the former Canal Zone. Among those attending the course were a number of Alvarez's key men. I remember giving the closing speech and later attending a reception for them at the Hotel Continental that evening. All of us were unaware of the trouble brewing back in Honduras.

The news came out the following morning, with word that General Walter Lopez was the new head of the Honduran armed forces. Later the same day, I received a message from Costa Rica: Alvarez wanted to talk to me.

When the phone hookup was finally made, the man on the other end of the line was an Alvarez who sounded in a far different frame of mind than the man I knew: alternately bitter, defeated, tearful, without hope, then violent, grasping for possibilities, beseeching me for support.

"What can I do for you?" I said finally, unable to think of anything that could unseal his fate.

"Manuel Antonio, call General [Paul] Gorman for me," he said, referring to the head of the U.S. Southern Command. "I haven't been able to reach him, but Manuel Antonio, please, tell General Gorman, tell him, tell him about what they have done to me, tell him that I am in hiding here in Costa Rica, tell him everything I have told you."

I did in fact get in touch with Gorman.

"Oh, yes, yes, we know about that, we know about that, thanks for the call," Gorman said, dismissing the whole matter and promptly changing the subject. I could see that Gorman indeed knew a lot about Alvarez's fortunes, and that nothing was likely to change.

All of this would be inconsequential except for the fact that not many days later I had a visit from a CIA agent, obviously aware that I was in touch with Alvarez.

"Alvarez is going to the United States," the agent said. "Please send him this money through the BCCI account." The gift was a large quantity of cash. I sent it to Alvarez and he went to live in exile in the United States.

I was fascinated by the whole process, but I just couldn't understand the Americans. They thought everything would be made all right with money. It was beyond cynicism; it was disconnected from reality: "Let's send something to pacify him, to take care of him and his wife and children—and to keep him quiet. He's done his job for us. And now it's over."

Years later, the Americans tried the same thing with me; two million dollars seemed to be the going price for a military commander to give up his nation's sovereignty. Alvarez was in the back of my mind—and all the money they could offer me wasn't enough to get me to leave Panama. It wasn't the only time they tried.

D'Aubuisson

The case of Roberto D'Aubuisson was far more complex, but boiled down to the same thing. Never mind morality—a foreign contact is useful when and if he matches up with U.S. policy objectives. D'Aubuisson had been a hard-line major in the Salvadoran army, so radically anti-communist, so extreme in his hatred of anyone even suspected of being on the left and so open about it that he was expelled from the corps for the sake of appearance. But, inside or outside the institution of the Salvadoran armed forces, D'Aubuisson was a military force to be reckoned with and he was always close to the United States. Although for public consumption D'Aubuisson was condemned and shunned by the U.S., privately he was embraced and never condemned by any key policy maker.

He came to Panama several times and we would have long talks, which were unavoidably and inevitably political. He was a tough, wiry, energetic man, anti-communist to the bone and oppressively military in manner. He walked and stood ramrod straight; even in informal situations, he was always stiff and starched, his pursed, tight lips ready to launch into a tirade.

It was evident that his principal reason for coming to Panama was not to meet with me, but to hold strategy sessions at the Southern Command. Panamanian intelligence was able to monitor what was going on at such events, even though we weren't invited in. There would be planning meetings with U.S. and Salvadoran officers, and sometimes Argentina would send up a military group to analyze the situation. In such settings, D'Aubuisson was frequently the protagonist. He would present his analysis of tactics and how things were going in the war. And he was given intelligence briefings by U.S. officials in return.

On one visit to my house, he brought whiskey and became increasingly loud and argumentative as the night wore on.

"Look, Manuel Antonio," he said. "You have the communists from El Salvador wandering around Panama all the time. I don't understand how you people here can give protection to these communists."

"And how do you know anything about it?" I asked.

"I have my own sources of information here, who tell me that the guerrilla commanders are always coming and going, whenever they want."

"Come on," I told him, "we're actually helping San Salvador by letting them come in," I said, making a joke. "At least when they're in Panama, they're not causing you any trouble. They're probably here partying. Life is different in Panama."

D'Aubuisson would not be deterred. He could be set off quite easily and would just flip. If you ever tried to break away from the constant theme of tactics in fighting the guerrillas and how to win the war, he would jump right back on the same track.

"No, no, no," he said crazily, almost jumping into the air. "They are directing the guerrilla war from here. This is their base of operations; they direct their operations and raise money and weapons in Panama. And this is where they have their contact with the Cubans."

What he said was not true. Panama was not providing support to the FMLN. He was saying that allowing them to come to Panama was tantamount to our supporting the war effort. Yes, the Salvadoran guerrillas came to Panama, but so did the leaders of many other guerrilla movements. So did their opponents, like D'Aubuisson himself. The leaders of these movements were very careful: they knew and we told them explicitly that this was open territory and that the world's intelligence services were all here, wandering around. But the rule was that nothing was to happen in Panama, that each of them was responsible for their own security, and we wanted no funny business; that this same warning would serve for every other country as well.

"Look, what are you telling me here?" I said. "Everybody is free to come and go in Panama. But nobody is launching any operations. We don't permit it."

"*Está jodido, pues*—that's fucked up," he said. "Toss them out or give them to me. Hand them over to me and nobody will ever know what happened."

The subject illuminated the personality of the man; his prosecution of the war was like a psychosis. And his attitude also foreshadowed what he was really doing. The United Nations, capping off years of human rights reports, said D'Aubuisson controlled paramilitary death squads until the day he died and was responsible for thousands of deaths of noncombatants throughout the 1980s. While D'Aubuisson never said so directly, he talked about "hitting the Marxists from all directions," saying, "The communists are like vermin . . . they must be exterminated," and if necessary, he would do so in a "scorched earth" campaign. These were the very words he used. And when he spoke, his eyes glistened with the ardor of what he was saying.

"Just let anyone try to stop us," he said. "They'll see what happens." He went as far as to talk about his military branch, separate from the political section of the ARENA—National Republican Alliance—party, which he had founded. "We have supporters getting anti-guerrilla defensive training," he would tell me.

When he talked about tactics, it was about his pride in his organization and intelligence capacity, in maintaining better files on people than even the Salvadoran military had. He said that his intelligence was based on his connections with the United States—he never said with what part of the U.S. government, he simply said the USA, and referred at times to exchanging information and keeping tabs with U.S. officials.

He felt himself empowered by U.S. policy, as did the Central American presidents, with whom—excluding, of course, Nicaragua—he had a more far-reaching relationship than has ever been told to do what he wanted with a perfect sense of mission. That was what he said whenever I met him. I once asked him if he feared international sanctions.

No, he said, because he had his flanks covered—by the knowledge that the State Department and the Central Intelligence Agency knew exactly what he was doing. He saw himself to be operating with the blessing of the United States, and he said he had the green light "to wipe out Marxist-Leninists," as he always put it. One time I remember trying to tease him into something.

"You're like pure black coffee," I said, "like a cup of black espresso, too strong, much too strong. You need a little bit of cream to balance things off. You're too extreme about this. Why don't you try talking with the other extreme? Why don't you talk to the Cubans, with Fidel's people?"

"Sure, I can talk with them and debate with them, no problem," D'Aubuisson said. "I'm not afraid to talk to them. I'm not afraid to talk to Fidel."

I remember very well the day that I introduced him to several members of the Cuban embassy in Panama. I had convinced D'Aubuisson to meet with the Cubans to discuss Central America.

The Cubans told the Salvadoran death squad leader that both sides should try to defuse the situation in El Salvador to end the bloodshed. While they supported the FMLN, the Cubans told D'Aubuisson, they saw them as an independent, autonomous force with their own principles and ideals. They also spoke to D'Aubuisson about self-determination for El Salvador.

I doubt that D'Aubuisson ever understood what they were talking about. It never reached the level of negotiations, but with such an extremist, even a talk like this seemed to be worth something. The Cubans ended up inviting him to Havana, and he said that he would be willing to go. But as far as I know, it never came to anything.

This was at the peak of the political violence—the disappearances and death squad activity in El Salvador. D'Aubuisson came more and more often, and it was no shopping trip to the duty-free zone, where so many tourists go in Panama City to buy perfume and wristwatches. He was coordinating his operations with the Southern Command.

Eventually, we caught them in the act—D'Aubuisson and the Southern Command, in violation of the Panama Canal treaties, began covert training of Salvadorans on Panamanian territory.

Early in 1985, the Salvadoran operations were heating up. Planes loaded with supplies were shuttling back and forth from the United States to the U.S. bases and then on to El Salvador. One day, about two dozen men arrived at Howard air base, Salvadorans without visas, traveling as military, saying they were going to a training course. The only problem was that the School of the Americas, the U.S. training center for police and military from Latin America, had been withdrawn from Panama, and the United States was not authorized to conduct military training for foreigners in Panama anymore. So what were they doing? Our officer on duty at Panama immigration let them come through, but reported it up the line. We presented a diplomatically worded complaint to the Salvadoran military: why were they sending personnel to Panama without getting visas? It was a question of reciprocity at the very least—Panamanians needed visas to go to El Salvador; the opposite was also true.

The complaint was filed and nothing happened. Then another group arrived, and they were denied entry. This time the generals at the U.S. Southern Command got involved, requesting entry for the Salvadorans, saying they were coming for a training course and asking for a visa. Retroactively, the Salvadorans also applied for visas at the Panamanian embassy in San Salvador, saying that they were on a group tour and that they were going to the Canal Zone.

Our intelligence branch had no trouble in finding out that these Salvadorans were traveling with fake documents. If you have a passport that says your name is Captain García, it isn't too hard to find out in San Salvador that there is no Captain García in the armed forces, no matter how hard you try to pretend. We were able to find out about it through our secret channels. Our operatives in the American zone told us this was actually a top-secret training session, combining instruction in intelligence, explosives, counterinsurgency, demolition training, sharpshooting, etc. The training courses were so specific that they lasted only three weeks at a shot. This was not general instruction. People came for their intended purpose, catered to each individual: snipers took sharpshooter training, explosives specialists took demolition training, intelligence operatives took intelligence training. Then they went on their way, back to El Salvador, for a little "freedom fighting." The United States trained the death squads at the U.S. Southern Command.

Oliver North

Despite all their money and friends of convenience like Alvarez and D'Aubuisson, the Americans just weren't doing too well with their wars in Central America. Early on it was clear to most in the CIA that I was not willing to help the Contras. Nevertheless, the Americans had for years come to me for help and advice, and when things started going badly for them in Central America, they tried it again.

The initiative came from the man known as the greatest of the true believers, Oliver North. In North's view, I was no different from men like Alvarez or D'Aubuisson, mere operatives who did his dirty work. North was a user of men. He would be the one to find friends of convenience, pay them off and discard them when their work was done. Like Alvarez, he also wanted to be the conqueror on a white horse. He wanted to be an American hero.

While I had two meetings of note with Oliver North—and I could see that he was indeed the brash, self-assured man people now know him to be—I had no idea at the time of the scope of his enterprise. I had to assume that the impetus for his searching me out came from the White House and CIA men I had dealt with over the years.

His first overture developed under unexpected circumstances. In 1985, Lieutenant General Robert Schweitzer, the director of the Inter-American Defense College in Washington, DC, invited me to give the institution's commencement address. The college brought in officers from Latin American militaries throughout the hemisphere—excluding Cuba, of course. The officers study and attend lectures for an entire term. This was the second time I had given a speech at the college and it was a pleasure to do so.

I thanked the general for his invitation, went to the commencement, gave my speech, sat through some formalities and went to a brief reception. This was all followed by an evening event, a gala party on a ship cruising the Potomac.

I was standing on the deck with a colleague when General Schweitzer called me aside.

"General Noriega, I'd like you to meet a colleague of ours, Lieutenant Colonel Oliver North of the United States Marine Corps," Schweitzer said, excusing himself politely after the introduction so North and I could talk.

I was surprised by the introduction and by North's presence, since I didn't think he had anything to do with the college staff. That was true, he said. He had heard that I would be attending this evening cruise and had sought out an invitation especially for the purpose of meeting me.

North may not have remembered, but I had met him several other times—in 1983, when he had accompanied Bush, and another time the same year when he had traveled to El Salvador with then Secretary of Defense Caspar Weinberger. On that occasion, I remember that the head of the U.S. Southern Command, General John Galvin, and I had agreed that we would give Weinberger the opportunity, as an old soldier from World War II, to review the troops. Weinberger had been touched by the gesture and reacted emotionally to the opportunity.

One other point: Weinberger apparently had been accompanied by another aide whom I just can't remember seeing—Colin Powell. If he had been there, Powell was far in the background, although he said in his autobiography that at this courtesy visit—at which we didn't exchange a word and at which I was paying honors to his chief—that I was "evil."

North got down to business. He described himself as being at the helm of the Contra supply effort. "We're in a war here, General. My orders come directly from President Reagan and Vice President Bush," he said, emphasizing his important, central role in all of this. North had apparently gotten to the cruise ship sometime before I did, and he was many drinks ahead of me. It had made him loose and talkative. It was evident that he wanted to leave me with the impression that he was not just any lieutenant colonel, but a special one, a man who even had the ability to give commands and do things that men of higher rank, even generals, could not do.

He made references to needing to get to know me, to having heard about my good work for the United States, and talked about how he was having problems in Miami because of allegations that people working for him on behalf of the Contras were also flying drugs. He spoke for a while like that, insisting that we would need to get to know each other. He was quite insistent and said that he would keep in contact with me and also with the Panamanian military attaché, who was standing nearby. I didn't say much, listened politely, and after a while we broke off. That was that. The whole thing left me a bit surprised— his brashness, his having sought me out—and I was wondering whether the whole thing was the word of a braggart who had had one drink more than he should have.

I brought up the matter in passing at a meeting during the same U.S. visit with William Casey at CIA headquarters. "Is it true what North says about his work with the Contras?"

"Oh, yes," said Casey. "It's true. North is who he says he is."

I had no direct contact with North for a year or more after that.

Then he approached me for help. In the summer of 1986, I got a call from Joaquin Quiñones, a Cuban American who would contact me on behalf of the National Security Council. I had met Quiñones through Pigua Cordobez, a Panamanian businessman; he was a political ally of Bush, a diplomat of some kind who had sought unsuccessfully the post of U.S. ambassador to Panama. Quiñones was represented to me as a messenger from the White House. At our first encounter, he had said that he was impressed by our military forces and that Vice President Bush was very much interested in Panama. Quiñones, like North and all the other envoys I met, told me that Bush was handling the Contras business directly.

Some time afterward, Quiñones came to Panama for a visit. He told me that Oliver North was visiting Iran and Israel and would be interested in meeting with me. They knew that I had a trip scheduled to Europe, so they suggested that North meet me on his return leg in England. I said that I had no problem meeting with him.

The meeting was at the Victoria Gardens, a hotel I was staying at close to the Panamanian embassy. I was accompanied by a young diplomat assigned to the embassy, named Jorge Constantino. I remember that we got together with the Americans at the left side of the lobby, toward the rear; there's a kind of alcove where they serve coffee. It's an isolated and private spot where you feel like you're in a room by yourself.

I recognized North easily from our previous meeting in Washington. He was disheveled, as were the men who accompanied him. He had the look of someone who had been traveling all night. He hadn't shaved and you could tell from his breath that he had been drinking. Richard Secord and John Singlaub were there too. They were both retired military men whom I hadn't met before, but whom I recognized later when the Iran-Contra scandal unfolded. Singlaub, I recall, described himself as chief of operations for the team; he gave me his card. Both men also looked unkempt; their clothing had the creased look of people who had been on the road.

I did have some forewarning of what this was all about, thanks to Mike Harari, my Israeli contact, a former Mossad officer based in Panama City. Harari had given me a general briefing about what they were up to, that they had been on a mission to the Middle East, including Iran. There was a story of a ship that had left Israel supposedly carrying food or candy or some nonsense like that. Of course, it was really carrying weapons to Iran.

I knew the possible reasons for this meeting after my previous contact with North. At the time, the U.S. Congress was ready to stop any covert operation that cost too much, took too long or in which Americans were liable to be killed. What the American government needed were intermediates who could handle clandestine operations on their behalf.

I am convinced that these were not freelance operations—both Bush and Reagan were always completely tuned in to and briefed on what was going on. Everything was handled at a distance by men like Dwayne "Dewey" Clarridge, who was the CIA regional chief for Latin America. Along with North, John Poindexter, Nestor Sanchez and others at the National Security Council, these men promoted a clear Reagan administration policy. The underlings always made sure to tell me they were asking for my help "in the name of President Reagan" or "in the name of President Bush." The president, they would say, "has authorized us to start supporting the military against the guerrillas in El Salvador and to launch attacks against Nicaragua." The problem for them was, we never agreed to participate in any of it.

Quiñones was also there, acting as translator. The atmosphere was quite cordial and respectful. North had a matter-of-fact, no-nonsense way of talking. He got right to the point, addressing me with the professional air of one military man speaking to another. He said he was worried that the Contras were not showing much combat ability and the United States was having trouble providing them with economic aid.

It was time for Panama to take a leading role in supporting the Contras, he said. In return, "There will be a clean slate; we'll forget about all the bad stuff we've heard," he said, referring to the political charges being planted in Washington by Panamanian opposition leaders. "We'll just forget about it." He made it sound like he was offering Christmas presents to an obedient child.

He said he wanted us to set up a commando operation to plant bombs, mine Nicaraguan harbors.[3] "What we need is a few spectacular acts of sabotage." I remember Quiñones translating the words "spectacular" and "sabotage." Sabotage, sabotage, sabotage—he repeated it more than once. He took out a piece of paper with a laundry list of things he wanted done: blowing up high-tension lines, acts of terrorism in Managua, mining the harbor. And he cast the Panamanian mil-

---

[3] North continues to maintain that the proposal to conduct sabotage operations in Nicaragua came from Noriega. Notebooks seized during the Iran-Contra affair make cryptic remarks about proposals by Noriega. But an authoritative CIA source says that Noriega never made such an offer. "He was seldom thought of" when it came to helping the Contra effort, "rarely asked and never provided any help whatsoever."

itary as his last hope. He had nothing else. The Contras had not been able to do anything.

"There's money in it for you and for Panama," he kept saying; "money to develop military projects, for more weapons, for whatever you need."

I thought North's proposal was ridiculous and never even considered it, not even for an instant.

"Look, the answer is that we just can't do this," I said. "I think you should face reality. The Contras have lost their opportunity, if they ever had one. The capacity of the Sandinista forces has grown and they are far superior in strategy and defensive posture. They have learned very fast. Their tactics are from the Soviet military, essentially a Soviet defense."

North betrayed no particular emotion as I analyzed the military situation, but his interest was piqued by my mention of the Russians.

"I need to get more information about this so I can pass it on," he said. "Give me an analysis and make it a good one. Explain everything you've told me about the Contras and the Sandinistas and the Soviet defense doctrine. I need to show something like that to Reagan and Bush, at least, because I'm responsible for what is happening."

He seemed to be taking what I had to say in terms of one military man talking to another. His attitude appeared to be: okay, you're not helping me on the ground, but we need a good military analysis of the situation. We need your expertise. This is the first time I've heard this.

I sent the document to him through Quiñones and I remember hearing no more about it until the discovery of the Contra scandal. Quiñones called me to say that the report was among the documents shredded in North's office. It was a more detailed version of what I said just a few months later in Tokyo before a group of diplomats attending a meeting of the Japan-Panama Friendship Association. In a carefully worded rebuke of U.S. policy, I said that we supported a regional settlement to the civil wars of Central America. "We face . . . the undeniable fact that the political and military crisis in Central America is being prolonged and, along with it, the economic crisis of the region is growing more acute," I said. "And the insistence on a strictly military solution undermines social programs, because the more that is spent on arms, there are fewer economic resources for hospitals, schools, low-cost housing and highways. In reality, what is happening in Central America, casting aside all literary adornments to explain it, is that the region is simply becoming an experimental battlefield for new military doctrines and concepts. . . ."

It was evident from everything I knew and from what was confirmed by meeting with him that North was trying to juggle a hundred chess pieces to try to make the Contra and Iran deals work. I only knew about one piece—me. I think he and his confidantes, men who also included Elliott Abrams, the U.S. assistant secretary of state for inter-american affairs,[4] and John Poindexter, were grasping for anything that would work; the Contras were not making any progress, the Honduras front was too visible and weak; the Southern Front was collapsing; there was limited money to finance the war. Perhaps Panama could make the difference. And when I refused, one has to conclude that the real reaction was vindictive, angry, filled with calls for revenge against the pawn who wouldn't play along. North pretended to his superiors that I was the one who had sought this meeting, that I was the one who offered to infiltrate Nicaragua and take up arms.

Just before North's unsuccessful 1994 campaign for the U.S. Senate in Virginia, I broke my silence with the news media and was interviewed about this subject on television in the United States. I repeated the story and told everything I knew. I am certain that my words helped him lose.

A Nobel Prize for War

The American establishment saw Panama's refusal to participate in their wars as the height of obstinacy. They grew angry. While a conspiracy of revenge against me began to germinate, they were forced to work around us when it came to their Central American operations. We could not control what the United States did at its Southern Command headquarters in Panama, although it was obvious that they were supporting the base's efforts in the region. At times, however, we were able to interfere. Meanwhile, we watched the United States mount op-

---

[4] Abrams pleaded guilty on October 7, 1991, to two federal counts of lying before Congress, as a result of investigations by Special Prosecutor Lawrence Walsh into illegal funding of the Nicaraguan Contra rebels.

erations to support the death squads in El Salvador and to mount counterrevolutionary operations against the Sandinistas from both sides of Nicaragua—Costa Rica and Honduras.

There was no greater contrast in the way two countries behaved, dealing with U.S. pressure to support the Central American efforts. By the end of the Bush era, the leader of one of the countries was a prisoner of war; the other won the Nobel peace prize.

Because of its strategic importance, Costa Rica replaced Panama as a mecca for intelligence and counterintelligence. Yet Costa Rica also basked in its international image of neutrality, being one of the few nations in the world that has no army. Costa Rica was boiling with all sorts of U.S. intelligence operations, issuing a license for example, so that a broadcast station called Radio Impacto could interfere with Panamanian radio during our election campaign. The Costa Rican government also was backing the Contra cause, although it didn't want this to be known.

The Costa Rican government allowed itself to be used by the United States to stage operations against the Nicaraguan government. This was something Panama had no intention of doing. With Costa Rican acquiescence in the form of direct authorization from its president, the CIA built an airstrip near the border with Nicaragua, with the help of an American expatriate named John Hull. From Hull's ranch, the United States armed the Contras' Southern Front, providing these Nicaraguan rebels with documentation, refuge, and storage of arms and, of course, looking the other way if they made money on the side with the trans-shipment of drugs within their arms operations.

Hull and his airstrip, we believed, were involved in providing logistical support for the infamous case of La Penca, the bomb attack on Eden Pastora at his jungle hideout on the border between Costa Rica and Nicaragua. Pastora was known as Commander Zero, the Sandinista fighter who split with his Nicaraguan rebel comrades after the July 19, 1979, overthrow of Anastasio Somoza. After breaking off from Managua, Pastora went into exile in Costa Rica and started forming his own group of guerrillas, which became known as the Southern Front.

Pastora survived the bomb attack on his headquarters, although an American reporter who had been interviewing him was killed. Pastora came to see me in Panama several weeks before the attack. He realized that he would always be a target for attack, although he gave no indication that he suspected there was an ongoing plan to kill him. I have read reports charging that an Argentine mercenary was brought in to kill Pastora, by the Sandinistas or the CIA or both, using the attacker as a double or even triple agent. Our investigation into the matter was inconclusive, although we found evidence that John Hull and the CIA had some knowledge of the event. While the Sandinistas had no use for Commander Zero and would have been willing to kill him, it was John Hull and Oliver North's partner, Joe Fernandez, the CIA station chief in Costa Rica, who had the greater motive. Killing Pastora was perfect, because it would cast blame on the Sandinistas, it would take away a loose cannon the CIA could not control and it would, perhaps, create a martyr to the Contra cause. They failed, although thanks to Costa Rica, the operations of Hull and the United States to subvert Nicaragua and Panama went on unimpeded.

I am particularly offended by the public image of then Costa Rican President Oscar Arias, who won a Nobel prize for his work in "consolidating peace" in Central America. Actually, Arias sold out to Washington and was able to win peace only with Panamanian help. We were repaid for this help with treachery when Arias had the gall to support and endorse the U.S. invasion of Panama.

I first met Arias when he was running for president. His predecessor and patron, President Luis Monge, had contacted me and asked that Arias be afforded the same warm relations that Costa Rica had enjoyed with Panama during many administrations. In particular, it became obvious that Arias needed money for his presidential campaign, and more money after he was elected for what he said were political campaign debts. We gave his successful presidential campaign thousands of dollars and then continued to give him money after that. He would occasionally call my secretary, Marcela Tasón, when he needed money, and he insisted that Marcela deliver it to him personally at his home. We asked for and expected nothing in return. This was support for an ally with whom we shared a common border.

When Arias became the major force in trying to arrange a Central American peace accord, he was stymied until I personally appealed to the Sandinista government to hear him out. On one specific occasion, I remember Arias came to Chiriquí. We met at the home of Dr. Jorge Abadía, a prominent Panamanian politician. Arias asked for our help in organizing the "Esquipulas Two" Central American peace conference. During a news conference there, he applauded and praised my work in that regard. Daniel Ortega, the president of Nicaragua under the Sandinistas, and his brother, Humberto, the defense minister, considered Arias to be a moral and ideological weakling. With my repeated and persistent intervention, they finally agreed to sit down and talk with the other Central American countries. Arias won the Nobel peace prize, then he allowed the United States to place antennas in Costa Rican territory to spy on Panama; he allowed American operatives to base themselves in Costa Rica to spy on us. The United States pressured him to drop his friendship with Panama and side with them against us. He was never a mediator or a peacemaker. He was for sale; he had become just another Central American president, like all the others dependent on the demagoguery of George Bush's new world order.

CHAPTER 6

Whose Enemies Are They?

THE REASON William Casey and Oliver North were so insistent that I support them in Central America was clear: in the past, I had been quite effective in dealing with one of the toughest problems for U.S. intelligence—communication with Fidel Castro.

My long, cordial relationship with Fidel Castro was not based on ideology; it developed as a result of a request by the United States. I first met Castro as a result of Cuba's capture of two mercenary ships—the *Johnny Express* and the *Leyla Express*, under the command of José Villa, a seaman of Spanish origin—at the service of the CIA.[1] Villa and his men sailed to the Cuban coast and staged a wanton machine-gun raid on the resort town Balnearios, killing a score and leaving many wounded. When Cuban gunboats counterattacked and captured the two ships, they took Villa into custody. Both vessels flew the Panamanian flag.

U.S. intelligence contacted General Torrijos soon after the capture of Villa and his men, hoping that Torrijos's friendship with Castro

---

[1] The two ships were based in the Caribbean and were used as staging craft for speedboat attacks, in which Cuban exiles raced to shore, spraying the coastline with machine-gun fire. On December 15, 1971, Cuban gunboats attacked the two ships and captured Villa, a Spaniard based in Miami, after seriously wounding him.

might help negotiations toward Villa's release. Castro and Torrijos had not yet met face-to-face. I was Torrijos's G-2 intelligence chief, a lieutenant colonel at the time, and had not yet met the Cuban leader. Torrijos first tried normal diplomatic channels, citing the origin of the vessels, but was rebuffed. The Americans asked him to try again.

I don't remember Torrijos's specific rationale for complying, but this was at the inception of the Panama Canal treaties, and helping out the United States on such a request seemed like a helpful and painless gesture of good faith.

So he sent Rómulo Escobar Bethancourt, a well-known diplomat who played a key role in the canal negotiations, on a special mission to meet with Castro in Cuba. Bethancourt, a friend of Castro, spent a month in Havana discussing the case with Cuban officials and, occasionally, with Castro himself. Fidel rejected any possibility of releasing Villa. The guerrilla attack had outraged all Cubans. They were traumatized by the killing spree, the coldness of the crime and the unrepentant, bloodthirsty demeanor of Villa. Not surprisingly, Rómulo came home empty-handed.

The Americans insisted still more. They had to keep trying to get Villa back. They asked Torrijos to make one more try. "This time," the CIA station chief said, "send Noriega."

At the time, not only did I not know Fidel, but I also had never been to Cuba and didn't know much about the issues involved. But there I was, on orders from Omar, bouncing along in a C-47 transport plane, on my way to Havana with two aides and a pilot, Alberto Purcell.

At José Martí International Airport we were cordially greeted by Manuel Piñeiro, the chief of the American section in the foreign ministry, known widely by his nickname Barbarroja—"Red Beard." We spent our first day engaged in diplomatic niceties. We were housed in a diplomatic guest house in a picturesque setting along a lake. Our hosts took us around the city, showed us films about Cuba, served dinner, offered before- and after-dinner drinks, more small talk, then a very cordial good-night.

The following day, it was the same routine: breakfast, smiling hosts, a tour of the environs outside Havana. "This is all very courteous and we thank you for your hospitality," I finally had to tell Piñeiro. "But, as I've told you, our specific and sole mission is to meet with the *comandante* and that's what I have to do."

"Of course, yes, we know, we understand, no problem," Piñeiro and his aides said. Then we started more tours and more dinners and another round of drinks—it was clear we were in a classic Cuban holding pattern. I was getting quite frustrated that second night and as I drifted off to sleep, I was wondering how much longer this could go on.

"Colonel, excuse me, but Fidel is here," said one of my aides, calling me after midnight. I quickly dressed and prepared to greet Fidel. There were presentations, protocol and small talk—a good thing, because it took some effort to shake myself awake.

I do think that Castro's famous late-night-entrance schedule was partly his method of catching people off guard, but was also simply consistent with his work regimen. This first encounter with Fidel Castro lasted until five in the morning; 90 percent of the conversation was about Panama, with Fidel asking lots of questions. How do the locks of the Panama Canal work? What is everyday life like for Panamanians, agricultural production figures, the methods used, the type of fishing, our governmental system, information about Torrijos . . .

I interjected one point of my own: details of a trip he had made to Panama. It was in the 1950s, during the tenure of my brother's leadership in the Federation of Students. Luis Carlos had spent time with him during the visit and kept some snapshots of the two of them posing with another young visitor, Che Guevara, at the old Hotel Central in Panama City. Fidel had no memory of the specifics, but he did remember the trip. It reminded him of the old days and it went a long way toward establishing our relationship. When I got back home, I sent him copies of the pictures.

Far from the image painted by his opponents and detractors, who wanted to portray him as crazed and distracted, Castro was easy to talk to. He spoke deliberately, listened and enjoyed the banter of conversation.

We spoke into the night, toasting with whiskey, then drinking coffee to keep going. Close to dawn, he stood up.

"Very well, tomorrow I'll come show you some of our housing projects. We'll take a little tour," he said. I remember looking at my watch. It was 4:47 A.M.

"*Comandante,* just to remind you, I do have a specific mission from General Torrijos; I need to talk to you about the *Leyla Express* and—"

"No, *hombre,* no," he said with a frown, cutting me off. "It is not possible that our relations, our communications have to be based on these miserable murderers, who have killed children and innocent people and who deserve nothing more than death themselves because of the savage way they operated." He then launched into a rapid-fire diatribe about the guerrilla attack.

"How is it possible that Torrijos could be asking me to hand over these murderers who have raised the indignation of all Cubans?"

His visit had been an exercise in psychology. Catch your opponent off guard (actually sleeping, in my case), set your own pace, parry and wait for his first move, then strike and leave him speechless.

He had won this first round easily.

All I could say was "Okay, we can talk about it tomorrow."

I slept for a few hours until, as he had promised, Fidel came around to pick me up, at midmorning, along with his bodyguard. One could say that it was yet another tour, but with Fidel at the wheel of his own jeep, it was a fantastic experience. There was nothing contrived about this day, yet it was spectacular. People would come running as they got a glimpse of us driving along, trailed very unobtrusively by a single car. Sometimes there would be spontaneous town meetings and gripe sessions. Fidel listened intently, no matter what the subject.

"Let's go take a look at some of our projects," he said. We drove along easily, chatting amiably, stopping at construction sites, meandering from village to village.

People crowded around; they were happy and friendly; some had complaints against bureaucratic delays—a shipment of cement hadn't arrived on time, or a document promised for such-and-such a date wasn't in yet. Fidel would gesture to his private secretary, right alongside him. A notation was made for follow-up later.

Fidel was the perfect tour guide. He explained everything as we went along. We went to a livestock station engaged in experiments to increase milk production. It seems there was a special cow that had been brought in from Canada—complete with comforting music and a beautiful stable. There was much talk, down to the smallest detail about the livestock, with the people that worked there. Always in good humor, but not falsely so; no polite laughter, just good-natured banter. The atmosphere was matter-of-fact.

Again, Fidel steered the conversation and I had no opening to discuss my mission; the only mention of Panama or Torrijos came when Castro wanted to make a comparison with what we were seeing: "What's cattle-raising like in Panama? How many hectares of land do you have per cow?" were some of the questions I remember.

"Well, I am not an agronomist or a rancher," I said, completely at a loss to come up with a good answer. "The only thing I can say is based on observation. We have a lot of land for grazing—all we need," I said proudly. "I would say that the ratio of cows to land is the maximum distance a cow can walk in a day as it grazes."

He was taken aback. "But that can't be; if the cows walk so much, they grow lean and milk production suffers," Fidel said. "The theory is that too much grazing land for cattle cuts back on their capacity to fatten and produce milk." So much for my ability to match Fidel's expertise in farm production.

We drove around all day and he dropped me off at the guest house after nightfall. After the explosion at the end of our first encounter, I was not about to launch into a discussion of my mission. So, agreeing we would see each other the following day, I simply said, "Remember, *Comandante,* we have other things to talk about."

"Tomorrow, Noriega, we can talk about that tomorrow," he said, waving his arm to dismiss the subject as he drove off into the night.

At the guest house, I was reunited with the others in my group, who had gotten their own tours, each with a chaperon of his own rank and station. This was the case on all my trips to Havana. Other than dinners and public events, Fidel and I always met privately. That is Castro's style.

That night we went to the Tropicana to see its famous cabaret show, with Piñeiro and his aides as our hosts.

The following day was filled with meetings and lunch with government officials. We had told our hosts that this day was to be our last in Havana; we were leaving for home the following morning. The day wore on and Fidel was nowhere to be seen. At night, there was a dinner offered by Piñeiro at our guest compound. Unannounced, Castro arrived as the meal was about to start.

It was a barbecue, in the back garden by a pleasant swimming pool. Fidel took me on a tour of the place. The house had once belonged to the Du Pont family, one of many expropriated buildings now used by the government for meetings and guest quarters. I told Fidel that I admired the decor and the artwork on display, an exhibition by Cuban artists.

"Choose any one you like and it's yours," Fidel said, in a grand gesture, motioning toward the works of art. I thought for a moment and selected a painting. But one of Fidel's aides objected to what the boss was up to. "*Comandante,* you can't give this away; it belongs to the state," she said. "You can't give away any of these paintings; they are government property and part of our national collection."

This was unexpected, since we were dealing here, supposedly, with what the Americans would call an autocrat, a dictator, a man who answered to no one. I wasn't certain what his reaction would be.

Fidel's expression didn't change. He nodded to Celia, his aide, calling her aside for a second. "Don't worry," he said. "Celia's right. We can find you a similar painting by the same artist." They did just that. I was impressed and never cease to recall this telling anecdote about a man and the power he wields. I thought about what I might have done in the same circumstance. It was an important lesson.

After dinner, the hours were ticking away and I was quite aware that unless I delayed our departure, this could be my last chance to win the release of Captain Villa. I was determined to keep my schedule. Protocol was fine, but I was not going to allow the rules of diplomacy to keep me in Cuba for a month, as had happened to Rómulo Bethancourt.

Fidel finally pulled me aside; he put his arm on my shoulder and we went walking off alone to the far end of the swimming pool, opposite from where the barbecue pit was set up.

"Okay, look, why does Torrijos want these guys?" Castro asked. "I can understand why he would want the ships, because they are Panamanian, but what can he want with these murderers? What relationship can he have with all of this?"

"To tell you the truth," I said, "he wants them because the gringos have asked him to do it. They insisted; they said to do everything he can to get them out. At the moment, he is working on the diplomatic strategy for the Panama Canal treaties; we want to do so from a position of strength. This is the kind of thing that comes across as a request for good faith in these types of negotiations."

"But who is behind it?" Fidel asked. "Who are the masters in this game?"

"I don't know who they are," I answered. "Torrijos was contacted directly. But call it what you want, CIA, State Department, the military, it's the same thing—the Americans want these guys back."

"The law requires that these men be tried, and everyone knows they're guilty," Fidel said. "They were caught in the act; these men are supposed to face the firing squad and no one here will cry for them. Public opinion is indignant—they demand it. I wish you could have seen what it was like. They mowed them down. Bodies of innocent people all over the beach—mothers, crying babies. He couldn't have chosen a more innocent location—a poor fishing village, no military, nothing. Poor fishermen and their families, and he just opened up with his machine gun."

Castro continued with a series of arguments against the idea, talking about the terrorists, what they were like, their arrogance, the cold-bloodedness displayed by Villa in particular. "Not even a sign of remorse . . . if he had the chance, he would have killed a thousand people . . . the indignation of the people who live there . . . the indignation of the people investigating the crime . . ."

"Yes, *Comandante*, I understand, I sympathize. We all understand this," I said. "But our request is based on a higher level, a political problem. And we think this will help change the balance. It is something that Torrijos needs badly. It shows the Americans his potential value when he comes to the negotiating table, that he's the man that has managed to do what no one else could have done."

We went on talking for a while and I still had no idea what the outcome would be. Suddenly, Fidel threw up his hands. "Listen, if you really want this piece of shit, take him. Tell Torrijos that he can have him."

He called Piñeiro over. "Okay, set it up for Noriega to take this garbage back with him," he said. And he added a sardonic joke. "We don't want him to get shot for coming home empty-handed." Once Fidel had decided, that was that. He mentioned something about having some explaining to do to the Council of State. But there were two possibilities: he either had given up arguing with me and made the decision without consultation, as a gesture of good faith to Torrijos, or he had consulted ahead of time and was enjoying the arguments before announcing the decision he already had made. I never knew which. Either way, this was another lesson in power.

We said good-bye to Castro right there at the guest compound. It was about midnight. By 5 A.M., we were packed and ready to leave. Cuban soldiers brought Villa as we arrived at the airport. We were taking our "little package" home with us. And I could see that he was an arrogant piece of work. As the Cubans brought him to the plane, they were cursing him, saying, "Son of a bitch, we hope you die of cancer," things like that.

Instead of keeping quiet, he was mouthing off back to them. "If I ever get back here, I'll have my machine gun ready for you!" he sneered.

"Try to come back and see what happens, you mother!" one of the soldiers said.

"Communist bastards!"

I'd had enough. I watched from the steps of the plane and was afraid that the Cubans were going to change their minds—or shoot him on the spot.

"Tape his mouth so he shuts up!" I ordered my men as he reached the steps of the plane.

Years later, the United States again asked me to intervene to win the release of a prisoner in Cuba. That top-secret case was even more embarrassing to the Americans. In 1984, during the first Reagan administration, the CIA, under William Casey, had sent Henry Pino, a Cuban-American pilot who worked at the Panama Canal, to take clandestine aerial photographs of the Soviet cosmonaut facilities in Cuba. Again, I sent word of our interest to Barbarroja. After several days of back-and-forth with Fidel, Pino was released.

These successes brought other requests from various establishment figures for the release of political prisioners. Fidel never turned me down.

That first contact with Fidel did what both sides had hoped: it cemented friendly relations between Cuba and Panama, gave Torrijos the immediate good-faith gesture he wanted and proved to the Americans that I was capable of getting the job done.

It heralded the start of serious relations between Panama and the Cubans, all propitiated by the United States. After this auspicious beginning, I was usually the liaison. My contact with Cuba also lessened Cuba's isolation, whether with the Organization of American States or other countries, for which Panama could serve as a conduit or third party.

It was a high-level relationship. Fidel and I were not trading secrets. My conversations with him were always political in nature—political analysis, political theory—and at times I had urgent requests from the Americans.

The Americans knew that I often spoke to Fidel and that any subject at hand would be dealt with seriously and securely. For instance, when they wanted to send a secret envoy, as they once did in the person of former Deputy CIA Director Vernon Walters, I would tell Fidel outright: "The Americans want such-and-such" or "The CIA says such-and-such." There was no secret about where the request came from. And he would answer as he saw fit. During the Sandinista period, during the Central American wars, Fidel and I spoke often. He was always concerned that the United States would invade Panama; he was always thinking about the number of soldiers the Americans had in Panama, the kinds of weaponry. He called it a kind of guillotine, permanently perched over Panama, that Panama was the "headquarters of Yankee imperialism." He was, of course, comparing our situation with that of Cuba. There were similarities.

But our first joint experience of an American invasion came with the U.S. attack on Grenada in October 1983. It was days after I formally had become commander of the Panamanian Defense Forces, succeeding General Ruben Dario Paredes.

The contact came hours after the U.S. began landing its marines on the beach in Grenada, where the Cubans had a military garrison and army engineers building an airstrip and reinforcing the island.

The United States had botched its invasion badly. It was laughable. They had no idea where they were; some marines had to use an Esso gas station map to find their way. Even though it was a small island, they got lost, and Washington was worried they would stumble upon an American medical-university compound and start killing students by mistake.

They wanted to scale things back, avoid bloodshed of American soldiers or pictures on television of students lying in pools of blood on the ground.

The first of a series of phone calls came from Casey; a number of other people, including Vice President George Bush, were also on the line. Bush, as a presidential candidate years later, would at first try to say that he had never spoken to me, that he never participated in this series of contacts on Grenada. Eventually, faced with the facts, his limp memory would improve and suddenly he would remember.

The Americans asked me to open up a line of communication with Fidel. The message was this: "We have obvious superiority of forces over the Cuban contingent on the island; please stay neutral, don't engage with the arriving U.S. troops. It is impossible to win. There could be an escalation; innocent civilians will be killed in the process."

In retrospect, of course, this concern about innocent lives stands in stark contrast with the wanton killing of civilians during the invasion of Panama.

I got in touch with Fidel and we had perhaps five or six rounds of calls back and forth. First I talked with the Americans, then to Fidel, sometimes alone, sometimes with other officials on the line.

I made it clear to all of them that I was transmitting an official entreaty from the United States. Fidel knew this in any case, but I made it explicit, saying that the United States was reaching out to him through me, that it was not a trick or double-dealing in any sense. It was a petition by the Americans because they wanted to save the American students.

Fidel was indignant and outraged.

"Why the hell are they asking this stuff now, when my information tells me they're already attacking the island?" he said. "How are they going to ask for us to consider alternatives when they're already on the beach?"

We went back and forth on this. Fidel's persistent answer was that it was too late to negotiate since the American troops were already on Grenada. He would make no commitment to the Americans. Nevertheless, when the time came, he took the hint. He didn't have that many men on the island; certainly not enough to repel an invasion, but enough to cause trouble, just enough to fight back, provoke injuries and death among the civilian population. Although he did not tell the Americans what his decision was, his position became obvious. He chose not to fight. The Cubans on Grenada did not raise their weapons. I am proud to say that my intervention with Fidel, without a doubt, saved the lives of American students that day.

Grenada ended up being a precursor of the Panama invasion in miniature. The Americans could no longer tolerate Prime Minister Maurice Bishop. He had gone over the line: he was becoming friendly with Fidel Castro; he was expressing socialist ideas. He manifested a Third World vision and would not listen to "reason."

So the Americans decided to eliminate Bishop. They called their invasion of Grenada a "multilateral force," but this was a transparent subterfuge to justify their intervention. The blueprint for the invasion was much like that for the invasion of Panama: plan an overwhelming attack; conspire to kill a leader and blame it on his own countrymen; pretend that you are doing it to restore democracy. In Panama, the plan was to kill me and blame it on the Panamanians.

Bishop was killed and that was the way it was going to be in Panama; co-opted members of the defense forces would be goaded to kill me. Only, in Panama, things didn't follow the entire script. I survived.

Moammar Gahdafi

My contact with Gahdafi was different and quite unique. I first met the Libyan leader on a mission to Tripoli for Torrijos in the mid-1970s. It was part of Omar's plan to reach out to the Third World and establish Panama as an independent country among other nations. The idea was to establish contact, set up lines of common interest and arrange for a later visit by Torrijos himself. I was accompanied on that first trip by several members of the National Guard, including Colonel Armando Contreras, Lieutenant Colonel Armando Bellido, and Major Cleto Hernández, who was an especially able aide-de-camp, speaking both French and Arabic.

Gahdafi knew little about Panama and it was my job to tell him what we were all about: I brought maps, gave him an atlas as a gift and spent a day describing the strategic importance of the Panama Canal. He marveled at the thought of the canal and Panama's rivers and lakes. He swooned at the idea of so much fresh water, comparing Panama with his desert home. It was a learning curve for Gahdafi, but the more he heard, the more he expressed solidarity with us. I had long, very interesting conversations with him.

With the different visits over the course of time, I had the chance to see him in several phases—his military phase and his Islamic phase. His identification with the religious system took him back to his roots, and he set himself up in a tent in the desert. I also saw him at his house, the same one that was bombed by U.S. warplanes when Reagan attacked Libya. His wife and children were in the house and an infant child was killed. The United States didn't express regret and said that the child wasn't his, but only an adopted baby.

I had the opportunity to know him as political leader, supporter of Third World countries and as a military man. I was there when he issued his credo, *The Green Book,* during the country's annual liberation celebration. The event included a great military parade, and they displayed their entire arsenal. I was on the reviewing stand as Gahdafi's special guest.

In this incarnation, I saw Gahdafi the military commander, leading his people, motivating them—at the time, he was in the middle of a border conflict with Egypt and was defying their army.

His philosophy was to put his ideals into action. Libya set out to help liberation movements around the world. He had a ministry dedicated to doing this. And that operational aspect was important to us. Our goal was to create sympathy for Panama's position and support for passage of the canal treaties internationally. That's why we approached Gahdafi and other leaders of nonaligned countries.

He understood our mission. He was an intelligent, well-mannered person in the sense that he knew how to listen, ask informed questions and respond. Those are, after all, hallmarks of an educated person, and I recognized these qualities in both Gahdafi and Castro: to know how to listen, to know how to explain oneself, to ask a question and to have the patience to hear the answer.

After several visits, we finally arranged for Torrijos to visit Libya. Gahdafi received him at his office. We went on a tour of the country. He took us to an oil-processing facility, to the university, to the land-reform projects and to a desert station where they were at the time planting wheat by using an irrigation system. It was a successful visit, capped off by the signing of cultural treaties.

In all, I made ten trips to Libya and was always received by Gahdafi in an atmosphere of sympathy and respect. I maintained contact with him after the death of Torrijos; it was not, as the Americans would have it, some subterranean, mysterious contact, and it had nothing to do with espionage. These were political contacts, aboveboard, a meeting between leaders, man to man. In times of crisis for either one, we called each other by phone. When the United States attacked him, I called to find out about the situation there. He was obviously very upset. He had lost a child.

Throughout this association, I took Gahdafi as he was, the leader of a sovereign country under attack by the United States. When I was under political attack during the last months before the invasion, he called every week to express his support and concern. In September 1989, he invited me to attend the commemoration of the Libyan revolution. My daughters Lorena and Thaís represented me in Tripoli. In the course of time, Libya had broadened its diplomatic representation in Panama; they gave it some importance, adding a cultural office and building a small mosque downtown. They also had economic interest and were planning to develop operations in the Free Zone, where they had purchased commercial space.

There was never any involvement in terrorist training. We made that clear to the Americans and the Israelis when they expressed concern. We said that our relations with countries like Libya showed our neutrality and our sovereign right to choose our friends and allies. We were developing open, aboveboard commercial relations with many countries. Our goal was to have Panama as an open trading center for the commercial benefit of all; if we had relations with all these countries, it was unlikely that Panama would become a target for the terrorist activity of any one of them.

The Shah of Iran

*"The United States seeks not friends,
but servants."*—Simón Bolívar

The philosophy of open borders and maintaining friendships on all sides became complicated on at least one occasion: when the United States asked us to give refuge to Mohammed Reza Pahlavi, the shah of Iran. Allowing the shah to come to Panama was a goodwill gesture to the United States. It fulfilled no Panamanian business or strategic interest, and, for the first time, it opened us to the possibility of terrorist attacks from the Middle East.

In fact, our image suffered as a result, at least among student groups and nationalist parties, who chanted in favor of the man who overthrew the shah, Ayatollah Ruhollah Khomeini. The only advantage was in international prestige—we were helping the United States solve a problem and we were receiving quite a bit of notoriety on the hit parade of fleeting fame. Everybody was talking about Panama, if only because of the shah.

The first overture for the shah to come to Panama was early in 1979, shortly after his fall from power. The argument by some was a financial one—in return for asylum, the shah could be expected to invest heavily in the country. In February, the shah's son, Prince Reza, came to Panama City for a visit in which he could examine investment opportunities. In November, Bernardo Benes, a Cuban-born banker in Miami, contacted Ricardo de la Espriella, who was vice president under President Aristides Royo, and asked if the offer to visit Panama was still open. The shah had arrived in New York from his asylum in Mexico on October 22, 1979, to receive medical treatment. On November 4, Iranian students and militants seized the U.S. embassy in Tehran, along with a number of hostages. The Carter administration was looking for a quick departure for the shah and was considering Austria and South Africa. Was Panama still interested? De la Espriella said he believed it could still be done.

On November 30, Ambler Moss, the U.S. ambassador to Panama, was asked by the State Department to make an inquiry. By December 1, he was able to tell Washington that General Torrijos would agree to give the shah refuge if President Carter asked him to do so. The president's aide, Hamilton Jordan, was dispatched secretly to Panama and joined Ambassador Moss for a meeting with Torrijos. Torrijos went along with the idea and offered two possible hideaways—a mountain ranch in Chiriquí and a house owned by Gabriel Lewis, former Panamanian ambassador to the United States, on Contadora, the resort island just off the Panamanian mainland. I took an inspection team to review both locations, and the shah's men chose Contadora. There were then negotiations with the shah and with the Americans about security arrangements. The shah wanted substantial security guarantees and communication with the outside world. The United States offered special electricity-generating equipment and long-distance telephone lines, which the shah rejected, fearing his phones would be tapped.

After super-secret preparations, the shah was flown to Contadora on a Twin Otter aircraft on December 15, 1979. He took up residence in the chalet owned by Gabriel Lewis, who at one time owned the island.

When news of the shah's arrival became known, we faced student protests in Panama City and criticism around the world. Contadora had become an exotic destination with a newfound reputation. It's name was on the maps, but tourism declined 60 percent. Who wanted to face armed guards on the beach?

The shah's security forces in Panama were men who had been well trained in Europe, the Middle East and the United States with both commando and intelligence experience in the field. At their highest count, there were more than three hundred members in the force, most of them operating fixed control points on four shifts, once we set the shah up at his quarters on Contadora.

Several times, there were attempts by terrorists to penetrate the security cordon and reach the shah; at least one occasion involved a zealot on a suicide mission trying to sneak into Panama with false documents. With the ayatollah declaring that killing the shah would be a sure route to heaven, we were certain that there would be such an effort and our guard was always up. There were at least six cases in all involving various plans to break through the security net. There were also several nighttime overflights with a goal of attacking the shah as he slept. None was very professional and none got very far.

Our security followed the principle of conducting operations in a way that would never alarm the subject we were protecting: we deployed plainclothes operatives at key locations, we used wiretaps, we monitored airports and the coast, often employing agents who didn't seem to be intelligence officers but instead tourists, gardeners or common workmen who blended into their surroundings. The Iranian team was confused and intrigued by our subtle, almost invisible method of operation, since their approach was the classic man-to-man bodyguard protection. "Where is this security that is handled so we can't even see it?" the Iranians wanted to know. For that reason, at the outset, relations were strained between our Panamanian forces and the Iranian team. After a while, however, they recognized that our measures were intricate and worked, and they became accustomed to depending on our operation. They praised our security apparatus and started calling us magicians among security operatives. That was much in contrast with the shah's decision to reject security measures from the Southern Command or any other U.S. federal agency.

The shah didn't trust the United States, fearing that their monitoring of his planning, contacts and relations would be used against him. He told me that his relations with the Americans left a bad taste, a feeling of lack of sincerity, lack of friendship and help when he needed it most, during his exile in the United States, despite their historically unconditional support.

Within the context of a man whose world had been broken apart, the shah was personable and natural in the way he conducted himself, sad and inconsolable, yet calm and coming to terms with his life. I saw the shah every day, mostly when his own security detail retired for the night. He would ask questions about Panama, a place he knew nothing at all about. He spoke often of what he had done for his country. He asked us what the latest news was from Iran and would sometimes turn on the shortwave radio we had given him to monitor news reports from Europe and the Middle East. I remember one time he heard on the Zenith shortwave that the Ayatollah Khomeini had executed a number of generals from the shah's disbanded army. He cried when he told me about this.

He spoke in a low voice, with a dark, far-off look in his eye. He was never at all effusive nor did I ever see him smile. He slept in an upstairs bedroom in the chalet, and his valet and bodyguards slept on the floor at the entrance to his bedroom. His wife, Queen Farah Diba, slept in a separate room downstairs. He had two Dalmatians, each the size of a newborn calf, but quite docile.

It was evident that he was a man educated in another era, and was used to the trappings and privileges that went along with being the *Shahanshah,* Son of Suns, King of Kings. He moved with an imperial air and was used to the finest foods and accommodations. He never touched money or carried any worldly possession.

He liked to have a close-cropped haircut, so once a week we sent around the National Guard's barber, Sergeant Santiago Ardines, who would give him a trim. Farah Diba also had special visits from a hairstylist. My wife, Felicidad, introduced her to the stylist Giovanni, who would also come around frequently. Farah Diba was cordial to my wife, giving her her own gold cigarette case as a birthday present, emblazoned with the royal crown.

The couple's sons would visit now and then. One of them, Cyrus, went on a tour of the canal locks on one occasion, traveling to the countryside. The captain of the plane he flew in gave him the controls during the flight. Cyrus had flown ever since his father had given him a plane for his fifteenth birthday. I recall that he was given honorary Panamanian air force wings when he landed.

Farah Diba loved to chat on the telephone long into the night. She also played quite a bit of tennis, took long walks and went waterskiing. One day there was a ruckus among the security guards—the scuba-diving team, to be exact—because they spotted her waterskiing in the Pacific. The divers got as close as they could and enjoyed the view—she was a very attractive woman.

If anything could be said about the shah, it was that he was a wanted man. Killing or capturing the shah would have been a trophy for the Iranian government and its supporters. Meanwhile, the Ayatollah's revolutionary government did everything possible in diplomatic and legal terms to have him returned to Iran.

In retrospect, it's clear that General Torrijos never would have handed him over to the Ayatollah. He did allow speculation on the matter and participated in formal meetings with lawyers, hearing arguments and such; this was designed to avoid any violence of the kind that the Americans had faced once they protected the shah. Torrijos told me that the only way anyone would ever capture the shah was on his way out of Panama, headed somewhere else.

When the time finally came for the shah to leave Panama, it was on the insistence of his twin sister. The shah was in the middle of a complicated political argument about his medical condition. His doctors, including the American heart surgeon Dr. Michael DeBakey, mostly agreed that his spleen was cancerous and needed to be removed. The argument was over where to do the surgery.

The Americans rejected surgery back in the United States, fearing further protests if the shah returned to U.S. territory. The second option was to conduct the surgery in a Panamanian hospital, but the shah's family and advisers would not hear of it, even though the shah was hospitalized for a time at Paitilla Hospital, one of the best in the country. There was also a suggestion that the surgery could be done at Gorgas Hospital, a U.S. medical institution in the former Canal Zone. Panamanian physicians led by a military doctor, Carlos García, opposed this option, partly because it would violate Panamanian medical procedures, but mostly because García disagreed with the diagnosis of the Americans that an operation was required or that the shah could even survive such an operation. Behind it all was the inference that it would be convenient for the Americans if the shah died on an operating table in Panama.

The shah's twin sister settled matters. After long talks with Jihan Sadat, the wife of Egyptian President Anwar Sadat, the offer was made for the shah to go to Egypt. This came despite strong protests from Washington. The shah's sister was a domineering figure who wanted nothing to do with any of us. No one liked her, least of all the security team around the shah. Her influence was such and she argued so much that her brother finally gave in and agreed to move to Egypt. Once she had convinced him, she left with twenty trunks of clothing and other personal effects.

I was in Chiriquí on March 24, 1980, the day of his departure, which came so suddenly that I didn't know exactly when it was happening. There, on the border, I received a message that he had to speak to me urgently. On the flight down to Panama City, I learned that he was leaving. I arrived just as he prepared to board the plane that was to take him to Cairo. He was already on the steps of the plane when he saw me. He put his arms around me (something that was very much out of character for him) and said that he had been looking for me all day and was relieved to see me before his departure. "If you had been here, and had been told what was going on, I would have felt secure with your assurances and never would have given in to leaving," he said. As he spoke, his eyes seemed the saddest eyes I had ever seen, and he was close to tears. He was feverish as he shook my hand in a final farewell. One could see the shadow of death on his brow.

The shah's brief period of exile in Panama was a strangely emotional experience for all of us. We developed a certain affection for him, a sense of pity, perhaps. The experience, however, was mixed. Panama and the island of Contadora had become known worldwide, but the promise of a boon for investment hadn't panned out. The shah invested nothing at all. We had won the respect of the world's intelligence services for our efficiency and expertise. Torrijos had demonstrated his faithfulness and honesty in the international political arena; if there was calculation in so doing, it simply was to show the Americans that he was willing to work with them. On the other hand, of course, the loss of prestige in the Third World and among Islamic countries was pronounced. But now that the canal treaties were a reality, Omar wanted to nurture his friendship with the Americans as a platform for regional leadership. He thought he had a role to play as an honest broker. But his plan was tragically cut short.

CHAPTER 7

A Death
in the Family

DESPITE THE EFFORTS OF Torrijos, there was no indication at the start of the Reagan administration that he was receiving any respect from the U.S. government. In particular, his efforts for rapprochement with Fidel Castro were scorned by Washington. Torrijos thought that he could serve as a conduit to bring Cuba back into the fold. "Every moment of Cuban isolation equals years of shame for the American continent," he said on more than one occasion.

Reagan, who had just been elected, saw this as further justification for his opposition to the canal treaties.

"Frankly it is incredible that we are thinking of taking the critical step [of turning over the Panama Canal] when Torrijos maintains such close relations with Fidel Castro and the Soviet Union," Reagan said. "We are faced with a man who systematically violates the rights of his own people. He and his group came to power at the point of a bayonet by toppling an elected president. He now controls the press, has proscribed the political parties, with the exception of the Communist Party and his own, which is controlled by the Armed Forces."

His vice president, George Bush, agreed. "Torrijos is becoming a Latin American Gahdafi by supporting and providing financial aid to terrorist guerrillas. He has opened headquarters for liberation and terrorist movements, hidden in Panamanian embassies like those of Libya, the Polisarios and the PLO."

General Torrijos had called routinely into command headquarters from Río Hato on the Pacific coast that Friday morning, July 31, 1981, to check in.

We had a skeleton staff on duty, as was the custom; our extended weekend started after 11 A.M. on Fridays.

"Nothing new, General, sir," I said to him.

So little was going on that we drifted away from official subjects, nothing to do with the military or politics at all. Plain gossip, mostly about secretaries. One of them was the beautiful Celia, Torrijos's favorite, with her ebony skin and long eyelashes. Then there was another one of the secretaries, who had married Lichito Castrellon, Torrijos's helicopter pilot. The newlyweds were off on their honeymoon.

It was a relaxed time for all of us now that the treaties were signed and passed. The average workload at the general command had decreased noticeably. Omar had gotten much more involved in politics. He had said that signing the canal treaties was like earning his master's degree; now he was going to work. He was developing a plan of action for the future. Part of his plan involved identifying up-and-coming civilian and military leaders. Young intellectuals were sent to study in England, the United States and elsewhere. He met with the old guard of the Democratic Revolutionary Party, urging them to develop new strategies for the future. He was also choosing prominent members of the military, assigning them to social action projects—farming development, welfare and political education programs in peasant areas.

Anybody who says they knew exactly what Torrijos had in mind would not be telling the truth—he never told us. But we could see what he was doing.

On the personal level, he had a backup plan. He had set up a modern, comfortable office for himself in a duplex adjacent to his house in Altos de Golf. He invested money to purchase antennas and other gear so that he could set up a national TV network.

Torrijos had time for everything; he was happier than I had ever seen him, more lighthearted and joking around all the time. He was watching his family grow, thrilled that his new grandson would be baptized with his name, Omar Efraín, proud of his new daughter, Tuira, given the indigenous name of Panama's largest river.

Omar's schedule involved meetings with athletes, native artists, composers and folksingers. Distinguished visitors from Colombia and Venezuela were always passing through—there were always two places set for visitors at the beach house. Torrijos loved to offer hospitality to guests.

He was becoming a statesman with a diverse group of political visitors. In the weeks prior to his death, there was a delegation from the Nicaraguan Sandinista leadership. "Get out of the trenches," he told one of the leaders. "Make it a political battle, the guerrilla war has been won," he told his Nicaraguan guests, who were deferential because Torrijos was one of their oldest supporters. There also had been a visit by American General Vernon Walters. Walters had served as deputy director when George Bush was chief of the intelligence agency. It was part of a reconciliation with U.S. intelligence agencies. For the twelve years after the U.S. involvement in the 1969 coup against him, Torrijos had shunned intelligence officials. Now, following ratification of the Panama Canal treaties, he had signaled the change by giving a medal to Arthur Esparza, the chief of the U.S. Army 470th Intelligence Group, for his efforts toward passage of the treaties.

Torrijos was becoming an important world player; his mediation could have cooled the fires and averted the dirty wars that, with billions of dollars of American aid and support, killed more than 100,000 people.

Torrijos had taken some time off at his getaway beach house in Río Hato and from there decided to take a drive with a small group of people to the town of Penonomé. He told the local commander, Major Elías Castillo, to set up a get-together with friends, local politicians and military leaders. He then ordered that his Twin Otter aircraft be flown in from Río Hato to pick him up. The idea was that he would make an impromptu visit to Coclecito, a small farming community he had special affection for across the mountains along the Atlantic coast, then come back for the evening festivities. Torrijos had funded a kind of social-economic commune for farm families in Coclecito, with experimental crops and a project to raise Brazilian Cebú cattle.

The quick decision left El Cholito Adames, who was due to be rotated out, with the job of flying Torrijos on the hop back and forth.

Everyone knew the drill when Torrijos was in the area. The schedule was always subject to change and invariably announced at the last minute. There was no flight plan.

That was the last anyone saw of Torrijos. When it got late, Castillo became concerned and called ahead to Coclecito. He found that the plane had never gotten there. The air force started checking the vicinity, well aware of Torrijos's penchant for changing his mind and not telling anyone. They radioed the nearby settlements of Santa Isabel, Salvador and others, but no one had seen the general. They even called Cali and Chocó, Colombia, in case Torrijos had gone off on a surprise visit.

By nightfall, Colonel Florencio Flórez, second in command, declared a national alert. The air force, under Major Alberto Purcell, immediately started a search-and-rescue operation, working into the night with no trace of the missing plane. The next day, the first information came from a peasant in the area of the valley of Cerro Marta (outside the assumed flight path to Coclecito), who reported the sound of an explosion around the time the plane was assumed to have gone down. Purcell sent reconnaissance planes and helicopters, which found the tree-covered crash site, the plane's front section burrowed into the side of the hill, the fuselage sliced off by trees. Torrijos and his entourage had been killed instantly. Cutting a path through difficult terrain, an infantry rescue team accompanied by a pathologist, Dr. Ruiz Valdes, reached the wreckage and identified the charred remains of Torrijos through dental records. The rescuers carried the bodies down from the mountain as the nation heard the news.

The judicial and legal investigations were handled by Attorney General Olmedo Miranda, one of Torrijos's best friends, who had known him ever since the days they served together in Chiriquí. The military team responsible for maintaining the Twin Otter aircraft conducted its investigation in conjunction with an international air safety team. No evidence of sabotage was found, despite rumors of U.S. involvement.[1]

Torrijos's tomb is at Fort Amador, not far from the Panama Canal, which he wrested from American control, changing the course of Panamanian history.

---

[1] Plots to kill Torrijos were first disclosed by Watergate conspirator John Dean during testimony before the U.S. Senate Watergate Committee in 1973. Later, during the 1975 Senate inquiries into operations of the CIA during the Nixon years, chaired by Senator Frank Church, there was additional testimony and documentation of U.S. plots to kill Torrijos and Noriega.

Life After Torrijos

No one in the military command was prepared for Torrijos's death. He was our leader, and his charismatic style dominated the military institution. It was as if we lived under a paternalistic umbrella in which certain basic tenets—the structure, style and substance of our lives—were all taken for granted. I was certainly content with the status quo and I assumed the other members of the command were, as well. After all, there was no thought of a time when he might not be our leader.

Succession, style and command structure were not things we talked about. There was an established order of succession: first Florez, Paredes, Colonel Armando Contreras, then me. My life was organized within that system—I actually was younger and had fewer years of service than many other officers. I was content with the pace of my career.

Florez took over as interim leader without a struggle, as if Torrijos was still guiding the system; his ascent was the natural order of things. Florez was the son of a famous leader of the Panamanian National Police and was a graduate of the Nicaraguan Military Academy in the time of General Anastasio Somoza. He was a simple soul, calm spirited, a good athlete. He tried to maintain a good relationship with everyone he came in contact with, to make friends wherever he could.

Florez was not up to the job of commander. He had difficulty assuming the place of such a dominant personality as Torrijos. He didn't feel like the commander, nor did he adopt the title due him, general of the National Guard. He retained the rank of colonel like the rest of us and didn't even move into Torrijos's vacant office, which remained as a kind of ghostly reminder of him.

At first, there was no problem. In the weeks after Omar's death, we closed ranks, much like a family pulls together after a parent dies. The survivors cooperate to keep the house and the family structure intact. Each of us had his job to do, concentrating on maintaining the system as Torrijos intended it. That structure, after all, was the only one we knew.

After a while, though, as in any family, reality set in. The guiding force of Torrijos's leadership grew dim. Florez was unable to remain in power. On March 3, 1982, Paredes, next in the chain of command, was promoted to general and assumed the post of commander in chief, which had seemed vacant ever since Torrijos's death.

I was never close to Paredes; rather, our relationship was that of superior officer to subordinate. He had been in the military longer than I and it was always assumed that he would be commander first. He was capable of great loyalty to his friends and family. He held his family, particularly his sons, as all-important in his life.

Immediately after becoming commander, Paredes set about his further goal of becoming president of Panama. Late in 1982, he summoned Contreras, me and Díaz Herrera to a meeting where he declared his plans, along with a twist. He said he would resign his command in early 1983 so that he could run for the presidency the following year. But, he said, Contreras would not be his replacement. "Contreras has come to the moment when he must retire," he said. "Noriega will take over the command."

I don't know how Paredes had decided this or whether anyone else knew. I can only say that this was a total surprise and the first time I had heard that I would be bumped to the head of the line.

Ultimately, Paredes failed to garner the support he needed and his presidential candidacy collapsed.

On August 12, 1983, two years after the death of Torrijos, I assumed the rank of general and commander in chief of the National Guard. It was undoubtedly my proudest day.

My power came as a result of the Revolution of 1968, after which a new constitution was promulgated, stating that "the government shall exercise power in harmony, jointly with the National Guard." The armed forces were designated to uphold the affairs of state so that laws could be enacted and carried out. It was a division of efforts: bureaucratic administration, paperwork and economic theory, international relations and protocol were handled by the president of the republic; internal affairs, civil defense, emergency management and labor relations were handled by the commander in chief of the armed forces.

This Panamanian structure had historical roots. Since the foundation of the Republic of Panama, the administration of Panama was of key concern and interest to the United States; having a commander in chief in charge of public order, blessed by the United States, made the canal a lot easier to control. The United States essentially imposed the structure and personality of the Panamanian government from the very beginnings of the country in 1903.

In Panama, civilian and military power were condemned to work hand in hand. I had learned this by studying Panama's past. Throughout our history, politicians have fallen back on the military as the final arbiter.

Faced with the indecision of the civilians, the failure to get to the root cause of problems in the country, we saw the civilian power structure turn time and again to the military.

As a young officer, I remember many labor strikes in which the civilians were unable to take decisive action. They turned to the National Guard; we were the ones who had the contacts within the unions, who would be able to establish a dialogue with the union leaders, prevent strikes and look for solutions to their problems. This gave us a natural leadership role.

This is no surprise, considering Panamanian history. What we call the traditional political parties are really interest groups founded by the wealthy families, who were always allied with the United States. Their overtures to the masses were confined to election time, when they were forced, as we say, "to bathe in populist waters."

Compare that with the Democratic Revolutionary Party, founded by the military under Torrijos, where the base of support was the people. They were accustomed to having direct contact with their leadership.

In any case, I had a clear vision of my power in terms of Panama: I understood the politics; I understood my base of support, both within the military and among the masses.

But what I did not accept was receiving orders from the Americans; nor did I accept being subordinated to the caprice and interests of Panama's economic power brokers.

CHAPTER 8

Neither Bowed
nor Broken

How did it all happen? What is the story behind my conversion from the darling of the U.S. intelligence community to the enemy who symbolized everything that was bad in U.S. politics? The answer is complicated but begins with a simple reality: I never wavered in my essential commitment to Panamanian nationalism. I never strayed from the conviction that my country was sovereign and had a right to decide its own future.

There was no double-dealing with the Americans, no involvement in killing political opponents, no drug dealing. My emergence as the enemy was the result of machinations by the American propaganda machine, combined with tactical mistakes on my side, opportunism by Panama's wealthy elite and the bloodlust of the U.S. government under Reagan and Bush, which, in turn, led to an invasion of my country.

The progression is not an easy one to track: there are a number of things to keep in mind. First, there was the peculiar nature of these rich Panamanians—English-speaking, American-educated patricians. These were people who sidled in with the Americans. They wanted to cozy up to power politics, be it via the U.S. ambassador or a visiting deputy secretary of state; and they made the Americans they wooed feel good in Panama, doing everything they could to make Panama City seem just as American as any true-blue American city.

These rich Panamanians hated the military and what we stood for. In the majority, we were not third-generation Panamanian patricians, whose mostly American or European ancestors had served the United States designs on Panama at least since the beginning of the century. We were people of color, mestizos who reflected the diversity of our heritage: Spanish, Indian and African.

Of course, the military was tolerated when it was only a police force, as it was in the early days, before men like Torrijos and Boris Martínez dared to take a nationalist stance and express our independence from the United States. But after the revolution of 1968, we were more than a nuisance to the monied class—we were a mortal threat. We sought economic, social and political equality for the same impoverished people they chose not to recognize. Liberation, nationalism and social welfare meant nothing to them.

This rift between us was ready to be exploited. Our Panamanian enemies soon had their chance. With the rise of the Reagan administration, there was constant, residual anger toward Panama and the successors of Torrijos for the passage of the Panama Canal treaties; there was concern that Panama could not be counted on to go along with the American anti-communist agenda.

The Panamanian wealthy elite made use of the ignorance of U.S. policy makers and the see-no-evil, hear-no-evil, speak-no-evil philosophy that reigned in the U.S. State Department. The rich power brokers said they were clean and we were dirty, that all corruption came from the military, that the wealthy bankers and car dealers and lawyers—men like Arias Calderón, Billy Ford and Guillermo Endara—were all as pure as mountain snow. The Americans figured it had to be so: these were their friends and dinner companions, their tennis partners. They all had so much in common, they had to be telling the truth.

Besides the connivance of the oligarchy, there was a second factor: the change in the perception of my usefulness to the United States. At first, I was still on the "useful" list for the Americans. I was regularly invited to Washington and elsewhere for meetings and to give speeches and provide analysis.

We had regular meetings with our counterparts at the U.S. Southern Command and coordinated with them in accord with provisions of the canal treaties. As we have seen, I continued to provide significant help to the United States on intelligence matters. I had excellent relations with CIA station chiefs in Panama: Joe Kiyonaga, Brian Bramson, Jerry Svat and Don Winters being among the ones I knew best. William Casey and his aides knew they could count on us when they needed us, and they respected us.

The Panamanian Defense Forces also gave strong, consistent support to the Drug Enforcement Administration. This was documented in the many interchanges of correspondence between me and my subordinates and U.S. officials. In addition, they recognized that we were not only cooperating, but providing intelligence that helped catch and target drug kingpins. In December 1984, one year after I became commander, Panama provided information to the United States on the activities of Jorge Luis Ochoa of the Medellín cocaine cartel and Gilberto Rodríguez Orejuela of Cali, who were setting up drug operations in Spain.

As a result, the two men were arrested in Spain for extradition to the United States. Mysteriously, because of U.S. negligence, Colombian authorities won control of the case and had both men extradited back to Bogotá, where they were swiftly released.

Shortly thereafter, Panama took another major step against the Colombian drug traffickers. The government voided the charter of the First Interamericas Bank in Panama City, after an investigation showed that it was being used by another Cali drug dealer, José Santacruz Londoño, to launder drug profits. The lawyer for the First Interamericas Bank was Rogelio Cruz, who became attorney general of Panama after the United States invaded Panama, and its directors were Guillermo Endara, the man installed by the Americans as president, and his associates Jaime Arias Calderón and Hernán Delgado.

The DEA drug fight in Latin America was greatly enhanced by Panama. We encouraged the participation for the first time of other countries in the region, who were skeptical about working with Americans for fear that doing so would allow spies to operate in their countries. I was the one who suggested and organized the first hemispheric drug conference at Contadora in 1982. It went so well that the United States decided to adopt it as an annual event. (The second year, the meeting was held in Venezuela.) Officials of the anti-drug campaign in the United States were able to hear there, for the first time, from the Latin American drug police themselves—their problems, their questions, their analysis. A great wealth of information was gathered and the contacts established were valuable, but only after the meetings were organized by me. Previously, Latin American countries had refused to share intelligence with each other, let alone with the Americans. Not only were there regional rivalries, but also they feared the United States would make use of information gathered to destabilize their governments.

But the winds of American intervention in Panama were already blowing when I took over as commander of the Panamanian Defense Forces. The wealthy classes alone would not have been enough to sabotage me. They needed a willing reception in Washington.

Operating on their own time schedule, and creating the facts as they went along, the Americans slowly moved toward attacking me and working with our Panamanian enemies for my downfall. First, I refused to play along with their game in Central America. I committed cardinal sins: I said no too many times. I refused to allow them to use Panama as a base for attacks on Nicaragua and rebels in El Salvador.

The closing of the Panama-based School of the Americas in 1982 was mandated as one of the first tangible changes under the Torrijos-Carter treaties of 1977–78. The United States was well aware of the provision, but the Reagan administration just couldn't swallow it.

As determined and proud as we were to follow through with Torrijos's legacy, the United States didn't want any of this to happen. They wanted an extension or a renegotiation for the installation, saying that with their growing war preparations in Central America, they still needed it. But the School of the Americas was an embarrassment to us. We didn't want a training ground for death squads and repressive right-wing militaries on our soil.

The basic U.S. proposal was for a fifteen-year extension in the operation of the School of the Americas. In effect, this would extend the U.S. presence in Panama against the spirit of the canal treaties. The only way we would accept such a school, I told them, was if it were reconstituted.

"We will make it a school for social development," I told the Americans. "It will have a Panamanian director. There will be classic military training, but also lessons in civic action,[1] health care, rural medicine

[1] The civic action plan, which included health care for the indigent, road-building programs and agricultural support, was cited by U.S. military attachés in Panama as being a model for Latin America.

and aid in creating peasant cooperatives." We wanted to convert this international monstrosity for repression and murder into something completely different. The United States was appalled—they wanted to train demolition teams and snipers and terrorist squads to fight the Nicaraguan government. I was adamantly opposed. And this became the first no that the United States heard me utter; it was a surprise for them that, sitting at the negotiating table with my friends, the Americans, I should say no; that I had the nerve to demand compliance with the letter and spirit of the Torrijos-Carter treaties. They saw it as disobedience on my part, and they took it very badly. "General," they told me, "you've taken a very radical position. What has happened?"

Barletta and Spadafora—a Palace Coup

The closing of the School of the Americas was the first no. I've already described the second no: it was my absolute refusal to help the Americans in Central America, capped off by my rejection of Oliver North's plans for us in Nicaragua. But there was one more incident—the murder of a government critic and a military plot against me within my inner circle, both of which led to the dismissal of Nicolás Ardito Barletta as president of Panama.

The United States agreed in 1984 to support Barletta as president. Barletta had been living for a long time outside of Panama, working for the World Bank. He was a student of Secretary of State George Shultz,[2] one of a number of U.S.-educated Latin American technocrats, like Carlos Salinas in Mexico, somebody operating in the field of international economics, studying the foreign debt, things that mattered to the United States. For that reason, and with the patronage of Shultz, there was a campaign in favor of Barletta's sudden candidacy.

This didn't bother me at all. In military command meetings, we had decided that it was a good idea for the civilians to take a stronger hand, especially in economic policy. We opposed Arnulfo Arias's candidacy from the Panameñista Party and so did the Americans. The old caudillo

---

[2] Barletta had a Ph.D. in economics from the University of Chicago, and Shultz was one of his professors.

invited me to his beach house just before the election campaign and told me outright that one of his campaign promises would be to dismantle the military—the same thing he tried to do in 1968.

With the support of the PDF and the PRD—Democratic Revolutionary Party—Barletta was elected by a narrow margin in 1984. That was what the Americans wanted. Arias complained that the election had been stolen from him, but his complaints were disregarded. The United States sent an official delegation to the inauguration; among those attending was former President Jimmy Carter.

With Barletta's presidency, I agreed that the military should take a less active role in economic and political affairs. Upon his inauguration, I told Barletta that we wanted to return to the barracks. "With your election," I said, the country "will dine on democracy for breakfast, lunch and dinner."

This was not to be. Barletta began to face criticism. There were general complaints that he was a terrible manager and a weak leader; he knew nothing about building consensus, neither in the legislative assembly nor among the people.

Barletta started mouthing U.S. economic analysis, which said that countries like Panama needed to impose severe cost-cutting controls to curb the government debt. The International Monetary Fund, in concert with Reagan administration policy, was pushing deficit-cutting measures throughout the hemisphere. The result was certain to be the loss of hundreds, if not thousands, of civil service jobs. Instead of creating political alliances, negotiating and selling this to the legislature and the country, Barletta simply announced his support for the measures and remained aloof. He was highly criticized; labor unions, especially those representing public employees, became restive, charging that he was surrendering Panamanian sovereignty to U.S. economic theory. His reaction was to run for cover behind the support and prestige the military could offer him.

But this was not the only problem; the political temperature was rising all around us. Barletta and I were both targets of someone who was plotting to undermine my leadership of the Panamanian Defense Forces.

As reported in the book *Our Man in Panama,*

> with both the president and Noriega out of the country, Díaz Herrera decided to make the move he had been secretly contemplating since Noriega took over as comandante. He took the first steps

toward overthrowing Noriega. "I saw a great crisis coming. . . . I thought the opposition was going to take great advantage of that death. So, with Noriega away, I tried to see if I could orchestrate something against Noriega himself, something inside the barracks and with the politicians at my side. I went out on a limb, with the PRD and the armed forces, to see if I could pull off a putsch against Noriega," Diaz Herrera recounted.[3]

On the morning of September 16, 1985, the news from home was a shock: Hugo Spadafora had been found murdered over the weekend in Chiriquí. I was out of the country in Europe for several weeks, attending a military-naval-affairs conference, and traveling between England, Paris and Switzerland.

I immediately contacted Barletta at the presidential palace. He told me about his working plan to investigate the crime. I also spoke with a member of the Legislative Assembly, Alfredo Orange, who was a close friend of the Spadafora family. I assured him that the investigation would be carried out and that I would give it special attention on my return.

Spadafora was a homegrown Panamanian who had studied medicine in Italy, then ran off to Africa as a militant in the Angolan war of liberation prior to Angola's independence from Portugal, in 1975. When he came home to Panama, he joined a local leftist student movement; he took the code name Dr. Zhivago.

Spadafora became an informant for the National Guard; investigators from the National Department of Investigation were able to identify and disband the leftist organization he belonged to, based on the information he provided. It was during his informant phase that I had my first contact with Spadafora. I was serving at the time as captain in charge of an elite infantry brigade called the Pumas de Tocumen.

Over the years, I got to know him well and helped advance his career when I could. I saw him rise from youthful informant to vice minister of health to the head of a Panamanian brigade that volunteered to help the Sandinistas overthrow Anastasio Somoza in Nicaragua. As the Sandinista march to victory gathered strength, Spadafora and the Vic-

[3] Dinges, *Our Man in Panama*, p. 224. The account is based on Dinges's interview with Díaz Herrera. Accounts of a coup were also published in *The New York Times*, James Le Moyne, October 2 and October 5, 1985, and in *The Village Voice*, February 6, 1990.

toriano Lorenzo brigade were there. History found Spadafora marching toward Managua and the eventual victory of the Sandinistas alongside Commander Zero from the south. But Daniel Ortega and Tomás Borge and the main column of the Sandinistas were advancing from the other direction, and they beat Zero to Managua. That broadened the animosity between Eden Pastora and the rest of the Sandinista leadership. Spadafora was left on the short end. As the Americans began organizing the Nicaraguan Contras in the 1980s, Spadafora was there too.

Spadafora worked with the Contras. As he also established arms-dealing contacts in Central America, inevitably he brushed shoulders with both the American establishment on one side and drug dealers on the other, both trading arms for drugs.

At this point, Spadafora's intrigues already were a mixture of ideology and criminality, dependent only on the singular goal of making money. Having set up base in San José, Costa Rica, he made a slow transition from rebel fighter to businessman and wheeler-dealer.

We maintained an active intelligence-gathering operation in Costa Rica, both because it was a border country and because it had become spy central for various spy agencies. Spadafora was one of a number of Panamanians operating in Costa Rica about whom we received regular reports. He was not singled out for special observation, nor did we consider him a threat or a major player in the intrigues of Central America. The CIA also was hard at work gathering intelligence in San José. Our information indicated that the CIA did not take Spadafora as an important player either, but they did know what he was up to.

Over time, Spadafora fashioned himself as my enemy and as a critic of the Panamanian Defense Forces. It was apparently because of a decision by the Panamanian controller general to cut off Spadafora's longtime monthly cost-of-living stipend, which had begun during his days running the Panamanian brigade for the Sandinistas in Nicaragua. That stipend amounted to roughly two thousand dollars a month, about what he earned in the mid-1970s after he got the job as vice minister of health. Eventually, however, the controller general's office objected, refusing to sign vouchers to pay rent for a new apartment Spadafora had set up in Panama City. Spadafora deeply resented this, considering it a personal affront, and started denouncing us. This was no ideological conversion or political decision: he was insulted and decided to seek revenge.

Nevertheless, Spadafora came and went from Panama City to San José freely and frequently, without fear of harassment. His final, fateful trip, however, came under circumstances still not understood.[4] The 1993 murder trial in Panama on the Spadafora case showed the extreme doubts surrounding the case. I was named originally as a co-defendant, along with nine other men; no evidence was presented against me at the trial, which took place in Chiriquí during the government of Guillermo Endara, the opposition leader made president by the Americans. The jury, despite political pressure, responded to the lack of evidence and acquitted seven officers, including Major Luis Cordoba, with whom supposedly I was in touch during the murders. Two military policemen from Chiriquí, Francisco Eliezer González and Júlio César Miranda, were convicted and did confess to the crime. I was convicted in absentia, even though all of the officers who would have had to serve as my liaison if I were involved got off scot-free. Convicting me was obviously the result of political pressure, part of the syndrome of blaming me for anything that happened in Panama.

In early September 1985, according to testimony at the trial, Spadafora suddenly decided to return to Panama. For unknown reasons, he went the long way, the difficult land route, instead of doing it the easy way, via scheduled airlines that fly from the mountain-ringed Costa Rican capital to the lush banks of the canal along the Pacific coast in less than forty-five minutes.

Spadafora's widow said her husband had received a phone call from Panama City, summoning him. "Get back here" was the message. "Very big and important things are about to happen."

It later became clear that a coup was being planned against me, and the plotters wanted Spadafora's help.[5] I could not have suspected that the death of Spadafora coincided with what was later re-

---

[4] U.S. journalist Martha Honey reported on the BBC that she had tea with Spadafora in Costa Rica two days before he was killed. She said that he was collecting funds and men for the Nicaraguan contras and that he was connected to suspicious people who could have been involved in an internal drug trafficking dispute among several factions. Another journalist, Leslie Cockburn, said that her sources indicated that Spadafora could have been killed because of a dispute among various drug trafficking groups.

[5] A cousin of General Omar Torrijos, Díaz Herrera later went into exile in Venezuela.

vealed to be a half-baked plan by Díaz Herrera to raise a rebellion against me.[6]

The investigation into the death of Spadafora indicated that he traveled from the border by bus with González. Witnesses said they saw the men travel together and share lunch in the town of Concepción. González, whom everyone called Bruce Lee, was an Indian, Asian in appearance, skilled in martial arts like his movie star namesake. He was one of a number of Indians from the local Guayme tribe who were on the local constabulary, an auxiliary branch of the defense forces.

Spadafora's widow, Arihanne Bejarano Acuña, testified before a Panamanian judicial investigation on January 6, 1986, that "Hugo traveled to Panama under the name Ricardo Velazquez. My family, his friend Victoriano Morales, and a contact named Julio Valverde knew about his trip. Valverde had visited him one day earlier. Hugo decided to go on his trip to Panama on the morning of Thursday, September 12. Walter Chavez and Jorge Beade had told him to be careful with Julio Valverde, that Julio had betrayed Hugo."

At the trial, González was silent while prosecutors described how the crime was committed. When it was his turn to speak during the reconstruction of events, he confessed: he took Spadafora to an isolated location, tied him up and killed him. "I was there, I met him, we took the bus together . . ." He testified without emotion; neither did he say why he had committed the act.

Also a defendant in the case was Lieutenant Colonel Luis Cordoba, the military commander in Chiriquí. He had been a loyal officer and probably believed at the time of the killing that he was protecting the military institution by hiding what he knew. As he sat there listening to the testimony, it dawned on him how much damage he had done by covering up González's deed.

So when González was through, Cordoba broke his silence. He stared directly at "Bruce Lee" as he spoke, in a loud voice so the jury would hear every word. "My sin was that I knew what you had done, but I kept quiet about it," he said.

[6] Díaz Herrera initially confessed "I caused . . . the ouster of Barletta . . . to justify . . . what I had plotted against Noriega." He later recanted, according to government documents quoted in the book *The Noriega Years* by Margaret Scranton (Boulder: Lynn Rienner Publishers, 1989; p. 89).

"Up to this point I protected you and was silent. I never accused you, but it's all over. I'm not helping you anymore. You're the one who did it, 'Bruce Lee.' I never got an order to do this, and I never gave you one. You killed him. Tell them! Did I give you the order?"

"Bruce Lee" looked away and said nothing.

And that's the way it was left. Cordoba helped cover it up, fearing that the defense forces would be blamed, but neither received orders nor ordered nor participated in the crime.

Years later, even after the 1993 trial was over and the murderer was identified, there still remained doubts. Was it a simple case of robbery? Was it a contract killing, based on a double-cross in an arms deal? Was it retribution stemming from the Central American wars? No motive was ever revealed.

There was one more defendant at the 1993 trial, a young captain named Mario del Cid. Del Cid was found innocent of all charges. No relation to Luis del Cid, my former aide, he was caught up in the Spadafora case. According to him, Díaz Herrera had invited him to join in the rebellion against me. When Del Cid refused, he said, Díaz Herrera took revenge by implicating him in the Spadafora murder. It was pure reprisal from Herrera, del Cid said, but he remained in jail for four years before the case even went to trial.

This series of events occurring in my absence gave birth to a web of lies. Out of nowhere, Major García Piyuyo, the Panamanian attaché for police affairs in Costa Rica, extradited from Costa Rica a German man who claimed knowledge of the case. Speaking on national television, the German provided unusually detailed information about the Spadafora killing, and Díaz Herrera played him up as if he were the key to unraveling the entire case. But our investigators took a look at his claims and determined they were pure fabrication. The German disappeared from sight as quickly as he surfaced.

Barletta, already in trouble with the leadership of our Democratic Revolutionary Party because of his plan to embrace IMF budget-cutting recommendations, now got involved in a constitutional dispute about whether he had the authority to convene a commission of inquiry about the Spadafora incident.

I had completed my visit to Europe and flew finally to New York, where I had promised to meet with Barletta, who was preparing to attend the UN General Assembly. When I got to New York, we made several attempts to meet but were thwarted by scheduling problems. Barletta and I both had meetings; he met on economic matters with Shultz and other officials. I met with foreign leaders, including Premier Felipe González of Spain.

While something told me to stay in New York and talk to Barletta, my concern about the situation back home won out. It was nighttime when I got back to Panama City. At the arrival area at the military section of the airport, I found a group of legislators waiting for me, demanding Barletta's head. They were fed up and said the assembly wanted nothing more to do with him.

Barletta arrived from New York the following day. We sent a helicopter to the airport and brought him directly to command headquarters for consultation. The meetings were in my office and lasted most of the day; attending were Barletta; Jorge Abadía, the foreign minister; Colonel Marcos Justine and Rómulo Escobar Bethancourt. The proceedings were an airing of the situation and the charges.

Barletta's responses were slow and deliberate. I was there to listen, serving as moderator for the discussions, which continued through lunch, occasionally extending outside my office, up and down the corridors outside.

Barletta tried to debate the issue on a higher level, using economic and political reasoning. He mentioned neither Spadafora nor the investigations nor anything of the sort. He spoke about his future and his political support, and one thing stood out. "If you people get rid of me, you'll be replacing me with Delvalle, a member of the oligarchy; you'll certainly have no friends in his circle. You will be sorry if you get rid of me.

"Do you really want to replace me with a *rabiblanco*?" Barletta asked rhetorically. (*Rabiblanco*—"white tail"—was our slang term for the wealthy oligarchy in Panama.) "Are you sure about that?" he said, arguing that he was still a viable president and the best insurance the PDF had. Time proved him right.

It was clear that the Americans knew what was up. Halfway through the meeting, I received calls from both Nestor Sanchez at the National Security Council in Washington and from U.S. Ambassador Everett Briggs.

"Listen, Tony," Sanchez said. "I hope you're not really going to dismiss Barletta. This is going to touch off lots of tremors back here; they're not going to like it." He was very conciliatory—not surprising, since we had often worked together cordially on other issues. I can't say he was a friend, because there are no friends in such matters. But I can say we had maintained good professional contacts in the past, when he was in the CIA and later at the State Department.

"Manuel Antonio, as your friend, I must tell you it will never be forgiven at the State Department; they will view it as if you had staged a coup. You are going to have problems, many, many problems as a result.

"Think about it, think it over," he said. He didn't say any more, but he definitely had made his point.

Briggs was more blunt: Barletta should be left alone. The U.S. ambassador was no friend, but he had been identified to me as more than an ambassador—a CIA contact as well. He said he was passing along a little free advice from Shultz himself. "Don't do it," he said. "Don't do it."

I told both Sanchez and Briggs that it was impossible for me to keep Barletta as president. I tried to explain the domestic political atmosphere and the pressure for him to be ousted. Understanding none of this and disinterested in Panamanian politics, they didn't believe me—they saw this simply as my once again saying no and turning against them.

Well into the afternoon, no one had budged in their positions. Barletta asked to speak to me in private. Everyone left and he addressed me in the same friendly manner in which we always treated each other.

"Tony, can't you help me? Isn't there anything you can do?"

"That's it, Nicky. There's nothing I can do," I said. "You've heard how they all feel."

The debate lasted for hours, but finally Barletta relented when he understood that our decision was firm. He announced his resignation.

I undoubtedly could have used my influence to maintain Barletta in power, but the political cost would have been great; everyone was lined up against him.

Two months after Barletta's dismissal, in December 1985, I received a message from General Galvin, the head of the U.S. Southern Command, that John Poindexter, the president's chief of staff, would be making a stop in the former Canal Zone en route to elsewhere in Latin America. He wanted to meet me at Howard air base. I didn't know who Poindexter was or what his objectives for the meeting might be.

I agreed to meet him, unaware that I was about to be subjected to one of the most arrogant, empty-headed performances ever staged by an American government official. Later, I found out that local CIA and U.S. military representatives at the U.S. embassy had tried to brief Poindexter before our meeting, but that he had been disinterested. He didn't want reality or substance to interfere with what he had to say.

"I am here representing President Reagan and George Shultz," he began, soon after we were ushered together into a meeting room at the air base. Seated no more than six feet away from me, he puffed on a pipe and spoke coldly, his eyes never meeting my gaze. "By the end of this year, Barletta must be returned to power and Panama must terminate its role in negotiating peace in Central America,"[7] he said. He sat there arrogantly, puffing away in a display of bad manners, wearing a loud, ugly sport jacket that seemed to fit his obnoxious demeanor. But his words were worse than the image he made. I remember being fascinated by the way that his eyes focused off at an angle the entire time he sat there, looking at some indistinct point in space.

My aide, Lieutenant Moisés Cortizo, did the translating for me, but was having trouble maintaining his composure. "Panama should break relations or diminish relations with Cuba, as well as limit the Cuban presence in Panama. The Panamanian military doctrine is a bad ideological example for other armies in the region. . . ."

On and on he talked, focusing on that imaginary point somewhere over my shoulder. Cortizo, a West Point graduate, and several other Panamanian officers present tried to catch the eye of the U.S. embassy representatives in the room, who also looked away, probably wishing they were somewhere else.

Even though Poindexter was not man enough to look at me, my

---

[7] Panama hosted the first attempt at a homegrown mediated solution to the bloody civil wars in El Salvador and Nicaragua. The negotiations, on the island of Contadora, served as a blueprint for an eventual peace initiative joined by the United Nations, but never warmly embraced by the Reagan administration.

gaze was fixed on him as he went through his tirade. Several times I had to stop Cortizo from allowing his indignation to boil over—he could hardly hold himself back. General Galvin, who had come along for the meeting, had to make sure that tempers stayed under control.

When Poindexter finished, I continued looking straight at him. I hardly knew how to take his rude, threatening, outrageously ill-mannered, disconnected performance. But I answered him.

"You are a high-ranking official from Washington, but you are very much misinformed," I began. "Whatever information you think you have, your words are worthless; your words and threats are an insult. The United States owes a debt to Panama and to me for the always respectful relationship we have enjoyed these many years. Leave, go back wherever you came from, but find out about Panama before you ever bother speaking to me again—have somebody brief you on the truth of this relationship."[8]

Poindexter's startling performance made it clear that the U.S. relationship had changed drastically. Washington was hostile and incapable of dialogue. They wanted to dictate and Panama was not responding the way they wanted.

Now that Barletta was out, we were no longer compliant with U.S. policy. Panama was an outlaw regime—I had said no once too often; I could no longer be trusted. For our part, we started to miscalculate the Americans—we did not understand that the United States had become our enemy. We did not understand that the enemy would go to any lengths to control us, to destroy us.

---

[8] CIA station chief Donald Winters met with Poindexter before the Noriega meeting, along with General John Galvin, the head of the U.S. Southern Command. Winters was "struck by the fact that Admiral Poindexter showed no interest in discussing General Noriega the individual nor the message he was supposed to deliver. He merely puffed on his pipe and asked about the monkeys and the vegetation . . . About an hour later, I received a phone call. 'Who was that man?' Noriega asked. Noriega had no idea of Poindexter's role nor status and had been subjected to a lecture delivery and then departure by Poindexter."

CHAPTER 9

Plomo o Plata[1]— The Offer I Couldn't Refuse

G ENERAL, I HAVE A PLANE waiting for you right now," said William Walker, the State Department official assigned to get rid of me, one way or the other. "You can pull together family members, friends and anyone else you like, pack some things and leave for the airport. I am authorized by the president to give you two million dollars immediately, along with a medal commemorating your years of fine service."

The scene could not have been any more ridiculous. Walker and Michael Kozak had asked to meet me on March 18, 1988, two days after a coup attempt carried out in coordination with the CIA and the Southern Command. The timing was more than coincidental; the Americans were close to the coup leaders, Colonel Leonidas Macías,[2] our chief of police, and Major Augusto Villalaz, who had been working with U.S. Air Force intelligence. PDF intelligence efforts routed out the conspirators and all were arrested. When the coup failed, they went to an alternate plan: convince me to leave on my own.

---

[1] Literally, "lead or silver"—that is, the choice between being shot or taking the money.
[2] Macías had ardently supported Noriega when Delvalle tried to have him removed on February 25, 1988.

The meeting was held at a defense forces house at Fort Clayton, one of the houses that had been turned over to Panamanian custody under provisions of the canal treaties. This had a nice symbolism for us. Also in attendance for the Panamanian side were several members of the general staff: Rómulo Escobar Bethancourt, the veteran diplomat who had negotiated with the Americans during the canal treaties, and my American lawyers, Neal Sonnett,[3] Raymond Takiff and Steve Collin.

Walker and Kozak, both veteran State Department officials, were accompanied by a third man named Steve Pieczenik, who just sat there staring at me strangely. I was later tipped off that he was some sort of a psychiatrist whose job it was to psychoanalyze me by watching how many times I blinked and how many times I cleared my throat. The theory was that they could then figure out my weak points and set up psychological operations against me. I found out about this from one of our doctors, Carlos García, who by chance knew this man and had asked what was going on. "Listen," Pieczenik had said. "The general is more straight than Kozak and Walker. They're the crazy ones."

Walker repeated his offer. "Okay, we have a plane waiting for you right here, gassed up and ready to go to Spain. You can leave, take all the people with you that you want; if you need money, we'll give you money; if you have friends you want to take with you, that's okay too. Anything you want. We'll even give you a medal for your service to the United States, if you like. Just leave the country. The Spanish government agrees and is awaiting your arrival. It's all been arranged."[4]

And that was it, bare-boned and on the table, no preamble, just: "I am authorized by Shultz and President Reagan; you can read it right here in this document," he said, handing me a piece of paper that said that these men were their official negotiators and representatives.

These men actually thought that I would go for it. They probably hadn't read the CIA biography of me, where they would have seen evidence that went against the resident belief that I was a self-serving sot who only cared about money. "Noriega is intelligent, aggressive, am-

[3] Sonnett, a prominent criminal lawyer, resigned from the defense without explanation following Noriega's capture.

[4] Walker, deputy assistant secretary of state for Central America from 1985 to 1988, didn't remember offering Noriega money. "Two million dollars doesn't ring a bell. We offered him a plane and anyone else he wanted in his entourage, but I don't remember money. . . . I can't swear that no one else offered him something."

bitious and ultranationalistic. He is a shrewd and calculating person," the biography says. Being a nationalist is not compatible with selling yourself and your country down the river for two million dollars.

I was intrigued: had they actually brought two million dollars in a suitcase? I was recalling how several years earlier they had used me as intermediary to pay the same amount of money to Gustavo Alvarez, the deposed Honduran military commander. In my case, they saw that I wasn't a willing victim. The coup attempt hadn't worked and I wouldn't go quietly.

I had a fleeting thought that Walker and Kozak could probably be arrested under Panamanian law for attempted bribery, with the money being confiscated by the attorney general's office. It was with great restraint that I didn't start to laugh as Walker talked on; when he finished, Kozak spoke, to give it the final touches. "This is the sensible approach," he said, trying to take the hard edge off the conversation. Kozak had known us for years, having been a longtime friend of Rómulo Escobar.

I managed to contain myself and say almost nothing. I looked around the room. "Thank you for coming, gentlemen. "We have a lunch with President Solis Palma,"[5] I said. "We can reconvene after that."

It was true that we had a luncheon meeting planned with Solis Palma, but my words were a stalling tactic rather than anything else. We didn't even discuss the proposal during lunch, feeling that it was too absurd to warrant consideration.

About two hours later we went back to Fort Clayton and sat down with Walker and Kozak and the psychiatrist whose job it was to watch me blink. They looked at me expectantly. I told them what I could have told them straight off: that this was an unacceptable insult.

"You obviously have come here thinking that this is your colony and that you can push us around like chess pieces however you choose," I said. "Panama is a sovereign nation and I am its military commander. I've always treated the United States equitably. You have no right to talk to me like this." I told them to get out of Panama.

American foreign policy is probably always as cynical and simplistic as it was in the case of Panama: "capture the tyrant, restore freedom and democracy, stop drug dealers from killing our children." Simple

[5] Manuel Solis Palma, the onetime student activist and Noriega adviser, became president on February 26, 1988, after Eric Arturo Delvalle fled the country into exile.

slogans make it easier for the American government to win support from the public, who are mostly ignorant about what's really happening outside their own isolated spheres.

There are two other slogans that the Americans respond to. One comes from *The Godfather*—"making someone an offer they can't refuse"; the other is almost the same, though it comes from the language of the drug traffickers: *plomo o plata*—"lead or silver"—"choose the money or we'll fill you full of lead." Both can be used with absolute precision to describe how the Americans decided to deal with me: they would either pay me to leave the country or they would have me killed.

The money offer was a surprise; the plots to assassinate me were not. I knew they'd considered killing me and Torrijos during the Nixon administration. They saw these as viable alternatives: the Americans wanted to reassert their ability to control Panama and the Panama Canal and rid themselves of the defiant leader of an army they had created but could no longer control.

One plot by the Americans would have involved Colonel Eduardo Herrera Hassan, who had been our ambassador in Israel. Parallel to meeting with me, the Ameraicans flew Herrera to Washington and asked him to raise a mercenary force on the Caribbean island of Antigua and infiltrate across the Costa Rican border into Panama. These men would stage an assault; if I happened to die as a result, would they have been sorry? Herrera ultimately declined. Years later, Delvalle told friends that he vetoed the plan when it was proposed as being too macabre and too violent. Innocent people would have been killed, and Delvalle told Washington that he would not support the operation.[6]

O̲nce the United States made the decision to force me out of office, the only thing that could stop them was my resolve and the world of appearances—since they had laws against overthrowing governments and killing foreign leaders, everything had to be secret. But I admit that the trouble they had brewed up was wearing me down.

---

[6] Walker said he recruited Herrera Hassan to overthrow Noriega, but the operation never materialized. "We thought that maybe if a rival group rose up, they might be able to knock Noriega out of the box," Walker said in an interview. "By that I don't mean kill him, but take over. . . . I could understand his thinking it was an attempt [to assassinate him]. . . . I guess he could think that's what anyone rising against him would do."

First, Ronald Reagan signed a series of secret orders that would lead to my ouster. They were known as Panama One through Five. Several of these directives involved mounting and funding the opposition against me. Panama Five included repeated, unsuccessful attempts to mount military action against me and, failing that, a plan to have me killed.[7]

The directives may have been signed by Reagan, but the operation was the result of plotting by a committee of Panamanian exiles and State Department officials. Gabriel Lewis Galindo, a onetime Torrijos and defense forces ally, was the Panamanian most responsible for plotting against me. Lewis was motivated by revenge after I vetoed his claim to a million-dollar commission for participating in the sale of the government-owned Hotel Contadora to the Japanese Aoki group; Lewis took it personally and decided that he and other members of the economic power elites would never be able to control the economic future of the country as long as the Panamanian Defense Forces continued to stand in the way of their business ventures. As long as I wouldn't interfere in his economic plans, Lewis would surround me with attention and coordinate meetings for me with high-level American business and political leaders.

Lewis knew the workings of Washington better than any other Panamanian. The public relations lobby he created in the United States now became a powerful force against us, setting out to unite opposition to us in the State Department and the Congress. When he started working to overthrow me, so did the lobbying firm of Arnold and Porter, which once represented us. Lewis and the chief propagandist at the law firm, William D. Rogers, a former canal treaty negotiator, used what they knew about Panama to their advantage, publicizing twisted information and attacking us on all fronts. They knew who our friends had been in the United States and now influenced those friends so they would turn against us.

Lewis's most important ally in the Reagan administration was Elliott Abrams. It was Abrams who had failed so badly in Central America,

---

[7] While portions of the covert action plans remain secret, they included funding a guerrilla insurgency to oust and possibly kill Noriega, a plan to run a parallel Panamanian government under Eric Arturo Delvalle from U.S. military bases and a $10 million fund for the 1989 election campaign. For a further description of the U.S. plan, see Scranton, *op. cit.*, pp. 130–42.

working with Oliver North on trying to invade Nicaragua and destroy the Sandinistas. Abrams also had revenge in mind for my having rejected North's request for helping in their maniacal plans. Walker and Kozak worked for Abrams.

My dismissal of Barletta played right into their hands. Barletta's vice president, Eric Delvalle, took over as president on September 28, 1985. Things went along smoothly for the first few months. Delvalle dropped the plan to link up with the International Monetary Fund; labor relations improved and the legislature and the entire public sector were put at ease that there would be no mass firings of civil servants. I always got along well with Delvalle, the heir of a sugar-growing empire. We had known each other for years, since he had been a good friend of my brother, Luis Carlos.[8] I saw Delvalle as a practical, intelligent man. He was close to Gabriel Lewis; Delvalle's daughter and Gabriel Lewis's son had married. Nevertheless, the two men had a falling-out and I sided with Delvalle. Eventually, succumbing to family pressure and with the United States applying extreme economic threats, Delvalle moved to the Washington camp.

The tide turned on February 4, 1988, when the United States issued a drug indictment in Florida. The indictment named me along with the Medellín and Cali cartels in a massive plan to ship drugs to the United States.

I soon realized that the Americans would use the indictment as part of a cynical little maneuver to encourage Delvalle to move against me. On February 25, 1988, three weeks after the indictment was issued, Delvalle was coaxed by Lewis, Abrams and company to issue a decree, with no legal basis, declaring that I was relieved of my duties and that Colonel Marcos Justine was to replace me as commander in chief.

This was also humorous, bordering on the macabre. We had monitored Delvalle's preparations for the announcement for several days and even knew where he had taped the address that was to be broadcast that afternoon on nationwide television. We decided to take no action against the broadcast or Delvalle, preferring to gauge public reaction instead.

[8] Luis Carlos died of natural causes in 1984.

As I sat in my office along with a number of associates, waiting for the broadcast, I was reminded of the time almost twenty years earlier when Silvera and Sanjur tried to oust Torrijos and there were premature congratulations all around. "Who will be congratulating Delvalle now?" I wondered.

His speech came on the air as planned. "There is no other alternative but the use of the powers that the constitution gives me, to separate General Noriega from his high command and to hand over the leadership of the institution to the current chief of staff, Colonel Marco Justine," Delvalle announced.

The response was complete and utter silence—no one took Delvalle seriously. Justine, who sat back in his chair, stared at Delvalle as if he were crazy. From Justine's house, Delvalle just drove on, stopping home long enough to pick up his bags; without delay, he closeted himself at the U.S. Southern Command and prepared for exile in the United States.

The Reagan administration now used all the means at its disposal to discredit me and the military. The drug charges were one method. I saw this indictment as part of U.S. pressure tactics and never took it seriously. I first refused to even consider legal counsel in the case and then finally allowed my subordinates to choose lawyers—Raymond Takiff, Frank Rubino, Neal Sonnett and Jack Fernandez—through contacts with Americans in the Canal Zone. And the Spadafora case was another tool, manipulated into a cause célèbre: because of public relations, a single, unsolved murder started to take on more importance in the United States than all the thousands upon thousands of murders taking place under U.S. auspices throughout Central America. The Spadafora card was played with the help of journalists who dealt unquestioningly with all the propaganda and listened to the rantings of Spadafora's brother, Willy, who found a life for himself in the notoriety surrounding his brother's death.

To add to the pressure, the Abrams-Lewis team began weaving a system of news leaks about corruption. They planted information describing impossible charges of hidden wealth and a network of supposed colleagues who were controlling massive stocks of money. Corruption became the constant drumbeat of the Americans, as if Panama under my control had invented the concept in three short years, as if it would disappear as soon as they invaded my country.[9]

---

[9] The U.S. Drug Enforcement Administration reported that in the post-invasion period, money laundering and drug dealing were rampant in Panama, far worse than before the invasion.

Corruption is endemic to Latin America; it didn't start with the Panamanian military, and it didn't end with its demise. If anything, without the control we supplied, corruption without an armed forces in Panama was worse than ever.

The corruption charges were interesting in light of what happened after Delvalle moved into exile in Miami, purportedly establishing a government in exile. Taking his cues from Elliott Abrams, Delvalle, along with the Panamanian ambassador to Washington, Juan Sosa, now had power over millions of dollars in Panamanian funds deposited in U.S. banks.[10]

What they were trying to do with me was exactly what they had done so many times before, in Guatemala, in Nicaragua, in Grenada. So it had been in Haiti with Baby Doc Duvalier.[11]

The United States orchestrated the formation of the Civic Crusade, essentially the work of the U.S. embassy chargé d'affaires, John Maisto, the diplomat who was brought in from the Philippines to work the same magic he had produced against Marcos. This was ironic.

Shortly after Marcos's overthrow, the Reagan administration had asked President Delvalle to grant asylum to Marcos, but the president decided against the U.S. request, largely because of the strong negative response from students, intellectuals and others. I did not interfere in Delvalle's decision process on whether to give asylum to Marcos, even though doing so would have ingratiated us once again in the eyes of the Americans and could have defused the coming plot against us.

Maisto trained the Civic Crusade on how to organize street campaigns, how to burn tires and organize protest marches. He sent leaders of the Civic Crusade on a field trip to Manila along with a priest designated by Archbishop Marcos McGrath and gave them a briefing on how the destabilization campaign there had worked. Aurelio Barría, one of the Civic Crusade leaders, was singled out in particular by Maisto and received a briefing on the sequence of events that led to Marcos's fall. They started implementing similar actions one by one—

[10] In 1988, the General Accounting Office (GAO) complained that it was unable to audit the $10 million fund controlled by Delvalle and his aides to be used for maintaining the Panamanian embassy and consular expenses in the United States. The State Department and the Treasury Department refused to provide details to the GAO, saying it was the Panamanians' responsibility.

[11] Jean-Claude Duvalier, Baby Doc, left Haiti for exile in France in 1986. He assumed power on the death of his father, François Duvalier, Papa Doc, who ran the country from 1957 to 1971.

a perfect copy. Once again, the American motto, "If it works once, try it again," and the Kissinger refrain, "To solve a problem, you have to create the problem," carried along U.S. policy.

Despite all these efforts, the Civic Crusade never mustered the support of the vast majority of Panamanians, who came to refer to the crusade effort with derision as "the protest of the Mercedes-Benz." We were not threatened by their actions in any major way, nor did we do anything other than maintain standard police controls of demonstrations to avoid public disorder. Of course, we were criticized for this as well, as if no police or national force had the right to maintain control. Many crusade leaders left the country in voluntary exile, fearful of a fight, but not because of any action by the Panamanian Defense Forces.

The Americans piled on a series of increasingly severe economic sanctions, designed to force us into bankruptcy; they expected that the pressure would make it impossible for us to meet our government and military payrolls. The most important sanctions were elimination of the quota for importing sugar and its derivatives, the freezing of assets of private banks and the National Bank of Panama in the U.S. Federal Reserve system and creating an escrow account for receiving funds owed to Panama in the United States, including payments due Panama under the canal treaties. Eventually, the United States blocked outright all our exports to the United States, accounting for two-thirds of all our export revenue. It also restricted exports to Panama and called on its trading partners to do likewise.

As the sanctions continued, the United States accomplished what it wanted: it forced a massive recession, unemployment, lack of market for agricultural goods and scarcity of manufactured products. It created an unjustified crisis on a massive scale.

We organized to resist the economic pressure, but at a terrible cost. The American policy was designed to turn Panama from a thriving, healthy country into an impoverished shell. Prices soared, people lost their jobs, all because of a cynical policy by a small group of men out for revenge.

Our response was to publicize what the Americans were doing to us and find ways to become self-sufficient. It was difficult, but we managed to pay our state payroll, never missing a day; we were even able to pay year-end bonuses. We managed to stay liquid and to meet government debts and we also were able to maintain key public services for health care, the poor and highway maintenance.

We organized subsidized-care packages for the poorest communities, sent out military civic action teams to enhance agricultural production and took measures to eliminate black-marketeering at all levels.

On the international front, we went for help where it was available. The Americans used all means at their disposal to discourage their European allies and Japan from doing business with us. So we established ties with the PLO, North Korea and the Soviet Union, looking for diplomatic and economic support. These were all ways of seeking economic and political independence. Panama had been a country whose foreign relations were under the umbrella of the Department of State. Set free from that obligation, we made deals, much to the chagrin of the United States. We signed an agreement with Moscow, for the first time giving Aeroflot Airlines landing rights in Panama. We also signed a fishing agreement with the Russians, which gave their maritime fleet rights to operate in our waters, increasing their business in the region. Of course, to the Americans this meant that the Russians would be able to spy on them more easily, since some Soviet fishing boats also carried electronic surveillance. The Americans passed along their dissatisfaction through diplomatic channels, but they were hardly in a position to make demands. We didn't care what the United States thought.

The sanctions were a cynical exercise orchestrated in much the same way that the United States imposed sanctions on Cuba and Haiti. The result was unjustified interference in our economic affairs; the effects were felt in reverse proportion to how wealthy someone was. The rich businessmen of Panama City may have suffered economic problems, but it was the poor people of San Miguelito who had less to eat. Was this fair or was it another type of invasion by the United States, an invasion of our right to economic independence?

Considering our resources, we were doing a pretty good job of fending off the American Goliath. There was, of course, rising popular discontent. But most of that was caused by the economic hardships provoked by the Americans. It was the same cynical approach used by the Americans with Fidel Castro in Cuba: willfully destroy the economy, and then blame the leadership for an inability to maintain proper standards of living. Despite everything thrown at us, there were jobs and food for Panamanians throughout the crisis.

The secret policy directives focused on a number of fronts; the sanctions and political action were followed by attempts to subvert the military. And in each case of military subversion, the U.S. tried to use military pressure as a lever in their attempt to negotiate with me to leave power.

The visit by Walker, Kozak and the psychiatrist was not the first attempt at negotiations to get me to leave office. At the same time that the Abrams-Lewis team was working on coup plots and veiled assassinations, they orchestrated a visit by Carlos Andrés Pérez, the former president of Venezuela. Carlos Andrés had been Panama's ally during the canal treaty negotiations. After having been out of office for ten years, he was now campaigning for reelection in 1988 and sought to enhance his image at home by focusing on his value as a Venezuelan statesman in the international arena.

Carlos Andrés's effort seemed like a welcome surprise, since he had been our friend and ally during the Panama Canal Treaty negotiations. But my friends at the CIA—with whom I maintained close contacts throughout the crisis—told me that the Venezuelan statesman was now fronting for the Americans.

"Leave everything to me," Carlos Andrés told Washington. "I can deal with Noriega."

Carlos Andrés flew to Río Hato air base on March 7, 1988, accompanied by former Colombian president Alfonso López Michelsen and Carlos Pérez Rosagaray, a close Colombian friend of the Venezuelan president. We met at a thatched-roof party hut at Río Hato. Carlos Andrés quickly started singing the same tune being sung by Walker and Kozak. "It is high time for the military to withdraw from politics," he said.

By our final meeting on March 29, it was obvious that Carlos Andrés was under pressure to deliver his promise to the United States that he could "take care of Noriega." Retire, he said, hold free elections without the PRD or the military. Archbishop Marcos McGrath, the leader of the Panamanian Catholic Church, would serve as guarantor of a transition period to civilian control. Perhaps through his own ignorance, Carlos Andrés did not know that McGrath was far from neutral.

The meeting was inconclusive, but Carlos Andrés was not to be deterred. He just went home and announced that I had capitulated and would retire, thanks to his mediation.

I then rejected his remarks as the lies they were. Carlos Andrés told his American benefactors that I had reneged on his agreement, that I was stubborn beyond all bounds and that, perhaps, an invasion was the only way to get me out of the picture.

I was reminded of what Torrijos had to say. "All Venezuelans have dreams of being Simón Bolívar," Omar said.

How true was Torrijos's analysis. It was evident that this man wanted to make his historical mark. There he was, bragging about how *he* was talking to the Americans at the highest level, how *he* would take care of everything. There were perhaps three separate meetings. Each time, Carlos Andrés flew to Panama, then went back to report on progress to his friends in Washington.

And in the end, what a great inheritor of the mantle of Simón Bolívar, the Great Liberator, who sought to unite Latin America, to free it from the yoke of colonialism. Carlos Andrés Pérez, oozing with his own ego-inspired problems, promoted illegal intervention in a fellow Latin country by the greatest colonial power of them all. Carlos Andrés became an accomplice in the U.S. operation to wipe out the Panamanian military and kill hundreds of Panamanian civilians.

But the Americans persisted. In April, Kozak came back; Walker and the psychiatrist were conspicuously absent. The first thing Kozak did was issue a mild apology for Walker's behavior. Seated before the Panamanian delegation, he said that he had felt bad about the previous visit. Walker, he said, had not been very diplomatic and it had indeed been an insult. And then he launched into the same proposals, all aimed at having me retire from the military and leave Panama.

Kozak was more respectful, playing the good cop to Walker's bad cop, but the proposal was essentially the same: I would agree to leave Panama for six months, retire from the armed forces and not participate in any way in presidential elections scheduled for May 1989.

This time, I admit, I was ready to accept the possibility of a deal; I was growing weary of all the pressure.

I knew I had strong opponents with voices that spoke loudly in Washington, but the campesinos and the unions were supporting me—it was not my popularity that was at stake, nor my physical health, nor stress or anything like that; there was no personal problem. I was simply weighing the balance of the country in the international scheme of things. The screws were being tightened on us to an extent that hadn't taken place in any other country, not even in Cuba. I thought perhaps I could negotiaté with Kozak to reach some form of détente and an end to the craziness. If I was the one person who could bring about the change, perhaps it wouldn't be so bad to retire.

Kozak proposed that we continue to negotiate, under certain conditions: complete confidentiality during the talks and written proof that the United States would drop the charges against me and stop trying to have me arrested or killed.

We asked to split up the political and legal aspects of their proposals. Our American defense attorneys, Takiff, Rubino and Fernandez, talked with U.S. Justice Department negotiators about the legal aspects of the case. Rómulo Escobar and members of the military command negotiated with Kozak and his aides about the substance of what they had to propose. The meetings lasted for several weeks. Finally, on May 25, we reached a deadline imposed by the United States: Reagan was on his way to a summit meeting with Mikhail Gorbachev and wanted to be able to announce an agreement that would end the Panama crisis.

What he wanted to do was answer Gorbachev's call for perestroika with an example of how the United States was now working to make peace throughout Latin America. "Now that Noriega is leaving Panama on such and such a date, only Cuba is still outside the list of hostile governments." That was their plan. The only thing was, I didn't know about it. So they went ahead with their agenda and worked on it within their own time schedule, not within mine.

On the legal side, everything was set; they agreed that U.S. Attorney General Edwin Meese would petition the federal court for dismissal of the baseless charges against me, that they would prove that the dismissal was granted and that there would never again be any other charges of any kind.

But the political issue was not resolved. I had misgivings and doubted that my departure from the political scene would really solve anything. Many friends and military colleagues agreed with me.

I was free to decide for myself, but the general staff, in particular, argued that Panama would face instability if I left; there would be a perception that Panama was again capitulating to American imperialism. This, in turn, would bring political and economic turmoil and the

Americans would impose a new government with their own chosen members of the oligarchy—a change that they alone would say had taken place "democratically." The armed forces would be under the control of this new government, if they existed at all.

I wavered, still fed up and sick of the whole thing. And the Americans were pressuring me at the deadline. Reagan had already left for Russia and Shultz had held back, waiting for word from me. "Come on, let's go," Kozak said. "President Reagan is waiting for you to sign." I could take little solace from the fact that, at that moment, my decision held up the weighty matters of a superpower summit. That day, the defense forces general staff met at our offices on Calle 50 and read Kozak's proposal. They rejected it outright, giving me their full support and advising me not to accept.

I thought about it and finally went back to the Americans. I entered the room where they had gathered and looked around at everyone. "No," I told Kozak. "I won't do it."

I cannot regret my decision and I have no remorse for my actions, but I am deeply pained by all that has happened; my only consolation is that at least I did not hand over the country. The end result was the same—the Americans imposed a government and disbanded the armed forces. But it took an act of war to do it, blasting through the neutrality treaty and all bounds of civilized behavior. No one rolled over for them, least of all me.

The Americans were livid. They regrouped and stepped up all manner of provocations and interference in our affairs.

Our posture was to avoid confrontation by all possible means. When we didn't take the bait, they became more and more blatant in their actions, conducting activity that they knew was in open violation of the Torrijos-Carter treaties. They systematically began to abrogate every provision of the Panama Canal treaties.

They sent illegal air, land and sea patrols into our territory, all of which are specifically banned in the canal treaties. They staged maneuvers at will, and buzzed the ground close to population centers. The area close to the U.S. bases suffered all sorts of indignities. In one incident, a U.S. helicopter that was flying too low crashed into a poor area of town, destroying houses; every time a plane flew overhead it shook the straw off the roofs of peasant huts; cattle scattered in fear. And there were chronic traffic accidents, caused by unauthorized American convoys traversing Panamanian territory without regard to civilians. The Americans, under treaty regulations, should have asked permission when they took out convoys on the road, but they rarely did.

To raise tensions, they sent U.S. soldiers walking around Panama dressed in their uniforms, a clear treaty violation. It sounds like a small detail, but the presence of uniformed U.S. soldiers in Panama City streets was more than illegal; the Americans used it as a symbol of their impunity and our powerlessness when they decided to exercise their will. When we protested, there was no response. We understood the process; we knew their modus operandi. These were scripted provocations, and we warned our people not to be drawn into conflict. What other country would be subject to such indignities—we were at the will of an occupying army. Small wonder that I would later be confused by the military activity on December 20, 1989—we were facing a *permanent* U.S. invasion!

Despite all of this, some U.S. diplomats and the intelligence community in particular disagreed with Washington's policies. Ambassador Arthur Davis maintained cordial contacts with us until the very end. This was in marked contrast to the behavior of John Maisto, his deputy, who was the official designated to plan and carry out the civil disobedience campaign against the government. Maisto's idea of diplomacy was to ban all official contact between embassy staff and Panamanian military. Then, content with his isolation and ignorance, he would hold policy meetings at the U.S. embassy in which he berated me for being irrational and incapable of dialogue.

Davis's genteel manner was of little value. Policy was being controlled out of Washington. Davis had so little power that he was unable to control even his daughter, Susan, who had become active in the campaign of the Civic Crusade. She staged protests, banged pots and pans and became the darling of the international news media by passing along half-truths and gossip designed to sabotage the Panamanian government.

Lines of respectful communication were closed, with very few exceptions. At one point Senator Christopher Dodd came to see us, seeking the release of some prisoners. American visitors, whether Dodd or negotiators from the State Department, always took the same line. There was one solution—my resignation, my departure from Panama; that was what they were all trying to sell.

CHAPTER 10

The Manipulation of the Panamanian Elections

Kurt Muse

"*Comandante*," said one of my aides excitedly, bursting into my office one day in 1988. "*Tenemos un gringo*. We have a gringo—and he has all sorts of radio gear and documentation in English."

The gringo was a young American employed by the U.S. government named Kurt Muse; his mission was to set up a clandestine radio and computer operation to subvert the May 7, 1989, Panamanian elections.

The discovery of Muse and his secret installation was not only a coup for our intelligence services, but it was also a special opportunity to shed light on what the United States was really up to. For me the U.S. covert action was tantamount to the Watergate break-in or the theft of the Pentagon papers in the United States: Reagan and Bush had been caught red-handed violating our sovereignty.

And more than anything else I could say about the incident, I have to admit one sober fact: our mishandling of the capture of Kurt Muse was a fatal error for which I alone must take the blame. Immediately upon his capture, we should have cried foul before every international forum around the world, then postponed the elections because of U.S. meddling.

Muse had come to Panama perhaps a month or two prior to his capture. Quickly he began testing radio equipment; we began getting indications that our military communications were being tampered with. We set out to track the source but realized that we did not have the skills and expertise to do the job.

We sought advice, consulting with the Cubans, Israelis and East Germans; we picked up the necessary equipment we needed and sent teams for quick training courses in those countries to learn the latest techniques in catching high-tech invaders.

Our men came back after a few weeks with the equipment and skills to track down the culprits. Later, the Americans, in the midst of their embarrassment once the Muse affair was revealed, tried to divert attention from their illegal activity by planting the story that the Cubans were responsible for catching Muse, as if to say that Panamanians didn't have the intelligence and know-how to do it. But this was not true. Panamanians did the job all by themselves. And we were very proud of our accomplishment.

Homing in on radio signals was relatively easy, since Panama City is on flat terrain. The method was to send out monitoring equipment in several teams and to start circling the city, listening for wayward channels, always selecting the most likely time for the interference to take place. The surveillance team, despite its importance and prestige, was operating secretly for fear of being detected by the Americans. To avoid leaks, not even our own G-2 intelligence officers knew about their operations.

Before long, they scored a hit—the jamming signals had been found. Next, the monitors began running smaller and smaller concentric circles until they narrowed their target down to three high-rises in the Cangrejo section of town. Painstakingly they kept up the vigil until they reached one building, then one individual apartment. Inside was a very frightened man who said his name was Kurt Muse.

He was caught cold-fisted and red-handed. We found paperwork with plans for the operation, antenna equipment, sophisticated gear that could easily be disguised inside a guitar case. Within minutes, the notification came to me.

Muse was important, that became clear immediately. He was not a spy at all, really, just a communications specialist sent with the necessary equipment. I never saw him in person, but I remember my impression from seeing him on television: tall, slender, with a terrified look in his eye. He had no weapons, no protection; several accomplices happened to be away when we seized the building and they slipped out of the country. He had nothing and no one to fall back on since, officially, the Americans wanted to pretend he didn't exist. But Muse could describe the entire operation, and we had plenty of evidence backing up what he had to say. Quite a find!

We sent in an evaluation team to interrogate him, holding him for a while in isolation, discovering the details of the operation. Muse, realizing he had no lawyer, no contact at all with the outside world, needed no encouragement to open up. He was quite talkative.

The operation, he said, was intended to intervene in the election, providing phony radio and TV programming before, during and after to show that the opposition parties were winning no matter what the truth was. The idea was to provoke a swift, sympathetic reaction for the opposition at home and overseas, to report an opposition victory in the elections before ballots were collected. They wanted bogus reporting on all levels, creating the impression that everything had been decided in favor of the Americans and their candidates.

The Americans must have known right away that we had Muse, but didn't say anything until we made the announcement. One thing was clear: the Americans needed to free Kurt Muse. He was charged with espionage against the nation, a very serious crime under Panamanian law, as it would be anywhere else in the world. The United States declined to say that he had military status, since that level of military espionage was tough to defend. It was easier to defend him under civil law, with his rights to a lawyer, to visitation, food, etc.

First they sent the consul to see him, treating him like any other American from the old Canal Zone—a sailor who had too much to drink and got into a bar fight or something. Next, they sent along people who signed in at the jail as Muse's relatives, but we knew that these were neither cousins, nor brothers and sisters; these were government operatives, sent in to check on him and give him one specific instruction: "Don't talk!" And when they found out to their dismay that he already had talked, they switched to plan B: "Say everything you confessed was a lie, that you were coerced."

We monitored his jailhouse conversations with these so-called family members. "Shut up, don't talk!" they said. "It's all a lie, you were pressured," they said. "It was under duress."

But there was no duress, no pressure. The technical details of what he was doing were right there in our hands; so was the documentation to make the gear work. Nobody could have defended themselves against this: we had the goods.

Muse was such an embarrassment to the United States that his rescue from Modelo Prison was the prime mission of none other than Delta Force itself more than a year later—the first operation planned in the 1989 U.S. invasion of Panama.

He had been presented to reporters and confessed to what he had done; it was a blow to the United States, but they never acknowledged that he was a CIA agent or a DIA agent or paid at all by the United States, as if he were an extraterrestrial that just appeared suddenly from nowhere.

Colonel Marcos Justine was the one person to argue strenuously for us to cancel the elections. He said we should play it up big, protest and put Muse up for a public trial. He said that this was the exact moment to say there could be no elections, because the United States had conspired in our domestic politics and we needed to investigate how far they had penetrated our system.

Justine was right. Looking back, I see that this would have been the key moment to have shown the whole world how the United States was manipulating not only the electoral process, but all of Panama's internal affairs.

I miscalculated in not denouncing the U.S. more strongly, along with all the evidence we had gathered. We could have appealed to the international community, then called off the elections and demanded international sanctions against what the United States was doing to us. And I decided against it. Why? Because I thought the Panamanian people would understand this blatant interference in our lives and vote against the candidates that the United States supported.

That was logical as far as it went, but I wasn't taking into account what else the Americans had in store for us. They provided money, organization, advisers, propaganda and the strategy for the candidates that they endorsed.[1] Guillermo Endara, the Civic Crusade candidate for president, and his running mates were so evidently puppets of the United States that a sense of disgust rose about them among the Panamanian masses.

If the Americans were as certain as they said they were that the government candidate, Carlos Duque, could be easily defeated by Endara, they certainly didn't show it. The United States, under the secret Panama Four operation, allocated at least $10 million for destabilizing Panama prior to the elections.

Jimmy Carter

"*Hola, General, cómo está?*" said the very recognizable man with an always pleasant demeanor, a strong American twang filtering his words in Spanish. It was several days before the May 7 elections; Jimmy Carter, accompanied by his wife, had come to see me at my office in Fort Amador.

Carter's Spanish was good enough so that the three of us could meet privately, without the need for interpreters or aides. Mrs. Carter spoke little, but jotted down notes on a writing pad. I didn't think much about it, but I suppose this encounter was unique for an American president, past or present. He could actually speak a language besides English. Perhaps, we had always hoped, he could also understand and respect a country other than his own. That was not to be.

Carter had come to Panama as the head of a delegation approved to monitor the elections. He and his aide, Robert Pastor, along with officials from various other groups had pressured us to accept such monitoring. We had been reluctant to do so, seeing it as a question of basic national sovereignty. I had argued weeks earlier with Pastor and others that, given the United States' attitude, this would just be another infringement on our rights. We were under siege by the Americans, even though we had no civil war, as did other countries in the region. In addition, we did have popular elections every five years. We preferred following the Mexican political model. The United States up to that

---

[1] Financing and propelling the opposition campaign was acknowledged in the Panama One through Five presidential findings, including a $10 million election-financing payment.

point had never sent election monitors to Mexico, which was neither second-guessed nor chastised seriously in Washington for its voting system. Why should we be different?[2]

Taking that line in what I assumed were confidential talks with Pastor, I was irritated to learn that he would quickly brief the news media on parts of our conversations, including my reluctance to accept American-influenced election monitoring.

When, under pressure, we finally went along with the idea of having foreign observers present for the elections, Pastor found that he was not on the list of approved visa applicants. Carter called me on the phone about that, and Pastor was added to the list, not without my complaint about his breaking confidences.

I first met President Carter in the course of the canal treaty negotiations and found him to be an honorable man. He realized that the United States could not continue to occupy a strategic piece of land on foreign territory and call it its own. He was a man of vision.

I truly liked Carter, but I saw his role as that of a figurehead more than as the person who would actually be out doing the monitoring at the polling places. That, I assumed, would be handled by his staff.

"General, it sounds like the government is going to lose," Carter said. He apparently had already met with the opposition. I told him that I disagreed and I showed him why.

First, I said, after the Muse incident there was no reason to give credence to anything the United States said or did concerning Panama. They were the ones commissioning the polls, which showed our Democratic Revolutionary Party in third place, sometimes even in fourth. We thought what they were doing was so blatantly cynical, so evident, that people would see through it. They always listed Ricardo Arias Calderón, one of the Civic Crusade's two vice-presidential candidates, as the most popular politician in the country. Nobody believed that.

"We take our own surveys, precinct by precinct, and we're especially strong in rural and poor areas," I told him, pulling out some charts that had been prepared.

[2] Mexico's ruling Institutional Revolutionary Party, which hasn't lost a presidential election in more than fifty years, is perennially charged with voting fraud. But, as Noriega knows, the United States is muted in its comments about the Mexican electoral system, for fear of damaging its stability.

"I doubt you'll win," Carter said, showing himself unmoved by what I had to say. I could feel that he was under the influence of what Gabriel Lewis Galindo, the opposition, and the U.S. embassy were saying. The meeting was short and Carter was noncommittal.

Afterward, I was surprised to find that the Americans had somehow bugged our entire conversation. Carter, of course, traveled with a security contingent that included Secret Service agents. But one member of the team was stationed outside the office, out on the grass, behind the building. We had a man working close by him, pruning trees and cutting brush with a machete. The U.S. agent didn't realize that the gardener was also a PDF soldier assigned to the CIA liaison officer nearby.

"The agent had the officer wired somehow," said a member of my intelligence team. "While he was doing the cleaning, the gardener could hear everything the two of you said." I was surprised and thought it would be unbecoming of Carter or his wife to carry in a bug to a private meeting. We never found out whether that was the case or whether, perhaps, a special long-distance listening device was used.

I didn't see Carter again after that, but his complicity with the American plan became more and more clear. On election day, he apparently went to election headquarters and complained that he had seen a blatant case of falsifying a ballot.

Magistrate Yolanda Pulice, the head of the electoral tribunal, said that his attitude and behavior had gone beyond his usually polite demeanor. Marching into the election office, Carter was heard by workers to berate one official, "*Señor, usted es un ladrón.*" ("Sir, you are a thief.") She rightly complained that this was interference in our affairs; the right approach would have been to file a formal complaint and allow an investigation. But Carter and the other election monitors fell into lock step with the U.S. embassy and the political opposition.

Carter didn't come back and speak to me directly about his complaints. He spread word that aides prevented scheduling a meeting with me and that I had refused to see him, which was not true. He and Pastor, his aide, had my private telephone number and were accustomed to calling me without intermediaries of any kind. But they never called.

While we did not have a sophisticated electoral tallying system, it was not a secretive operation. Overlooked by all the critics was the fact that representatives from all political parties participated in the count. Both at precinct and headquarters, government and opposition poll watchers sat side by side.

The opposition charged that the voting was fixed, so their supporters started hijacking uncollected ballots, delivering them to Archbishop Marcos McGrath, who was well known for his enmity toward the government and the military. By law, ballots not signed by the election commission headquarters were not valid. But McGrath claimed that he had most of the unsigned ballots at the archdiocese, which was doing its own count with its own computers and its own election operation—it sounded a bit like the Kurt Muse operation. The problem was that the Church had no relationship to the official election board, which was designated by Panamanian law as the official arbiter of election results. How did anyone know that the ballots they would then present to the world were legitimate? The only answer could be based on the prejudice propagated all around us: the answer was, the gringos would say, "Archbishop McGrath is an honorable church leader."

Major Manuel Sieíro, the chief of the Chorrera military garrison, caught people at the local parish in the act of running an illegal voting and ballot-counting operation right inside the church grounds. The official raided the operation and seized evidence. In that way, we were able to show what was happening in many parishes—that the church was following the orders of McGrath in openly supporting the opposition.

Marcos McGrath, the Man

Who was Marcos McGrath and why was he not to be trusted? He was a constant, pernicious accomplice of both the Americans and the opposition, whose influence cannot be underestimated. The leader of Panama's Catholic Church had a long-standing hatred for the Panamanian military, the Torrijos revolution and everything they stood for.

He and his minions lent support to the opposition parties, railed against the government from the pulpit and attended planning sessions with the United States against the military. McGrath presided over a divided Church in Panama—not everyone of the cloth shared his collaborationist, pro-American attitude. But his role ended up being decisive and pivotal in the fall of Panama and, ultimately, in delivering me into the hands of the Americans. The pulpit under McGrath became an open tribunal for preaching against the constituted government, violating the religious dictum "Render unto Caesar that which is Caesar's and unto God that which is God's."

He despised the liberation theology movement and dismissed or transferred priests who supported such liberation theology ideas as a church of the poor. Thus it had been in the case of Padre Héctor Gallegos, a rebel priest who ran afoul of landowners and disappeared in the province of Veraguas in 1971. Gallegos, a follower of the Colombian guerrilla priest, Camilo Torres, was inspired by the teachings of liberation theology and issued harsh criticism from the pulpit against the oligarchy and landowners of Veraguas, citing them by name as he spoke, charging them with usury and making unfair profits.

The landowners lashed out at him in return. The attacks became personal. Someone destroyed an electric generator at his house.

Suddenly, Gallegos disappeared. Everyone was certain that he had been killed. Torrijos appointed a prosecutor, Olmedo Davíd Miranda, to investigate the disappearance. He gathered evidence, questioned people, and even detained Alvaro Vernaza, a relative of Torrijos. The Church also conducted its own investigation, bringing in foreign investigators.

No trace of Gallegos, no evidence, was ever found. There were attempts to name me as being involved, but it didn't work. It was convenient for McGrath to blame the military because they couldn't come up with any relationship, reason, or motive to name anyone else. They started the rumor that Torrijos had ordered the murder of Gallegos and that I supposedly pushed him from a helicopter. No evidence, no reason to charge Torrijos, no motive—it was the landowners who hated the priest, not the military. It was nothing more than the drumbeat of the Church against the National Guard, and against Torrijos.

This was one of many great disputes between McGrath and Torrijos. There was a palpable hatred between them. Torrijos despised the man and I know the feeling was mutual. On the other hand, we protected McGrath and accepted his version of events when a car he was driving in the hours before dawn ran over and killed a person on the street.

McGrath was more an American than a Panamanian, and he never renounced his U.S. citizenship. He was born in the Canal Zone and spoke Spanish with an odd gringo accent. He ordered parish priests to denounce the military from the pulpit.

I was invited one day for lunch at the apartment of McGrath's brother, Eugene, a decorated American hero in World War II who had fought at Iwo Jima. Eugenio had been married for a time to the Hollywood actress Terry Moore, a former wife of Howard Hughes.

At lunch, the archbishop pulled me off to chat. I remember that the apartment was on the eleventh floor of the Roca building overlooking Panama Bay. As we spoke, the archbishop stood at an angle, half looking at me, half at the ocean. "Isn't it true, Colonel, that Torrijos is the one responsible for this Gallegos business?"

I looked firmly at McGrath and reminded him that his own assistant, Monsignor Legarra, was in charge of the church's investigation. "He works for you; you should trust and respect his word," I said.

McGrath just looked away. "What a lovely view this apartment has," he said.

I promptly told Torrijos about this conversation. He reacted confidently. "Well, now," he said. "I know just what I'm going to do." Torrijos took McGrath's interference in the political process seriously and passed along a complaint via diplomatic means to the Vatican investigative office, headed by Monsignor Pinci.

When Torrijos died, the archbishop thought he would deliver the coup de grâce. Torrijos's body was borne in procession to the portals of the National Cathedral. Those accompanying were shocked to hear McGrath speak as he met the procession at the steps: "You never wanted to give me an appointment to meet with you," he said, speaking to Torrijos one last time. "And now you come here without having asked me for one." It was an enmity that lasted unto death. At the religious ceremony, McGrath even went to the extent of mispronouncing Torrijos's name, calling him "Omar Efraín Torres."

To my lasting satisfaction, I can say that it was Torrijos who had the last word, even after his own death. I was not yet commander of the armed forces when Pope John Paul II came to visit Panama in 1983. Ricardo de la Espriella was president, and we had scheduled a small audience with the pope at the presidential palace. Those attending were the president; Monsignor Laboa, who was the Vatican ambassador to Panama; my wife and I; and my predecessor as commander, General Ruben Dario Paredes, along with his wife.

The audience consisted mostly of speeches by the Panamanians present. The pope sat quietly, mostly just staring at us deeply and sternly. When the allotted time was up, all the others began filing out and the Holy Father touched me lightly to stop me for a moment as I passed by. He placed his right hand over his heart. "I am grateful for your cooperation," he said quietly, looking at me. That was all he said. Thinking about this, I suddenly realized that Marcos McGrath had been investigated and would never, ever be named a cardinal of the Roman Catholic Church.

Evaluating the impossibility of coming up with an electoral count and facing mounting protest, we called a meeting at the presidential palace. President Solis Palma, the electoral commission—including magistrates Luis Carlos Chen and Yolanda Pulice—Colonel Justine, Darisnel Espino and Carlos Duque were present. The options were few—cancel the elections or declare a military takeover. My goal and my preoccupation were finding a solution that would avoid the loss of Panamanian lives. So we did what we should have done months earlier: we canceled the elections.

Canceling the elections did succeed in breaking the American strategy: as long as there were no election returns, the Americans could continue provoking street protests, hoping for and spurring on new provocations and violence. But it was all too late.

I had been forced down a dead-end street. If only we had canceled the elections after capturing Kurt Muse, the course of events would have been far different.

Martyred by Someone Else's Blood

During the election count, from May 7 to May 10, there were daily Civic Crusade demonstrations organized and spurred on by John Maisto and the American embassy. It was evident that they intended to instigate an uprising, but the masses never joined them. So they decided they would do it alone. It was a sacrifice for the wealthy. The demonstrations were conducted during business hours—nine-to-five protests in the banking district, centered around Calle 50. They never took place far from there, and were always programmed at predetermined times of day: the *rabiblancos* were encouraging their employees to hit the streets for an instant rally in front of the TV cameras. There was a distorted notion that Panama was close to revolution. All eyes focused on Calle 50, where the protesters arrived in their Mercedes, and their perfume-soaked women waved starched white handkerchiefs. Instead of going to play tennis or find a game of poker at the Union Club, they would drive down to Calle 50 for a few hours of protest. And when they got hot and tired in the evening heat, they could always send down their maids to do the protesting for them, carrying along their Teflon-coated pots and pans to bang a phony protest rhythm. It didn't sound like the fire-hardened, blackened iron pots of San Miguelito or of the poor neighborhoods. There were no protests there.

The rest of the country was actually peaceful and quiet. The poor people of Chorrillo, San Miguelito, Caledonia and everywhere else in Panama—people who couldn't afford a day off—went to work, went to the movies, bought their lottery tickets, went out dancing and went to sleep, living life as they always did.

Was it because the people were repressed in those areas by the demons, me and the Panamanian Defense Forces? Or was it because they had no reason to protest, that the protests were manufactured by vengeance-seeking white bankers and businessmen in collusion with the Americans?

The demonstrators became increasingly active. The first few times, they agreed to march in the street, but only after much prodding by Maisto and company at the U.S. embassy. And they met with such little success that we thought each attempt would fizzle and be their last. We were wrong.

They set up one last desperate march on Wednesday, May 10, again organized and forced upon the opposition by the Americans. With very few supporters on the streets, Guillermo Endara, Ricardo Arias Calderón and Billy Ford (the other vice-presidential candidate)—fearful of taking a stand, having little prospect of success—hopped into their van and began a small motorcade down to Casco Viejo, the old part of downtown Panama City. All along the route, they were in touch with their American embassy benefactors via mobile radio.

The reluctant procession rolled downtown along Avenida Central toward Casco Viejo, where international TV cameras were waiting.

The Americans were pushing their gutless Panamanian stooges to the limit, because they intended to create a scene.

The provocation came in the form of a human life. It happened that the U.S. embassy had lent bodyguard Alexis Guerra to work with the opposition candidates. Guerra was an employee of a company called Tesna-Mimsa, a security firm whose sole contract was with the U.S. embassy. Guerra was considered a traitor by those who knew him in the military and the police force. He had sided with the enemy and was on loan to the opposition candidates, working this day to protect Billy Ford.

The atmosphere was volatile as the caravan reached the end of the road, down to the waterfront at Santa Ana Park. The police were under orders not to shoot, to avoid being provoked into action. These were standing orders.

But shots were fired, and regardless of how and why, the responsibility was ours—the officer in charge had failed by not controlling the situation.

The incident could have been provoked by the march participants or by agents planted in the crowd or among the troops—and it could have been PDF soldiers who had been bought off. The Americans employed agents provocateurs on the streets to stir up trouble. Many of them were Puerto Ricans, members of the U.S. military in civilian clothes. For example, an American army colonel, Chico Stone, went frequently to such events as a civilian, wearing his baseball cap and blue jeans. Stone was expelled from the country for attending civilian rallies. We arrested some of the Puerto Ricans at one rally, camouflaged as if they were Panamanians. That was how they worked.

When it was over, Guerra was dead, his blood splattered all over the sparkling white *guayabera* of Billy Ford. Was Guerra the target? Was it intentional? It was part of John Maisto's plan.

It is an understatement to say that this did us no good. I knew that the world reaction would be devastating, but there was nothing I could do about it. Bad as it was, it was even worse because we had redoubled our efforts to avoid the constant provocation hurled at us by the Americans. Common sense dictates that if you are counting election ballots and have hopes that your side can win, you should not simultaneously be out on the street beating up the other side's presidential and vice-presidential contenders. This would be the very thing that the opposition would want us to do, in order to pull victory from almost certain defeat. And the bloodletting that day took the process over the edge.

The reality was that a bloody photo of Billy Ford, transmitted around the world, was the product of a plan to create a victim. The Americans saw it as good fortune that Ford would have his clothing stained with blood, to make it seem as if he had been injured and was the victim of violence. He did nothing to correct the impression. He was a martyr with someone else's blood.

One week after the balloting, the Civic Crusade tried a Sunday general strike. It didn't work. They had no support. The Americans saw that their plans had been stymied. Endara, who said he had been lightly injured in the fracas at Casco Viejo, was left to his own devices. Comically, the rotund lawyer announced a hunger strike, saying he would eat nothing except for the Host when he went to Mass. The joke went around that he was praying all the time so he could take as much communion as possible, because nobody noticed any change in his sizable frame. Other than that, we had burst the balloon and Panama quieted down. There was no civil strife in the country. Our main problem was the escalating military provocation from the Americans, and the escalation had hardly begun.

CHAPTER 11

"But There Shall Not One Hair of Your Head Perish"[1]

*B*oom. The thud of a rocket grenade pounded the stone walls of the military command center in Chorrillo. I tasted dust and could smell the burning powder that exploded just outside my window. *Boom.* Another shock, tracking closer to the little alcove room where I lay motionless on the floor. Would the next one hit closer, penetrate the small window, tear open the wall? How many minutes before I die?

It was October 3, 1989, and I was certain I would be killed any second by the barrage of rocket fire exploding beneath my window. All that I had been through, all the fortunes and trials had come to this: I lay prone on the floor of a small room at my office in command headquarters wondering what death would be like.

I got to my knees long enough to pray. "Dear God, if I die here, thy will be done." Rockets shook the room. Between thoughts of death, I searched for a way out, summoning my reserves of discipline and power of reasoning. You are a soldier, I kept telling myself, fighting my emotions. Analyze the situation.

A loudspeaker penetrated the din. "You are surrounded. All of your units are with us. Urraca, *presente,* Machos del Monte, *presente,* Battalion 2000, *presente.* You must surrender. There is no escape."

I was listening to voices telling me to surrender, punctuating the

[1] Luke 21:18

explosions and weapons fire. I winced with the concussion of each blast, wondering whether I could still think, still complete the next thought before the end came. *The windowpane is all that separates you from the street and the grenades. It's just a matter of time. These guys are coming in.*

The attack is too strong, too close.

No, you're a soldier and you are fighting. Think, man, think.

But the attack is overwhelming. There is no time. . . .

The human mind cannot always be controlled; it jumps about, it paints things as being all lost, and then, if you let yourself be convinced by what you are seeing and what your mind is telling you, you really are defeated. Flashes of the previous few days went through my mind as I tried to figure out who was behind what was happening.

The previous Sunday was a day of celebration for the baptism of Jean Manuel, my daughter Sandra's son. There were friends, politicians, members of the military, all gathered at the church.

Something was in the air. As we sat in the church for this beautiful celebration, we could hear military operations in the distance outside—tanks rumbling and helicopters flying nearby. I assumed it was routine security for the event and protection for the general staff. But when one helicopter buzzed close overhead, creating a racket inside the church, I motioned to Major Moisés Giroldi, a well-liked, personable, highly trustworthy officer, who stood to one side of the chapel.

"Giroldi, find out what's going on," I said. Then I remembered that the staff had brought along fireworks to celebrate the baptism. "And take some of the firecrackers with you. The next time there's a flyover, set some off."

A helicopter pilot can't distinguish from the air whether ground explosions underneath him are weapons being shot at him or fireworks. And gunfire from the ground can take out a helicopter. Giroldi followed my orders. This little ploy worked. The helicopter did one more flyover and was drawn away by the crackle of the fireworks. Having done that, I turned back to the reverence of the moment without giving it another thought.

That night, I slept at my room at headquarters, as I sometimes did. Not for any special reason—I sometimes stayed at the command headquarters if I had an early meeting. I went home for a bit Monday morning, freshened up and spent the rest of the day at Amador, where my field office was located.

My security team sensed trouble, and Eliecer Gaitán, my trusted aide and security chief, was especially on edge. I trusted him implicitly, and do to this day.[2] He was highly intelligent, trained at the Argentine Military Academy, an excellent intelligence officer. He had been in the UESAT—antiterrorism forces—and later transferred to my personal-escort detachment. Within the detachment he had diverse duties: he acted as a kind of military administrative liaison for me with the various military units; he also functioned as military attaché, supervising logistical arrangements. He had been trained by the Argentine military attaché Colonel Mohamed Seineldin, to prepare for military instruction at our planned Institute of Military Studies.

Gaitán was born in my home province of Chiriquí. He came from a line of Panamanian military officers, people with a good tradition—a good family. Eliecer Gaitán had a great future ahead of him, a professional career cut short by the U.S. invasion.

Gaitán's versatility became a liability for him. I began to depend on his expertise and gave him power that went beyond the chain of command. His direct superiors saw him as a threat because of his capacity and because of the confidence I had in his performance. He was often bad-mouthed by his superiors because of his brusque style and the ability he had to walk up to a man of higher rank with the cachet of authority.

Among his other skills, he was a fine investigator. And so it was that prior to the October coup, he was highly suspicious. Giroldi's name kept coming up in conversations, connected to dark rumors about troop movements and protests. Gaitán could be tough and direct. He went straight to Giroldi, who, as a major, was a much higher ranking officer than this young, brash captain, that very Sunday. "What's going on, Giroldi?" he said. "I hope there's no funny stuff going on. Let's not play games," he warned.

I arrived at headquarters early Tuesday morning, varying my sched-

[2] Gaitán took refuge in the Vatican embassy after the invasion. He was at that location when Noriega was tricked into taking asylum there on December 24, 1989. Gaitán escaped from the embassy prior to Noriega's surrender and was able to evade capture by the Americans, leaving Panama for exile.

ule and route, as I always did, for standard security reasons. My body-guard, Iván Castillo, had also arrived. At around 8:30 A.M., my personal physician, Dr. Martín Sosa, was in the process of doing a routine medical checkup, and I remember vividly that he had strapped the blood pressure sleeve around my arm and was taking a reading on the mercury. We started hearing indistinct explosions in the distance. Sosa laughed as he watched my pressure go up on the gauge; it seemed like something from a movie or cartoon. He stopped laughing when the full force of the mortar-and-grenade attack began moments later.

Sosa was there with me, along with Castillo, as I conducted this inner dialogue.

You are a soldier; analyze your situation. You have seen two military divisions outside—the Urraca and the Dobermans—where is your support?

I asked Sosa and Castillo what they thought. They said that maybe it was a battle for power between forces; that was wrong. Both battalions were lining their tanks up around the building, aiming right at us. Voices were telling us on the loudspeakers that all the other battalions were joining ranks with the rebellion. Yes, we were surrounded and yes, there was an intense barrage, I told myself. But there should be opposition out there.

I heard them say that I was surrounded and that everybody had united behind them. Intellectually, I began to realize that it probably wasn't true. But they kept repeating it and it started sounding like it was true.

What if, just what if, they were lying?

Bullets, shells and grenades were hitting the facade all the while. We were in a tiny alcove, just big enough for a bed, a bathroom and a changing room like many military barracks have for officers. Just the three of us there, isolated, pinned down in a heavy barrage for what could have been several hours.

When the barrage had begun, we had gone looking for telephones but the lines were dead. I remembered the private line I had in the alcove, a phone no one knew about. I was able to call my office to give Anabel Dittea, a member of my staff, the emergency code words: *Primero de Mayo.*

I considered it likely that I still had supporters and that my phone call had put a counterattack plan into action, that loyal troops would organize a rescue. So, if they were lying outside and if my phone call had done what it was supposed to do, maybe there was still a way out of this mess.

I found out later that I was right. Very few units had joined the rebellion. The contingency planning had worked. Battalion 2000, under the command of Major Federico Olechea, was coming to the rescue, and along the way Primero de Mayo had mobilized the transit police. The Machos del Monte regiment, based in Río Hato, an hour away, also got the call to come into Panama City to help repulse the attack. The main force of the regiment flew into Paitilla Airport and was now close to the center of action. All of them evaded the Americans, whose waffling support for the coup helped us regain control.

One of our best strokes of fortune came as a result of action by Marcela Tasón. She was on her way to work when she came upon the whole thing in progress. Her son was a member of the antiterrorism forces. She tracked him down and went out with him on his motorcycle to round up supporters. They found Porfirio Caballero, who was our chief demolition specialist. Caballero piled some rocket grenades in his car and headed for the high-rise apartment buildings overlooking headquarters. Soon, he had a commanding view of the rebellion, and he and several people he had rounded up started launching rocket grenades at the rebels below. The rebels, in turn, seeing rocket fire from behind them as they attacked my position, figured that my supporters had been able to mount an air response. Peeking out the window, I saw one rocket hit an adjacent building, which caught fire, but I had no idea what was going on. I know it got some of their men—an ambulance came in to take out some wounded.

Suddenly there was absolute silence; next I heard the sound of scuffling inside the perimeter of headquarters. I was on an upper floor, and the ground level had an open patio large enough for trucks and equipment. The attackers were inside the building and would come to get me.

I decided to leave the anteroom and go into the front room of my office. Dr. Sosa was there; Castillo had gone out into the general headquarters area and hadn't returned.

"Well, Doctor," I said jokingly, "here we are, just the two of us. I just don't know. I figured you'd be long gone by now."

He was silent.

"You always seem to be there at just the right moment," I continued. "Here you are, about to be a witness to history in the making. . . ."

I was interrupted by pounding on the main door to my quarters.

"*Mi general,* come out, come out, open the door!" said a voice I could not immediately recognize. "It's Armijo. Come out. Please don't shoot."

Roberto Armijo was a colonel and I immediately assumed he was leading the rebellion.

"Okay, what's going on?" I said through the door, maintaining a calm, measured tone.

"Listen, *Comandante,* I have to tell you . . ." he addressed me properly as *Comandante,* this I could hear. But the rest of what he said was muffled and distant.

"Well," I said, "come in, Armijo. The door is open."

There was silence. No movement toward the door. I could tell that Armijo and whoever was with him were afraid to see what they would find when they came in.

"Listen, the door is open," I repeated.

"No, you open it," another voice replied.

"But the door is open," I said. "Come in."

Silence again, then the hesitant question, "You're not holding anything?"

"Ah, hell, open the door!" I told them impatiently.

Finally, they complied. I remember that the door opened from the outside inward, so I stood back a bit and got my first glimpse of the rebels.

"Lieutenant, is this possible? You of all people?" I said to one of the junior officers nearby, a man I remembered promoting just two months earlier. I looked at this man, but I meant my remarks to be heard by Giroldi. "Exactly what military school do you come out of?" I asked.

I immediately began sizing them all up, and slowly, confidently walked out into the main patio surveying the scene. Most were speaking in that thick-tongued way people have when they've had quite a bit to drink. In the hallway, down toward the stairway that led to the main floor, I saw nothing but strewn wreckage. Lieutenant Colonel Aquilino Sieíro stood holding one arm as if he had been grazed by shrapnel; Lieutenant Colonel Luis Cordoba was at the bottom of the stairs, apparently under arrest, and still siding with me. I walked along the hallway and saw eyes averted as I looked at each man. I continued down the stairway, utter silence all around me, my left hand in my pocket, my briefcase in my right hand. The main floor was huge and I could see tanks had pulled in close. I walked past them until I came right up to Giroldi, the obvious leader of the rebellion, who was at the rear of this tableau, wearing only a T-shirt and trousers, down there on the main patio. In comparison, I was in full uniform, very much showing the men who their commander was.

"You are firing at your own men; you are firing at yourselves," I said, in a measured, forceful tone, looking around at all of them. "Your own men. Can't you see that the Americans are behind all this, that they are using you in their game? Can't you see that you are just pawns of the Americans, up there watching all this?" I gestured up to Ancon Hill, right above us, where the U.S. Southern Command had a perfect line of sight to view everything that was going on.

We could always tell when the Americans were watching and listening to us; we would always see the orientation of their radar antennae shift about 30 degrees. That's the way it was—the Americans were playing Big Brother up there, watching everything.

"Manipulation by the Americans," I shouted at them. And I looked at each one individually, calling him by name. "You, look at you," I said to one after the other. Every one of them lowered his head. "Miguel, José, Fulano, Solano, why are you here?"

Nobody said a word. I had been walking all this time, unimpeded, right out of the main area onto the street, where the tanks were, and I did the same with the tank commanders, talking to each one.

I could see that there was no firm leadership; they were confused. I turned back to Giroldi; he was not drunk, like many of the soldiers obviously were. He stood there, firm but nervous. He seemed very pallid and his twitch was acting up, curling his lip involuntarily.

"*Comandante,* you must understand. They are blaming you for what is happening to us these days. I'm very concerned about you. Be an example for us, show them; because, without you, the men cannot function, and this country can go no place."

Strange, disjointed words from the leader of a coup. He made no sense.

"Please," he continued, "let's move inside."

We went to an area where the other rebel officers had isolated a group of my closest men, including about a dozen members of my escort unit, forcing them to the ground, facedown on the floor. Among them was Castillo, who had been quickly arrested by the rebels when he left my office in search of an escape route.

I saw Gaitán there, lying on the floor. He had been seized as he attempted to come to my aid. Rodolfo Castrellon wanted to use his helicopter to help me, but it was captured as well.

I remember the fear in the eyes of the rebels; none of them could directly return my gaze. No one touched me or changed his polite, deferential tone when addressing me. It gave me a measure of my position and my chances. Far from the sense of being lost, on the verge of death, I now slowly was able to dominate and exert my authority. I started to retake command. I could feel the tide turning, the power of the situation returning to my side.

I looked around and gestured to the men before me. "Okay, fine, let's negotiate. What is it that you want?"

Giroldi stammered and said nothing. He wanted to confer in private with Sieíro and Armijo, following the chain of command even though these superior officers were at the moment his prisoners. They pulled aside and argued a bit, out of earshot. Armijo finally came over, delivering Giroldi's message.

"Everyone who has completed his term of duty should retire," Armijo said.

"Agreed," I said, knowing they expected me to argue since I was on the list of people soon to retire. "What else?" They just looked at me, then walked off and started arguing among themselves.

The more talk, the more obvious it became that they were not in as strong a military position as they let on. My own units were still free outside the perimeter.

The rebels were behaving wantonly. They had begun taunting their captives—my men lying on the ground. In particular, Gaitán was having trouble. He had been captured outside, was dragged in and was periodically being kicked in the ribs. Javier Licona, a captain in the cavalry, had a special hatred for Gaitán. "You, Gaitán, you were a big man last night, warning us not to try anything." Licona dragged Gaitán in front of everyone, threw him to the ground and was going to murder him right there. I ran over and pushed myself between the two men, standing nose to nose with Licona. I had no weapon, nothing, one man facing down another. "You'll have to shoot me before you shoot him," I said, gesturing to Gaitán on the floor.

Licona looked at me for just an instant, averted his gaze and backed off. He left the building. I later learned that he ran straight for the Southern Command, pleading for help. Sources told us that Licona's plea won a sarcastic response from General Marc Cisneros, the head of the U.S. Army forces at the Southern Command.

"Well, Captain," the Mexican-American general said in a saccharine-sweet, flowery way. "You're a bit late. You and your dear friends are already surrounded below; there's nothing we can do to save them now."

When Licona fled, something changed in the room. Giroldi and the others stood there, waiting for me to speak. I looked at all of them and spoke in a loud voice so the rest of the men could hear me.

"You don't have control here," I said, staring at Armijo. "Reinforcements are moving in; the Machos del Monte are already on their way. Companies are defecting. You might as well face reality," I said, gesturing this time to Giroldi.

Another captain came into the room, agitated. "Let's get out of here, let's take one of the trucks," he said to one group of rebels. They started to force members of the general staff onto a nearby troop transport, among them Sieíro, Miguel, Aleman, Daniel Delgado, Carlos Arosemena, Moisés Correa, Theodore Alexander, Rafael Cedeño and the rest of the general staff.

I found out later that this abortive act was part of the plan to imprison most of my senior staff, the majors and colonels, and then to deliver Lieutenant Colonel Luis Cordoba and me separately to General Marc Cisneros at the U.S. Army command.

I had to act quickly. I moved ahead of them and began giving orders. "Nobody's leaving here; get out of those trucks *now;* get down from there," I shouted, pushing them.

"You don't have the capacity to rise up against this *comandante,* not one of you!" I again shouted, looking around at all of them. "Not one of you has the balls to go against me."

All around headquarters, my men were taking the upper hand. One of Giroldi's lieutenants came in.

"Major, we have one man killed and another wounded; they're starting to take over," he reported. "We have to start to answer the attack. We'll be slaughtered here."

"Major," I told Giroldi, speaking in an even, soft tone to him. "You've lost it; you're not in command. You and your men must surrender."

Giroldi knew that I was right. Perhaps he could handle his own unit, but he didn't have charge of the men around us. Everyone was wavering. Soon, I had more men on the floor of the headquarters than the rebels did. Marcela's ploy with the rockets and the code transmitter to Mrs. Dittea had worked. The rebels were defecting in the face of what they thought was a massive air counterattack. They were absolutely distraught.

Eventually, Giroldi called me back into the side room where he and the other rebels had been. "Okay," he said, "let me go—I don't know where to go, but just let me go."

I looked at him and remember feeling a mixture of pity and disgust. "Man, just get out of here," I said, waving him away.

Within minutes, however, he was under arrest, seized by some of my now victorious men, who had gotten up from the floor and were dusting themselves off. The tables had turned. The rebels fled, or pretended they had never been rebels at all. They sought out friends and begged forgiveness. But my men raged with fury, having felt themselves at the brink of death. The adrenaline was flowing. They saw Giroldi trying to leave and, despite his protests that I had dismissed him, dragged him back before me.

"*Comandante,* this man cannot go," they said. "He must pay." Giroldi was unlucky; his presence had become an issue and my options were limited.

"*Comandante,* please, let me go back to my wife; she's waiting for me," Giroldi begged.

"Giroldi," I said to him, "you didn't act alone in all of this, did you? I want you to tell me the truth. Tell me all about it." I went walking off with him, not far from the others.

Moisés Giroldi had been a fine soldier, the man least expected to participate in a coup. In fact, he had been instrumental in putting down the 1988 coup attempt by Macías, Villalaz and company. He also had shown great loyalty and personal warmth toward me. He was pleasant; he didn't speak excessively and when he did it was with precision, very slowly.

He had been close to me for some time. Not only had I been the best man at his wedding no more than about a month earlier, but my wife was instrumental in scheduling the ceremony. Giroldi and his bride, Adela Bonilla, had been living together for some time.

Giroldi was the kind of officer who enjoyed camaraderie. Any time he showed up at headquarters, he made it a point to come over and visit with me and shoot the breeze. The talk was not personal, but about military matters. I considered my relationship with Giroldi a relaxed, cordial, respectful association.

It was difficult to think that he was now the leader of a coup against me, especially with the deference he continued to show. He was obviously nervous and on some form of medication, which caused his eyes to blink uncontrollably. But he dealt with me properly throughout the coup attempt and never threatened me personally during this entire uprising, even though some people claim that was the case. He never held a machine gun to my face, nothing of the kind. And, unlike some versions, I never held a weapon on him or anyone else there. All around us, there were drunken soldiers, some drunker than others. Not Giroldi. He was respectful and never carried a weapon during the uprising.

A doctor had been treating Giroldi for hypertension, I had been told, but he was taking amphetamines against all medical advice. His face was reddened and he was agitated, more frightened than one might expect a soldier like him to behave. All of this was even more confounding, considering my relationship with the man.

During my brief talk with Giroldi that day, one thing became clear: a sizable conspiracy had been mounted, largely through the efforts of the Americans. Giroldi was only the most visible protagonist in that conspiracy. As I began to realize how deeply this could go, I wanted to use Giroldi's information to root out the conspirators. But after speaking for only a short time, there was an interruption.

"*Comandante*," called one of my men, staring hard at Giroldi as we talked. "You're needed over here."

Inevitably, there were charges that I killed Giroldi, but it was not so; neither did I order his death. I had every reason to keep him alive. Even though we had been in an extremely tense situation in which the rebels had launched this massive assault against us for hours, it was not our practice to murder our fellow Panamanians. Throughout history, the penalty for such rebellion was exile, not death.

When I left the *comandancia* that day, it was with the knowledge that everyone had their respective responsibilities. The investigations included an inventory of personnel and equipment—who and what was missing. It was all programmed and it was not for me to do; the chain of command meant that I would receive and review a report from each unit. I asked for an idea of how many men were wounded, how many in the hospital, and then I let everyone get to their own work.

It started to rain and I began walking, trying to get away from the general vicinity of headquarters. Mentally, I had already recovered, and was thinking about the political side of things. I had won a battle, and I saw that the chain of command was operating; I had extricated myself from the portals of death itself. Headquarters was secured and my command of the situation was complete.

I returned to my office at Fort Amador, and my staff arranged my schedule so I would have maximum visibility and people would know that I was well and firmly in command. My first stop was a political rally in Santiago de Veraguas; my supporters were on the street and there were cheers and applause. By nightfall, all the world was talking about what had happened, reconstructing and often fabricating what had taken place.

After Giroldi's death, his wife was provided with U.S.-paid lodging at the Chateaubleu Hotel in Coral Gables, Florida. American diplomats encouraged U.S. newspapers to meet with her. She told interviewers that her husband had said that they might have to kill me in the course of the coup[3]—not as an actual assassination, but rather an attack on the headquarters by Panamanians, spurred on by the Americans, in which the United States could innocently watch the news footage of my body being carried out of headquarters. "I blame the North Americans for my husband's death. They only had to show off their power and equip-

---

[3] See *Divorcing the Dictator* by Frederick Kempe (New York: G. P. Putnam and Sons, p. 376). Noriega vehemently denies most of this account, by his rivals and enemies, but endorses the comments made by Giroldi's wife.

ment and his coup would have worked. There would not have been a confrontation. No Panamanians are so stupid as to confront the North Americans."[4]

Following the U.S. invasion, there were a series of trials in Panama, airing the deaths of Giroldi and the other rebels. I was tried in absentia—no surprise, since all of my opponents were in power.

The Americans had failed to accomplish their goal—eliminating me, coaxing an assassination from within. The United States realized that it had not found the means to get rid of me. The political violence had failed, the economic sanctions had failed, the military option had failed. The option of having the government in exile authorize Eduardo Herrera to come back with a team of insurgents had failed. All these options, conceived and paid for by the U.S. government establishment, with American tax dollars, had failed. Now they knew that they would have to take matters into their own hands.

They prepared for invasion, but made one more attempt at negotiations; within a day of the coup, Michael Kozak contacted my American lawyer, Frank Rubino, asking for another meeting. The problem was that I still could not accept being bought off by the Americans. When that message became clear one final time, the invasion was the only option left to them.

In mid-December, I was declared head of state, because the situation had brought us to what amounted to a war footing. We were living in a state of war—with constant provocation by the Americans, constant threats—and this was an emergency measure, a wartime measure. This is what I repeated on December 15, 1989. My words were twisted by the Bush administration, which was looking for as much justification as it could find to invade Panama. I said that a state of war existed because we were under siege, but it was not a declaration of war. The speech was seized upon by the United States, which made the absurd claim that I was declaring war.

It's the same with the other image of me from that time, my appearance at a meeting of Latin American historians, during which I was given the machete used by soldiers fighting for independence with Simón Bolívar in Ayacucho, Peru, in the 1800s. This Anficto-nico Congress in August 1988 was attended by delegates from all the

---

[4] Kempe, p. 393.

countries touched by Bolívar's march of independence. The machete is the symbol of the men who fought to liberate the Americas from Spanish domination; in Panama, it is the symbol of the campesino, of the campesino's right to work and of his work in the jungle. I raised it high, as a proud symbol of Latin American—and Panamanian—independence.

CHAPTER 12

Searching for Daylight

I STOOD ALONE on the morning of December 20, 1989, and gazed out from a promontory that gave me a cruel vantage point of the invasion. To one side, across the hills, I could look in the direction of Tinajita, where we had a major barracks. There was an aerial bombardment, the sound of tracers whooshing through the sky, small-arms fire and explosions. The sky glowed and shook periodically. The invasion was in full bloom and there was no means of control or coordination.

After the confrontation at the airport and our escape from the 82nd Airborne's perimeter, we received a radio message from the man I identified as J.F., detailing the points of enemy infiltration, including the possibility that some of our own bodyguards had been bought off by the Americans. I ordered dispersion of our forces and a mobile defense, along with the distribution of more than two tons of armaments, including rocket-propelled grenades and mortars. We shut down communications to avoid detection by radio monitoring. From that moment on, our forces initiated, according to plan, a variety of independent elite commando operations, commanded by Captain Gonzalo González, Captain Heraclides Sucre, Gaitán, Porfirio Caballero's explosives specialists and the detachment of alpha and beta squads of the

"Silver Fox," one of our top men. For their own protection and concern about reprisals, I do not identify J.F. or Silver Fox here.

We stopped at Balbina Periñan's house. She was on an official trip to Ecuador. A number of armed fighters were there, but we were pinned down in total darkness. In the distance you could see flames coming from the direction of Chorrillo; you could hear the sound of planes and helicopters racing by, but all we could do was lie low and wait for daylight to see what was happening.

I spent the night pacing, peering through the windows, listening to the explosions. Former President Solis Palma called from Venezuela at one point; Periñan answered, but the line cut off and the telephone no longer worked after that. San Miguelito offered a view across to Tinajita, but also down toward the city below. Suddenly, I saw tracer fire, the sound of weapons and then a helicopter careening to the ground in flames.

The fighting was particularly fierce in our vicinity. The general staff had gone to Tinajita, the last place the command should have gathered. The barracks was nestled on a hill amid humble Panamanian homes. It took a pounding. The first attack at Tinajita missed the barracks and bombs fell among the nearby houses, killing civilians.

The company based at Tinajita was known as Los Tigres—the Tigers. For a while, they were able to hold off the Americans; by 5:30 A.M., helicopter gunships had left the barracks in ruins.

Bush and his cowardly war machine used Panama for target practice. Contending that they had to destroy our ability to fight them in the skies, for example, the U.S. Air Force chose the Río Hato air base for the world's first wartime test of the Stealth bomber. We were a proving ground for the Gulf War, which was to come later.

Lacking any anti-aircraft support of any kind, a sense of impotence overcame the Panamanians, both regular army members and the poorly armed members of the Dignity Battalions, who had begun to put up a disorganized resistance. With our command structure cut, never expecting an air attack, Panama was unable to do anything against the world's greatest military power. Hardly a surprise.

It was an overnight war, filled with Panamanian heroes facing insurmountable odds, filled with neighbors and friends tending to the needs of the fighters and their wounded, because they were patriots who believed they had the duty and the right to defend their homes, their land and their countrymen. At dawn, there were many dead.

In Panamanian terms, the invasion was the equivalent for us of Pearl Harbor: a strong, devastating aerial attack. Panama's Institute of Seismology reported 417 bomb explosions in the first fourteen hours of the invasion. Had it been a land assault, we would have had the capacity to defend ourselves better. One thing is certain: the numbers of dead—Americans and Panamanians—had to be more than was reported by the U.S. military and the Panamanian opposition government installed by them.[1] On the American side, an unreported number of helicopters went down. I saw two in San Miguelito; there were reports of two or three more during the attack on the *comandancia* and in Panama Viejo, the ruins of the old colonial city of Panama, which was being used as a hideout where a small group of my men had been conducting nighttime raids and maintaining contact. When you start adding up these deaths along with the people killed at the airport in our skirmish, you get close to the total number of Americans reported killed during the entire invasion—twenty-three. It had to be more.

There was blood and destruction on the Panamanian side. Around the headquarters complex in Chorrillo, fire turned children, mothers, fathers, the elderly, entire families, into ashes as they slept; people trampled the wounded as they fled the flames. Hundreds, perhaps thousands of dead, much more than the 320 people the Americans and their shameless Panamanian stooges claimed had died. No one has been able to determine the number of Panamanian dead. The Americans said that the Panamanians set fire to their own people in Chorrillo. What cynical, outrageous lies! The Americans painted a picture of the Dignity Battalions as gangsters who fought against their own people. This was pure propaganda, no better than anything the Nazis and imperial Japan used against the Americans in World War II.

A t around dawn, we saw three Blackhawk helicopters descend in a field not far from the house. We assumed that they were deploying troops in the area. It was time to move. The only option was to circulate—look for our men and try to reconstruct a plan.

We were using a taxi. I had changed from my uniform into civilian clothes. I was wearing jeans, a shirt and a cap. I was also carrying a gun,

[1] The number of Panamanian deaths was reported by U.S. and Panamanian officials as being between 270 and 400 dead. Some Panamanian groups put the toll as high as 4,000, but could not document their claims.

some grenades and other gear. We went out looking for Gaitán and his men, our special urban squads, but it was all chaos in Panama City.

The Americans had knocked out long-distance communications. Television and radio had already been commandeered by them, and they were broadcasting propaganda and misinformation about the fight and about who had surrendered. They were using a Panamanian folk song called "El Fugitivo" as a signal that they hadn't found me yet.

It was all psychological warfare controlled by the occupying forces. They would announce, "So-and-so has surrendered, and is at such-and-such an embassy," that "Liberation forces are mopping up isolated guerrilla operations" in Colón. In between news items they would play "El Fugitivo." They still could not find me.

We switched our base of operations to a house near the Church of San Francisco. I tried to strategize what to do next.

One of those accompanying me voted for us to stop trying to fight. "*Jefe*, this isn't going to work," he said. "You have to go to the Cuban embassy. You'll be safe there. Face it, it's all over."

I said no. The best thing was to set up operations in the mountains. I had received information telling me that the coast was clear to the Cuban embassy. My family was there and I could have snuck in and taken asylum. We spoke by telephone with the Cuban ambassador, Lázaro Mora, who said he would accept whatever decision I made.

"We've got to get to the hills and set up a base," I said. "We've got to regroup our forces."

We made telephone contact with some of our political allies and proposed that we go to the presidential palace, but the majority didn't like the idea. We spoke with Darisnel Espino, who reported on a confrontation between U.S. soldiers and a group of Panamanian civilians and military led by Luis Cordoba and Nivaldo Madriñan, who were holed up in the Avesa building on Via Brasil avenue.

There was no rest; I had to find a way to escape the city.

The next morning, the Americans were tightening their command of the situation. They had started house-to-house searches for anyone they could interrogate and, most of all, for information about me. After a while, it became too dangerous. We had to move. We operated between several safe houses and also used the cemetery in Río Abajo.

We had to be very careful, for fear that any suspicious activity would tip off the Americans. We tried to stay away from windows, to avoid loud conversation, to limit the use of running water and toilets. All we could do was wait for nightfall. More and more people were venturing out onto the street; American MPs were everywhere.

We established a communications channel using two women, code-named *"Micaela"* and *"Garganta."* They forwarded messages to and from Micaela's husband, who stayed by the telephone. We received a report on the night of the twentieth that two U.S. tanks and radio transmitters had been destroyed, and that there were several American casualties.

We were able to confirm the transport of heavy weaponry to clandestine locations for eventual use against the invaders. One mortar operated for a time from the inner patio of the National Institute, the secondary school I once attended. While the new U.S.-installed government was being sworn in on a U.S. base in the old Canal Zone, units from the Machos del Monte battalion launched an attack that blocked them from getting to the legislative assembly building.

There were also several actions that were not carried out, including an attack in Colón on the Pedro Miguel Locks. We denied permission to carry out this mission, to avoid the death of Panamanian workers there. Also, one commando unit stormed the Marriott Hotel along the waterfront, seizing American journalists as hostages. Fortunately, the leader of the group did not harm them; the only journalist killed during the attack was a Spanish photographer killed by the American military.

At one point, I got to a telephone and taped a message that was broadcast for a while on Radio Liberty, which still supported us. It was basically a rallying cry, calling on loyal Panamanians to oppose the invasion in any way possible. Mario Rognoni, a longtime member of the PRD and a strong supporter, was at the radio station, along with Ruben Murgas. Murgas and Rognoni said that the president, Francisco Rodríguez, had taped an on-the-air message as well. Now, Rognoni suggested, we should try a live broadcast. I agreed and we started talking. Within minutes, I heard a pop on the phone line and a tremendous explosion in the distance. The Americans, monitoring the broadcast, had bombed the radio station. I was left holding the phone. Rognoni, I found out later, was unhurt in the attack.

The news was bleak and demoralizing. It was overwhelming. There were fewer and fewer reports of fighting, and most of the remaining resistance involved skirmishes or sniper attacks. I was trying to get to Chiriquí. Guerrilla action was the only alternative at this point. Yet I wanted to be pragmatic—I was looking for odds in my favor.

Although we had quite a good stockpile of ammunition, those responsible for distributing it had failed to do so, neither to soldiers at home nor reservists nor members of the Dignity Battalions. None of our potential supporters was armed, although many were coming around looking for weapons. In Panama City, in Chiriquí, scattered around the country, were substantial stockpiles of weapons. The caches sat in hiding, unused and undetected.

Chiriquí, Río Hato and Battalion 2000, for example, our best fighting units, had a cache of sixty thousand rifles, eighty tons of ammunition, rocket launchers and mortars. The invaders never discovered the stockpiles of guns, nor our ammunition stores.

The head of the U.S. Southern Command, General Maxwell Thurman—"Mad Max," as his troops knew him—was simply speechless when our men finally surrendered and identified the arms stockpiles. "Well, this all must have been contraband, intended for sale on the international market," he said. But he was wrong. It was our own materiel, for our own use. He never had a clue. Thurman died in 1995.

If a rear guard had been able to organize in Chiriquí and Veraguas with commands in the other provinces, we might have regrouped. But all of our provincial commanders and staff were under tremendous pressure. General Marc Cisneros, the chief of the U.S. Army in Panama, was working with Archbishop McGrath to negotiate surrender without further resistance, reaching out to the zone commanders one by one, arguing that resistance was futile and would result only in more bloodshed. They threatened to bomb Chiriquí, Bocas de Toro and other cities if the commanders did not surrender. What the Church argued was perhaps true: lives were saved. But it was also true that McGrath was a collaborator with an invading army. It was no surprise; he never considered himself a Panamanian.

While all this was going on, Bush appeared on television to praise the invading troops and to say his cowardly invasion—all that a wimp with an inferiority complex could be capable of—was a liberation. The mission, he said, was to capture me and "bring me to justice." He was lying.

The Americans, with their twelve thousand soldiers permanently stationed in Panama, didn't need to send another twenty thousand men if the goal was really to capture me. If that were the case, they could send one hundred men or Delta Force to capture me—or, more likely, kill me.

If killing me is what you want to do, you put a one-million-dollar price on my head and pay somebody to do it. If you want to capture me, you offer the same two million dollars you were going to pay me off with and you save all the money that American taxpayers had to invest in their little invasion. The reason the Americans didn't do this was Orwellian. The Americans have a law that prohibits the assassination of foreign leaders. Evidently, of course, they have no law against invading a sovereign country and killing hundreds of men, women and babies. No, the invasion was not intended to capture me. They wanted me dead in any case like they had Premier Maurice Bishop of Grenada dead. The invasion was intended to destroy the Panamanian Defense Forces and to guarantee that the Panama Canal would be in the friendly, Anglo-loving hands of a Panamanian puppet government by the time it was to be turned over by the United States on December 31, 1999.

By Saturday, December 23, communications were isolated and we could see that we were getting more and more hemmed in. We knew that the Americans were conducting house-to-house searches in their attempt to track me down. They launched attacks on one house in San Miguelito, and destroyed the Torrijos memorial house on Calle 50 and several others, based on information about where I had taken refuge.

When the circle tightened even more, we moved to what I knew would be the safest place we could find: the cemetery at Río Abajo. I was sure that the Americans would be too scared to go in there at night: Americans are afraid of death even during the day, let alone in the shadows. (The best insurance is always to stay in a cemetery. It is time tested and proven. But I know that after the Americans read this they'll put it in their manual of procedures: "Search the cemeteries overnight!" They'll force a squadron of quivering soldiers to search every graveyard, and the men will be spooked beyond belief by the silence and peace they find there. Consider it a hint for the next invasion.)

The city was evidently subdued by the third night after the invasion. I heard almost no gunfire, only the sound of an occasional car, helicopters overhead and the incessant engines of an airplane that was handling communications and tracking over the city.

We were analyzing several options. First, I received information relayed from the same contact I had used as the invasion began. This time, from inside the U.S. embassy, came the message: "Exit battlefield. Evasion and escape or death!" From the Cuban embassy came word that the situation was still dangerous and threatening, that American troops still had the building under siege. There was also word about at what time the guards surrounding the embassy would be fewer in number—Ambassador Mora approved of the option for us to go there. But my intuition told me to discard this option—I did not want to create a pretext for an American attack on the Cubans. I was in fact told later by the Vatican emissaries that Thurman said he would have attacked the Cuban embassy to take me into custody, understanding that this was a violation as flagrant as the Iranian occupation of the U.S. embassy in Tehran ten years earlier.

The Libyan embassy was also threatened and under siege. Several of my escorts circulated in the city and were able to analyze the American roadblocks and the teams searching for me. They came running back for me, fearing the worst. The city was surrounded and our escape route to Chiriquí was closed. We decided to move.

Before doing that, however, a message was relayed to me that Monsignor José Sebastián Laboa, the papal nuncio, wanted to talk to me. I'd maintained contacts with Laboa previously and we had gotten along well. He was trustworthy, I thought, being a man of the cloth and not necessarily linked politically with the right-wing, collaborationist archbishop.

As I remember the Laboa episode, I recall what an acquaintance, businessman, Roberto "Papa Bobby" Motta, said to me: "Tony, there are three kinds of truth in the world—your truth, my truth and the truth."

Laboa's truth was that he was going to help me as a friend, having returned from his interrupted vacationing in Europe, and that he could pick me up undetected in his limousine and sneak me into the

Vatican embassy for a meeting to discuss the situation. By this time, the
city was so tight that travel, with or without my disguise, was impossible. He was to send a car to the parking lot of the duty-free store in Río
Abajo. We had taken a vantage point in our car that gave us a view of
the parking lot without our having to go out into the open.

At the appointed time, we sat in the car, watching the parking lot
from a safe distance. The car hadn't arrived. We circled and went
around the block, but there was still no car. "Let's get out of here,"
one of my escorts, Ulises Rodríguez, said. "I don't think we should be
doing this; it could be a trap."

The fourth time we circled around, I decided to go out in the open
and look for the car. They had told me that Laboa himself would be
waiting for me. My plan was to use the car to get out of the area and
not go with him to the embassy. With the diplomatic protection, I considered going to the hideout at Panama Viejo. I also knew that Lieutenant Colonel Cordoba and Lieutenant Colonel Madriñan were
operating freely with his small squadron. I had other plans as well, but
none of them included going to the Vatican embassy. From my perspective now, I am convinced that Laboa unwittingly saved my life by
diverting my plans.

Finally, I saw the nuncio's limousine, the Vatican flag on the left
bumper. I approached it and saw two men in front, a driver and a man
I presumed to be Laboa. I opened the rear door. I looked more closely
at the man in the bishop's robes and discovered that it was not Laboa
but Father Javier Villanueva, a Spaniard who was McGrath's aide and
an outspoken opponent of mine. Also in the limousine was Laboa's
secretary. My heart sank and I might have bolted out the door had
Villanueva not held out an explanation, and had I not seen that the
man in priestly robes driving the car was actually a lieutenant from my
security contingent. I felt somewhat relieved and smiled.

"Monsignor Laboa sent me to come get you," Villanueva said, trying to allay my fears. "He's waiting for you at the nunciature." I felt a
bit more relaxed, but I still didn't trust Villanueva. I knew that he had
been one of those who had used the pulpit, in his case the Church of

Cristo Rey, as a political forum, haranguing against the military and the government and calling openly for protests.

I was still carrying my sidearm, some grenades and an AK-47, and I brought them in the car with me. Ulises Rodríguez started getting in the car too, but the man disguised in front stopped him. "You can't get in, only the general," he said in a gruff, hoarse voice. "Be careful, *jefe*," the escort said and followed us.

Just after getting into the car, we spotted a heavily armed convoy passing by loaded with guns, rifles, and telescopic and night-vision scopes. They headed straight for the dead-end street we had just driven out of minutes earlier. The Americans raided the chalet where we had stayed but found few traces of my presence—a red beret with the word COMANDO written on it and a pair of black paratrooper boots I had worn. "Negative, Mission Fugitive," the U.S. soldier reported back to the invasion headquarters. The special ambush operation had failed once more.

In the confusion, we drove around without an obvious destination. "Are you going to take me where I want?" I asked Villanueva.

"Let's meet with the monsignor first. He's just come back to town to meet with you." Well, I thought, the Vatican embassy is a safe haven and there was no harm in going to talk to Laboa. Of my few options, at least it was an open door, although I was still not thinking of asylum. We drove along barricaded streets. The route was circuitous, but within minutes we had pulled into the courtyard of the Vatican embassy.

One of the first men I saw at the front door was none other than Eliecer Gaitán. "What's going on?" I asked him.

"The nuncio is inside" was all he said.

I was going to get my rifle, but Gaitán said he would get it for me. "I'll take it out when they put the car in the garage," he said.

I went inside and encountered a busy scene. There were many other people there, all in civilian clothes.

Those present included Father Velarde, who was our chaplain; Jaime Simmons, a prominent banker, and his children; Gaitán and ten members of ETA, the Spanish Basque movement, who had been given asylum in Panama. There was also a strange Cuban man whom I didn't know.

But once inside, they told me that Laboa wasn't there. "I've come to talk with Laboa," I said. "Where is he?"

"He had to go out, but he'll be back," one of the bishop's aides said.

I had little time to react to what he said, because I soon became aware of a distant rumbling sound, growing closer, gaining in volume. It was the sound of heavy equipment outside, tanks rumbling along the street. I started to go outside to retrieve my weapon. "Don't worry, we'll get it later," Laboa's secretary said. The limousine pulled away and the sound of the machinery grew louder. Tanks were approaching the gates.

What I had seen as an open door was a neatly designed trap, along with the prospect held out to me that something good would come of this. There were to be no negotiations, no simple little meeting, and there was evidently no escape. I was surrounded, thanks to the traitors working for the Americans.

CHAPTER 13

Caught
in the Trap

I HEARD THE SOUND of aircraft, more tanks and soldiers moving in, installing barricades. It seemed that within an instant, they had organized a siege on the place, complete with loudspeakers barking orders.

Only then did Laboa appear.

"I was out of the country when all this happened, and I raced back," he said, ushering me into a small anteroom downstairs.

"I thought perhaps I could be of some help. Can I offer you some wine?"

I was thirsty and said I preferred a beer instead. There was none.

"You're obviously tired; why don't you sit here and rest for a while and we'll prepare your room," Laboa said. "Monsignor McGrath had been staying here, but he's gone now."

"What's the matter, didn't he want to see me?" I asked, making a small joke.

"Well, you know how it is," said Laboa, grimacing.

"I don't want you to consider me here under asylum," I said. "I don't want you to tell anyone that I have asked for asylum, because I have not. I am here against my will. Tell no one that I have come here in any official capacity at all."

"But I've already told the Americans you're here," he said.

I walked out into the main hall of the embassy.

I was taken to a bedroom upstairs that had obviously just been abandoned by McGrath. It still had the fetid smell of cigarette smoke. I could see that the churchman had been using the Vatican embassy as a command post. In his hurry to avoid seeing me he had left behind a number of things on the small desk—notes with names and messages, several telephone numbers. Ironically, the boy cleaning the room was the godson of the newly installed president, Endara. He took away all the papers. I sat down and started to make some telephone calls. Villanueva quickly ordered that the phone be removed.

In time, it became evident that Laboa's concern was not to act as neutral negotiator but to concentrate all his energies on convincing me to give up the fight.

During this time, I think that Laboa was actually in worse shape than I was. First there was the subject of the deafening rock music. The Americans placed huge loudspeakers outside and started playing scorching, diabolical noise almost immediately after they laid siege to the embassy.[1] It was a roaring, mind-bending din, although I was off in my own thoughts and meditations and paid little attention. There were a number of nuns who served as cooks and aides at the residence, and they were all very tense and distressed. But none so much as Laboa, who was really the one to crack under the torturous music. He appealed to Cisneros directly to cut the music off, saying he couldn't think about negotiating with that infernal noise.

Later, we were able to reconstruct the game played by the Americans. Our ambassador to Sweden, Elmo Martínez, had an apartment right near the nuncio's enclave. Elmo, who was home on leave, could focus down on the street below and observe Laboa and Villanueva meeting with the Americans. Villanueva in particular was passing along information daily to the U.S. Army about everything that was going on inside the Vatican embassy. Villanueva was a very nervous man, the compulsive sort. He was a snake, ill-mannered and obnoxious with the people at the embassy, deceptive and distant in the way he spoke. I could see that he was an informer, that he was telling absolutely every detail of what was going on; anything anyone said would be reported back to Cisneros. He

---

[1] Surrounding an embassy in this fashion is a violation of international law.

provided written reports to Cisneros, he spoke with Cisneros. If we used the telephone, he went running down immediately to the gate, calling for the Americans. Collaborator that he was, he also drew up a map showing the layout of the embassy, including the location of my quarters, so the Americans could plan for what they wanted to do. We have photos showing Villanueva meeting with the Americans at the gate of the embassy, giving them the map. My room was in the rear, flanking another building. Right behind the room was a parking lot. Once informed by Villanueva, they repositioned themselves with monitoring equipment and telephones so they could be as close to me as possible.

Although it was obvious that Villanueva was informing on me, he made efforts to talk to me. He was seen quarreling with Laboa's assistants and did everything he could to toss around his authority. The Basque exiles especially detested him.

He acted as if we were supposed to know each other, but I told him I had not even seen a picture of him before.

"General Thurman is very upset that you were able to slip through his surveillance," he said. "He's asked Monsignor Laboa and me to hand you over for better or for worse."

"And just who the hell are you supposed to be, anyway?" I asked sarcastically, copying the tone with which the Basques treated Villanueva.

"It's no surprise; you're just like the Basques," he said. "You are one of them. You've been protecting those wretches for ten years. But I am the representative of Archbishop McGrath."

"Why don't you go say hello to Thurman and Cisneros for me?" I said, dismissively. "Tell them the guy they were supposed to kill is alive and well."

Every day, surrounded, we could hear the tanks and the airplanes and helicopters and the sound of chanting demonstrators, the same demonstrators as always, with their fancy cars. The poor folk were not in support of this, nor did they have anything to celebrate after the Americans invaded their neighborhoods and killed their friends and relatives.

As the days went on, I was wondering how long the standoff could last. One possibility was that the Americans would eventually downgrade and drop their guard; I would have to wait them out. Alternatively, if I had to surrender, I would at least surrender to a Panamanian. But the Panamanians placed in office by the Americans didn't want that. Their attorney general, Rogélio Cruz, said that if I turned myself over to Panamanian authorities, they would have no way to deliver me to the Americans; the Panamanians definitely wanted the Americans to take me and solve their problem.

I asked Gaitán if he knew where the weapons were that I had brought into the embassy—the grenades, the AK-47 machine gun. He said they were gone; someone had handed them over to the Americans.

I had access to another weapon, an Uzi, thanks to Lieutenant Colonel Arnulfo Castrejón, who had arrived at the Church residence some time after I did. He was able to smuggle in the weapon through his brother, a doctor, who visited him daily. Eventually, the brother was allowed to take Castrejón home, and the Uzi stayed with me. I did the best I could to hide it, but this wasn't easy. I was in a very sparsely decorated room, with a desk, a bed and nothing more. So I put it between the mattresses of the bed.

I considered the Uzi a defensive weapon and, under the circumstances, surrounded by the American armed forces, this seemed logical. I never for an instant considered taking hostages, nor killing Laboa or anyone else, although Laboa himself told me that the Americans were circulating such rumors. Laboa laughed at the idea. He knew that this was something I would never do. Neither did I even for an instant think of committing suicide. I can't relate to the idea of killing myself; I was using my gray matter to come up with an escape plan, and I was analyzing the odds of coming out alive. Death was only to be an option in the line of fire.

Finally, on January 2, Laboa called a meeting. Gaitán and Colonel Nivaldo Madriñan, the only other top-ranking officer in the embassy with me, were also there. He said that he saw no other option than for me to be seized by the Americans, because the next day they were going to remove immunity and the doors would be open.

"The Americans will let in the mob," he said. "They'll do the same thing they did to Mussolini"—that is, they would hang me and leave me strung up for everyone to see.

"But how can the Americans declare that this residence no longer has immunity?" I asked. "It isn't up to them."

"Well," he said, "there's nothing I can do."

In fact, once he decided to invade Panama, George Bush was trampling all over international law, along with his new allies installed in the

Panamanian foreign ministry. They had disregarded diplomatic immunity, raiding the Nicaraguan embassy, abusing the Cuban ambassador and violating the grounds of the Libyan embassy. They had organized a mob in front of the Peruvian embassy, where some PDF officers had taken refuge; people in the crowd threw Molotov cocktails, threatening to storm the place and drag the exiles out.

I reminded Laboa that at the beginning of the ordeal in the embassy he had read to me proudly a salutory letter from the Panamanian lawyer Dr. Materno Vasquez congratulating him on offering asylum, advising him of the principles of international law and the details of the Geneva Conventions and describing how these principles offered a legal foundation for what he was doing as chief of a diplomatic mission. I reminded him of the initial diplomatic response from the Vatican, invoking my right of obtaining refuge, just as the United States at that very moment was offering shelter to a Chinese dissident in Beijing, despite the demands of the Chinese government.

I called the Cuban ambassador, Lázaro Mora, and asked if they were doing the same thing at the Cuban embassy; that is, threatening to take away its immunity. "No!" he said emphatically. "They cannot do that . . ." and the telephone line suddenly went dead. I had taken advantage of the phone lines being turned on by Cisneros so arrangements could be made for the uniforms they would bring me when I was captured and in their custody. When the Americans heard the gist of the conversation, however, the line was quickly turned off again.

Madriñan started to protest and Laboa was ready to argue. The bishop was looking for the support of my aides; surrender, he said, was the only option.

"What about Spain?" I asked.

"They refuse to give you asylum," said Laboa, who was close friends with the Spanish ambassador.

"Okay, what about Cuba?" Laboa never gave me an answer. Obviously, he never contacted the Cuban embassy, even though Mora was prepared to accept me. The truth was that the United States made it clear they didn't want anybody to offer me asylum.

I left the meeting and started to prepare myself mentally for what was likely to come. I knew I had a weapon to defend myself. The Uzi was my insurance, I thought, because if the mob or the Americans were going to come in, at least three or four would go with me before I was lynched. That was the American plan, not the Panamanian plan. Thurman had planted the idea with Laboa. Once diplomatic safeguards were removed, they would find a pretext to shoot. Thurman warned that he would do nothing to block the mob of fifty to seventy people that they had ringing the embassy—it was Thurman who brought up the specter of Mussolini and the lynch mob.

I went up to my room and reached between the mattresses. My Uzi was gone. Someone had found it and delivered it to Marc Cisneros.

I was left to ponder what Laboa had said. "Look at it as losing one battle," he said. "Accept that and prepare yourself for the legal battle ahead. The only way now is legal recourse—impartial justice, untainted by politics. Your lawyers have been calling me and are awaiting you with optimism for the legal fight ahead."

Looking back on it all, my choice was capture by the Americans or to face a long-term future there in the Vatican embassy or, perhaps, an eventual attack by the Americans.

I could not blame Laboa for what had happened. I had known him for a long time; prior to this, our relations had always been professional and honest. We had worked with him on sensitive investigations, and when he asked us to keep confidences we did and still do. He was an affable man, a generous host and a good conversationalist. Laboa carried out his instructions from the Vatican as far as he could, based on international law. In many ways, Laboa saved my life. But he was a victim of intrigue. Analyzing things as dispassionately as I could, it was obvious that Laboa, pressured by McGrath, Cisneros and Thurman, had decided to deliver me over to the U.S. invaders. He was not waiting for an emissary from the Vatican, a priest who was also a specialist in international law, who had been dispatched to meet with us and help analyze the case. I understood Laboa's psychological profile; I knew he was nervous and vacillating in his political decisions. This was something that McGrath also knew. Laboa had another weakness—he feared public criticism. He ended up being hurt by the whole affair. The Vatican transferred him to Paraguay, the demotion to a distant outpost seemingly a rebuke. From there, he sent word through a mutual Panamanian friend, Lissí Arrocha: "Tell the general that he has my admiration. Send him my regards—and tell him I'm sorry."

Staying in Panama under the government's jurisdiction was not a legal option: the attorney general, Rogélio Cruz, refused to assume any responsibility, even though he contended that they had charges pending against me in the Spadafora case and others.

The next day, January 3, 1990, everything was done with precision. All that Laboa did and said was part of a cover story to prepare the way, psychologically, to turn me in. Laboa said as much afterward, that he had to use a little subtle psychology to be able to fulfill his mission. They brought me a uniform. I changed and went downstairs at around 6 P.M. A line of people had formed at the door, first the nuns, the Basques, the Panamanians and finally Villanueva. It was deeply moving and the human emotions were varied: tears, forceful handshakes, almost suffocating embraces. The wife of one of the ETA militants asked that I not be turned in. At the end of the line, Villanueva extended his hand to me. I looked at him, saying in a voice loud enough for all to hear, "We will see each other again."

I remembered what Laboa had told me: "Our only assurance and loyalty is that God will never abandon us." He gave me a Bible and placed a rosary with a cross on it around my neck. I was forced into an American helicopter at the start of the trip to Miami.

The details after my capture have been well documented. The real story of how the American justice system railroaded me into a long jail term has not.

CHAPTER 14

Judases Are Not Made, They Are Born

ONCE I WAS IN THEIR HANDS, the United States had to figure out what they would do with me. Their real plan had been to have me killed and to blame it on the heat of battle. Now, in custody, I was too visible to be killed outright. They invested a lot of time and a lot of money in their invasion, and now they were investing even more time and money scrambling to resurrect their flawed and insupportable drug indictment against me.

The 1988 drug indictment had little significance for me, but I soon understood that this was what they would use to justify taking me into custody. I recalled conversations with DEA and CIA contacts, who all agreed there was documentary evidence that showed how I had worked with the United States to stop drug trafficking.

Ray Takiff, the enthusiastic lawyer who had dealt with the charges in various international forums on my behalf, was strangely absent when I arrived in Miami and was taken before a tall, white-haired federal judge named William Hoeveler. My last contact with Takiff had been when he called me at the Vatican embassy, advising that I surrender, saying he was concerned for my safety. What Takiff neglected to tell me was that he had been working as a paid informant for the U.S. attorney's office in Florida for several months. He failed to mention that he had two employers—me and the U.S. government.[1]

Suddenly, I found myself in the United States. Isolated, ignorant of the American legal system, I discovered to my surprise that Takiff was no longer my lawyer. In court I met another of my lawyers, Neal Sonnett, who told me that he was resigning the case, gave me his calling card and told me we could speak privately by phone. I had no idea what he was talking about and never did call him. That left Frank Rubino, Steve Collin, Jack Fernandez, office manager Cristina Machin— Jack and Cristina were the only members of the team who spoke Spanish—and Jon May, whom I had never met before.

My secretary, Marcela Tasón, had a lawyer too. His name was William Kunstler and he was representing her on a separate matter. I didn't know who Kunstler was; I didn't know that he dealt with political cases. But it wouldn't have mattered. I found out just recently that Kunstler said he had written a letter offering to be my lawyer for free. I never received that letter.

The United States failed to kill me, so it resorted to character assassination instead. Once that was accomplished, producing a guilty verdict was easy.

I see the pattern clearly. The United States focuses on the issue of the moment and constructs a fantasy to justify its designs. One day it was me; the next it was Kim II Sung. "An unknown quantity, a communist," say the policy makers. "Let's put him in the pantheon of the Hitlers, along with Saddam Hussein, Moammar Gahdafi and Fidel Castro. Let's give him an image: the hate-ridden Oriental, or the drug-crazed madman who wants to destroy humanity."

That's what U.S. policy is all about, if you can call it policy. It's based on creating answers for the establishment, regardless of whether Republicans or Democrats are in charge. It's the establishment that counts. Once again, I am reminded of Henry Kissinger's refrain, "In order to solve a problem, you must first create the problem."

In the period covered by the drug indictments against me, 1982 through 1985, the United States knew it was failing in its attempts to

---

[1] Takiff was the chief informant in the Operation Court Broom case in Miami, which rooted out corruption among local state court judges. Takiff and the U.S. attorney's office claimed during the Noriega drug trial that Takiff did not try to mislead Noriega as to his relationship with the government.

impose its will on Nicaragua and El Salvador. The Reagan administration was desperately worried about losing these wars, about Americans being killed; they sought in Panama a more direct solution to their problems. But what could Panama do to help the Americans, with their anti-communist ideas, in their failed attempts to control insurgencies, based on faulty concepts of what Central America was.

The Americans panicked; they started thinking about Panama as a possible way out of their problems. If I wouldn't help them fight, then I could help them another way. Panama and I could be the scapegoat.

First the Americans circulated rumors about corruption in the military, about untold millions I supposedly had in secret bank accounts. When nobody listened, they pushed the issue into American newspapers and on American television. It was a classic psychological operations scheme. They did a good job.

Soon after the rumors and newspaper stories, Mario Rognoni from the Democratic Revolutionary Party approached me with the idea of appearing on American television to present a more positive image about Panama. By this time, I had no confidence in reporters. I was more afraid of them than I was of my political opponents. But Rognoni persisted and, against my better instincts, I accepted.

The reporter was Mike Wallace, a man I now know to be the epitome of sabotage journalism. At the time, I had never heard of him. Wallace and his team set a trap. They had certain questions they told me they were going to ask and they did. Then, as my aides and I kept asking them to stop the tape, Wallace started asking questions about things I wasn't prepared for. For instance, they had a supposedly secret transcript of my meeting with John Poindexter. Wallace handed me the transcript, which was in English, so I turned it over to Major Moisés Cortizo, who was acting as my interpreter, as he had during the meeting with Poindexter. Cortizo answered Wallace's question.

We were naive, and we fell into their trap. We were thinking politics and *60 Minutes* was thinking ratings. They manipulated the interview and then edited the tape to make me look as bad as they possibly could. What a noble profession!

After that, I realized I could not trust news interviews. Any interview I gave was short and on the run, so I could avoid being caught in the same trap twice. I was dealt with in the media based on American prejudices and deceptions, no matter what the truth was.

It was a gradual crescendo of propaganda discrediting me personally, bringing up innuendo about drug cases in which, in fact, we had co-operated with the U.S. Drug Enforcement Administration. We tried to counteract the propaganda by publishing the letters of commendation, the evidence from the U.S. officials that we were providing assistance, so that there would be a public record of what we were doing with them. We had letters, commendations and lists of drug traffickers captured in joint operations with the DEA.

The United States manufactured an entire vision of money laundering and drug dealing that revolved around me. As proof they offered trumped-up charges about my supposed clandestine wealth and all of the intrigue surrounding my supposed accomplices.

First, U.S. prosecutors charged that Panama had created a haven for laundering drug dollars. This was false; the Americans imposed the status of banking haven on Panama for their own purposes. U.S. businessmen wanted their own version of Swiss banks and convinced their friends in Washington to play along, with help from their wealthy Panamanian banking allies.

It was none other than Nicolás Ardito Barletta, protégé of George Shultz, who, with then President Demetrio Lakas, created special Panamanian banking privileges in the 1970s, along with bank secrecy laws that rivaled Switzerland's. Buoyed by a freely convertible U.S. dollar, Panama maintained the largest banking sector in Latin America, all laid out and planned by the United States during the oil boom of the 1970s and 1980s. There were petro-dollars everywhere, mostly from the Arab countries.

As a result, all sorts of side businesses developed. Shell companies were created, existing in name only in Panama for tax shelter purposes. Lawyers like Guillermo Endara—later installed as president after the U.S. invasion—prospered when they specialized in creating and participating in these shell companies on behalf of foreigners, for a percentage, of course.

So the bank secrecy act, propelled by the United States, fostered the growth of money laundering. Any drug dealer or any terrorist organization was permitted by Panamanian law to anonymously maintain accounts in Panama. Nevertheless, when the United States needed banking information on such people, they came to me for help. I personally opened our books to the United States, countermanding our laws so that they could see our accounts without having to sue anyone or enter into negotiations—just on grounds of good faith and law enforcement.

Things changed when Omar Torrijos took power and started criticizing the banking system. "American money is sleeping here, but it isn't making Panamanian babies," he would say. There was no long-term financial benefit to Panama. And it gave the United States a hammer with which it could punish our country. When they wanted to hurt our economy in 1988, for example, they simply pulled their money out of the banks. The banks closed, lateral businesses went bankrupt, people were forced into unemployment and we fell into a deep recession.

After charging me with being responsible for money laundering, the Americans next charged me with amassing obscene quantities of money and of cavorting with mystery men who helped me do this.

Key among the shadowy men was Mike Harari, a former Mossad agent who acted as a sales agent in Panama for much of our military procurement.[2] He was a friend and contact, but I had no business relationship with him at all. Much was made in the news media of Harari's presence in Panama and it was all grossly exaggerated. Harari was never my adviser, nor did Israelis ever have a permanent advisory or security role within the Panamanian armed forces. He arrived in Panama during the time of Torrijos and was well known by men who would be Israeli prime ministers, Menachem Begin, Yitzhak Shamir and Shimon Peres.

It was prior to the signing of the treaties and Torrijos secretly wanted to use these Israeli purchases to obtain materiel for our secret plan to sabotage the Panama Canal, in the event that the canal treaties were not signed. This presented a problem, however, because Israel's client status with the United States required that it inform the Americans whenever it sold technology to third countries. Obviously, Torrijos didn't want to arouse Israeli suspicions, so the first attempt at doing business with Harari went nowhere.

---

[2] Harari was assigned to hunt down those responsible for the murder of Israeli athletes at the Munich Olympics in 1976. His search led him to Lillehammer, Norway, where his commando team killed a waiter in the erroneous belief that he had found one of the Arab terrorists responsible for the Olympic massacre.

Later, Harari sold us airport emergency lights, and sometimes he helped us buy Uzis, riot control vehicles and other weapons from his government's military production company, Israeli Military Industries. He operated as an agent and I assume he earned a percentage of sales. This was all done publicly. In the sale of emergency lights, for example, his bill was unpaid at the time of the invasion; Endara's U.S.-installed government ended up paying for the lights, because it was a valid charge.

Harari acted as agent for maintenance equipment on Boeing 727 aircraft. He also had a widely publicized plan that he never completed, which earned him many political enemies. It was a magnificent project, to convert Paitilla Airport, which is a small, downtown Panama City airport, into a shopping and apartment mall. He would then build a new facility on recovered land down the coast, creating a new peninsula for the airport.[3]

Harari always got us the best prices. Sometimes he represented the Israeli government–owned industries; other times he was an agent for other Israeli businesses in Panama. And sometimes he helped us organize specialized training courses from the Israeli military—special forces, scuba diving and commando training.

Harari also set up visits to Israel for Panamanian businessmen. In one such case, I introduced him to an acquaintance, Roberto Eisenmann, the publisher of La Prensa, who would later become a key source of opposition to me and the defense forces. On my request, Harari hosted Eisenmann and his wife twice on an Israeli tour.

In the final phase of the boycott and tensions leading up to the invasion, the United States asked Israel if they could use Harari as a mediator for my departure from power. The indictment against me was already in place and the Americans were threatening Harari with a subpoena if he stepped on U.S. soil. But nothing ever happened. I believe it was because the Israeli premier at the time, Yitzhak Shamir, asked the Americans to keep Harari out of the spotlight.

Finally, I was told, Harari was spirited out of Panama by the Americans when the invasion took place. That showed that he was probably more valuable to the Americans than he ever was to Panama or to me.

---

[3] In the 1990s, the Panamanian government picked up on the same proposal and prepared to carry it out.

Mike would have been a good witness on my behalf at the drug trial. But Israel thought that might be embarrassing and he never showed up.

There were other so-called mystery men: my friend Carlos Wittgreen was supposedly a conduit for funneling money to me. This was not true. I had no economic relationship with him. He was doing business with the Cubans involving import and export, but it was not at all of the scale that people have said it was.

Then there was Jorge Krupnik, a man under the magnifying glass of the international investigative agencies: he was an arms supplier and had a connection to Colombian rebel insurgent groups. Colombia filed protests with us several times about his activities. Interpol, the international police information service, was tracking Krupnik, and information was exchanged between Panama and Colombia about him. Krupnik was also mentioned by Floyd Carlton, the government's star witness against me, as having been involved with shipping arms to El Salvadoran rebels in the 1980s. To my knowledge, that is untrue. Carlton also said that Krupnik was an Israeli intelligence agent, but I never saw any evidence to that effect and Krupnik denied this to me.

The Americans, however, used the names of Harari, Wittgreen and Krupnik in connection with my allegedly having amassed great illicit wealth. This was always based on innuendo and, upon investigation, always disproved. A report in the *Miami Herald*, for example, said that the Americans had no basis for the charges that I had stolen and hidden away millions of dollars.[4]

The list of wealth supposedly included vast riches on four continents: the ones I remember are a castle in France, an apartment in Brazil, a penthouse in Japan and a hotel in Orlando. What a feast for the prosecutors, what a wealth of stories for the news media! It ended up being a famine, although the debunking of these illicit wealth stories has never been publicized very much.

Investigators went to the apartment they said I owned in Brazil and found that it belonged to Raquel Torrijos, Omar Torrijos's widow, who lives there.

Next, they went to Tokyo and found that the penthouse I supposedly owned there was actually the official residence of the Panamanian

---

[4] "U.S. May Have Overstated Noriega's Wealth," by Andres Oppenheimer, *Miami Herald*, January 22, 1990, p. 1.

ambassador to Japan. I stayed there when I visited Japan to discuss commercial prospects for the Panama Canal, something that made the Americans very nervous.

As for the hotel in Orlando, it belonged to the Riande chain, which also owns the Hotel Continental in Panama and a hotel on Miami Beach. The Riande chain has disclosed its officers and shareholders, showing that I am not on the list.

Finally, there was the case of the French castle. I have visited France and have been a guest at some fancy places, but never a medieval castle.

The chief of state and commander of the armed forces has considerable clout in Panama; you live like a king. You take away the king's crown and he no longer lives like a king. It was inherent in my position and my mission for Panama that I travel around the world. Who paid for hotels and travel and meals? I was the leader, and the government paid when the leader traveled.

How different is this in any other country? Was this the justification for an invasion and a drug trial? Was the Panamanian system on trial, and did the United States have the right to decide what trappings were given to Panama's leaders? Furthermore, they were trappings of state and they remained with the state, just as happens anywhere else. Does the president of the United States take his limousine and his presidential jumbo jet with him when he leaves office?

The United States government and the prosecutors at the drug trial against me perpetuated an idiotic game. They tried and convicted me by saying that they had shady evidence of personal wealth. And since the world accepted their propaganda—I was the devil, the drug fiend—this money must be bad money. If I have any money at all, it must be from drug dealing, because everybody knows that I am who I am . . . but what does everybody know? How do you know anything about me? What is the basis for an indictment in U.S. federal court for misappropriation of funds and amassing drug profits? What is the basis for an invasion and forty years in jail? In the final argument of their drug case, the government prosecutors, rather than telling the jury to convict me as a drug dealer, declared, "Convict this dictator!"

CHAPTER 15

"Political Overtones" and a Drug Trial

I T IS DIFFICULT FOR ME to defend myself against the indictment that resulted in my being sentenced on September 16, 1992.
The United States government saw this as a great victory, over what I
am not sure. Drug dealing in the United States goes on unabated; in
Panama, without a legitimate military force, it is far worse than it was
in the 1980s. Now cocaine is rampant and Panama is an important stop
on the opium trail.

In any case, drug charges do not give one nation the right to invade
a sovereign country and kidnap its leader. This was not dealt with at
the trial, because Judge Hoeveler said he wanted to minimize the "political overtones" of the case.

He would have been hard-pressed to do so. The trial supposedly was
about me and drug trafficking. But it was really about abuse of political power. I was convicted because the system that invaded Panama
and killed my countrymen—while perhaps hundreds of its own were
killed—needed me to be convicted.

My initial tendency here was to avoid discussing the specifics of the
drug case. I was not involved in any such activities and have few means
available to me to disprove a fabrication of the magnitude I faced. But
I have considerable insight as to what the United States was up to in its
drug conviction. And I wish to set the record straight.

First of all, Panama, as I have written, was serious in its commitment to halting drug trafficking. The charge in the United States that Panama looked the other way for drug kingpins doesn't match with the evidence. Our chief drug investigators during the period in question, Captains Jorge Latinez and Luis Quiel, were widely respected by their American counterparts for their skill and professionalism. Under my command, drug investigators infiltrated drug operations and interdicted traffickers of all kinds and nationalities. U.S. prosecutors at the drug trial argued cynically that our government was involved in drugs because we didn't catch the main drug dealers; yet, by those standards, Colin Powell, George Bush and every U.S. administration since the 1970s should also be indicted, since Pablo Escobar, Jorge Ochoa and their smuggling ally, Gustavo Gaviria, all lived in the United States. They said we were a small country, unlike the United States, which was true. But we also had limited resources, and within our limited resources, we did an extensive job in slowing down the multibillion-dollar drug trade when it tried to move through our country.

Second of all, as the leader of a sovereign country, I had every right to order my men to infiltrate drug cartels and buy cocaine themselves; the DEA does it every day and they did it in Panama. Should the DEA be charged with a crime for buying cocaine to develop drug cases? Should I have charged DEA agents with a crime for doing that in my country? Whose laws was I required to protect and who should decide how those laws are applied?

The situation in the so-called U.S. drug wars remains the same. The United States is still the greatest consumer of cocaine and heroin on the planet, but continues to pressure other, far less economically powerful countries to do what it cannot do. If the United States cannot stem the demand for cocaine, how can a relatively poor country stop the supply? The governments of Bolivia, Colombia, Mexico and Peru, to name a few—Panama has never been a significant factor in the narcotics trade—will never be able to fight the economic power of the drug dealers. The United States knows this, yet uses its economic power to declare who is complying with U.S. drug policy and who isn't, using the hammer of trade "decertification," which can be counterproductive by forcing political instability, hurting legitimate business and forcing even more drug trade. By all standards, the United States should decertify itself—it has done nothing significant to stop the drug trade.

For me, the trial falls into four main areas of evidence: testimony surrounding the government's star witness, Floyd Carlton; testimony about the seizure of a cocaine-processing laboratory in the Darien jungle; testimony about meetings I had with Fidel Castro; and a supposed trip I made to Medellín, the capital of Colombian drug trafficking.

Floyd Carlton Caceres

My principal accuser at the drug trial was Floyd Carlton Caceres, a Panamanian pilot. Carlton testified that he paid me hush money so that he could ship four loads of cocaine from Colombia to Panama and onward to the United States in the early 1980s. I believe him when he says that he was transporting drugs. But I had nothing to do with it.

I had been told by the Drug Enforcement Administration and by the CIA that Carlton, who had delivered guns for the CIA to pro-American Nicaraguan rebels, was an undercover drug agent who should be left alone. The word came when our agents had arrested Carlton on an international warrant issued by the Peruvian Investigative Police. "Release him to our custody," DEA Station Chief Arthur Sedillo told Latinez, his Panamanian liaison.

"Carlton works for us, we're taking care of him," Sedillo said. "Let him go about his business; we will monitor his operations."

So, instead of being subjected to a pending Panamanian indictment and instead of being extradited to the jurisdiction of Peruvian authorities as we had intended, Carlton was released in Sedillo's custody without any documentation whatsoever. The United States never gives documentation to lowly countries like Panama. All they do is ask you for a favor—and you go along with it or you reject it, but you never learn the details, nor the results, nor what deals have been made.

Much of the information about Carlton's work for the United States was given to my attorneys, but was blocked from use because of something called the CIPA—the Classified Information Procedures Act—which limits the use of secret government documents.[1] Knowledge of this challenges the whole basis of the trial; Carlton was a man who was known by both sides as an informant.

---

[1] The Classified Information Procedures Act, 22 United States Code, under which courts decide how classified government material is handled during a public trial.

Documents concerning Panama's drug interdiction activities, as well as numerous intelligence files and archives, disappeared; it is well known that before even trying to capture me, U.S. military intelligence officers went to my offices, seizing any documents that could embarrass the United States or be used to help in my legal defense. These were all illegal acts in the course of an invasion that violated Panamanian sovereignty.

At the trial, Sedillo, like his fellow agents James Bramble, Thomas Telles and Fred Duncan, all former DEA station chiefs in Panama,[2] didn't have the guts to tell the truth.

How do I defend myself, when the records of all these relationships are either stolen from Panama or shredded by the government or blocked from even being mentioned in trial by a judge who consistently decides to deny entry of secret documents that would help my case?

Colombia

The same is true about a supposed trip that the U.S. government said I made to Colombia in the summer of 1983. They used this as the heart of their contention that I had been taken into the fold as a friend and confidant of Pablo Escobar and Jorge Luis Ochoa and company, all the drug bosses of the Medellín cartel, men I have never met.

At the trial, the American prosecutors acted as if I could travel to Colombia like a guy named Joe Smith, without the governments of Colombia and Panama knowing about it. For the chief of Panamanian intelligence to travel to a friendly country such as Colombia would require prior notification. It would have been known and I would have been unable to travel without government security or without the attention and participation of my hosts.

The entire story of this alleged trip is the creation of two convicted Colombian drug traffickers, Roberto Striedinger and Gabriel Taboada, who were among the traffickers who figured out the obvious: testify against me and get out of jail free. Since the trial, Striedinger, having fooled the judge and the jury, has gone back to Colombia after serving

---

[2] The men were all DEA special agents in charge in Panama from the late 1970s through the 1980s.

less than five years of a thirty-year trafficking sentence; Taboada, who was in the same Miami prison as I was for a while, became a government informant. Following the trial, he charged a DEA official with corruption, but an investigation in Washington dismissed Taboada's charge.

These two men were loose with the facts. But when you try to pin them down on when I would have been in Medellín to meet with the drug bosses, they say they can't remember the exact day. That is convenient, although since the United States confiscated all of my files and destroyed my command headquarters, I had no way to present a diary or agenda of my activities.

I certainly did go to Colombia in 1983, invited by the Colombian army to attend their jungle training school in Cali. Proof of this is also classified information, under lock and key and considered secret U.S. government security information.

It was impossible for me to go anywhere in Colombia without either notifying the Colombian intelligence services or being detected by the armed forces or by journalists. I was too high-profile, especially in June 1983, when I was in the final stages of the process that would make me commander of the armed forces in October of the same year.

Once I got to Medellín, according to the U.S. government, I was supposedly helping Fabio Ochoa, the youngest brother of Jorge Ochoa, buy a sports car. The concept is stupid: to think that the Medellín cartel with its billions of dollars would ask me to help them get a sports car, something they could get from any embassy in the world. Moreover, that months before I was to assume the position of general of the Panamanian Defense Forces I would travel secretly to Medellín, knowing that the Colombian military, with which I had a close relationship, would find out and be insulted and publicize the affront, probably telling the United States. Look at the logic of it and decide for yourself.

The head of Colombian military intelligence from 1981 to 1985, General Manuel Mejía and the leader of the Colombian Armed Forces, General Manuel Samúdio, were prepared to testify to this at the drug trial until the Americans, famous for pressuring and bending Latin politicians to their will, forced them to desist.

Speaking about Colombian intelligence: in my conversations with agents and officials from the Colombian Department of Administrative

Security, DAS—their combined equivalent of the FBI, CIA and DEA—I was told that their agencies saw persistent links between the U.S.-created Contra rebels in Nicaragua and the Colombian drug dealers. "Americans know what the Contras are doing, that they're working with the Colombian narcos," one Colombian drug agent told me. The problem was that without investigative assistance from the United States or some other government, they could not prove their case. They knew that it was politically impossible for one branch of the U.S. government to investigate another—which is essentially what would need to happen for such a charge to be proved. But they did see what was going on.

Cuba and the Drug Trial

On June 11, 1984, I received an invitation from Fidel Castro to visit Cuba. Such visits happened periodically, and when they did I invariably made a courtesy phone call to the CIA station chief, advising him of my trip, offering my services if the United States had any messages to pass along. By this time, all sides realized that I was a faithful broker in communicating between the United States and Cuba.

So I contacted Don Winters, the CIA station chief in Panama at the time, telling him that I was planning a quick trip to Cuba and asking if he had any messages for Fidel. We both treated the matter as strictly routine.

The timing of my trip was interesting enough for the director of the CIA himself, William Casey, to travel to Panama to brief me on the U.S. position on Cuba, asking that I push Fidel on certain issues. At a meeting at Governor's Beach outside Panama City, Casey outlined U.S. interests. Prime among them was the problem caused by the refugees of the *Mariel* boatlift—the thousands of Cubans who had been allowed to flee that Cuban port for the United States several years earlier on rafts and boats.

Would Cuba negotiate the return of some of the *Marielitos*—as the boat people were known? The United States wanted to return those among them who were criminals and social misfits and who were provoking serious problems in U.S. prisons. The U.S. goal was to convince Fidel to take some of them back. This type of negotiation went on before and after, and I was always available to the United States when it came to meeting with or passing messages to Castro.

This portion of the story was available at the drug trial. Winters was a witness at the Miami federal court, although his testimony was cut short. The government didn't want to let the jury hear about my friendship with so high a government agent, let alone with the director of the CIA. So they blocked most of Don's testimony and substituted several paragraphs of summary. I doubt if the jury, facing a year of proceedings and a mountain of papers, paid much attention. My friendship with the CIA remained concealed from the jury and the full extent of my emissary role to Cuba was not revealed. Documents held by the U.S. government, but suppressed and kept from the jury under the CIPA provisions, include a description of Casey's trip to Panama to meet with me about Castro.[3]

The United States has not admitted to this day that they asked me to arrange a visit to Cuba for a secret emissary to discuss these matters further. Fidel accepted. Sometime later, I spoke with U.S. ambassador Vernon Walters, who told me he made the trip.

At the drug trial, the entire Cuban relationship was woven into a pack of half-truths—or full-blown lies. José Blandón, the former Panamanian consul in New York who became a prime mover in the fabricated prosecution, twisted the facts around to help the U.S. government. The U.S. version, thanks to Blandón, was that Castro was to help mediate a situation that involved the discovery of a cocaine-processing laboratory in the Darien jungle, not far from the Panama-Colombia border. My trip to Cuba, said Blandón, was a hurried one, since I supposedly feared that there would be retribution from the Medellín cartel.

Blandón and the American investigators said that I had been paid four million dollars to allow the establishment of the drug laboratory and that its destruction meant that the Medellín cartel had been double-crossed.

Our forces didn't know the drug lab was there. When it was discovered, we contacted Colombia and dealt with it on an official level, in-

---

[3] There is no mention of drug dealing in any of this information; CIA station chief Donald Winters said he had no indication and no reason to think that any narcotics deal was discussed.

cluding the turnover of those captured in the raid to the Colombian government. My trip to Cuba had nothing to do with it either, and I did not discuss the subject with Fidel. The Darien lab was uncovered on June 24, thirteen days *after* my Cuba trip was set up.

The proof is in the CIA documents and in the word of Don Winters, who was not allowed to provide ample testimony. The real version of this trip alone destroys the U.S. indictment against me and shows that at a key moment, I was not involved in drugs in any way, but was taking political action on behalf of the CIA and the United States.

The attempt to link Panama and Cuba to the cocaine trade was nothing new. But it was not based on reality, nor was the argument developed to support the thesis very logical.

The argument was that I was conspiring with Fidel on drug matters and that both of us had full knowledge and control of drug trafficking in our countries for years.

The evidence came from the testimony of convicts who actually admitted dealing drugs. These men were offered leniency and tickets out of jail in return for the favor of implicating me or Castro in their affairs. The U.S. government put out the word to hundreds of men in its custody throughout the prison system: "Your sentence could be commuted if you testify—the truth doesn't matter, just come in and testify."

In the case of Blandón, the situation was particularly foolish. Part of the evidence he used against me was a photograph in which he, Fidel and I are seen attending a reception in Havana. Shocking, a photograph of Castro and me standing together! I must be guilty of drug dealing!

Blandón was not a drug dealer. But he was a man who turned against me for spite, after being dismissed from his post as Panamanian consul in New York. His web of lies was so twisted that, although his information is central to the trial, he was considered so unreliable that the prosecution never dared call him as a witness.[4]

---

[4] José Blandón was under federal protection during much of the Noriega trial. He had been a key source in developing the charges against the Panamanian leader, but was not called to testify because of conflicting accounts he gave. Jack Fernandez of the Noriega defense team said that the government took Blandón off their list of witnesses after they learned that Blandón had turned over to the defense documents and proof that favored Noriega. The government was also concerned about his role in the CNN tapes scandal, in which Blandón circulated tapes of Noriega's telephone conversations, which were smuggled illegally out of prison.

The federal prosecutors in Miami thought their method of operation against me was so successful that they tried the same thing against Cuba, hoping to ingratiate themselves with the anti-Castro exile community in Miami. So why not use Carlos Lehder,[5] the pathological liar, who admitted he never met me or Raul Castro, and who is in jail for life and is called by some prosecutors dangerous, unreliable? Why not use him as the heart of your case against me and against Raul Castro? These men are your enemies. These men consort with communists. Political pressure halted the proceedings against Castro. When the government heard that my lawyer Frank Rubino was going to take the case against Raul, the same prosecutors who devised the case against me actually came in three times to ask my lawyers to see if I would testify against Raul and Fidel. Of course, if they had wanted to go to the extent of asking me to testify, it meant they really had no evidence at all—this business of plea bargaining, bartering with somebody in return for a deal. But if they had had even the slightest evidence, they wouldn't have come to me. In any case, I said no: I was prosecuted for political reasons, and my moral and ideological convictions are above the methods employed by such men in the guise of U.S. justice. These men, who thought they could trade in lies and dishonor, made a mistake when it came to me; and without me, their crusade against Raul and Fidel Castro foundered and went nowhere.

Julián Melo and the Darien Lab

Colonel Julián Melo was involved in the construction of the Darien lab. He has told me that he was trapped into becoming the fall guy for other Panamanians—*rabiblancos* including the Tribaldos, Méndez and Barletta families—and I tend to believe him.

As an officer in the Panamanian Defense Forces, he was someone we would call *un vivo*, a wise guy, a live wire, always involved in everything. Within the National Guard, under Torrijos, he had occasional

[5] Carlos Lehder, reputedly the most important Colombian drug dealer ever captured by the United States, is serving a life sentence for shipping drugs from a Bahamian island he owned to the United States. Lehder testified at the drug trial that Noriega was a major drug dealer, although he admitted he had never met the Panamanian leader. In return, he received a transfer to a lower-security prison, U.S. protection for his family and the promise that he might have his life sentence commuted or transferred to another country.

disciplinary problems because of his style, and was punished by being sent to be military attaché in Colombia. It was easy for him to make friends there; he was able to develop contacts without trouble, which is what being an attaché is all about. He did his work well—he had studied in Colombia and knew the place.

Melo claims that he was entrapped and lured into the drug business by a group of wealthy financiers of the cocaine trade in Colombia, notably by Ricardo Tribaldos, who ended up testifying at the drug trial against me.

Melo became friendly with Tribaldos and his family while in Colombia. He sometimes assisted them when they had financial trouble or other problems, but always within the bounds of the law, whether in obtaining contracts or in other business dealings. But the Tribaldos family had other types of business as well—they had gotten into drug dealing with the Medellín cartel and laundering their profits in Panama.

Melo says that he was an unwitting accomplice in the construction of the Darien laboratory and, again, this is plausible. Basically, Tribaldos was asked by his Medellín benefactors if he could use his contacts in Panama to guarantee and protect the construction of a processing facility on the Panamanian side of the border with Colombia. Tribaldos said he could, but that Panama was asking four million dollars in protection money.

I never had any involvement with this. Melo agreed, saying he was the contact for Tribaldos; while admitting involvement, he said he never got the money either. Melo also asked the Medellín cartel to have me assassinated while in Europe in July 1984.

Even Tribaldos acknowledged that when he testified. He said that he was the one holding the money and he was the one who told Melo that he had been paid. Tribaldos was the true point of contact with the Medellín cartel, duping them into believing they had paid four million dollars for protection.

While Tribaldos did testify at the trial, Melo did not, interestingly enough. The federal prosecutors, Michael Sullivan and Myles Malman, secretly flew Melo into Miami, went quietly to the hotel room they had reserved for him and had a long talk. They found out, to their dismay, that he wanted to tell the truth. To their horror, Melo gave a completely different version of things, one which ran counter to the prosecution strategy. "Noriega knew nothing about it," said Melo. "Tribaldos and I worked alone. We hid it from him."

This didn't help the prosecution, so they turned on him. "We don't want to hear this. Tell the 'real story,' " they demanded, that is, a version of events that would help their case. Melo refused. The prosecutors were so threatening that he expected to be dragged off to jail at any moment.

Sullivan and Malman walked out, stripped him of his spending money and left him holding a hotel bill without money of his own. They realized that Melo would eventually be in touch with me and that meant they had to reveal to the court and to my lawyers that he was in town. The law said they were duty-bound to inform us of the meeting; they did so, not out of duty, but out of fear that they would be caught if they did not.

So Rubino went to see Melo at his hotel room. He told Rubino that General Ruben Dario Paredes had tried to coax him into testifying as part of a plea bargain for his son, Ahmet, who was also accused by the Americans. "They wanted me to testify against the general, but I refused," said Melo, visibly shaken. But he also refused to testify for the defense. The government intimidation job had its effect. He fled the United States, never to return, fearful that they would take reprisals against him for not playing along. He preferred to flee rather than face an indictment himself.

Topping off Melo's treatment, the prosecutors contended that our military system treated Melo leniently after the discovery of the Darien lab and this proved that we were a den of drug dealers. Actually, when the general staff saw the evidence, Melo confessed that he was working with the Medellín cartel. The Panamanian Defense Forces levied the maximum sanction against the disgraced colonel. He was dismissed from the armed forces, forfeited his rank, salary and benefits and was permanently banned from the military. Hardly a "light punishment," as the prosecution called it, in trying to show that I was an ally of Melo in some drug scheme. As with everything else, the prosecutors compared our laws with U.S. laws and said they were insufficient.

The fact was that Panama did not have a code of military justice, as does the United States, so there were no court-martials. It was interesting to hear the prosecution talk about the lack of a Panamanian court-martial before the uninformed jury, ignorant of Panamanian law, as if Panamanian law itself were on trial.

We also remanded the case to the Panama attorney general; Melo and those associated with him were placed under house arrest. Tribaldos and his other co-conspirators also were arrested.

The investigation showed that the laboratory itself had not been built yet. What our men found was a construction site, installations, an electrical facility, hammocks for the workers, but nothing of substance—no ether, no cocaine paste, nothing at all. There were only the inference and the deduction that someone was developing cocaine installations there.

Ironically, Melo and Tribaldos chose Panamanian attorney Hernán Delgado as their lawyer. Delgado managed to win a dismissal of the civil case. He had experience handling cocaine cases; he was also the law partner of Guillermo Endara, later to be sworn in illegally as president of Panama at a U.S. military installation, overseen by his U.S. protectors, on the night of the U.S. invasion of Panama.

Delgado and Endara, by the way, helped form a shell corporation in Panama for Willie Falcon and Sal Magluta,[6] who were allegedly the biggest drug dealers ever caught in Miami. Endara was listed as an officer of the shell corporation for Falcon and Magluta. After being named president in 1989, Endara, in consultation with Delgado and the Bush administration, denied any wrongdoing, saying he didn't know they were drug dealers. The men negotiated for immunity with the prosecution through their attorney, David Rosen, of Miami.

But Endara's activities were a matter of public record. Panama had become a narcodemocracy. "The nation's new president, Guillermo Endara has for years been a director of one of the Panamanian banks used by Colombia's drug traffickers," reported the *International Herald Tribune* on February 7, 1990. "Guillermo [Billy] Ford, the second vice president and chairman of the banking commission, is part owner of the Dadeland Bank of Florida, which was named in a court case two years ago as a central financial institution for one of the biggest Medellín money launderers, Gonzalo Mora. Rogélio Cruz, the new attorney general, has been a director and lawyer of the First Interamericas Bank owned by [Gilberto] Rodríguez Orejuela, one of the bosses of the Cali Cartel with [José] Santacruz Londoño . . . in Colombia."

---

[6] Falcon and Magluta, former speedboat racers, were found innocent in early 1996 by a federal jury in a U.S. indictment that charged them with smuggling tons of cocaine into the United States from Panama in what officials called one of the biggest cocaine cases ever conducted in the United States.

The Spanish paper *El País* said on October 26, 1990, that Endara was linked to at least three companies that worked with Interbanco, a bank investigated by the DEA for drug trafficking. "This connection presents a problem for the president, because the DEA has charged Interbanco with laundering drug money."

That was not the only reference that linked Endara to criminal activity. On August 19, 1994, *La Estrella de Panamá* carried a front-page story headlined ENDARA IS A CRIMINAL. It quoted an accusation by the president of the Panamanian parliament, Arturo Vallarino, who said that the method in which Endara approved government contract franchises was illegal. "We have to come to the conclusion that the man serving as president is a criminal; we can't permit the theft of millions of dollars in public money because of these franchises."

El Nuevo Herald, the Spanish-language edition of the *Miami Herald*, explained in an article on August 20, 1994, that Endara was giving these contracts to companies that he represented. It also quoted Vallarino as saying that "the public knows and realizes that the president is really behind the million dollar contracts."

On December 20, 1994, the fifth anniversary of the invasion of Panama, *La Estrella* also reported that Endara, who by that time had left office after the election of Ernesto Pérez Balladares,[7] paid thousands of dollars a month to members of his family from government funds:

"His mother-in-law, Carolina Díaz de Chen, had a salary of $5,000 a month, the daughter of the ex-president, Marcela Endara de Yap, received $3,000 a month, his son-in-law, Javier Yap, received $2,500 a month and [his sister-in-law] Mayra Díaz received about $900 per month."

In the end, the United States government got what it wanted. The details didn't matter. The drug case was stitched together against me in the same way that all the evidence was put together against me over a decade. Once it was decided that I was the problem, that I was the one who had to go by all means—if subterfuge, murder and lies were required—so be it.

---

[7] Ernesto Pérez Balladares won the presidential elections in May 1994 on the Democratic Revolutionary Party ticket, defeating Arnulfo Arias's widow, Mireya Moscoso and Panamanian singer and actor Ruben Blades, who had faltered in a third-party challenge for the presidency.

All I sought was independence for Panama. I thought Panama had the right to its own sovereignty and the right to break free of "the chains of colonialism." Those can be empty words, but I think that in Panama, they are appropriate. The same accusations of drug trafficking surfaced against other Panamanian leaders who dared challenge the United States in the battle for Panamanian sovereignty. General José Antonio Remón, during his term of office, from 1952 to 1955, was accused of drug trafficking prior to his assassination by an American sniper. Similarly, the Nixon administration accused Torrijos of drug trafficking and convened a grand jury to hear evidence against his brother, Moisés. The charges against all of us were lies. The lies against Remón ended with his murder; those against Torrijos disappeared with the approval of the canal treaties.

In the United States, chances are, if you saw me, it was in the most unflattering circumstances. Close to the invasion and during the trial, the video would show me raising something that looked like a sword. The image said I was angry, aggressive, belligerent. Repeat it a thousand times, over and over on American television, in New York, in Washington, and you win the psychological war. But the image was a fraud, softening the American people to the idea of attacking a dangerous enemy, supposedly poised to fight.

I could not find a way to explain the images or the frauds to the American people; I did not understand America. I had no way to explain these injustices in the living rooms and halls of power in New York, Washington and Miami. Perhaps Americans thought we were arming our soldiers with machetes to fight the United States.

Here I sit, waiting and hoping for my first encounter with the system of fair play. I wait here, in the faith that human fair play will overcome politics and that people will come to understand the colossal injustice of what has happened. It is the great tragedy of a great nation that decided it could control the rules of the game and destroy lives because it was the establishment and there was no other. The United States set out under George Bush to create a new world order, which was nothing more than a new subterfuge for becoming an international policeman. Nevertheless, I survive, struck down and persecuted, but neither despairing nor defeated. The United States has imprisoned neither my soul, nor my ideals, nor my faith, which exists in a flight of eternal liberty. "For what seems to be God's foolishness is wiser than human wisdom, and what seems to be God's weakness is stronger than human strength. Now remember what you were, my brothers, when God called you. From the human point of view few of you were wise or powerful or of high social standing. God purposely chose what the world considers nonsense in order to shame the wise, and he chose what the world considers weak in order to shame the powerful. He chose what the world looks down on and despises and thinks is nothing, in order to destroy what the world thinks is important. This means that no one can boast in God's presence."[8]

I assume my responsibility as head of government and commander in chief of the Panamanian Defense Forces during the treacherous attack by the United States on my country; no one can avoid the judgment of history. I only asked to be judged on the same scale as the treachery and infamy of my enemies, foreign and domestic. So here I am, a traveler making my way down the long road, certain that the final chapter of the Noriega story is yet to be written.

---

[8] 1 Corinthians 1:25–29. *Holy Bible. Today's English Version* (American Bible Society).

AFTERWORD

Manuel Antonio Noriega probably will always be judged according to the refracted vision of the beholder: for some, he will remain the devil; for others he will be less so as the sordid manipulations swirling around him become ever more apparent.

His narrative is just what it appears to be—the version of one man, whose reputation has often been overinflated to mythic proportions. There can be much debate over Noriega's account of his political life. It is certain that some of his accusations are accurate.

On the key points, I do not think the evidence shows Noriega was guilty of the charges against him. I do not think his actions as a foreign military leader or a sovereign head of state justified the invasion of Panama or that he represented a threat to U.S. national security.

This is a story about creating an image of guilt. If you strip away the costly U.S. campaign that inexorably attaches Noriega's name in history to drug corruption, you find a prosecution that went overboard to convict. So many U.S. agents searched hard and long to convict Noriega, only to come up with the tainted and contradictory words of a brace of felons who won their freedom in return for testifying for the government, whether or not they knew anything about Noriega. For the prosecution, the standard of proof sometimes seemed to be less whether they were telling the truth than whether their stories would get by.

All of this did great damage to the U.S. criminal justice system. For that reason, I challenge those who say that the details of Noriega's case didn't matter: that he was dirty, that any means used to convict him were satisfactory. "I have no evidence, but nothing will dissuade my absolute conviction that he was involved in drug trafficking," said former Ambassador Briggs.

There were three main reasons for the invasion, which had nothing to do with legitimate security interests: the wimp factor, that is, Bush's desire to counteract a growing image of weakness and protect his approval ratings, Panama's failure to help the United States with Iran-Contra and the right-wing U.S. concern that the United States would soon lose influence over the operations of the Panama Canal, with Japan waiting in the wings.

In these pages, I provide comments on Noriega's claims, his relationship with the United States, the Spadafora killing and the drug charges, along with a perspective of the U.S. invasion of Panama. In brief:

• Noriega's description of the plan to use explosives to sway opinion in the Panama Canal Zone in late 1976 squares with published information that an American army sergeant may have been involved in such an operation. At the time, the use of C-4 plastique was not widespread, and such explosives, which were used in the bombings, would likely be of U.S. origin. The CIA station chief in Panama in 1976, Joe Kiyonaga, died in 1988; his sons, John and David, both attorneys, said they knew nothing about the incident. The Defense Department and the CIA, responding to Freedom of Information requests, either said they had no information or that they would not acknowledge such information even if they did. Noriega's account is the only one describing involvement by then–CIA director George Bush. I found no confirmation of Noriega's account. I sent a letter to the former president, asking if he participated in the planning for the bombing, in preparation or training, whether he knew about American participation and whether he discussed the case at any time with Noriega. Bush's spokesman replied by telephone: "According to his recollection, the answer is 'no' to all five questions. But to make sure, he sent your letter to John Deutsch [director of the CIA]." Several days later, the spokesman phoned again, saying, "The CIA has nothing to add to what President Bush already said."

• On the controversial June 9, 1971, slaying of the Reverend Héctor Gallegos, investigative reporter Seymour Hersh reported that U.S. intelligence concluded that Noriega was personally responsible for the rural priest's death. Noriega is familiar with the reports, adamantly denying them and calling for any evidence to be made public.

• On the death of Torrijos, there are charges and countercharges concerning the plane crash that took the Panamanian leader's life. U.S. officials in Panama at the time of Torrijos's death who were familiar with the investigation into the crash conclude that there was no foul play and that pilot error may have caused the accident.

• U.S. intelligence sources confirm Noriega's accounts of meetings at their behest in Cuba; intelligence documents obtained through the Freedom of Information Act confirm Noriega's overtures to Fidel Castro concerning Central America and the *Mariel* boatlift, as well as his subsequent debriefing by William Casey. They also agree with his assessment that Casey would have blocked prosecution of Noriega on drug charges. I asked Colonel Matías Farias, the former U.S. military chief of protocol in Panama, about the relationship between Casey and Noriega. "I remember meeting Casey one time when he came to the Southern Command," said Farias. "As soon as he got off the plane, Casey said, 'Where's my boy? Where's Noriega?' "

Donald Winters, the CIA station chief in Panama for two years starting in 1983, said he was authorized by the CIA to describe his relationship with Noriega and what he knew about Noriega's contact with Casey. "I was present during three meetings between the two men, two in Washington and one in Panama, and can attest that the relationship was neither close nor personal. Casey was always well briefed (normally by me) as to how he should deal with Noriega."

• Intelligence officials deny that Panama or U.S. territory in the Canal Zone was used to train Salvadoran military or death squad members. But those denials may not settle the issue. Secret and compartmentalized U.S. operations in Central America during the 1980s took the concept of plausible deniability—the art of being able to lie because no witnesses could prove otherwise—to new levels of cynicism. Interviews with well-placed U.S. military personnel indicated constant efforts to deceive the American public about the relationship between the Salvadoran military, paramilitary forces and U.S. advisers and trainers.

214 ★ MANUEL NORIEGA and PETER EISNER

Panama certainly was used to circumvent other congressional mandates on El Salvador, such as the limit on the number of U.S. advisers in the Central American country. The military and the CIA played loose with the concept of "in country," ferrying people in from outside El Salvador for the day and having them spend the night elsewhere. They similarly disregarded other provisions, such as the rule that U.S. advisers not carry rifles nor operate in the field against Salvadoran rebels.

In 1985, *The New York Times* published a front-page story detailing armed U.S. C-130 reconnaissance overflights of Salvador operating out of Howard Air Force Base in Panama; the newspaper printed a photograph of one such plane, painted black and without any military markings. Independently, sources claimed that the fifty-caliber machine-gun fittings onboard these planes needed frequent replacement because of overheating from intense firefights. A key U.S. adviser told me that the United States manipulated the use of Panamanian and Honduran territory to make it appear they were complying with stated congressional controls on participation in the Salvadoran civil war.

• The U.S. government knew well that the 1984 presidential election was irregular, filled with corruption charges and probably was won by Arnulfo Arias. Nevertheless, the Reagan administration endorsed the election of Barletta, not only sending a message of complicity to the Panamanian people, but to Noriega. The irony of Jimmy Carter attending the 1984 inauguration, then criticizing the 1989 election process, is notable.

The May 7, 1989, elections were annulled before an election count could be completed, but there was agreement across the spectrum that, for whatever reason, Noriega's candidates would have lost. Summing up the response was Marco Gandasegui, a Panamanian political analyst with strong nationalistic sentiments who vigorously opposed U.S. policy in Panama. "I think it's clear that the government lost, or else they wouldn't have annulled the elections. You have to remember that the people were not voting so much in favor of one side or the other; they were voting negatively. The people who voted for the opposition were voting against the economic malaise that the country had fallen into; those who supported the government were voting against men they perceived as being too closely tied to the United States."

• Carter aide Robert Pastor rejects Noriega's account of attempts to set up a meeting following the May 7, 1989, elections, saying he was denied access to the Panamanian general.

• Plainclothes thugs circulated in open vans around Panama City on the day that presidential and vice-presidential candidates were beaten in the Casco Viejo section. While no individual was blamed for the killing of Alexis Guerra during that incident, it was widely believed that PDF soldiers were responsible. There were cases of police mistreatment of protesters during the election period.

• In the death of Colonel Moisés Giroldi after the October coup, there was sensationalistic reporting that Noriega had pulled the trigger himself in killing Giroldi. That charge has been discredited; it is believed likely that Captain Eliecer Gaitán ordered the execution of Giroldi and nine other coup participants, in a preemptive warning to all future coup plotters.

Noriega and the United States

Retired U.S. Air Force Colonel Matías Farias is not shy about his qualifications for giving political advice. In the course of his twelve years as a political adviser to the U.S. Southern Command, Farias has used his skills in understanding Latin America to counsel the governments of half a dozen countries, along with providing guidance to his superiors in the U.S. military. "I don't want to inflate myself, but it came to where people knew that I was someone to listen to. I'm the one that told them that Daniel Ortega would lose the elections in Nicaragua to Violeta Chamorro; I'm the one who told [Chilean dictator Augusto] Pinochet to allow civilians to take over. . . . He listened to me and everything was fine. I have a reputation for knowing what I am talking about."

So he was not surprised when he got a call one day in February 1988 from General Manuel Antonio Noriega. "My problem was that I needed to get permission from my superiors to be able to talk to him. It went all the way up to Admiral William Crowe, the chairman of the Joint Chiefs of Staff, and took three days before they gave me the okay."

The timing for the United States and for Noriega was crucial. Noriega had just been indicted on drug charges in the United States; Panama's civilian president, Eric Arturo Delvalle, was preparing to side with the Americans and call for Noriega's ouster. Noriega had maintained only casual contact with Farias over the years. But now, the

Cuban exile's special ability literally and figuratively to speak the language of Latin America was in demand.

Farias drove to Noriega's command headquarters on Avenue A in Chorrillo. He was ushered into Noriega's office, where he found the general wearing camouflage fatigues. They shook hands, then sat down alone.

"Colonel, it is said that you are the chief political analyst for the Americans here. You are the one they depend on. I'd like your advice as well. How do you see the situation?" the general asked.

"General, I must be frank with you: the situation is deteriorating. Every system has to pay a political cost for staying in power. And now the military is experiencing that reality. Unfortunately, the Panamanian people want a change."

Noriega listened intently as Farias spoke, and then responded evenly, obviously wanting to probe the matter deeply. "Colonel, everyone must understand that Panama has changed from what it was twenty years ago. The poor people now have a chance; they have more access to power, to wealth; the masses of Panamanians now have a future."

Farias nodded in agreement. "But the problem is one of perception," he said. "The people have the feeling that the defense forces have their hands on everything—"

"But the people have a civilian president who does make his own decisions," Noriega said.

"General, regardless of what you and I think, the people feel that the military has to back off. It is their perception; it is a reality for them. You may say that you have your supporters, but you no longer have a majority. The people are tired; if an election were held today, you would lose it heavily, probably by three to one."

"Is that what the Pentagon and the State Department think?" Noriega asked. "What about my friends in Washington?"

"General, you may have friends in Washington, the same ones you always had; but for the first time, you have some very powerful enemies. I don't think the situation is going to change."

Within days of Farias's meeting, on March 15, 1988, a group of Panamanian officers, led by Major Leonidas Macías, staged an abortive coup against Noriega. Macías and his co-conspirators were captured and imprisoned. U.S. officials were forewarned, and while Farias said he was not party to the plan, Noriega assumed that he was. The two men had no further meetings.

Nevertheless, Farias is one of a number of U.S. officers who break ranks with the prevailing wisdom about Noriega and his Panamanian Defense Forces. U.S. military analysts gave the PDF under Noriega high marks for professionalism.

Indeed, independent assessments by U.S. military sources said that Noriega had upgraded an organization that started out as a police force into the military organization it needed to be in order to protect the Panama Canal. "Noriega brought the PDF into the twentieth century," said one U.S. officer. "The goal was incorporating the military into canal defenses. I was personally disappointed with the invasion and the decision to dismantle the military."

Significantly, the officer said, under Noriega's tutelage the PDF developed far-reaching social programs. "I don't think there was a better civil affairs unit in all of Latin America. They sent doctors to remote villages and taught agricultural techniques to peasants. I think this was a very serious, well-intentioned organization."

General Woerner, the Southern Command chief until the fall of 1989, agreed with several key assessments by the men who had day-to-day contact with Noriega and the PDF. "Overall, I never saw any credible evidence of drug trafficking involving General Noriega," he said. "My analysis was that the U.S. policy of isolating Panama and its military was counterproductive to U.S. interests."

It was Woerner who, forced into retirement for refusing to invade Panama, had a concise answer to the question, Why did the United States invade Panama?

"The invasion was a response to U.S. domestic considerations," he said. "It was the wimp factor."

A declassified defense department intelligence report in 1976 described Noriega as a "Caucasian with apparent Negroid trace, 5 feet 6 inches tall, 150 pounds, medium build.

"As a student at the Instituto Nacional, he was active in socialist youth activities and became a member of the Panamanian Socialist Party, a Marxist-oriented group . . . inactive since the mid-1960s. . . .

While attending secondary school, Noriega wrote a number of nationalistic poems and articles which were published in local newspapers."

Large portions of the intelligence document were blacked out by
censors, including areas dealing with Noriega's private life and personal acquaintances. But the document does say that

> Noriega has maintained a friendly and cooperative relationship with
> U.S. military personnel since prior to joining the National Guard in
> 1962. . . . He has a decided preference for U.S. style food and a par-
> ticular fondness for hot dogs. He likes the finest brands of Scotch
> with water. He chooses his friends carefully when drinking. He does
> not like coffee and would rather drink tea or juice. He does not
> smoke, but chews gum. He likes caramel and taffy type candies.
>
> No [police] record available. Noriega admits that he and fellow
> high school students used to throw rocks at the Panamanian Police
> during his high school days. It can be concluded that any arrest
> record was destroyed after he became the National Guard G-2 (in-
> telligence).
>
> Noriega is a (Catholic), but his religion has little, if any, effect on
> his military or political views. Noriega is intelligent, aggressive, am-
> bitious and ultranationalistic. He is a shrewd and calculating person.
> Although loyal to Brigadier General Torrijos and respectful of his su-
> periors, he berates peers and subordinates, often in the presence of
> others. He has a keen mind and enjoys verbal "jousting" matches
> with U.S. contacts. He is a persuasive speaker and possesses rare
> common sense. He is considered to be a competent officer with ex-
> cellent judgment and leadership ability. He has long been one of
> Torrijos' principal political deputies and has played a significant role
> in shaping international policies of his country. With his experience
> as G-2 since 1970, which includes control over the National De-
> partment of Investigations (DENI), concerned with internal security
> and criminal investigations, and the Immigration Section of the
> Ministry of Government and Justice, Noriega seems assured of
> maintaining a role of "power broker." It should be of no surprise to
> some day find this officer in the position of . . .
>
> In the event of a confrontation between the U.S. and Panama's
> current regime Noriega would be a capable adversary, but it is be-
> lieved he would endeavor to maintain a limited liaison contact with
> certain U.S. officials as has been his policy in the past. Noriega feels
> the U.S. should "normalize relations with Cuba as a means to com-
> bat Cuban fanaticism." Past reports reveal Noriega's belief that "the

best way to control your enemies is to maintain close contact." The organization of his G-2 offices reaches out to all sectors of the public domain and provides collection of raw data and intelligence which permits Noriega to be the best informed individual in Panama. He is often selected to represent the Government of Panama on diplomatic trips and/or on important military conferences and negotiations abroad. He is considered to be one of the most powerful figures in Panama with close ties to Torrijos.

He is a man of action and not afraid to make decisions. For example, in January 1970, he refused to allow hijacked aircraft to be refueled and in the subsequent attempt to capture the hijacker, the young man, a mental case, was shot and killed without quarter. This incident, the only recorded hijack attempt in Panama, served to earn Noriega the grudging respect of the public and gave advance notice of his capability. Subsequently in 1970, Noriega directed the pursuit of a small terrorist/guerrilla band with helicopters.

Noriega is an aggressive leader. He is respected by friends and feared by enemies. He depends upon his intelligence organization and close relationship with Torrijos for the maintenance of power. He is considered to be at the top of the list of several likely successors to Torrijos as commandant of the National Guard should that position become vacant. Some observers view him as the possible future dictator of Panama. He was instrumental in Torrijos' counter-coup of December 1969 and since 1970 has been the leader of one of two informal officer "cliques" within the National Guard. His personal financial status appears excellent. Although his record of association with U.S. military goes back over 15 years, he is becoming increasingly distant toward the U.S. He maintains open channels with Cuban, Soviet, Chilean and other political representation in Panama. He is probably the second most powerful man in Panama and, therefore, possesses almost unlimited military and/or political potential.

During the Torrijos period, Noriega was a relatively low-key presence. Rumored to have the country wired, with some sort of intelligence information on almost everyone, he became a shrewd and trusted player behind Torrijos.

U.S. intelligence officials said that Noriega never earned the reputation as the brutal leader of a police state. U.S. human rights information never pointed to massive concerns with civil or human rights abuses. True, members of the oligarchy often did not fare well under

twenty years of Torrijismo. There was no love lost between the supporters of Arnulfo Arias and the Panamanian military. In all, estimates
were of three hundred political exiles from 1968 to 1989. That was
less than the number of refugees fleeing their homes in El Salvador
every day for several years at the height of the guerrilla war.

What about repression on the streets? There were incidents, but
even during protests by the Civic Crusade, said one U.S. military analyst, there was always an attempt by the Panamanians to maintain the
peace. "I always felt that they tried not to have confrontations."

One of the street commanders monitoring the protests, ironically,
was Eduardo Herrera Hassan, later brought in by the United States
after the invasion to reorganize a Panamanian police force. "Herrera
was bending over backwards to avoid violence. But where do you draw
the line between civil disobedience and keeping the peace? I never felt
like there was a lot of oppression."

It was impossible to say that Noriega was wildly popular on the
streets of Panama; he was not. Noriega underestimated the power of
the Civic Crusade, which was much more broad-based than he realized. Panamanians saw their country in contrast to Central America on
one side and the wealth of the Americans on the other. There were no
wars and little violence in their country of two million; no killings or
death squads as in El Salvador, no guerrilla attacks or civil war as in
Nicaragua or Guatemala. People looked around them and saw that
their lives should have been better. Where was the prosperity they
hoped for; why had the promise not been achieved? People blamed the
Panamanian Defense Forces, even before the U.S. pressure and all the
more later; with the U.S. economic sanctions, they were squeezed
harder than ever. There wasn't much Noriega could do but the un-
thinkable—sacrifice sovereignty in return for economic growth and go
into exile. It was a terrible bargain and he refused.

Questions about Noriega and the Panamanian human rights record
began being raised with the deterioration of Panamanian-U.S. relations,
linked directly to the Reagan administration's pursuit of its dirty wars in
Central America. By the late 1980s, the United States had failed in its
policy of arming the Nicaraguan Contras to overthrow the Nicaraguan
Sandinista government. U.S. intelligence officials who were close to the
operations in Central America said Noriega was peripheral to these
activities. Significantly, however, when Noriega was asked by Oliver

North to participate in the dirty wars by mining Nicaraguan harbors, he says he refused. North has claimed that the offer to participate in Central America was a Noriega initiative. North's own associates, however, reject this. "I love Ollie," one associate said. "But he knows that the idea was his alone. Noriega refused to go along with it."

"Unfortunately, the problem with Ollie is that you can never believe anything he says," said Vince Cannistraro, a former CIA deputy regional director who was second in command to North on the National Security Council.

The story of the Noriega meeting with North in London was further complicated when special prosecutor Lawrence Walsh released copies of North's notebooks, which indicate that Noriega was the source of the offer. There are opposing views on the significance of these notebooks, which indicate a detailed contact with Noriega regarding the Panamanian leader having offered to take action.

Cannistraro and other U.S. intelligence officials said that offer would have been out of character. "That's the Ollie North factor. Ollie having discussions with people and exceeding his brief was a common thing. That happened a lot. He was doing all sorts of strange, curious things. We know that now. I would tend to believe Noriega."

If there was one man who epitomized the U.S. policy in Central America during the period, it was not North, but Elliott Abrams, the assistant secretary of state for inter-American affairs. Abrams had turned his office into a soapbox for railing against communism in Nicaragua and El Salvador.

"Mr. Abrams's attitude descends from the notorious pronouncement made nearly a century ago by Secretary of State Richard Olney: 'The United States is practically sovereign on this continent, and its fiat is law upon the subjects to which it confines its interposition,' " wrote historian Arthur Schlesinger, Jr., describing Abrams as "an official with no visible qualifications for the job, who is both disbelieved on Capitol Hill and disliked by Latin Americans."[1]

---

[1] "Monroe Doctrine Fails Again" by Arthur Schlesinger, Jr., *The Wall Street Journal,* April 21, 1988.

Abrams says that when he entered office as assistant secretary of state for inter-American affairs in July of 1985, he sought "a hemisphere-wide human rights policy to deal with Stroessner, Pinochet and Noriega. It is also the case that Noriega's behavior was getting worse all the time."

At first he was stymied in his attempts to change official policy toward Noriega, with the Department of Defense and CIA arguing they were satisfied with the status quo.

"The DOD argument was that this is all intellectual nonsense: Noriega is our ally in protecting both U.S. citizens in the Canal Zone and the canal itself. The CIA said—we work with what we have.

"Why did State win this battle? I think the answer is drugs—once it became clear that the amount of drug trade was increasing.

"Let's be clear here, I was in charge of the policy," Abrams said.

Rumor and raw intelligence about Noriega and drugs carried more weight than persistent information linking Nicaraguan Contra weapons shipments to drug flights in Honduras and charges of drug corruption in El Salvador's military. Panama was a convenient target and a good escape valve to divert attention, because Reagan and Bush administration prestige was involved. The United States was pumping billions of dollars into El Salvador and Honduras to fight Nicaragua's Sandinista government and El Salvadoran guerrillas, looking the other way while the Salvadoran military trampled human rights in its country and keeping up the funding to the Nicaraguan Contras in their CIA-orchestrated effort to overthrow the Sandinistas.

Abrams and the Reagan administration, more than 100,000 deaths later in El Salvador and 50,000 deaths later in Nicaragua, were cynical enough to imply that their policy succeeded. "We were not playing to win, we were playing for a tie, and that's what we got," said one well-placed U.S. participant in the U.S. Central American operations.

Central Americans left Abrams and the rest of the administration out of the real solution to Central American problems. Where Abrams conspired repeatedly and secretly to foment a U.S.-led invasion of Nicaragua, the Central Americans waged peace. Noriega was friendly both with the Costa Rican president Oscar Arias and with the Nicaraguan President Daniel Ortega, convincing the reticent Ortega that meeting with Arias on what would become known as the Contadora Peace Plan was a good thing. Contadora, an island off the coast of Panama, was the venue for the first Central American meeting to find a solution to the regional civil wars of the 1980s.

The United States first rejected, then grudgingly went along with the Central American peace process. But Abrams and company, so identified with the anti-Nicaraguan cause, were incensed. They aligned with a small group of Panamanian antimilitary elite bankers and businessmen to lash out at Noriega as having locked Panama in the grip of military repression. To whatever extent this was so for the white, English-speaking upper classes, the story among the working class was different. In twenty years of military rule, impoverished and, importantly, mostly African-origin and mixed-ethnic-Panamanians for the first time were coming into their own. Sons and daughters of slum dwellers were obtaining a secondary-school education, were advancing to the University of Panama and were becoming civil servants, doctors, lawyers and university professors.

Some of these new educated masses adopted leftist political views; this estranged them from the political mainstream—the right-wing populist politics of Arnulfo Arias's Arnulfista party and the center conservative Christian Democrats were the major players. Instead, sharing the nationalism of the newly constituted Panamanian Defense Forces, the new Torrijista-raised middle class somewhat reluctantly sided with Noriega. One distinguished, well-spoken young doctor told me that he was proud to support Noriega in the May 1989 elections, not as a vote for corruption, but as a vote against the United States and in favor of Panamanian independence.

But the United States never wanted to hear much about Panamanian sovereignty. Lost in the indignation about the May 1989 elections, which were canceled by Noriega, was the obvious and well-documented reality that the United States has always helped manipulate the Panamanian political scene. Americans looked the other way in 1984 when questionable balloting procedures produced a presidential election victory for Nicolás Ardito Barletta, a University of Chicago–trained economist and sometime protégé of then Secretary of State George Shultz. His opponent was Arnulfo Arias, by then an octogenarian, perennial candidate seeking the presidency for a fourth time. Arias's fascist, racist views were an embarrassment to the United

States.[2] His frank admission to Noriega that he would try to abolish the military—as he had done in 1968—brought strong efforts by the ruling military to ensure that he would not be elected. Former U.S. ambassador Everett Briggs said in an interview that the United States was content with Barletta becoming president even though the Reagan administration knew that he was not fairly elected. "Barletta really was Shultz's student at the University of Chicago," Briggs said in an interview. "Everybody believed that Arnulfo Arias had won by a hair. The analysis done for me by the embassy staff was that he probably beat Barletta by less than 10,000 votes. But even the more responsible politicians in the opposition were willing to give [Barletta] the benefit of the doubt."

Also ignored by the resident wisdom about Panama under Noriega was that his strongest opposition in the United States came as a result of defections from the ranks of his supporters. Gabriel Lewis Galindo, for example, had worked side by side with him and Torrijos during the negotiation of the 1978 Panama Canal treaties. But Lewis and the Noriega camp had a falling out over personal financial matters. Lewis became an archenemy of Noriega and one of the inner circle of anti-Noriega plotters, who had the ear of Elliott Abrams back in Washington. Also on the list of disaffected plotters was José Blandón, the Panamanian consul in New York, who was deeply insulted when Noriega stripped him of his post. Abrams said he based his pursuit of Noriega on Blandón's charges about drugs. After months of searching for evidence against Noriega and coming up with nothing, "suddenly the answer was 'yes, we have the evidence.' The difference was Blandón."

Blandón was also close to Deborah DeMoss, the Machiavellian Latin America specialist on the staff of archconservative Senator Jesse Helms of North Carolina. DeMoss was able to use Helms's position on the Senate Foreign Relations Committee to promote Blandón's charges that Noriega was dealing drugs in association with Fidel Castro and

---

[2] Arias was elected president for the first time in 1940. "He espoused fascism and racism; he opposed and persecuted minorities, particularly English-speaking West Indians, whom he wanted to deport in order to purify Panama's racial structure." In his inaugural speech, he said, "The words 'democracy,' 'liberty,' 'liberalism,' are so bandied about nowadays that they have no meaning. . . . The demagogic concept that all men are free and equal is biologically without foundation" (Scranton, *op. cit.*, p. 51).

Colombian drug lords. Other members of the committee, including Democratic senators Edward Kennedy and John Kerry, were persuaded to publicize the Noriega charges in the name of sounding firm in prosecuting the supposed U.S. war on drugs. While many of Blandón's accusations about Noriega have become part of the historical record, his fabrications and outright prevarications were considered so dangerous that U.S. government prosecutors did not even call him as a witness at the Noriega drug trial.

None of this adds up to justification for a U.S. invasion. All of the alleged reasons—supporting democracy, blocking drug trafficking, protecting the honor of a woman, responding to Noriega's alleged declaration of war—were lies.

Spadafora

Colonel Al Cornell, the military attaché at the U.S. embassy in Panama, rushed into the office of the chargé d'affaires, William Price, with the startling news: the decapitated body of Hugo Spadafora had been found under a bridge in Chiriquí province.

"Did you hear the news?" he asked. "Somebody's killed Hugo Spadafora. This is a big problem for this government and this military."

"What's the big deal, Al?" asked Price. "He's just some left-wing Torrijista. No big deal."

"I'm telling you, Bill, this is going to have long-term repercussions for this government. This thing is going to cause big-time heartburn."

Cornell and other U.S. officials investigated the case. "I find it hard to believe that Noriega was involved," he said. "I don't think Spadafora was a great threat in any case. Only a fool would have done something like order the killing. He's no fool; he's a smart guy and a very bright street fighter."

Don Winters, the CIA station chief, agreed with Cornell that there were big problems. But he doubted Noriega's involvement. "First, it doesn't follow Noriega's MO," he told friends. "The Panamanian military doesn't kill people. Exile is the most common method of dealing with enemies; for them, getting tough is a little bit of roughhousing and their predilection for shoving things up the rear ends of people to humiliate them. But that's about it."

226 ★ MANUEL NORIEGA and PETER EISNER

The U.S. investigators on the scene saw proof beyond a reasonable doubt that two auxiliary policeman in Chiriquí were responsible for the killing. They were unable to find a clear motive. Perhaps, Cornell said, the underlings thought they were doing their boss, Noriega, a favor by getting rid of Spadafora.

"Well, possibly," said Winters, but he doubted that. Spadafora was no real threat to Noriega. Despite irritating news reports and columns written by the Panamanian exile, he really had very little impact in Panama.

All of them discounted reports that Spadafora was killed before he could deliver secret information about Noriega to the U.S. embassy in Panama City. They described Spadafora as a low-level intelligence contact for the United States. If he had special information about Noriega, which they doubted, he could have delivered it in San José, Costa Rica, where he lived. In any case, he certainly would have had multiple copies of the information. No such information has surfaced. Floyd Carlton, however, told DEA agents after his arrest in Costa Rica that he had provided Spadafora with information to be passed along about Noriega.[3]

Despite reading news reports on the subject, the men never saw any credible information that Noriega was involved. "At the most," said Colonel Matias Farias, "one could say that Noriega participated in a cover-up, or at least allowed the case to go unprosecuted. But I don't believe he was involved."

Any time Cornell, Farias or the CIA station chief at the time, Donald Winters, were questioned by colleagues or friends, their contention of Noriega's lack of involvement was met with disbelief. Hadn't they seen the National Security Agency transcript of the conversation Noriega had with his commander on the scene, Major Luis (Papo) Cordoba?[4]

"I don't know anything about that," Farias said. "Neither do Cornell and Winters. And if they don't know about it, you can be pretty sure it doesn't exist."

---

[3] An account of Carlton's relationship with Spadafora is found in *Our Man in Panama*, pp. 210–15.

[4] The alleged text of the NSA intercept had Noriega talking to Major Luis Cordoba. "We have the rabid dog," Cordoba said. "And what does one do with a dog that has rabies?" Noriega answered. In *Time of the Tyrants* by R. M. Koster and Guillermo Sánchez Borbon (New York: Scribners, 1990; p. 28).

Without a doubt, linkage of Noriega to ordering the Spadafora killing was the most significant item cited in rallying opposition to him both in Panama and the United States. Indeed, even when federal Judge William M. Hoeveler pondered the possibility that Noriega was innocent of drug charges against him, he told me that he was placated by the knowledge that Noriega was a bad character, in any case—"he was involved in the Spadafora killing."

The judge's assumption of the resident wisdom about the Spadafora case prompted a deeper look at the background of the charge that Noreiga ordered the killing of Hugo Spadafora.

Interviews with government officials and journalists who wrote stories about the Spadafora killing have failed to develop an original source for the NSA transcript.

All published reports I could find concerning the alleged National Security Agency quote were traced back to Guillermo Sánchez Borbon, whose column in the anti-Noriega newspaper *La Prensa* first published charges of the general's involvement in the killing. Sánchez Borbon said candidly in an interview that he could not confirm the source of the quote and that his book about Noriega, *In the Time of the Tyrants,* was not entirely true.

"It was not an objective book, it was a combative book. It has its inaccuracies," he said. Stopping short of saying the National Security Agency reference was invented, he said he had never heard the tape nor seen the transcript of such a statement.

Sánchez Borbon's American alter ego, novelist and raconteur R. M. Koster, was deeply involved in creating the popular impression in the United States and elsewhere that Noriega had ordered the killing of Spadafora. An expatriate writer and onetime nominee for the National Book Award, Koster has lived in Panama for forty years. His most recent novel is *Carmichael's Dog,* in which the title character is host to an infernal demonic universe whose members sometimes leap out of the ear of the pooch into the brain of the master.

As a young man in the 1950s, Koster served in the U.S. Army 470th Intelligence Brigade, based in Panama. He is a Democratic Party activist, and attends most party conventions as an expatriate delegate. At the height of U.S. anti-Noriega policy, he was one of a select group of English-speaking informed sources, tipsters and fixers used by U.S. foreign correspondents, including those of *Newsweek, Newsday* and

The New York Times to provide background on the Panama scene. Most recently, Koster is a source for a John le Carré novel about Panama, which portrays Panamanian military and political life.

His role as independent pundit was questionable. Koster penned the English version of the story about the National Security Agency intercept, first in a 1988 *Harper's Magazine* article, later in their joint post-invasion book, *In the Time of the Tyrants.*

Three U.S. military and intelligence sources, Winters, CIA station chief in Panama, Dewey Clarridge, his superior at the CIA in Washington, and Cornell, the military attaché in Panama, all on post at the time of the Spadafora killing, said they had never heard such an intercept and did not believe it existed.

In the same Panama book, Koster—who sometimes ghost-wrote the Sánchez Borbon column under the byline "El Gringo Desconocido" (the Unknown Gringo)—admits to having met in Washington in 1988 with members of the Bush administration's National Security Council, calling for the U.S. invasion of Panama and likening Noriega to Hitler.

" 'How are we going to get Noriega out of Panama?' Senator Kennedy's aide Gregory Craig asked R. M. Koster in January 1988.

"The same way we got Hitler out of Europe," he writes, continuing in the third person.

> Six weeks later, Koster was in the old Executive Office Building in Washington, saying much the same to staffers of the National Security Council. The indictments made the breach between Noriega and the United States irreparable, no matter what his remaining Washington friends might wish. The United States could not leave Panama for twelve years, until the appointed time for handing over the Canal to the Panamanians. Noriega would not leave unless he was forced to. The people of Panama couldn't, so the business would end in U.S. military action. The sooner this happened, the fewer people would die.

Despite promoting this tack, Koster says that this was not "advocating a course of action," but rather "predicting an event."

I interviewed a number of journalists, politicians and government officials who either reported Noriega's alleged involvement in the Spadafora case citing other sources, or as a given without documentation.

Murray Waas, a freelance journalist, wrote an article in *The Village Voice,* citing the *Harper's* article. "I got it from the *Harper's Magazine* piece by Sánchez Borbon," Waas told me. "I probably should have checked it better. I'm getting this sick feeling in my stomach that I didn't check it hard enough. . . . I assumed it."

Koster said he had gotten the NSA intercept report from Sánchez Borbon. Borbon said he didn't remember the source, but suggested investigative journalist Seymour Hersh; Winston Spadafora, brother of the slain Noriega opponent; or French intelligence.

Hersh said in an interview that he didn't know who Guillermo Sánchez Borbon was and that he received first word of the NSA quote about Spadafora years later in Panama while researching a possible film script in Panama for director Oliver Stone. The U.S. intelligence sources denied that Winston Spadafora had received any information on an intercept from the United States and doubted that there was any French report on the subject.

Carlos Rodríguez, a former Panamanian vice-presidential candidate and anti-Noriega political lobbyist in the United States, said he had heard the report from Roberto Eisenmann, Sánchez Borbon's boss at *La Prensa.* Eisenmann said he didn't know where the report came from, but always assumed Sánchez Borbon had come up with the story.

The manager of U.S. foreign policy in Latin America during the Reagan administration, former assistant secretary of state Elliott Abrams said he did not know the source for the Spadafora report. But he said, "Official reporting as I recall it made it clear. I would say my memory of this was that the Spadafora affair was the first crack in the Panamanian Defense Forces."

Briggs, the U.S. ambassador to Panama at the time and an avowed Noriega enemy, said he doubted the existence of such a National Security Agency intercept. "I don't remember intelligence reports or any privileged reporting on the case. I think it's entirely possible that Sánchez Borbon made the whole thing up."

Dwayne "Dewey" Clarridge, the retired CIA chief for Latin America, shed light on several points. He said that there was never any evidence linking Noriega to the Spadafora death. "It's ridiculous, I would have known about it, but I didn't because there was no evidence and no intercept."

The entire affair, he said, including the drug charges against Noriega, were "a travesty." In the case of Oliver North's charges that Noriega offered to attack targets and assassinate Nicaraguan Sandinista leaders, he subscribed to the theory that one of the many unofficial intermediaries used by North's makeshift Contra operations was brokering a deal to convince North and Noriega to work together. Noriega said the intermediary, Joaquin Quiñones, a Miami-based Cuban exile, was his constant pipeline to North. But Quiñones, who died in 1990, was never on the NSC staff and apparently was bartering influence between the two men.

A Trial Outside the Trial

Other than the government witnesses against Noriega and those officials and opponents in Panama who said he "must be guilty" of drug charges, I found few people close to the situation who thought the drug conspiracy charge was valid. Fernando Manfredo, longtime Panamanian deputy director of the Panama Canal Commission and a respected political figure, defended the general. "No, there was none of that," Manfredo said, asked about drug trafficking. "Perhaps some money laundering, but not directly by Noriega. But as for drug dealing, no, that's not Noriega's style."

Eduardo Herrera Hassan, the former officer under Noriega who was almost drawn into plots to kill his former boss, said he didn't think there was evidence linking the general to traffickers. "I never saw or heard any evidence of it," Herrera said.

The denials of Noriega's involvement in drug dealing came from disparate quarters. Agents of the CIA, the Israeli Mossad, the Defense Intelligence Agency and the Drug Enforcement Administration men who were close to the action in Central America said that the Noriega drug charges were trumped up.

At the DEA, there was much consternation over the drug charges. The Noriega trial produced a major rift between the DEA district office in Miami and the field agents who had worked in Panama for the previous decade. The field agents had grown close to their Panamanian counterparts, who helped them haul in drug busts and sometimes protected their lives. When they protested the drug indictment against

Noriega, they were told they had been duped by Noriega's intelligence apparatus.

One former DEA official told me in private that he did not think Noriega was guilty, then appeared at the drug trial to leave a far different picture. Averting his eyes, the DEA officer downplayed praise of the Panamanian Defense Forces' drug efforts, contained in frequent written commendations sent to Noriega and his aides.

The trial threatened to be undone when one of the DEA sources, apparently upset that he was being pressured to provide a deceptive impression of U.S.-Panamanian drug interdiction efforts, leaked a file that contained a trove of previously unrevealed cooperation between the Drug Enforcement Administration and Noriega's forces. The cooperation was so extensive that it had been given a code name: Operation Negocio, or "business" in Spanish; revelation of this material broadened the scope of Noriega's cooperation with the United States, both as a paid Central Intelligence Agency informant and in helping to halt major drug operations in the middle to late 1980s.[5] Some of the same DEA operatives who testified against Noriega paradoxically told prosecutors that Operation Negocio was an effort to identify pilots and planes flying drug money into Panama from 1983 to 1987.

James Bramble, who served as the agency's liaison to Panama from 1982 to 1984, was known to be concerned about charges of drug trafficking that took place allegedly in Panama during his watch. It was Bramble who flew to Darien near the Colombian border in 1984 with Noriega's chief drug agent, Luis Quiel, to examine the site of a major cocaine-processing laboratory that had been destroyed.

While Bramble previously claimed that he was certain the laboratory was found by accident and was not a result of illegal activity by Noriega or Quiel, he gave no such testimony at the drug trial.

The drug conspiracy indictment was mostly the work of the U.S. attorney in Miami, Leon Kellner, and an honorable, tough-minded assistant U.S. attorney named Richard Gregorie, whose single-minded goal of halting drug dealing ruffled feathers in Washington when he suggested before Congress that politics and lack of commitment from policy makers was blocking progress in the campaign to stop cocaine trafficking in the United States.

[5] "He Was Our Guy" by Peter Eisner, *Newsday,* December 15, 1991, p. 1.

While Kellner's goals were largely political, Gregorie was uncompromising. Gregorie's campaign to investigate the drug business in Miami, in cooperation with the Drug Enforcement Administration, coincided with intense efforts in Washington to fund the Contras. It has been widely reported, but not widely documented, that many of the pilots, clandestine airstrips, contract air lines and operatives working with the effort to fund the Nicaraguan Contras were also showing up in reports on drug investigations. Men like Floyd Carlton Caceres and César Rodríguez, both later implicated in the Noriega case, were transporting drugs for the Medellín cartel and guns-for-hire in Central America.

But the Contra wars were not on Gregorie's watch. He was chasing the drug dealers who were poisoning the streets of America; every individual off the street was a small victory in that war. If the victory against the tons of drugs coming into this country involved using evidence linking Noriega to the crime, all the better.

There was never any chance of bringing Noriega in for trial; the considerations that a U.S. attorney would analyze in deciding to threaten to take someone's liberty away did not apply. Noriega was an unpopular figure; linking him to a trial would bring publicity that could lead to convictions and more drug trials. The fact that the indictment mentioned Noriega didn't matter in terms of having to prove the allegations; no one would have to present evidence against him, anyway.[6]

Then Washington, under Abrams at the State Department, disdaining Gregorie's idealism, saw an opportunity. After refusing to cooperate or even listen to his warnings about the extent of cocaine trafficking in the Americas, suddenly Abrams paid attention; the indictment was a perfect foreign policy tool to meet other ends.

Gregorie never was told about how close his investigation into the drug business came to the heart of Iran-Contra. "If that were true, if the government was hiding behind a smokescreen the whole time that I was investigating drugs, and they knew that the men I was interviewing were also working for them, then that would be a major scandal,"

---

[6] John Lawn, DEA administrator when the indictment was issued, testified at a 1988 Senate hearing on narcotics that the document was not backed up by sufficient evidence. Lawn wrote letters praising Noriega for broad help in the drug wars, but testified as a witness at the drug trial that the letters were routine and not significant.

Gregorie said in an interview. "But nobody ever told me that and if that was true, I was kept in the dark."

But Gregorie also never expected his indictment to yield a trial against Noriega and neither did reluctant policy makers in Washington. After the invasion, with the sudden prospect of having Noriega in custody, the drug accusations became a useful—indeed, the only—means of justifying his capture.

By then, Gregorie was out of the U.S. attorney's office. He watched the Noriega trial from the sidelines.

The principal source in his drug investigation, ultimately leading to Noriega's indictment, was Carlton, who turned state's evidence after being captured in Costa Rica and testified before Congress and in intensive debriefings with Gregorie about the drug business. "Floyd was always solid and everything he said always checked out," said Gregorie.

The original blueprint for the Noriega drug conspiracy and most of what is assumed about his guilt is based on the testimony of Carlton. It was taken by all advocates of Noriega's guilt that Carlton told the truth. He had sufficient motivation, however, to be lying about Noriega's relationship to his operations. He was promised a free ticket out of jail, the right to remain in the United States, along with his family and a domestic servant, entry in the Federal Witness Protection Program, continued financing from the U.S. government and retention of his private pilot's license. Carlton had been captured by the United States in Costa Rica on January 18, 1985, for drug trafficking in an operation that included two other key witnesses in the trial—a former Panamanian diplomat and businessman named Ricardo Bilonick and an admitted American marijuana dealer named Steven Kalish. Noriega's G-2 investigators provided evidence that helped in the apprehension of all of these men. The men were operating through a company called DIACSA, a private plane dealership that worked alongside Bilonick's Inair at Paitilla Airport, with two State Department contracts totaling $41,130 to fly humanitarian aid to the Contras.

Carlton said that Noriega threatened him with jail when he brought up the subject of drug trafficking in a conversation in 1982. For reasons that were unclear, he said Noriega suddenly agreed to receive $100,000 for each of four cocaine shipments that Carlton handled. In return, however, Carlton acknowledged under questioning that he

neither informed Noriega about the timing or location of such shipments, nor did he receive Panamanian protection.

But the larger questions about Carlton had not been revealed: that
he was employed by the United States in the Contra arms-smuggling
pipeline and that his activities were known both to Noriega and to the
United States. That connection, blocked from revelation at the drug
trial, made it unlikely that Noriega would choose this known clandestine U.S. operative as his partner in cocaine dealings.

At the trial, Judge Hoeveler angrily blocked attempts by Noriega's
lawyers to delve into Carlton's pro-Contra arms smuggling. Rubino
hit Carlton with a series of questions about his gun-flying activities,
asking if they were ordered by Oliver North. Hoeveler sustained prosecution objections and grew testy as Rubino persisted. "Just stay away
from it," he snapped.

Rubino also produced a tape transcript in which Carlton lashes out
at Noriega for having him imprisoned and seizing his airplane. Carlton
acknowledged the conversation, which took place at the time he was
in U.S. custody testifying before a Senate foreign relations subcommittee.

"Do you remember referring to General Noriega, saying, 'That bas-
tard took my airplane'?" Rubino asked. "Did you say . . . you were
going to 'thank' General Noriega and then start laughing . . . Is not
this your opportunity to get your revenge?"

Carlton appeared before a U.S. Senate subcommittee with a bag over
his head to prevent identification and possible reprisal by drug traffickers. Reprisals or not, the employ of such men in the drug trials of the
1980s was a spectacle that fed the frenzy about how to fight a supposed
drug war. A supposition in the war was the naive notion that men like
Carlton, Bilonick and Noriega's other accusers had turned state's evidence for some purpose higher than getting out of jail. Carlton,
Bilonick and Kalish, like many of the witnesses against Noriega, served
only brief jail terms. U.S. prosecutors measured the testimony of these
felons and thieves, not against the truth, but against whether their versions of events could be contradicted easily. They looked into the limpid
eyes of these trusty prisoners and found what they saw to their liking.

The system left Floyd Carlton with only one logical choice: insert
Noriega's name in his confession of drug dealing and reap the benefits
of the plea bargaining system. Instead of serving a lifetime in jail for his
crimes, Carlton was allowed to keep his drug profits, retained his

pilot's license, won a new identity and a clean slate, hidden somewhere in the United States.

"It's the only way we have to prosecute drug criminals," said Gregorie. "It's an imperfect system, but what do you expect? You're not going to find Boy Scouts to testify against drug traffickers. And you're not necessarily going to have the standard types of evidence. You have to make deals to get testimony from people on the inside."

Gregorie's argument goes on to say that such testimony becomes valid when many such witnesses provide information that coincides on basic facts. And that is precisely where the Noriega prosecution fails.

Carlton's testimony at the trial was surprisingly weak, did not jibe with the testimony of Kalish and Bilonick and was subject to impressive impeachment by the Noriega defense. In the end, his testimony—the underpinning of the original indictment—was an afterthought; the DEA created a new ad hoc case against Noriega. Carlton was only one of twenty-six witnesses at the trial who were felons who won leniency, were paid and kept their drug earnings in return for testifying against Noriega. Most could not testify that they had met Noriega or even had firsthand knowledge of his alleged drug dealing. The trial divided the Drug Enforcement Administration between those tasked with convicting Noriega—"We had no evidence, so we had to do our duty and convict him anyway," one of these agents said—and those who leaked information showing that Noriega had worked with the DEA.[7]

Many of the original witnesses against Noriega were allowed to remain in hiding, because prosecutors and DEA investigators feared their questionable versions could be revealed as lies. Boris Olarte, a convicted marijuana dealer from Colombia, was supposed to testify that he had given Noriega four million dollars for a drug deal. In fact, it was his testimony before a grand jury that created the prosecution theory in the case—that greed had driven Noriega to sign up with the Medellín cartel, demand millions in protection money, then hide his participation in the affair behind his office. But the prosecution realized to its horror that Olarte's testimony was inconsistent with other witnesses'. Olarte, who was arrested by Noriega's anti-narcotics forces and, like Carlton, might have revenge as a motive, could actually sabotage the case by describing the wrong four million dollars delivered at the wrong time by

[7] For a factual account of the trial proceedings, see *The Case Against the General* by Steve Albert (New York: Scribners, 1993). For a complete and well-researched version of the charges against Noriega, see *Our Man in Panama*.

the wrong man. Olarte was allowed to flee to Colombia because of an alleged mistake by a veteran federal agent who had him in custody. The twelve-member jury never found out about Olarte. The prosecution argued successfully to Judge William Hoeveler that Olarte was not germane to the case.

Olarte was not alone in testifying about the four-million-dollar payment to Noriega: Carlton, Kalish, Ricardo Tribaldos and Noriega's former aide, Luis del Cid, all gave conflicting and mutually exclusive accounts of delivering alleged cartel protection money to Noriega.

If, for example, Carlton was delivering relatively small quantities of drugs on behalf of the cartel under Noriega's protection in late 1983 through a clandestine airstrip, why was his business partner paying to ship far greater quantities directly through a Panama City airport, in a much easier operation?

Both Carlton and Bilonick claimed separately that they were responsible for developing Noriega's relationship with the Medellín cartel. They contributed to at least three different explanations of how Noriega allegedly received four million dollars from the Medellín cartel, each contradicting the other. Another version was expected to come from a drug dealer named Ramón Navarro. Navarro died in an unexplained one-car crash in rural Dade County Florida months before the start of the Noriega trial.

Carlos Lehder, a Colombian drug dealer condemned by other U.S. prosecutors as a liar, was brought in to testify against Noriega, even though he had never met him. Gregorie was appalled that Lehder should be brought; Robert Merkle, the U.S. attorney who prosecuted Lehder in Tampa, was livid when he heard a deal had been struck. "This man is an enemy of the United States; he is an unrepentant, pathological liar." Lehder won a secret deal with the government in which he was withdrawn from the maximum-security Marion Federal Penitentiary, along with a vague promise that he might be able to get out of his life sentence. In 1995, Lehder wrote a letter to Hoeveler, threatening to recant on the grounds that the government was reneging on its bargain. After the trial, a juror told a reporter that he had been most impressed by Lehder's testimony.

Another witness, Gabriel Taboada, wrote the judge, also threatening to recant. Several other witnesses have recanted to friends and associates since the 1992 drug trial, saying the information they gave at the trial was based on a script supplied by prosecutors. Their words were shielded by journalistic pledges of keeping material off the record, or by their unwillingness to step forward for fear of continued government harassment.

"The whole case was a fabrication and I know Noriega didn't do what I was asked to testify he did at the drug trial," said one of these witnesses. "I doubt if any of the charges against him are true."

This witness said he was coerced by the government to testify in order to get out of jail. "I have a life, but they still watch me," the witness said.

While Noriega's lawyers were stymied in every attempt to bring up politics at the trial, politics could not be separated from the proceedings. Then U.S. attorney Dexter Lehtinen and Michael Sullivan, the lead prosecutor in the case, were both told by Justice Department officials in the Bush administration that Noriega had to be convicted at all costs. They put out the word to potential witnesses among the prison population that a get-out-of-jail-free option was there for the taking.

In late 1995, as the case moved toward a federal appeals court, Hoeveler was petitioned by the defense to hold a new trial. A key witness in the case, Ricardo Bilonick, had been brought in to testify as a result of bargaining between the U.S. attorney's office and Colombia's Cali cocaine cartel.

A onetime Panamanian diplomat, Bilonick operated an air-transport business in Panama called Inair, which sometimes handled weapons deliveries and other clandestine operations for the CIA. That line of inquiry was censored out of the Noriega trial. But Bilonick admitted that Inair did indeed transport drugs for the Medellín cartel.

Federal prosecutors admitted negotiating with Joel Rosenthal, a former U.S. prosecutor turned indicted lawyer for José Santacruz Londoño, leader of Colombia's Cali drug traffickers, to win Bilonick's testimony. Moreover, they acknowledged the allegation that the Cali cartel may have paid Bilonick $1.25 million to induce him to testify.

In return, the government agreed to recommend leniency in a separate drug case involving Luis Santacruz (Lucho) Echeverri, the half-brother of José Santacruz Londoño, leader of the Cali cartel. With Bilonick's testimony, they bartered eight years off Lucho's twenty-three-year trafficking sentence. Secret negotiations between the U.S. prosecutors in Miami and Joel Rosenthal.

Rosenthal and other Cali representatives landed Bilonick after they went out shopping for a "dynamite witness" who would be a valuable-enough catch to bargain for leniency.

"I believe that you should give Lucho credit if Bilonick comes in and pleads guilty," Rosenthal wrote to then U.S. attorney Myles Malman and his partner in the Noriega case, lead prosecutor Sullivan. "I cannot stress to you how critical it is to this agreement that my client's role and identity be kept secret. He cannot withstand the exposure."

"Remember, the appearance will be that you have made a deal with the Cali cartel to secure the cooperation and specific testimony of a witness against the Medellín cartel," Rosenthal told the prosecutors.

"The conduct of the prosecutors in this case is so reprehensible, so lacking in moral compass, that it nearly defies rational analysis," Noriega's attorney said in a court brief. "Before this case, it would have been inconceivable that our government would enter into a mutual assistance agreement with a criminal organization. Yet the documents now before this Court prove without doubt that the United States Attorney's Office contracted with the Cali cartel for a 'dynamite' witness to be used against General Noriega."

Judge Hoeveler did not concede in public that a fraud had been committed by the prosecution, but he did recognize the seriousness of the charges about winning testimony as a result of using cocaine cartels as a mediator.

"Bilonick's testimony hurt Noriega very badly; so did the testimony of Kalish," Hoeveler said, amplifying on a statement he made at Bilonick's sentencing hearing. "I think by anybody's standards, he was one of the more important witnesses the government presented in the trial of the case, providing some essential connections that were not otherwise provided. . . . Those things were, I am sure, important to the jury."

The problem was that if Bilonick and Carlton worked together and were employed by the Medellín cartel, as they testified, why would Carlton be shipping several hundred pounds of marijuana to the United States via a clandestine airstrip, paying Noriega $100,000 per flight in cartel money, while simultaneously Bilonick was shipping tons of cocaine directly into Panama City's Paitilla Airport, with payments of $500,000 per flight to Noriega?

The answer, said Noriega's defense, was that both men were lying—Carlton, to please the U.S. attorney's office, save his skin and win revenge against Noriega; and Bilonick, because he was paid, and perhaps threatened, by the Cali cartel in return for his testimony.

Judge Hoeveler denied the defense motion for a new trial. He said "the evidence presented at the hearing is troubling," but not serious enough to force a new trial. Privately, Hoeveler told me that he hoped the U.S. 11th Circuit Court of Appeals would rule on the case quickly, believing that ultimately the questions surrounding the Noriega case would and should be handled by the Supreme Court.

Death

I covered the Panamanian elections of 1989, the deteriorating relations with the United States, on through the October coup. On December 20, I was home with my family, preparing for the holidays, when I received a call from a friend in Washington. Our mutual Pentagon source, he said, was telling me to get to Panama immediately, that the U.S. invasion was about to begin.

I had just returned from a long stint in Colombia, where I wrote about the death of Gonzalo Rodríguez Gacha, the notorious don of the Medellín cartel. My later reporting would show that U.S. government advisers participated in the killing of Gacha, although President Bush would later deny any official U.S. role.[8] From my vantage point in Bogotá, I could not fully perceive the drumbeat and rhetoric building against Noriega. It seemed incredible to me that such an attack would actually take place; I did not believe the United States would invade Panama. I refused to take the advice of my source, even though I knew the information was authoritative.

By midnight, I knew I was wrong. I had to wait two long days before a journalists' charter could fly to Panama to cover the invasion. Our Lockheed 1011 jet was hit by rifle fire from snipers below as it landed at Howard Air Force Base in the Canal Zone.

The U.S. military would not allow journalists to venture out of their perimeter and held the two hundred–odd reporters on that flight in protective custody overnight before releasing us. The next morning,

[8] "U.S. Got Gacha" by Peter Eisner and Knut Royce, *Newsday*, May 4, 1990, p. 1.

the scope of the invasion was clear. Despite sniper fire and isolated skir-mishes, the Americans had applied massive force that left the country devastated and the Panamanian Defense Forces decimated. In Cho-rrillo, the slum that surrounded the Panamanian Defense Forces head-quarters, there was only charred wreckage from a fierce firefight that destroyed a neighborhood of shanty dwellings. The Americans said few civilians died, hardly any of them in Chorrillo. But some civilians claimed they trampled over dead bodies to flee for their lives that night. A blasted vehicle contained the carbonized remains of a human being, the body almost melted by whatever had attacked him.

Wherever there was death or destruction, the U.S. military assured reporters that it had been caused by Noriega's men or by Dignity Bat-talions, whom Noriega described as civil defense but the Americans dismissed as thugs. This carbonized body was that of a member of the Dignity Battalions, we were told, although I doubt any identification was possible or had even been attempted. Using the words "Dignity Battalion," I assumed, justified the remains being there, making the death a little more acceptable.

To find out more about the death, I went to the central city morgue at Santo Tomás Hospital. It was Christmas Eve. Small groups of peo-ple, mostly women, huddled outside the morgue, oppressed by the fetid smell of death in the tropical sun. They wailed and sobbed, hold-ing handkerchiefs to their mouths as they tiptoed around pools of blood to enter the rank-smelling morgue and search through the bod-ies. The odor of death in the tropical heat would linger with them.

One of the women was looking for her brother, a navy lieutenant who had left home the night of the invasion and had not been seen since. She stood about fifty paces from the entrance to the morgue, a cement ramp-way surrounded by tropical contrasts—palms, bright flowers, casting oc-casional shadows across the entranceway. She waited for nothing but the courage to summon up a move toward the door. Her whimpering breath mingled with the sounds of others, whispering, turning away from the wind, which carried the terrible scent on the breeze, on to the city and the Pacific Ocean, where its essence was never quite gone.

A hospital official checked a list; her brother was not on it. "Go home before you look here; wait another day," the official told her.

The sun slipped intermittently behind clouds that dimmed the trop-ical heat. The shade was good, but by afternoon, when the sun was bright again, the stench was overpowering.

Her brother had come home on December 20, 1989, the Wednesday afternoon of the U.S. invasion, to the family house in a nice section of the humble San Miguelito district and stayed—for a while. He spoke a bit, but in the hours before it became clear that Noriega was out he had kept mostly to himself, pacing in the yard or in the small living room. Then he had slipped away from home to go fight the Americans. The family feared he would now be one of the nameless dead, so she and her sister had come together to the morgue.

In the office, blessedly, air conditioners relieved the ever-present smell. There was a small Christmas tree on the desk, a poster reminding Panamanians to make cornea donations to the eye bank, and a prayer: "Lord, discover my solitude that I may later work with Thee for the salvation of the world."

"Can we see the list of bodies brought in since Friday?" the older of the sisters said, placing a paper towel over her nose as she approached an orderly. "Go to the chapel tomorrow," the worker said. "They will have pictures of the dead from all over the city." It was a relief for the sister that she would not have to enter; the seventy bodies had been piled on top of one another, and trying to identify each one was a grisly task.

As she left the building, she glanced left and saw a body wrapped in embroidered cloth. "How do people work here?" she asked softly, half to herself. "How can this be happening?"

Standing nearby was another woman, a stranger seeking solace and giving some. Her daughter had been killed by a sniper's bullet at a downtown hotel. She had come to recover the body. "She was twenty-five years old, so young," the woman said, struggling to speak. "Bullets were flying everywhere. And one came through the window and got her here." She placed an index finger in the furrow of her brow.

A doctor came along with another list of the dead. "What is this list?" someone asked. "It is the dead we have registered here," said the doctor. It contained the names of more than one hundred people who had died in downtown Panama City in the seventy-two hours since the December 20 invasion of Panama. "But please understand," the doctor said, grasping my arm. "This does not include the babies and children. You must understand me." He then walked hurriedly away, ignoring a request that he explain what that meant.

The Americans and the Panamanians who took power when Noriega was overthrown said 326 Panamanians were killed. A doctor at the

American Gorgas Hospital in the old Canal Zone said the number was impossibly low. The number and the reality had become a political affair—some declaring the low figure, some declaring ten times more deaths, but none fully justifying their claims.

"It is not the quantity of the dead," said Juan Mendez, the executive director of the Washington-based independent human rights organization, Americas Watch, when asked how he would recommend solving the question of how many people died. "It is a question of why anyone had to die at all."[9]

While Noriega stood on a promontory and watched the firefight in Panama City on the first night of the invasion, Roberto Miller Saldana lay dying. Miller Saldana and four fellow transit policemen were standing at a small highway guard post near Howard air base when the first wave of U.S. troops arrived. Miller Saldana was one of the three thousand or four thousand members of Noriega's Panamanian Defense Forces who was no soldier at all. Miller Saldana was a cop on the beat.

When the Americans began pouring out of the U.S. base, Miller Saldana and his friends on duty nearby started to run. He didn't make it; the others did. So the likely first casualty of the U.S. invasion of Panama was a Panamanian policeman shot in the back. His cousin, Milsa de Hastings, told about Miller's life between gagging breaths outside the morgue. It was her grim task to identify Roberto's body.

"He was a transit cop—he wouldn't fight, he wouldn't resist, all he had was a pistol. One of his friends called us—they made it, he was the only one that didn't. I guess he just didn't run as fast as the others."

When Miller Saldana's wife, cousin and brother-in-law, Walter Valenzuela, arrived at the hospital, security was tight. U.S. soldiers wearing camouflage gear and greasepaint checked identification of those entering and exiting the grounds. There was confusion about where to receive information on the dead. The information desk had

[9] Americas Watch, analyzing the Panama and Gulf Wars, said, "In a little over a year, the United States has engaged in two wars, and in both of them it has refused to comply with important humanitarian obligations. It is a matter of great concern to us that military triumphalism appears to be inhibiting the American public from examining this troublesome trend." *News From Americas Watch*, April 7, 1991, p. 14.

ceased reading out the list of names, and anxious people were unsure where to go to search for missing family members.

Finally they were allowed to walk into the makeshift morgue. They found the ghastly scene of bodies splayed upon bodies, blood congealing on the floor and splattered on the walls, flies getting caught as they flicked at the sticky red pools. After stepping around the room, they found a tag with his name and looked over the remains. Walter walked back from the morgue. "It was him, I got a good look," Valenzuela said. "There were two bullet holes in his back."

On a tour of Panama City, I observed that the damage was extensive. The key military buildings of the Panamanian military were gutted. The headquarters of the National Investigative Police, the DENI, was a shell. Along city streets, fires burned, vigilantes bullied people and anarchy was evident. Every road was blockaded by citizens protecting their property and by U.S. soldiers, who patrolled only strategic checkpoints.

Later, the U.S. military commander, General Maxwell Thurman, would face criticism for failing to protect Panamanian civilians. Americas Watch said the United States violated its obligations under the Geneva Conventions. "With respect to the United States forces, our report concluded that the tactics and weapons utilized resulted in an inordinate number of civilian victims, in violation of specific obligations under the Geneva Conventions. The attack on El Chorrillo, and a similar attack in an urban area of Colón, were conducted without prior warning to civilians, even though the outcome of the attack would not have been effected by such a warning. Under the Geneva Conventions, attacking forces are under a permanent duty to minimize harm to civilians. We concluded that the command of the invasion forces violated that rule."[10]

One young man who fought in the Panama war was a nineteen-year-old American paratrooper named Manny, a Hispanic kid from Arizona. I met with Manny at Fort Bragg, NC, interviewing him on condition I not use his full name. The experience of the Panama in-

[10] News From Americas Watch, April 7, 1991, p. 10.

vasion left emotional scars; he saw his life running an endless news-reel in the seven seconds it took to jump from a U.S. Air Force C-130 transport into the brief but confusingly fierce battle at Río Hato airfield.

It was now the stuff of his recurrent nightmare: fires were blazing below him in the darkness; as the land came up beneath him, and amid the sparks of gunfire and explosions, he had the comforting feeling that it would all be quick, that death would be rapid and numbing.

Suddenly there was gunfire and blood all around—four people dead on the highway. And in the transition from sleep to consciousness, he realized again that it was no dream. It was the invasion of Panama, and he was the killer.

"I look back at Panama, and I think sometimes that I'm too sensitive, maybe too nice for the job. I was always taught that human life was sacred. To me, the hardest thing is having to deal with the fact that I took another life—a couple of them. . . . It bothers me to see these guys [who have never seen war]. It doesn't faze them at all."

Manny's one-night war, the night of the Panama invasion on December 20, 1989, went far beyond anything he could have prepared for. Manny went through hell that night.

When the jump was over, he was stuck with tons of equipment on his back, a turtle rolled over on its shell. He struggled free, marveling at being alive, and ran till he found some other men.

They mounted a roadblock on the Pan-American Highway, which cuts straight across the Río Hato airstrip. "We had been told to shoot at anything that moved. And all of a sudden a car came through. It jumped the road parallel to the runway we were guarding. They wouldn't stop, so we lit the car up right there on the runway. And we didn't know exactly who was in it. But since I spoke Spanish and all, I had the lovely job to see what we had gotten. We were thinking that they might have been Machos del Monte, but they weren't. Right there—*boom, boom, boom, boom*—all four of them bought it."

Manny and his companions tried to tell themselves that maybe these were spies or special forces operatives, but the truth was evident. They were two teenage couples out on a date.

"There was a lot of blood. . . . Not a pleasant sight, not a pleasant sight at all. But what are you going to do? If you would have hesitated, with my luck, it would have been a carload of heavily armed infantry types who would have handed the rest of those guys up. I couldn't see myself having to deal with the fact that because of my hesitation four or five good American boys died.

"I'd like to go back to Panama, maybe with my father, take a look in other circumstances—tell the people that I didn't go down there to kill Panamanians, not by any stretch of the imagination. I'd like to do that."

There was disagreement about exactly what happened at Río Hato. U.S. spokesmen said there was fierce fighting, but Panamanian civilians said the attack was a one-sided assault by U.S. troops, with only a minimal response from Panamanian fighters, mostly in the first moments as they saw paratroopers landing against the moonlit sky.

After that, they said, most of the Panamanians and students at the school ran off into the bushes and kept running. Apparently a few Panamanian soldiers stayed around for a day or two, taking occasional potshots or directing mortars at moving targets.

A U.S. intelligence source in Panama agreed that there was little resistance after the parachute landing at Río Hato. "There was some firing at first, but there really wasn't much of a fight," the source said. "They either surrendered or mostly fled to the hills."

One of the witnesses to the attack was Javier, a thirty-nine-year-old civilian teacher at the air base. The teacher said that after he was captured, he saw one student whose intestines were split open by a horizontal burst of automatic weapon fire. That student, he said, appeared gravely injured. He said he also saw several students with lesser bullet wounds. He overheard Americans talking about their losses. "They said six had died," he said. He had seen two dead paratroopers.

A special forces soldier gave a tour of the quarters of the officer in charge of the military academy. It was evident that someone had burst into the room, tossed in a grenade and fired a headboard volley of machine-gun fire at the major. Pieces of brain were scattered in pools on the floor. I was told that several students were killed and perhaps these were the remains of one of them.

An American soldier stood outside and spoke to me when no one else was around. "When do you think Bush will be satisfied with what he's done and let us go home?" he asked.

U.S. military planners said they came to Río Hato highly armed—with Army Ranger paratroopers, helicopters and special forces units—

because their aim was to carry out a quick operation inflicting the fewest casualties and suffering the fewest losses possible. Río Hato was considered critical to the United States because it was home to two units of the Panamanian Defense Forces considered to be among the most loyal to General Manuel Antonio Noriega.

"What they wanted was a coup de main [overwhelming shattering blow] and they put all the force in there and the equipment," said a high-ranking military source in the U.S. Southern Command in Panama.

Descriptions of the operation at Río Hato from both Panamanian and U.S. sources show that the poorly trained Panamanian Defense Forces were totally unequipped for the sophisticated attack launched by the United States.

Panama seemed a proving ground for American military mobilization. It marked the debut of the multibillion-dollar Stealth bomber in combat, fighting an enemy that had no radar to be fooled by its supposedly low profile, no planes or rockets with which to challenge its domination of the airways. The debut was not a glowing success: two bombs dropped and both missed the airstrip. One was a dud, leaving a crater near a barracks; the other fell on a village about a quarter of a mile away.

"You could probably do without those [Stealth bombers]," said an officer at the U.S. Southern Command. "That was probably a political decision. Somebody had to prove it could at least fly."

Río Hato, which served as a World War II air corps staging point for the United States, had no home air fleet. In fact, Panama had no fighter planes at all and its few helicopters and small plane fleet were immobilized in Panama City moments after the U.S. invasion began in the early morning hours of December 20.

As evidence of the rudimentary, failed effort to protect the base, a U.S. infantryman who gave a tour of the battle site showed an overturned Panamanian personnel carrier in a ditch with an unused anti-tank weapon, probably the highest-power weapon available to the Panamanians.

"We don't know how it got there; maybe they were trying to get away and it flipped, but it wasn't hit," he said. Two days earlier, he said, they found a boot with part of a leg still in it in the cab of the vehicle.

A witness to the assault at Río Hato was visibly shaking when a tall American man approached him. Eyes to the ground, he would not speak. "Don't worry," the teacher was telling Baltasar, a twenty-year-old student who asked that his last name not be used. "He's an American, but he's a newspaper reporter. He won't hurt you."

Baltasar, who lived with his family in a bullet-scarred house in a civilian settlement about a mile from the Río Hato base entrance, said he saw many civilian injuries that night.

"I saw cars blasted," he said, pointing to the Pan American Highway, several yards from his house. "I saw them grab one guy a few days ago on his bicycle and throw him to the ground. . . . The Americans were just shooting at anyone on the road, taking prisoners and taking control of all the cars."

After the attack, Baltasar was taken with all the other males of Río Hato and neighboring towns to a detention center on the base. He was released after several days and returned to the ruins of his neighborhood.

"The soldiers came back afterwards, and they deactivated nine mines on this side of the fence," he said. "But on the side you are on, they didn't remove any mines; they didn't tell us where they are. They just told us to walk where we have already walked."

This was the Panama I saw during and after the U.S. invasion: no enemies among the barefoot poor folk huddled in tents behind barbed wire after their houses were destroyed; there was no guerrilla war, no high-and-mighty international agenda in Panama. I saw suffering and disgrace and I was embarrassed by the fear I invoked because I was from the nation of the conquerors.

Noriega's decline and fall, the U.S. invasion of Panama, the Noriega drug trial and conviction have been transcended, perhaps, by events of greater specific weight on the scales of world history. But for those who lived through the invasion of Panama, the death and destruction they suffered are universal. And for journalism, Panama stands apart as a microcosm of what can go wrong, a dismal lesson in how the resident wisdom can guide the course of events and misguide an understanding of what happened.

"There never was a just [war], never an honorable one on the part of the instigator of the war," Mark Twain wrote. ". . . statesmen will invent cheap lies putting the blame upon the nation that is attacked; and every man will be glad of those conscience-soothing falsities . . . and thus he will by and by convince himself that the war is just and will thank God for the better sleep he enjoys after this process of grotesque self-deception."

The death, destruction and injustice wrought in the name of fighting Noriega—and the lies surrounding that enterprise—were threats to the basic American principles of democracy. That will not change until history is repaired, until self-deception is replaced by common sense and chauvinism is erased by reality. My effort was to go beyond the obvious and the already written, to show that behind the complacent sense that nothing went wrong, much to the contrary, U.S. policy toward Panama in the 1980s was on an ignorant, twisted and deadly course.

Nothing makes a soldier so angry and can be so unfair as the suggestion that he is callous about having to kill; if he is balanced, a soldier hates to kill. He kills because he is so trained and so ordered. He does so with faith in his country, whatever country, and with anguish in his heart.

Soldiers were ordered to kill in Panama and they did so after being told that they had to rescue a country from the clamp of a cruel, depraved dictator; once they acted, the people of their country marched lockstep behind them.

It was left for the Panamanians and the few observers of that attack to ask how it could have happened. Mostly, the event receded into a vague history, forgotten and cast aside. But this was the United States of America, under whose laws the president and the Senate by a two-thirds vote in 1977 pledged to never again interfere in the internal affairs of Panama—Panama, a creation of Teddy Roosevelt; Panama, the prototype of Manifest Destiny and the Monroe Doctrine.

The signing of the Panama Canal Treaty was a watershed in relations with Latin America; a decided turn away from past conduct and intended to establish a new relationship of equality not only with Panama, but also with all of the hemisphere. This was so much the case that the United States under President Carter invited the other countries of the hemisphere to sign the Panama Neutrality Treaty to cement a new regional partnership based on sovereignty and mutual respect.

To say that the situation on December 20, 1989, was so extraordinary that Noriega, whatever he did, was worse than Pinochet or Stroessner or any other dictator in Latin America or that Panama deserved what it received is to divert attention from the essential truth: the United States under George Bush invaded Panama because he had the power and was able to do so to meet his own agenda. Bush needed no declaration of war and any justification would do; he was convinced and self-deceiving in his decision; the consequences and the lives were beyond his consideration.

The shambles of U.S. actions and responsibility in Panama were the result of the actions of rigid and ruthless ideologues; Noriega was the target, but the responsibility lies with a country whose citizens should not be so complacent as to fall for the rhetoric. At the very least, the consequences must be analyzed, the impact must be seen and the culprits must be revealed for the sake of history.

APPENDIX I
The Conquest of Panama

Vasco Núñez de Balboa had already traveled some distance into the lands of the isthmus when upon this unforeseen journey he arrived at an area of peaceful Indians, living in the confluence of two great and navigable lowland rivers. The rivers were connected to each other by the laws of ebb and flow. The Spaniards observed that when the tides receded, the waters withdrew in a raging torrent toward the sea. The Indians told the conquerors that the river, which they called the Tuira, ran its course "to the great salty seas," something that made no sense at all to Balboa's troops. But when the tide rose, seawater ran upstream into the Tuira. This unique ebb and flow of the tides between the two mighty rivers can be seen still where the Spaniards built the fortress of Yaviza, a staging point for their continuing incursion into what would become known as Panama.

Yaviza was the same name the Spaniards gave to the natives, whom they heard shout excitedly, when the tide came in and they ran to fill their cauldrons with fresh water while they could, "*Yavi . . . za!*, *Yavi . . . za!*"—"The water is coming, the water is coming."

It was from this fort on the shores of the Río Chucunaque, which was fed by the waters of the Chico, which in turn ran into the greatest and most voluminous river of Darien, the Tuira, that Balboa set sail in

1511 for the west coast of Panama. The settlement was already known by the name Santa María de la Antigua del Darien.

Here, in an open field, in the shadow of the venerable walls, with the echoes of the river, by the ancient and forgotten first Spanish fortress on the isthmus, José del Carmen Mejía came as a teacher. His students were the people who lived nearby and he taught them no matter their age or previous education. Elsa and Alberto Ayala were there; so was Aida Moreno. Also sitting in the shade of the fortress were Fernando and Elicer Alguero; Manuel Aguirre; Chichi, Edy and Yolanda Lay; Teresa, Rafael and Hilario Mejía; Matías Ayala and one more—me, in the arms of my mother, María Felix Moreno Mejía. Dozens of young people, Choco Indians and others came to be educated by my great-uncle José del Carmen, who was the leader and culture advocate for the entire area, as well as a protector of the Indians.

Today there is still a humble reminder of those lessons—the school in Yaviza bears the name of José del Carmen Mejía, the little man of Darien. He was of Spanish ancestry, a descendant of Rafael Mejía and Fernando Mejía, who respectively married Ramona Peralta and Petra Morales, the most immediate relatives I had on my mother's side.

The Spanish conquerors hugged the northwestern coast of the Gulf of Uraba and advanced eastward along the islands of San Blas. The area is located above the Caserio Careta, later known as Acla, in the Bay of Caledonia. These were said to be the lands of Chief Careta, who surrendered to the power of the invaders. It was here, so the legend goes, that Careta showered Balboa with gifts, including his own daughter, Princess Anayansi, in a gesture of peace and friendship.

The Spaniards obtained reinforcements here and advanced farther to the northwest, unto the realm of the neighboring Chief Poncha, on the other side of the dividing mountain range. Faced with the presence of such supernatural beings of resplendent helmets and armaments, Poncha and his tribe fled without a fight. Now controlling the territory of Poncha, they marched to the southeast, to the lands of Chief Comagre, who was also subjugated. This broad conquest extended Balboa's control from San Blas to the upper and middle portions of the Chucunaque River. It was there in the lands of Comagre, at the foot of the mountains, on his western flank, gazing southward, that Balboa first saw those great salty seas mentioned by the Indians at Yaviza.

Historic narrative, sprinkled with legend, says that the Spanish, upon seeing the objects of gold and nuggets that had been given to them, raised so much commotion that in the excitement they began to fight among themselves. Gazing upon this spectacle, Panquiaco, the son of Chief Comagre, was both disgusted and surprised. "Why do you fight for such meaningless things given to you by my father?" he called to them, mockingly. "If you follow this path, after a quarter moon, you will find an immense expanse of saltwater, whose currents will carry you to a great land with an even greater chief, where you will find such stones lying all about." The route described by Panquiaco ends at the empire of Tihuantisurgo of the Incas, the children of the sun of Peru.

Balboa immediately understood. How could he get there? he asked. He sought information that he could transfer to his charts and maps— features of the land, rivers, valleys, soil types, vegetation, types of mountains, the chiefs in the area and the characteristics of their warriors, wealth, the women, the animals that inhabited the region.

With all this local intelligence, he asked the chief for help to undertake a journey that had become the dream of his very existence.

The number of men chosen to go with him on his quest was estimated to be one thousand. Balboa, excited with the greed for gold and for conquering new lands and kingdoms, returned to the territory of Careta and ordered his ships to set sail for Santa María to prepare for the great adventure.

With singular dedication of time and energy, all was swiftly prepared for their departure: a sailing vessel with two masts, twelve canoes, two hundred Spanish soldiers, a large number of Indians and a pack of hounds, among them the legendary Leoncico, which Balboa had brought from Spain.

The logistics completed, they weighed anchor on September 1, 1513, from Santa María. The ship's log indicates that they fought a headwind, arriving at the village of Careta on Sunday, September 4. They tied up the boat and secured its lines and placed the canoes on shore Indian style, upside down.

On Tuesday, September 6, they weighed anchor again and entered the vast unknown saltwater sea, which was the route toward the empire where gold could be found everywhere among the rocks.

They sailed away from the dominion of Careta, crossed over the dividing hills and continued on their way to Acla-Paso Caledonia, arriving once again in the land of Poncha, who on September 13 paid homage to Balboa. Balboa relaxed for a week in the hammock of the submissive chief. On the twentieth, he arrived in the lands of Comagre. From there he moved onward, already supplied with food, soldiers, spotters, carriers and guides, arriving at Chucunaque by way of Subcuti. Learning to make the type of raft built by the Indians and following their teaching, Balboa found the patience to wait for the cycle of high water to subside, to cast the rafts into the water at a 45-degree angle needed to make the other shore.

Once on the other shore, they advanced over the lowlands, flooded by the waters of the Chucunaque, which constantly overflows its banks. There were expansive lagoons formed all along the shore, with vegetation that they had never seen before.

The heroic pace of the conquerors, however, was under assault by implacable foes that battered the demigods from across the seas. The enemies were diarrhea, fever, mosquitoes, mange, ticks and insects of the jungle, the same things that attacked Felipe González centuries later on his visit to Panama. They struggled with the closed jungle, mysterious, indomitable; the permanent torrential downpours; damp, rotting clothing; the choking cough of musty heat; mud; poisonous vines. Nevertheless, the obsession with the road to the New World, toward the Empire of the Sun, drew Balboa on like a being possessed, hypnotized, pushing his soldiers on like a seer.

They entered into another area of unknown natives, who attacked the decimated caravan, burdened by the relentless downpours of September, the nights at candlelight awaiting a surprise attack by the Indians or wild animals, and the floods cascading down from the mountains.

Finally they reached the peaceful waters of the River Sabana, where Chief Quarequa and his indomitable warriors awaited them. Many Indians fell in the battle that followed, but Balboa's men finally subjugated the chief and his tribe. There on the River Sabana, which overflows its banks to nourish the mangroves, the poet José Santos Chocano was inspired to write this verse:

> . . . A horse came first
> Into the torrid mangroves
> when Balboa's throng rode in
> awakening the sleepy solitude,

*hinting beyond at
the Pacific Ocean, as
blasts of air brought the salty
spray to their senses.*

They camped on the river shore. Before the sun emerged over the blackness of the breaking dawn, Balboa, like an Olympian god, his eyes rolling with anticipation, shouted, "Up and onward."

As the hour approached noon, they came to the foot of the Arracuyala mountains and prepared for the ascent. It was a tortuous advance before they came to the highest plateau, where they rested as they contemplated the way upward. Balboa advanced with his men, lances pointed toward the peak. The conquerors were approaching the highest summit of Guayabito; from there, looking down upon the New World from a point measured as 100,200 paces by Fonseca the mapmaker, one could see a calm, utterly peaceful bay shaped like a horseshoe, glimmering in the midday sun.

The human eye was lost on the boundless surface of its immensity, sparkling with every possible shade of blue. That was the view to the south-southeast. These were the mighty salt waters whose currents would carry them to the Empire of Gold.

It was the South Sea. Spellbound, Balboa ordered his troops to ascend, and all of them, before the sight of the brilliant, silent sea, shouted, crossed themselves, fell to their knees, kissing the earth and raising their prayers to God for having led them to this happy end to their journey.

The ship's log registers the day as September 25, 1513, from the hill of Guayabito, Sabana plains; there, eighty soldiers of the Spanish crown, with an unknown quantity of Indians under the visionary command of Captain Vasco Núñez de Balboa, having come from the Atlantic and crossed the isthmus, discovered a new ocean, the Pacific. They had traced a route that 390 years later, in 1903, would become the crossroads of a nation.

APPENDIX II
A History of Intervention

Balboa was only the first of many conquerors. The Americans occupied Panama fourteen times over more than one hundred years, with many of the same kinds of extrajudicial proceedings and extensions beyond the limits of diplomatic and international law that characterized the 1989 invasion.

On June 22, 1856, for example, an event took place that became known as the Watermelon Incident, a great riot in the capital that left dozens killed and more than fifty wounded. It all began as the result of a dispute between an American and a Panamanian fruit vendor on the street. It was the first case in which a series of events led to diplomatic, military and economic reprisals by the United States. The United States sent a naval force to the isthmus, which anchored offshore while U.S. officials tried to pressure Panama (then known as New Granada) to admit that it was the only party responsible for the chain of events that led to the riot. On September 19, 160 sailors landed in the capital, seizing control of the railroad station for three days before leaving. Not giving up, the United States then sought to force the government to turn over sovereignty of all the islands in Panama Bay to U.S. control as compensation for the Watermelon Incident, as well as all control of the Panama Railroad Company. In the end, the United States did in fact oblige the government of New Granada to pay compensation for the incident.

There were other incidents in 1860, 1865, 1868 and 1873, all involving U.S. imposition of its naval forces on the isthmus. On September 27, 1860, the United States invaded Panamanian territory and interfered in its affairs. The event was the result of a public disturbance, after a domestic political demonstration. U.S. troops under the control of Commodore Porter came onshore from the USS *St. Mary* and occupied Panama City for eleven days.

On March 9, 1865, there was another case of U.S. intervention following a political uprising against the government of New Granada staged by Gil Colunge, a Panamanian patriot; U.S. marines, this time under the command of Captain Middleton, again disembarked from the same vessel and occupied the capital. As a result of that incident, Panamanians memorialized the saying, "I will not sell out my country." On April 7, 1868, U.S. marines disembarked once more, occupying Colón for four days. On September 24, 1873, marines occupied Panama City until October 6; the United States said that U.S. interests had to be protected on the isthmus, after supposed threats by a series of domestic political disturbances.

On January 18, 1885, the United States sent an invasionary force to Colón, commanded by Captain Lewis Clark. The United States had been asked to intervene by General Ramón Santo Domingo Vila, president of the federal state of Panama. His aim was to suppress a separatist movement opposed to the Colombian dictatorial government of Rafael Núñez. In the course of putting down the uprising, U.S. authorities hanged a rebel leader, General Pedro Prestán Colón.

On April 15 of the same year, U.S. forces from the USS *Acapulco* seized control of the Panama railroad from the Atlantic to the Pacific. Later the same month, the U.S. consul in Panama called for a military occupation of Panama to deal with rebel uprisings.

And then in 1900, there was another war and another invasion, with an interesting sidelight. It was known as the Thousand Day War and the Panamanian military leader was one General Manuel Antonio Noriega, my ancestor and the man after whom I am named. In the course of the war, the United States again took control of the railway line. In September 1902, U.S. forces led by Admiral Silas Casey invaded and occupied the ports of Panama and Colón for two months. There were a series of other actions, all leading up to the original Panama Canal Treaty. On May 15, 1903, U.S. forces from the USS *Wisconsin* seized and killed General Victoriano Lorenzo, leader of the popular militias for Panamanian independence. It was an attempt to eliminate a leader considered by the United States to be an obstructionist to their expansionist goals. On November 2, 1903, U.S. forces landed in Colón in a surprise raid designed by the administration of Theodore Roosevelt to supplant Colombian authority in Panama with an independent state. Behind the scenes was a Frenchman named Philippe Bunau-Varilla, who decided Panama would be an independent state without so much as waiting for a reaction from the parties really involved, Colombia and Panama. Panamanian independence was declared on November 3, separating it from Colombia. Panama had been part of Colombia ever since its independence from Spain following the War of Ayacucho, led by Simón Bolívar in 1824. Bunau-Varilla signed the treaty on behalf of Panama, although he was not Panamanian, along with William Nelson Cromwell, an American lobbyist working on the canal project. It was an early case of Panama's oligarchy submitting to U.S. interests to further their own economic interests. Independence came without so much as contacting Colombian authorities and by disregarding the 1846 Cipriano-Bidlack Treaty with Colombia, in which the United States guaranteed the "perfect neutrality" of the isthmus along with Colombian sovereignty.

On November 5, the USS *Dixie* arrived at Colón to reinforce the USS *Nashville*, which had been on station to protect the separatist state. Thus, the United States, via an invasion and occupation, enforced de facto Panamanian independence from Colombia. On November 18, the new de facto state was given its first president, Manuel Amador Guerrero, with the full support of the Americans. At the same time, the Hay–Bunau-Varilla treaty was signed, legalizing U.S. military intervention in the isthmus and placing the sovereignty of the Panamanian republic under its virtual control. On December 2, 1903, a provisional Panamanian government junta ratified the treaty, another act of U.S. intervention. Ratification of the treaty meant the virtual sale for posterity of the isthmus to U.S. control. On January 15, 1904 a constitutional convention created the first law of the new republic: the right and privilege of the United States to intervene militarily in Panama.

From November 14 to 18, 1904, the United States plotted against the commander of Panama's army, General Esteban Huerta, who sought to overthrow President Amador Guerrero and supplant U.S. forces. Guerrero became the scapegoat in a policy developed by the United States to convince the Panamanian oligarchy that there was no need for a homegrown army, that the Panamanian military was inherently corrupt and that they would be a permanent threat to civilian politics. Complying with U.S. demands, the Panamanian government signed a proclamation to disband the army.

Throughout the twentieth century, the United States has seen Panama as so strategically important that it never worried about or considered Panamanian sovereignty in establishing its political goals.

APPENDIX III
Recollections of
Professor Alberto Ayala Moreno[1]

The teacher José del Carmen Mejía was the first cousin of my maternal grandmother, Narcisa Mejía, who was married to Daniel Moreno, an adventurous man who had disappeared from family life, submerging himself in the whirlpool of the search for gold, the latex of the rubber tree and the harvest of sarsaparilla root, which grew in abundance in the jungle of the province of Darien and established itself in the richness of the fountain of natural resources in the region at the time. This teacher Mejía, with great social sensitivity, had elevated the cultural level of the area, improvising classes in the open air for children and adults and especially for the Choco Indians, who were accustomed to "giving away" their small children.

José del Carmen Mejía promoted the humanitarian and proper adoption of abandoned Choco children. I remember that our family had adopted a boy named Hernán, whom we treated as a brother.

María Felix Moreno Mejía had arrived, at a very young age, from Yaviza (El Darien) to the capital of Panama, and she worked in the industrial factory of the old French Bazaar, making clothes for men, in

---

[1] Alberto Ayala is a professor of education. A graduate of the University of Panama, he is the author of children's stories and educational material.

front of the Santa Ana Park. It was there that María Felix met Ricaurte Tomás Noriega, who was a public accountant for the governmental administration of the internal revenue. Noriega had been married twice and he had four adolescent children, three from the first marriage and one from the second. From this man, she became pregnant and gave birth to Manuel Antonio.

María Felix, a very attractive, good-natured woman, who had been queen of her company's celebration in the village of Yaviza, in commemoration of the patron San Jose on the nineteenth of March, accepted her role as a single mother.

Her family members tell the story that she was so happy and such a dancer that even being pregnant, about to give birth, she enjoyed the carnival; and, on that Sunday, watching the parade of floats and marching bands, she had to be rushed by emergency with the pain of contractions to the Hospital Santo Tomás, where she gave birth that same day in the maternity ward. Afterward, she left for El Darien, with her son Manuel Antonio, to attend to her mother, Narcisa, who was very sick and alone because her husband, Daniel, had disappeared into the jungle looking for gold, the rubber tree and the sarsaparilla.

Upon the death of her mother, María Felix fell ill from the punishment of the jungle region, malaria, which left her with tuberculosis. In order to avoid her son contracting the disease and by order of her doctor, she delivered him to the guardianship of her intimate friend and godmother, the teacher Luisa Sánchez, who afterward was transferred to the capital city and took the son of María Felix.

The teacher Luisa, a single woman, dedicated to her role as an educator, included the son of María Felix in her first-grade class, where he passed all of the regular material even though he was not yet of school age.

Manuel Antonio's mother died without him ever seeing her or knowing her love. Later on, with the authorization of his father, Ricaurte, his aunt Regina Moreno claimed custody of Tony Noriega. He was living in the same area as the public market, on the shore of the beautiful and historic bay of Panama, in the building at 27 North Avenue, above the construction company Ávila on the "hill to the presidency" adjacent to the January Second Plaza.

At 27 North Avenue we lived through the years of primary school and the years of secondary school in the cradle of Panamanian nationalism, the National Institute, called, with pride, the Nest of Eagles. There, in the top floor of the building at No. 27, stayed eight families in small apartments. Most were married couples who gave shelter to students that came from the provinces to study in the secondary schools in the capital. The top floor seemed like the busy honeycomb of a beehive when school let out, with the different colors of the uniforms of the boys and girls. In one of these rooms, Manuel Antonio was under the strictly ordered guidance of his aunt Regina Moreno de Delgado, whom he lived with, along with her husband, José, and his two cousins José Alcides and Yolanda Estela.

I, Alberto Ayala, the narrator of these events, lived with my mother, Flora Moreno Mejía, and my sister, Elsa America Ayala, in the adjacent apartment. The daily life of young students was common for all the residents of the neighborhood. That is, go to school, and then study together or separately in their rooms, or in the open spaces of the public areas such as the long, wide balconies that overlooked North Avenue and Thirteenth Street, which led to the old Secret Police.

The recreational games were on Saturdays and Sundays in the open spaces on the streets of the January Second Plaza, the Presidency of the Republic, the Plaza of France or in the areas used for skating or playing ball, or the beaches of Santo Domingo for swimming.

Since José Delgado was chief mechanic of Lefebre, a coastal trading company, Manuel Antonio and his cousin José Alcides learned about the ports of the Pacific Coast and the routes of the trading ships. Their school vacations were spent traveling from the ports of El Darien to the port of Pedregal in Chiriquí, passing by Mensabe and Guarare in the central provinces. They also spent seasons on the island of Taboga, where José Delgado came from with his enormous family.

These trips on board the trading ships developed in the boys culture and experience, not only from seeing the different regions and customs of the country, but also from hearing the stories and tales of the sailors on the ship during the two or three days and nights of sailing.

APPENDIX IV
Commentary by
Tomás A. Noriega Méndez[1]

My father, Don Ricaurte Tomás Noriega Vásquez, a certified public accountant, was first married to Doña Clotilde Méndez Uriño, the mother of Júlio Octavio Noriega Méndez, a civil engineer; Rubén Noriega Méndez, a pharmacist; and me, his first-born son. When Doña Clotilde died, Don Ricaurte married Doña Lavinia Hurtado, the mother of our brother, Dr. Luis Carlos Noriega Hurtado. His other child, Manuel Antonio Noriega Moreno, was my father's son with a young woman named María Felix Moreno. My father had me take María Felix to the hospital where she gave birth to Manuel Antonio; later I also was entrusted to deliver a monthly stipend from my father to María Felix. Years later, Doña Lavinia adopted Manuel Antonio. At his death, Don Ricaurte was an employee of the Controller General of the Republic, where he carried out his duties with honesty and professionalism. He was a stern, conservative man, and neither drank nor smoked.

Don Ricaurte's family tree includes another General Manuel Antonio Noriega, a participant in the War of a Thousand Days; my

[1] Tomás A. Noriega Méndez is a political science teacher and attended the universities of Panama and Mexico.

brother was named after him. Other relatives of note were Don Tomás Agapito Noriega Vega; General Benjamín Ruiz, a physician schooled in England and senator and governor of Panama; Judge José Gertrudos Noriega; and Dr. Homero Ayala P., a police commandant.

APPENDIX V
Remarks by General Manuel Antonio Noriega, Commander of the Panamanian Defense Forces, Before the Japan-Panama Friendship Association, Tokyo, Japan, December 12, 1986

The Japan-Panama Friendship Association was kind enough to extend an invitation so that I might come to talk with you on important issues of the day, issues of interest for both our countries. I am grateful for such an honor. Because I am conscious of my responsibilities as a Panamanian official and as a citizen. And this invitation gives me the opportunity to meet here such distinguished Japanese private sector leaders and very good friends with whom I share the goal of strengthening all the ties of friendship which unite the Japanese and Panamanian peoples.

Only some twenty-five years ago, Japan was a silent voice in the concert of international politics; but today, and although the Japanese may not wish it, your country has great influence in world affairs by virtue of its conduct and its example. In a certain sense, what Japan does affects the way of life of the rest of the world. All of the most important observers of the Japanese phenomenon concur in pointing out that economically, the performance and example of Japan are irresistible. The Japan of 1986 is a powerful force in international trade, in monetary and financial affairs, as well as in science and technology, thanks principally to the brilliant creativity and the hard work of the Japanese people.

It is an undeniable fact that as Japan emerges as a trans-Pacific economy, it will have to carry out an increasingly important role in the problems of international politics worldwide, since the Japanese today recognize very well that their domestic and foreign interests can coincide at times.

We Panamanians are struggling to modernize our society by eliminating vestiges of economic and social backwardness, which still affect some sectors of our population. We admire Japan's performance and example, which are founded primarily on a solid and profound scientific, technological and humanistic education. But we try to understand Japan as it is, not as other countries wish it were. We know that, within the immense interchange of goods, ideas and capital that its labor has stimulated throughout the world, Japan has its own strong personality.

We have before us two situations which flow toward common coordinates: on the one hand, the growing role that Japan will have to exercise in world affairs; and on the other, the facts related to the strategic location of the Republic of Panama, of such vital importance for free international trade and the maintenance of peace. Therefore, the concrete interests of our two countries compel us to examine seriously and responsibly all those situations which could affect, positively or negatively, legitimate interests which serve only mutual and equitable benefits for the Japanese and the Panamanians.

Central America

Because of its possible impact on the security of inter-oceanic transit through the Panama Canal, it is imperative that we first express our serious concern about the crisis that the Central American region has endured for seven years.

What occurs in all of Central America has to be of particular interest to the Republic of Panama. The delicate political-military situation in that region may impact negatively on the development and national security goals of the Panamanian nation. For this reason, the Government of Panama, together with its Armed Forces, has decided not to allow itself to become involved directly in any confrontation between groups or States in the region. Nonetheless, this decision by Panama implies neither passivity nor lack of interest. On the contrary, Panama has decided to participate actively as a mediator and as a moderating factor, through the efforts of the Contadora Group.

As is known, the Contadora Group worked intensely for three and a half years to reach agreement on a document known as the Act of Contadora for Peace and Cooperation in Central America, which was presented to the Foreign Ministers of the region on June 7 of this year and which was the result of a sincere effort to find possible formulas of conciliation.

Unfortunately, serious differences have arisen about international military maneuvers; control and reduction of weapons; and the level of national forces. These differences have produced stagnation in the initiatives of the Contadora Group.

In his Annual Report for 1986, the Secretary General of the United Nations, Javier Pérez de Cuellar, points out quite correctly the present situation in Central America when he states:

"The Central American crisis has deteriorated continuously because of the growing interference of conflicting ideologies and the attempts to impose unilateral solutions by use of force."

We face, then, the undeniable fact that the political and military crisis in Central America is being prolonged and, along with it, the economic crisis of the region is growing more acute. And the insistence on a strictly military solution undermines social programs, because the more that is spent on arms, there are fewer economic resources for hospitals, schools, low-cost housing and highways.

In reality, what is happening in Central America, casting aside all literary adornments to explain it, is that the region is simply becoming an experimental battlefield for new military doctrines and concepts such as, for example, that of the "violent peace."

Extraordinary efforts must be undertaken if we are to retain the hope that the Contadora process can still offer the best possibilities for a measure of peace in Central America. Perhaps an initial mistake in the Contadora efforts is that they had as their objective to find a single solution to all the conflicts in the region, both present and future, with emphasis on political and diplomatic measures, but without the participation of military leaders involved in those conflicts. And one of the difficulties with the peace formula of that group is due to the fact that the manner of regional conflict has not changed much since 1983.

At this time, most objective analysts have the impression that the "Central American conflict" has been reduced to a confrontation between two countries: Nicaragua and the United States of America.

We are convinced that the achievement of peace rests on the direct and fundamental responsibility of the sovereign countries of the Central American region, on the basis of mutual respect and on the political independence of each nation. We are also convinced, however, that a broader and more genuine peace will only be possible to the extent that real social progress is achieved for the peoples of Central America, the product, first of all, of a palpable social justice, but also of the development of their economic, human, and intellectual potential.

In this respect, the industrialized powers—for which the whole world is becoming a single economy—have an exceptional opportunity to contribute to and to participate in the reconstruction and strengthening of the economic and social structure of all the countries of Central America, through realistic and efficient cooperative programs, in both the public and private sectors.

Japanese-Panamanian Relations

Now I would like to turn to matters which are of more specific interest within the framework of our bilateral relations. I begin by pointing out, with great pleasure, that since the end of the seventies there has been between Panama and Japan a period characterized by cordial, friendly relations in all areas of cooperation. In the private sector, which you represent in such a distinguished manner, there has been an explosion of initiatives for the establishment of Japanese banks and firms which have chosen Panama as their center for international operations, above all for Latin America.

The Panamanian government has reiterated its sincere desire that the Japanese private sector continue to invest in Panama, and it offers all the security guarantees as well as the necessary incentives so that the Japanese private sector and its representatives can develop their activities without impediments of any kind, within the framework of Panamanian laws.

Within that broad program of cooperation, which has already had many important achievements, one which stands out is the request made for the financing of the Northern Corridor and the studies of the Southern Corridor, both projects of vital importance for the future development of Panama.

The Panama Canal

But unquestionably the most noteworthy matter in the relations between Panama and Japan today is our mutual interests with respect to the present situation and the future of the Panama Canal. These are key issues for my country and for the development of international transportation and communications.

It must be deeply satisfying for our two countries that the Tripartite Study Commission on Alternatives to the Panama Canal—which comprised Japan, the United States and Panama—has begun to work seriously and efficiently in its headquarters in Panama City. And we are sure that in the next five years this important Commission will present its conclusions and recommendations on the best alternative to the present Panama Canal.

As you will recall, the establishment of the Tripartite Commission was necessary in order to fulfill Article XII of the 1977 Panama Canal Treaty. This article grew out of the Panamanian view that the interoceanic Canal that bisects its territory is *not* to serve exclusively the interest of Panamanians or Americans, but rather that it is a major technological facility which should lend highly efficient service to the free trade of all the nations of the world, without discrimination.

True evidence of the responsibility with which Panama looks at the future of interoceanic communication is the willingness of our country to accept the undeniable fact that Japan is the country which possesses all of the qualities to participate in the studies of such a vital project for world transportation and trade. We have recognized, thereby, the legitimate interest of Japan in that project, first manifested by its pioneering leaders such as Shigeo Nagano, representing the business community, and Prime Minister Masayoshi Ohira, to whose memory I dedicate my greatest admiration and respect, and who distinguished themselves by their enormous efforts in the building of relations with Latin America and, in particular, with Panama.

The distinguished friends here present know that for historical reasons the issues involved in every aspect of our Canal are very sensitive for the Panamanian people, because the struggle to recover our full sovereignty and control over the Canal and the adjacent territory was difficult and long. Nonetheless, it has not occurred to a single Panamanian to object to the participation of Japan in the study of the alternatives to the Panama Canal. On the contrary, the Panamanian people view sympathetically the intellectual presence of Japan as one more guarantee of the high level of efficiency and objectivity to be achieved in the conclusions and final recommendations of the study.

The Tripartite Study Commission's principal objective is to analyze the inherent problems in the future of the Canal. We Panamanians, however, are interested in and concerned about the efficiency of the locks in the present Canal for the immediate future. At the present time the Canal is administered by the Panama Canal Commission, an agency in the Government of the United States of America. It is responsible for its operation and maintenance until noon, December 31, 1999, when those responsibilities will become the exclusive concern of the Republic of Panama.

The most serious challenge faced by the locks in the Canal, for the immediate term, is that of the increase in transits of larger vessels, which can only navigate the narrowest part of the Canal, the so-called Culebra Cut, one way at a time. This serious limitation increases the waiting time for ships at the entrances to the Canal, with the consequent increase in delays and the costs that navigation companies have to assume.

With the unavoidable objective of solving this problem, a proposal has been developed for the widening of the navigation canal at Culebra Cut to allow simultaneous two-way passage by deep draft vessels. Feasibility studies indicate that the project would cost about $500 million and that it could be initiated quickly.

Panama has been insisting untiringly to the United States government that it is necessary to undertake without delay the widening of Culebra Cut for the benefit of international transportation and trade. The hoped-for results have not yet been achieved. This situation is regrettable, above all when we see that several sectors in Japan have made known their interest in contributing to the financing and execution of this work.

With the same objective of facilitating interoceanic communication in the short term, the Panamanian government is already carrying out the first phase of the enormous project called "Centropuerto," which consists essentially of establishing an integral transport system of 55 kilometers in length between the Atlantic and the Pacific. The system would use the facilities of the Panama Railroad between the ports of Cristobal and Balboa for the rapid, low-cost transfer of goods and containers between the two oceans.

Panama expects that the "Centropuerto" project, which will complement the Canal and the trans-isthmian pipeline on its territory, will be operating within a few years in order to provide another alternative service for the benefit of the international community.

I have taken the liberty of opening this kind of parenthesis between the present and future of interoceanic communication through the Isthmus of Panama. You can thus appreciate in full detail the ceaseless efforts the leaders and people of Panama are making in order to deserve the confidence of the international community with respect to the efficiency and security of any better alternative to be found to the Panama Canal.

The Study Commission

As far as Panama is concerned, the work to be completed by the Study Commission on Alternatives to the Panama Canal is, then, a very important part of all the preparations that my country is making to take over responsibly, seriously and efficiently, the operation, maintenance and defense of the Panama Canal—or an alternate route—as of noon on December 31, 1999. The study is of transcendental importance for us Panamanians, because it is of such scope, content and reach that it will define in large measure the future of the Panamanian nation, as indeed the Panamanian Commissioners have pointed out.

It is important to bear in mind that the principal goal of the Study is to identify and evaluate the feasibility, from the technical, economic, ecological, social and financial perspective, of a plan to modernize the trans-isthmian transport system in Panama which can be executed as the *best* possible alternative to the present Panama Canal.

The best alternative, which will ultimately be identified, should allow for the maximum exploitation of Panama's geographic advantages. The international community, governments as well as organizations, have recognized already that the Republic of Panama's greatest natural resource is it geographic location.

Therefore, my country has every right in accordance with the norms of international law to exploit that resource for the benefit of all its citizens.

The alternative to be identified will be chosen from among the following:

1) The widening, improvement or modernization of the existing Canal by means of the construction of larger locks;

2) The construction of a sea level canal between the Atlantic and the Pacific;

3) The construction of another interoceanic transportation system on this Isthmus of Panama; this would be a non-hydraulic system such as railroads, highways, conveyor belts, ducts, etc.

At present, the Study Commission has already defined the reference terms for this Study and these were approved in the Final Report by the three participating governments. Work is underway on the administrative structure of the executive Secretariat of the Commission and on the planning of the Study, in accordance with a time-line chart with a continuous duration of five years.

On June 19, 1986, the Study Commission published the text of the "announcement for Request of Pre-qualification information." In it the Commission requested qualifying data from international consortia composed of companies and entities of the Republic of Panama, Japan and the United States of America interested in participating equitably in the development of the detailed plan of study, the execution of the feasibility analysis and the drafting of the final report.

I understand that the submissions of nine consortia presently are being evaluated for pre-qualification in accordance with the evaluation criteria approved by the delegations of the three member countries. Furthermore, this month, precisely December 16–18, the second meeting of the Council of Commissioners will take place, at which time technical, administrative and financial matters will be addressed. The Commissioners will also select the accounting firm for the Study Commission.

As you can see, Panama clearly has an enormous interest in the efficient completion of the Study, since it is the first time that our country is participating with other powers, on an absolutely equal level, in the most serious of decisions on interoceanic transportation through the Isthmus of Panama. It is fundamental to our national interest that Panamanian professionals have an effective role in the administration, supervision and execution of the study. It is not necessary to take into consideration the origin of the funds for said Study, because it concerns a multidisciplinary undertaking of high technical and scientific quality in which Panamanians will be able to apply their creative abilities, learning at the same time from the Japanese and American colleagues.

As the second user of the Panama Canal, Japan is interested in the efficient completion of the Study, as has also been manifested in a consistent and permanent manner since the creation of the Commission in September 1985.

Conclusion

One of the dearest traditions etched in the mind and heart of every Panamanian is his vocation to help in constructing a peaceful world on a solid foundation of understanding, cooperation and solidarity among peoples and States. For this reason, we Panamanians have always intended that our Canal—or any alternative project—be a bridge to peace and a step towards progress, that is managed in an efficient and entirely neutral manner.

Our concept of the national, technical and professional role which the Armed Forces should play in modern society has convinced us that the principal function of the military is more dissuasive and defensive than repressive and offensive. Therefore, our fundamental responsibility, in these times, is to promote, encourage and protect the circumstances which will ensure the atmosphere of peace enjoyed by citizens, as well as foreigners, who live together harmoniously in the territory of the Republic of Panama.

As Commander of the Panamanian Defense Forces and as a soldier, I must express my strongest and most sincere repudiation of violence, conflict and war.

"Never again war" was the solemn call by which Pope Paul VI challenged all representatives of all nations meeting in the General Assembly of the United Nations. And that challenge is deeply rooted in our Panamanian military doctrine with the concept of "Security without war."

Finding myself now in the heart of this great country, dedicated to the cultivation of peace, progress, work and understanding, I experience a very special emotion because I share the identical sentiment which already forms part of the Japanese national soul and which is a definitive feature of its culture. This great country has earned the respect and admiration of the community of all men because it has made peace a cult to be worshipped and identification with nature a national vocation of the highest spirituality.

Japan is a great country because it has solid traditions and convictions, it has patience, it has will power and a strong spirit like the steely mountain of the poet:

> *That resembles Mount Fuji . . .*
> *That violently resists erosion*
> *That withstands the mist.*

Thank you.

INDEX

GENERAL MANUEL ANTONIO NORIEGA became commander
of the Panamanian Defense Forces in 1983. He is
designated a prisoner of war in the United States
under the Geneva Conventions.

PETER EISNER is a former foreign editor and
Latin America correspondent for *Newsday*. He reported
from Latin America for *Newsday* and the
Associated Press for fifteen years, covering
the U.S. invasion of Panama, Central American
strife and the drug wars.

ABOUT THE TYPE

This book was set in Galliard, a typeface designed by
Matthew Carter for the Merganthaler Linotype Company
in 1978. Galliard is based on the sixteenth-century
typefaces of Robert Granjon.